Praise for Aliette de Bodard:

'An intriguing mystery, elegantly written . . . with carefully crafted characters both with layers and depth, de Bodard reflects the best and worst of human nature in her novel' *Guardian*

'Truly beautifully balanced: between new and old, birth and death, beauty and ugliness, inside and outside, beginning and, yes, ending. It walks the line, and walks it fine' Tor.com

'I have rarely read such a brilliantly executed piece of work . . . This is a must read for everyone who enjoys complex fantasies with well-developed characters and sophisticated worldbuilding' *Interzone*

'de Bodard aptly mixes moral conflicts and the desperate need to survive in a fantastical spy thriller that reads like a hybrid of le Carré and Milton, all tinged with the melancholy of golden ages lost'
Publishers Weekly

'The devastated Paris of Aliette de Bodard's novel is especially haunting. This is partly because de Bodard, a Nebula Award-winning French-Vietnamese writer, lives in Paris and can convey a visceral sense of immediacy to a ruined Notre Dame or the remains of the grand department stores, and partly it's because of the sheer lyricism of her prose' *Chicago Tribune*

Also by Aliette de Bodard from Gollancz:

The House of Shattered Wings

THE HOUSE OF
BINDING
THORNS

ALIETTE DE BODARD

This edition first published in Great Britain in 2018 by Gollancz

First published in Great Britain in 2017 by Gollancz
an imprint of the Orion Publishing Group Ltd
Carmelite House, 50 Victoria Embankment
London EC4Y 0DZ

An Hachette UK Company

1 3 5 7 9 10 8 6 4 2

A CIP catalogue record for this book is
available from the British Library.

ISBN 978 1 473 21261 9

Printed and bound by CPI Group (UK) Ltd, Croydon, CR0 4YY

MIX
Paper from
responsible sources
FSC® C104740
FSC
www.fsc.org

www.aliettedebodard.com

www.gollancz.co.uk

To my son the Librarian,
for waiting until this book was done before
deciding to come into the world

ONE
DEATH OVER FEAR

IN the House of Hawthorn, all the days blurred and merged into one another, like teardrops sliding down a pane of glass. Madeleine couldn't tell when she'd last slept, when she'd last eaten—though everything tasted of ashes and grit, as if the debris from the streets had been mixed with the fine food served on porcelain plates—couldn't tell when she had last woken, tossing and turning and screaming, reaching for a safety that wasn't there anymore.

And she couldn't tell, exactly, when she had last had angel essence, but she didn't need to. It was an emptiness within her, a feeling that someone had torn out a chunk of her heart and hadn't bothered to kill her afterward. It was . . . the presence in her mind like a tree of thorns, the inescapable knowledge that he was with her no matter what she did—that he had found her, dragged her there, that he would never let her go.

Asmodeus.

Madeleine stared at her hands, and found them shaking.

"You have to do better," Iaris said. Her smooth, ageless face was creased in a frown; the white of her doctor's coat in sharp contrast to the olive tones of her skin.

The door was, as always, locked, the windows barred, with only a pale, sickly light coming through. At least this time Madeleine wasn't strapped in the chair, but Iaris would do it again if she thought it was useful.

Everything seemed unbearably real, unbearably sharp: the red flowers on the wallpaper, the embroidered trees and birds on the bedcover, and the faint smell wafting from Iaris, bergamot and orange blossom and some exotic wood.

His scent.

Her hands were shaking again.

In front of Iaris, on the mahogany desk that stood between them, was a container filled with a fine light-colored dust: angel essence. Madeleine had hardly paid attention to it during the first part of the interview, but now she could barely see anything else—could feel the power, trapped and roiling in that small space—could almost taste it, the warmth of a storm sliding into her belly, the magic that would fill her to bursting, that would make her feel safe again. . . .

"Lord Asmodeus retrieved you from House Silverspires," Iaris was saying. "Twice." Her frown was disapproving again. "It wasn't so you could waste your life away."

Madeleine tried to speak, found only ashes on her tongue. She tried again, dragged words from some unbearably faraway place. "I didn't ask to come with him."

Asmodeus had linked Madeleine back to the House—without her consent, of course; he'd never stop for anything so trivial as that. He'd taken her back, made her his possession again, and imprisoned her here, to mold her to his wishes. To make her his tool, his weapon, and there was no place in his grand plans for an addiction to essence.

Iaris's face didn't move. "What you want is irrelevant. You're here. You're a dependent of Hawthorn. Not an angel essence junkie." She was human; Madeleine was sure. In spite of her name, in spite of the smooth skin of her face and hands: she didn't have the light, effortless way of moving of Fallen, their innate elegance, sliding through the fabric of the world like sharpened blades. But somewhere in her youth, she'd been too close to a Fallen, too long, and some of their agelessness had rubbed off on her, creating that odd, unsettling effect.

Madeleine didn't remember Iaris. But then, she'd paid so little attention to other people before she'd run away from the House.

"You will clean up," Iaris said. "Otherwise you're so much useless chaff, Madeleine. And no one in this House has time for the useless."

"I know," she said. She could imagine they did not, that Asmodeus had little time for anyone who did not do as he wished. She didn't need the threat, didn't need to feel the fear again: the threat-laden conversation they'd had shortly after he'd dragged her back, the touch of his hand on the scars of her calves, the knife resting, oddly still, against the skin of the back of her hand, drawing just enough blood. . . .

"Now, there is no substitute for angel essence," Iaris was saying. "We've weaned you off the drug. Whether you get strong again, whether you eat, whether you sleep, whether you relapse, is all up to you."

Madeleine wanted to relapse. She wanted, so badly, to reach out for the container with the essence—to lose herself in it, to forget where she was, why she was there. And yes, it would gnaw away at her lungs again, would kill her centimeter by slow centimeter, fill her breath with blood, but it was still better than whatever awaited her inside the House. Still better than belonging to Asmodeus.

It took all she had to hold herself still. Because they would never give her that container. Because it was a test, as everything else had been; something Iaris could write in her report, a little chart of how well behaved Madeleine was, day after day. Of how close she was to being normal, functional, if either of those words still had a definition that made sense.

"You have to learn," Iaris said, softly, "what makes you reach for essence. You have to recognize what kindles your need."

"I don't need to learn," Madeleine said, wearily. "I know."

Iaris raised an eyebrow. At last, she put down the paper she was holding, and looked at Madeleine as if seeing her for the first time. "Let's say you do know. Most addicts don't. They just want their next fix, the next rush of power, caring little what it costs. But, assuming you do, Madeleine, knowing is not enough."

Madeleine—aware, all the while, of the link to the House in the back of her mind, of Asmodeus's presence chafing against the least of her thoughts—said, softly, "I don't want to be cured."

"You would prefer to kill yourself slowly?"

She'd wanted to die. She wanted to say this, but the words wouldn't leave her throat. A death of her own choosing; a slow slide into oblivion, to a place where fear, and where old memories, didn't matter.

Iaris said, almost gently, "You're the House's now. And things have changed in the past twenty years."

They had. Another head of House, the purges almost a distant memory; the floors pristine waxed parquet, every trace of blood expunged, all the dead forgotten. But not Elphon.

She didn't need to close her eyes to hear his screams; to see, again, the spray of blood as the swords slid home into his chest, and to see him again, walking behind Asmodeus as if nothing had happened. As if he had not died, and risen again through a magic Madeleine couldn't claim to understand.

"You're safe here," Iaris's voice said, floating to her out of the darkness. "The House takes care of its own, Madeleine."

Iaris didn't understand. She couldn't understand. She hadn't stood in the drawing room watching Frédéric and Zoé and Elphon and all the other gardeners be cut down. She wasn't the one who had crawled through the streets of Paris, the cobblestones slick with her own blood, every movement awakening fresh pain in her calves, in her broken ribs, every agonizing gesture underlined with the same fear that he would find her, that his thugs would finish what they had started.

Twenty years. She'd escaped, had gained twenty years of freedom away from Hawthorn, but twenty years were as nothing to a Fallen. Of course Asmodeus had come for her, taken her back to the House.

"You're safe here."

She wasn't. She had never been. Here was everything she had been running away from, and she was back again, locked in a room and awaiting the pleasure of the Fallen who had made her life a living hell. There was no safety anywhere.

The smell of angel essence was unbearable now; the familiar promise of power. She reached for it without realizing she did so, feeling the warmth of it in her hand, the weight of the container. It didn't make any false promises, didn't tell any lies, would merely slide into her lungs with the ease of long habit, and the power of Fallen magic would fill her from end to end, banishing the darkness—

"Madeleine!"

Hands, trying to pry hers from the essence. She batted them away, struggled to raise the container to her mouth all the same. A trickle of power like honey down her throat—a sense of rising relief as it took hold—and then pain flaring up in her fingers and her palm, and she was on her knees, nursing a hand and wrist that felt torn apart, the warmth in her belly receding, ebbing away to leave only the sharp, sickening presence of the House in her mind.

She was hauled to her feet, roughly. Iaris stood, holding the container, angry.

"I told him this was a waste of time," Iaris said. She clenched her hand, grimaced as if something hurt. Had Madeleine harmed her? She couldn't remember what had happened in the tussle for the essence. "Once a junkie, always a junkie. No one has ever shaken an essence addiction."

Madeleine hung, limp, between the orderlies that held her. She tried to remember what it had felt like, to be free of fear, to soar, even for the briefest of moments. But everything smelled of citruses and bergamot, and all she could feel was the nausea, rising to swallow her whole, and there was nothing to bring up but bile, its taste drowning the distant fire of angel essence.

"This experiment is terminated," Iaris said, with grim satisfaction. "He'll have to find some other use for you."

No. She knew, all too well, what only other use Asmodeus could have for her; what only other use there was, for the weak, for the useless, the disobedient. No no no. She tried to speak, to get words out from the emptiness in her. But nothing came.

THEY strapped her to the bed before they left, tightening everything so much she could hardly breathe. Iaris's petty satisfaction, for it wasn't as if the room, with its furniture bolted to the floor, held anything that Madeleine could have used to hurt herself.

As Madeleine lay staring at the ceiling, braced against the sound of footsteps in the corridor, closing her eyes and trying not to think what might happen now, everything seemed to blur and recede into some faraway land. The flowers on the wallpaper became featureless shapes, the dim light from the window darkened into night, and the ghosts of the past rose to watch her with their empty eyes.

The gardeners: Elphon, with his hands covering the wound in his chest; Frédéric and Pierrette, their homespun shirts drenched with blood. Oris, her shy apprentice in Silverspires, with his arms marred by snakebites.

And the last one, who had not belonged to Hawthorn, who would never belong there.

Isabelle.

On the Fallen's chest were the two bloody holes that had killed her, but her eyes were the same—that brittle innocence that had gone too soon, that bright and feverish gaze of one not meant for this world.

Madeleine. Her voice was the keening of the wind, and she swayed and faded, as if a mere breath would have been enough to dispel her.

She didn't say anything else, but she didn't need to. She'd come back so that Madeleine could live, could save House Silverspires; to give her hope, a thing so small and so fragile it was doomed to be crushed.

Madeleine.

"I can't," Madeleine whispered to the emptiness of the room, and turned her face away from the blurred vision, praying to a God she only distantly believed in to forget her, too.

SHE must have slept—must have slid, unaware, into the yawning darkness—but she couldn't tell when the ghosts became dreams, or if they had been real at all. When she woke up, struggling to take deep breaths, the straps digging into her skin, her arms and legs deadened, day had crept into the room again, and it was empty.

Faint birdsong came from outside: Hawthorn's famed gardens, almost intact despite the war that had devastated Paris. The quiet gurgle of a fountain in the background—a statement of power that, in an age of polluted rivers and corrosive air, the House could afford to waste running water on an ornament—and, farther out, the giggles of children racing after each other in another, alien world.

Were children truly happy, in the House? Asmodeus was Fallen: he would never father anything on anyone, would never care for anything or anyone. *She'd* been happy as a child; but that had been in Uphir's time; before the coup that had raised Asmodeus to be head of House. Before the fear.

There was no warning, no footsteps or creaking of the waxed parquet. But the door opened.

She knew it was him before she saw him, when the smell of bergamot and orange blossom wafted into the room. She would have fled, if she could do more than futilely struggle against the tightened straps.

He was light on his feet. She heard his footsteps only when he neared the bed—a brief touch that made her want to scream, and the straps were undone, one by one—her lungs burning as they filled up with the air they'd been denied. She pulled herself up, trying to massage some feeling into arms and legs that had long gone dead, and he sat on the side of the four-poster bed, close enough to touch.

"Madeleine." He smiled, showing the sharp teeth of predators. "Take your time."

His face was smooth, ageless like that of all Fallen, his gray eyes shining with magic, his movements effortlessly graceful. He had square horn-rimmed glasses, his particular affectation: like all former angels, he had perfect eyesight. His hands were fine, elegant, with the long fingers of a pianist, though he played no instrument beyond the ecstasy and pain of others.

"Asmodeus." His name tasted like ashes in Madeleine's mouth. And, because in spite of everything, she still clung to what life she had, she added: "My lord."

"Respect? How charmingly adequate." He smiled again, as if he knew exactly how respectful she was. And why would he not? She'd never been a good liar. "Iaris came to see me. She was . . . angry."

Madeleine didn't dare speak.

"Mostly because you hurt her pride, I suspect," Asmodeus said. He patted the bed by his side, as if he expected her to sit there, but she didn't move, and he didn't make any comment. "And because—let's be honest— she never believed you would come through."

"And you did?" She couldn't hold back the words. They were unwise, especially said to someone used to unthinking obedience.

"Mortals can be surprising, more so than Fallen. You strive against so much in your brief lifetimes. I try not to make hasty judgments."

She stared at her hands again. They were steady, though everything within her was screaming that she should run.

As if she'd ever get far.

"Iaris is right in one respect, though," Asmodeus said. "There is little we can do with you at the moment." He stretched the fingers of his right hand, one by one, as if considering a particularly troublesome problem.

Her. She was the problem. He would take her into the cells, and finish what he had started long ago, break her as he'd broken those who rose against him. He would—

"You never left, Madeleine, did you? Always crawling away from the wreck of the House, never leaving the shadow of the past." He reached out, and laid a hand on her ribs, the ribs his thugs had broken, twenty years ago—fingernails, as sharp as knives, resting on her chest, above her madly beating heart. "You live and breathe fear, and there is no room for anything else."

"How—" She took in a deep, shuddering breath.

"You forget. Fear is a weapon, and I'm . . . intimately familiar with its use." Asmodeus's tone was sharp, amused. "So I'm going to offer you a choice.

"Look at me. How much do you fear me, Madeleine?"

She looked up into his eyes, because he would make her look up if she didn't. His gaze was gray, mild, uninterested, but there was fire in its depths, the flames that had engulfed him when he'd Fallen from Heaven, the heart of a monster who cared only about inflicting pain on others.

He'd come into her room one evening, blowing the acrid smell of orange blossom into her face—magic, his magic, pinning her to the chair in which she sat—the knife glinting in his hands as he'd explained, smiling all the while, the consequences if she tried to escape the House again . . . the cold touch of the blade on her arm, flaring into sharp pain as it parted her flesh . . . a deeper, harrowing pain as his spell slowly, excruciatingly squeezed her damaged lungs, a searing fire that made her convulse, except she couldn't move against his restraints, couldn't even draw breath to cry out. . . .

Her hands shook, her palms greasy, sweaty. She struggled to voice something that wouldn't be a scream. "You know."

"Do I?" He was silent, for a while. "We should have had this conversation earlier, but never mind. Things were a little hectic. I stand by my own, Madeleine. It's how the House works. It's the only way it can work. If you swear and keep fealty to me, if you do your best not to relapse, then I will protect you no matter what happens. All that fear—I will bring it to other people instead. Those who seek to harm you."

It didn't help. She tried to say something, to convey that being under his protection was as frightening as being hunted by him; but then she thought better of it. It would not change anything if she spoke up, and she'd never been one for pointless, suicidal bravery. "You said I had a choice."

"Indeed," Asmodeus said. He straightened his glasses on his nose. His gaze rested, for a while, beyond her. "You're my dependent, but you feel no loyalty to me. Quite the contrary. And I, in turn, have little use for you, as things are. If you choose to remain broken beyond anyone's capacity to heal, if you show no goodwill and pledge no loyalty"—he shrugged—"then I will release you."

The way in which he said it made it clear she wasn't going to walk out of Hawthorn, not on her own two feet. "How—"

"It matters to you?" His voice was sharp. "Surely death is its own goal, and its own reward. I will choose the manner of it. You might as well be of some use, after all, even if it's only for a few hours of my own enjoyment."

Death. The release she'd sought, all those years. But on his terms. "That's unfair," she said, before she could think. "No one chooses death over fear. No one—"

"No one? Be honest, Madeleine."

She could, indeed, endure pain, could endure many things if oblivion was the end of the path. But he would be the one who killed her in the end. He would bring her everything she had run away from; make every single fear, every nightmare, she'd ever had come true in the hours—stretched forever—before he finally deigned to grant her death.

It was no choice, and he knew it. It was the fear of what he might do, over the sick certainty of what he would definitely do.

Asmodeus rose, straightening the lapels of his dark gray swallowtail jacket. "You may think on it. I'll have food brought to you, should you see fit to eat." Faint disapproval in his tone; that was new. Or perhaps she'd just never noticed it.

"Wait," Madeleine said.

He stopped, halfway to the door. "Yes?"

"If"—she swallowed, trying to banish the taste of soured citrus in her throat—"if I choose loyalty—will I get out of this room?"

His smile was boyish, almost free of any sense of threat. Almost. "The House is busy. If you so choose, of course you will get out. In fact . . ." He paused, as if pondering whether to say more. "I will have work for you."

She said, because she had to, "You don't even know if I will keep my word."

Asmodeus turned to look at her, his head cocked sideways like a bird of prey. "You're a terrible liar, and an entirely too principled person. Of course you will keep your word. And if you don't"—he shrugged, again—"there is always the other option." He must have known, then, what she was going to answer. It was obvious. But then, as he had said, she was transparent; an open book that he, and others, had always read with ease.

"I—" It was no choice. There was no choice. And, in the end, she clung, so dearly, to the little she had. Angel essence was one thing, its heady rush making everything bearable, obscuring the inevitable ending. But to knowingly, willingly, walk into Hawthorn's cells with him . . . "I will pledge my loyalty to you."

AFTER they were done, Asmodeus went out of the room for a brief moment, and came back with the people who must have been waiting in the corridor for Madeleine's answer.

One of the two bodyguards behind him carried a tray of food that she set on the table, and then both of them withdrew, which left the other two people who had come in with Asmodeus.

One was a mortal woman, with some of that same smoothness to her face that Iaris had, except her exposure to Fallen magic must have been less, because her dark hair had sprinkles of gray, and her hands showed the first spots of age. She appeared a little younger than Madeleine, but must have been older in reality.

The other one Madeleine already knew. Or had known, once. Elphon had been her Fallen friend in the gardens of Hawthorn, and had died the night Asmodeus seized power from Uphir. And, somehow, he had been raised from the dead by Asmodeus, and now walked the earth as if nothing were amiss, oblivious to his past life and the connection between them. His loyalty to Asmodeus was absolute.

Her new minders, no doubt: she was certain she wouldn't leave this room without supervision.

Asmodeus gestured for the others to sit. They did, one in each uphol-stered chair, leaving Madeleine at the end of the four-poster bed. Elphon handed her the tray, which she balanced on her knees. The aroma of the food wafted up to her: some kind of vegetable soup.

"Eat," Asmodeus said.

She didn't feel hungry. She took Iaris's medicine before the soup, the white pill a day that kept her cough from returning, even though nothing would ever heal her wasted lungs, or give her more than a few years longer. The soup was scalding hot, and it made little difference. It was bland, much as if it had been boiled for too long.

They all waited for her to finish, in silence. When she stole a glance upward, she saw that neither Elphon nor the woman looked particularly at ease.

"You know Elphon," Asmodeus said. He wasn't sitting; he was lounging against the wall by the door, with the sated air of a predator, which he af-fected at nearly all times. Fallen were rarely harmless, but no one who saw him would ever underestimate what he was capable of. "And this is Clothilde. She's one of the House's magicians, and a member of the Court of Birth."

The intricate hierarchies of Hawthorn had never meant much to Madeleine. She set her spoon by the side of the empty bowl, and waited for the rest.

"I have a project," Asmodeus said. "Outside the House. One which requires a delegation."

Another House, then. She grimaced. "I don't understand why you'd send me."

"Not for diplomacy. We both know how abysmal you are at that," Asmodeus said. "That will be Clothilde and Elphon's work. You're part of this as . . . Let's say I need your skills. And your knowledge."

Alchemy, her former work? But Hawthorn had an alchemist, Sare, who would be more intimately familiar with the peculiarities and intricacies of making elixirs and charged containers from Hawthorn's live Fallen, or the remnants of its dead ones. It had to be about House Silverspires—her former House, the one that had cast her out. But that made no sense, either: Silverspires had been Hawthorn's enemy, but the events of seven months ago had left them bloodless and in ruins, barely capable of being a power in postwar Paris, much less a threat.

"I don't understand," she said.

"I need alchemy," Asmodeus said. "Among other things."

"Sare—"

"Sare is House alchemist. She has other work. And what I expect is rather basic: nothing that requires her expertise or skill. I'm sending a delegation of magicians, and I need someone to recharge their artifacts when the magic runs out."

Rather basic. Madeleine forced herself not to flinch at the casual dismissal: he was entirely right. Filling containers with angel magic was something she could have done in her sleep. "You said there were other things."

"Yes," Asmodeus said. His hand moved, gracefully, as if he were sketching something in the air; and, in answer, an image gradually coalesced between him and her.

It was the face of an Annamite woman: mostly human, and mostly resembling the old-fashioned pictures of the imperial court Madeleine had seen in the library of House Silverspires—thinned eyebrows over harsh eyes, a crown of black cloth with golden figures and beaded tassels, worn tight over the head, except that patches of the skin of her face had worn off, revealing the iridescence of scales, and that the nubs of deerlike antlers protruded through the crown.

It wasn't a face that Madeleine would ever forget, no matter how much essence she got high on.

"Ngoc Bich," she whispered.

"You *are* familiar with her, then. And yes: my affairs," Asmodeus said, slowly, softly, "are with the kingdom under the Seine."

The Annamite kingdom. The dragon kingdom.

"How do you know—?" Madeleine asked, and then fell silent. The dragon kingdom—the underwater power that lurked under the Seine, lashing out and killing Fallen and humans alike—was reclusive, its existence a secret. Isabelle had known, but Isabelle had a link to Philippe, who in turn was Annamite, and presumably better informed about a territory held by Annamite creatures.

"How do I know it even exists?" Asmodeus shrugged, an expansive gesture that seemed, for a moment, to drag ghostly black wings into existence. "We have long had an agreement with them, even in Uphir's day. And the time for their secrecy is ending. That means they are vulnerable."

Clothilde nodded. Her gaze, throughout, had not left Asmodeus. "You have Ghislaine down there already."

"As an envoy, yes. To smooth things out," Asmodeus said. "To gain allies and support, and win them around to the possibilities we're offering. But we have to make a formal offer, and that can't come from her."

Clothilde didn't look surprised. She'd probably been briefed ahead of time, unlike Madeleine. And she had at least a vague idea what was going on. "The terms haven't changed," she said: a question, a confirmation.

"No," Asmodeus said. "I see no reason for them to change. But you'll take Madeleine with you. She's been there before."

Madeleine had been there exactly once, with Isabelle, in a past that might as well be another lifetime: when Isabelle was still alive, when House Silverspires was still under threat and not a field of ruins. "And I'm not going to be told what this is about?" Madeleine said, more sharply than she'd intended, before she remembered whom she was speaking to.

Asmodeus raised an eyebrow, but appeared more amused than angry, as if watching a fish out of water thrash on land. "House Hawthorn will offer a formal alliance to the dragon kingdom. One sealed in the traditional manner. It has all gone somewhat out of fashion, but my perception was that Princess Ngoc Bich and her officials were still fairly traditional."

A formal alliance. Madeleine stared at him. He couldn't mean. He couldn't possibly mean—

And, when she did not speak, he did it for her. "Clothilde is carrying an offer of marriage to the kingdom. My marriage."

TWO
THE AFFAIRS OF DRAGONS

THUAN'S days in House Hawthorn were mostly routine, though the real purpose of his presence in the House was anything but. He looked young, much younger than he truly was: a teenager to most Westerners, and as such, his days were split between attending the classes dispensed by the Court of Birth, and doing odd jobs whenever the Court of Hearth needed an extra hand.

For the current week, he was seconded to the House's infirmary, which he found overwhelmed, with entirely too many patients battling anything from pneumonia to foul-smelling wounds. He carried bandages and syringes, and mirrors filled with angel magic, to the three doctors on duty, trying to avoid Iaris's bad mood, and found himself, finally, in the nurses' room, sharing a quick meal of sandwiches and verbena brew.

It was, like the kingdom, a much diminished place. Once, the room they were in would have had tiles with vivid patterns, and elegant furniture. Now the grout had yellowed, the tiles faded and cracked, and the table and chairs were old, dusty, creaking ominously as they leaned back into them. Too often patched, the lines of repairs clearly visible in bright light; of which there was so little in Paris.

"Sorry," Géraldine said, with a shrug, fingering her crucifix. "There are better days."

Her younger companion—Nadine, Iaris's daughter and Thuan's tutor in class—snorted. "With the old dragon on duty?"

Thuan tried not to wince, or react otherwise, at the mention of "dragon." There was no way Nadine or anyone else could know that he was more than he pretended to be. He had come into the House half a year ago, a waif rescued from the streets through the kindness of Sare, the House's alchemist; he was, to all intents and purposes, working his way into the House; hoping, like everyone else in the class, to be chosen to become a full dependent of Hawthorn.

Some nights, he offered a brief prayer to his long-dead ancestors that he would find what he was looking for before the allegiance ceremony ever happened. His disguise would fool many people—many Fallen, even—but the power swirling within him would never allow him to pledge allegiance to a House.

Not to mention, of course, that his aunt would kill him if things ever got to that point. Or, worse, resort to sarcasm.

"You do love her," Géraldine said. She poured tea for Thuan, and Ahmed, the other nurse in the room.

Nadine rolled her eyes upward. "Mother? Only when she's not breathing down my neck." She inhaled the aroma of her cup, and sighed. "She's been very busy."

Ahmed grimaced. "That time of year. Bad enough when it's the common cold, but this year we seem to be collecting pneumonia and dysentery."

"There's a difficult birth in Ward One keeping Iaris busy as well," Géraldine said. "Magicians' babies are always the tricky ones. Though last I checked, she'd admitted defeat and sent to the Court of Birth for a powerful Fallen. This one is clearly going to need to be helped along." She made a face. "Not to mention the cholera."

"The old woman in Ward Three?" Ahmed asked. "You don't think—"

"I don't know. But Iaris is worried," Géraldine said. "It'd probably be best if you didn't go there," she added, for Thuan's benefit.

Thuan shrugged. It was a water-based disease and, as such, had about as much chance of hurting him as the common cold. But they couldn't know that; their concern was genuine. Which would, if he thought too long about it, make him feel bad about the deception he was currently involved in; about being here for the kingdom's interest, and certainly not the House's. "Thanks." How was he going to bring the conversation around to the subject that interested him without raising suspicion?

"You heard the news?" Géraldine was already putting on her nurse's coat. Breaks were short, and she'd been there before Thuan had arrived.

"Which one?" Nadine asked, draining her cup. She threw a glance at the grandfather clock ticking away the hours in the corner of the small room.

"Iaris has terminated the experiment with Madeleine."

Nadine snorted. "She only tried because Lord Asmodeus asked. She can't refuse him anything."

"No one can," Géraldine said.

"You know what I mean," Nadine said.

Géraldine looked at her, sharply, and didn't answer. "Time's up," she said to Ahmed. And, to Thuan, a touch more kindly: "You still have a few minutes left. Finish your food. You look entirely too scrawny to be healthy."

"What did you mean?" Thuan asked Nadine, after they had both left. He knew her relationship with Iaris was fraught, but not why.

Nadine sighed. She leaned against the table, nursing the empty cup in her hand. "Mother was with him from the start, before the coup that deposed Lord Uphir. She . . . likes him." Her tone suggested that she didn't see why.

"And you don't." Thuan readjusted his topknot, pinning stray hairs back into place. He should have cut his hair before coming to Hawthorn—few Annamites in Paris wore their hair long, these days—but it suited him, and it would be such a hassle to regrow when he was back in the kingdom. He hadn't *quite* been able to overwhelm his vanity on the matter.

"Lord Asmodeus is powerful. He keeps the House safe. That's all I need to know," Nadine said.

Thuan had set aside the cup of verbena, which he didn't care for unless it came with enough sugar to cover the taste. *You're jealous,* he thought.

They're closer; closer than you are to your mother. It wasn't what Nadine would want to hear. "He's not a very likable person," he said. He'd never actually met Asmodeus, only seen him from afar—but the head of House Hawthorn didn't sound like the kind of person you wanted to take along on a crazy escapade into inns and houses of pleasure.

Nadine snorted, again. "You don't say." And, finally: "Mother wants to impress him. She wants his approval, like a child. Or a puppy. And she doesn't understand he doesn't care about her. She's just one more dependent to him, one more person he owns."

"She'll come round."

"When she hasn't in the thirty years I've known her?" Nadine set her cup on the table. "Unlikely."

"You're on edge," Thuan said. And so, now that he thought about it, were the other nurses. "Why? It's not the cholera or whatever else they've got brewing in the wards."

"Well, the cholera would be bad enough," Nadine said. "Since there's not much we can do to cure it." She shook her head. "It's nothing."

It wasn't. Thuan had to be careful: he was navigating a labyrinth more complicated than addressing the Secret Institute, back in the kingdom. At least in the kingdom he knew what was going on, who followed whom and why. Here . . .

A fish out of water, he thought, not without irony.

"You can't understand," Nadine said. "You'd have to have grown up here."

"Nadine, I'm going to become part of this House in less than a year's time. I can't remain ignorant forever." It was a lie, but there was no way he was going to tell her the truth. Not if he wanted to come out of this alive and whole. "Try me."

Nadine sighed. He thought she was going to say something about his being Annamite—his not belonging *here*, in the ruins of Paris, as if he hadn't been around for longer than she'd been alive—but instead she went on, staring at the clock. "It's Madeleine. And Clothilde, possibly."

Clothilde was one of the House's magicians, moving in circles so far above Thuan she might as well have been a star in the heavens. Madeleine he had never heard of until a few minutes ago. "What of them?"

"He's taking an interest. I told you, you wouldn't understand. Lord Asmodeus is the head of the House, but he's only a member of one court. The Court of House." The one that dealt with outside business and the relationships with other Houses. "And he's mostly left everything else alone. Until now. Perhaps because Samariel is dead, and he's lonely without his lover." Her voice was skeptical. "But he's been closeted with Clothilde, and insisting that Madeleine had to clean up her addiction to angel essence to become a full dependent of the House. Something is happening. Something big."

Angel essence. And something big. Thuan didn't like that, not at all. "Surely only for the good of the House."

"You don't understand!" The cups on the table rattled as Nadine pushed herself off. "The last time he took a genuine interest in internal House affairs . . . the gardens were dark with the ashes of funeral pyres, and the Seine ran red with blood."

"The Seine has never been red with blood," Thuan said, gently. The waters ran dark and deep, and blood would dissolve in the mess of spells and magical residue that had corrupted them after the war. Blood was, in truth, the least of the kingdom's problems.

"You weren't born then." Nadine shook her head.

He didn't correct her. "I've never seen any angel essence in this House." He wasn't about to let an opening go to waste.

"You're too young. And it's nasty stuff; trust me," Nadine said. "After you've seen a few addicts coughing their lungs out, and I mean that literally, you'll know to avoid it."

A memory, abrupt and unforgiving: a darkened room where dragons in human shape lay, writhing and twisting—the acrid smell of Fallen magic, mingled with that of vomit, eyes rolled upward in a face too pale and too skeletal to be healthy, the antlers on either side of the head translucent, veined with purple. He'd reached out, and one of them had snapped in his hands, with a crack like shattered bones, except that no bone should have broken that smoothly, that easily. And it had lain in his hands, still warm to the touch, still obscenely pulsing with life that should, by rights, have left it entirely. . . .

This, Second Aunt Ngoc Bich had said, *is what we have to deal with, nephew. And you will find out where it's coming from. Who supplies it, and why. And fast.*

The kingdom was under siege: weakened by angel essence, hounded by House Hawthorn's delegates. It wouldn't hold out for long, and Thuan was key to finding what was going on. The House of Hawthorn, after all, had the most to gain from a diminished dragon kingdom, and it would make terrible sense if they were the ones trading in essence.

Except that, so far, he hadn't made much progress at all. Some spy he made.

"I know about the effects of essence," Thuan said, quietly.

Nadine opened her mouth to speak, and then closed it, her eyes wide with an emotion he couldn't read. Too late, he realized it was surprise, tinged with the fear of having said too much; and he turned around, to meet the eyes of the man who stood in the doorway.

Not, not a man; a Fallen.

Thuan's body bent into a graceful bow before he'd even realized what he was doing: the full, elegant thing reserved for being in the presence of the emperor or the empress, which his tutors back at court had despaired he would ever master.

The Fallen raised an eyebrow. "New to the House, I see. I'm the first to appreciate signs of obedience, but there is such a thing as too much." He wore the colors of Hawthorn: a dark gray swallowtail jacket over matching trousers, and a silver tie at his throat, shining like a star before the fall. His gaze, behind the square horn-rimmed glasses, was impassive; but even though he held himself still, he radiated raw power. It streamed out of him like an exhalation, an electrifying effect that seemed to make everything in the room recede into insignificance. "Hello, Nadine," he said, as she straightened up from her own bow. "Your mother doesn't seem to be in her office."

Nadine shrugged, feigning indifference. "She's either in Ward One or in Ward Three. Difficult birth. Or cholera." How could she stand there and look away from him? How was she not drawn to him like a moth to a flame? Thuan fought his own body to a standstill, ignoring the *khi* element that swirled within him—water, rising like the beginning of a storm. He didn't want to get into a fight; couldn't afford to get into a fight.

"I know she sent to the Court of Birth for help," Asmodeus said, with a dark smile. He made a short, stabbing gesture with his hand. "Thank you. I'll look for her there."

When he left, it was as if someone had cut all the strings that kept Thuan upright. His eyes remained glued to the door; his body struggling to stand up again, every muscle threatening to betray him at the same time.

"Hey," Nadine said. "Don't faint on me, please."

"How—"

Nadine shrugged. "You get used to it." She stared at the bleached walls of the room without really seeing them. "Or pretend you do."

Thuan could pretend many things, but not that. He breathed in, slowly, shakily. He didn't smoke, and he didn't think they were allowed to smoke in the infirmary in any case, but he was seriously tempted. It was either that or run after Asmodeus, to get just another glimpse of him, just another acknowledgment from those cool gray eyes. . . .

What in the heavens was he thinking? He certainly couldn't afford anything like that. Keep his head down, Ngoc Bich had said. Find what the House is up to. Find where the essence comes from. That was the brief.

A brief that he was thoroughly failing.

"Anyway, you've made quite an impression," Nadine said. "Not bad for you."

As if he wanted to be remembered by the Fallen whose House he was busy infiltrating.

"No, not bad," Thuan said, still struggling to breathe.

Not merely bad. Potentially disastrous.

THREE
DELEGATIONS

ON the night before they were due to leave for the dragon kingdom, some-one knocked at the door of Madeleine's room. "Come in," Madeleine said. Not that it made any difference. She couldn't open the locked door, and presumably whoever was knocking had the key.

She didn't think it would be Asmodeus, who wouldn't bother knocking when he could come straight in, and indeed it was not.

It was Clothilde, empty-handed and with gray circles under her eyes that made her appear oddly older. She wore a neatly cut swallowtail jacket and trousers like a uniform. The old parquet creaked under her feet as she moved into the room. "I thought we should have a little chat."

"Go on," Madeleine said, wearily. It wasn't as if she could prevent her, or anyone, from dropping in.

Clothilde sat, not on the chair, but on the desk, her hands pressing down on the mahogany surface. "He's told me it's vital you don't relapse."

No need to ask who "he" was. "Or he'll kill me, you mean?" Madeleine, never particularly diplomatic, wasn't in the mood to make an effort.

Clothilde shrugged. She straightened the sleeves of her dark jacket. "We're going to have a lot to do in the dragon kingdom. I can't afford to keep a perpetual watch on you. Even though I will, since I have to." Her smooth face was expressionless.

"And you have a miracle solution?" Madeleine felt drained, already, with that familiar emptiness, a hollowness to the world that preceded a flash of craving. "Iaris said—"

"I know what Iaris said. I also know she wasn't trying very hard. And, for all her ill will, she's still a doctor. She has some principles which hamper her." Clothilde reached inside her jacket, and produced a container, which she flipped open. It was a mirror, its surface as dark and as roiling as a sea during the storm. "Fortunately for you, I don't."

Madeleine's mouth was dry. "This isn't—"

"Angel essence?" Clothilde shook her head. "No. You're addicted to the high, the rush of power. This is merely angel breath, trapped in a mirror."

She was all too familiar with it. As a former alchemist, preparing these had been part of her job: safeguarding Fallen flesh, making sure the magic inherent to all former angels wasn't wasted; that fingernails and teeth and eyeballs, and sinew and skin and flesh, were salvaged, preserved so that power could be passed on to magicians or other Fallen for their spells.

"Yes," Madeleine said. Didn't Clothilde know she'd already tried? "It's like warmth compared to a burning flame. Like ashes to a fire. It doesn't do anything." Angel essence wasn't simply preserved Fallen magic. It was refined, distilled from the brittle bones of Fallen until it had the potency of a wildfire.

Clothilde's face was unreadable. "Perhaps. If that doesn't work . . . There's something, somewhere, that will help you weather the crises. A pleasant smell, or a prayer, or the feel of a knife against your skin."

"How would you know?"

"He was right," Clothilde said. "You're such a terrible diplomat. Do me a favor, and shut up while we're down there? I need your knowledge, not an incident that jeopardizes everything." She was silent, for a while. "I don't know about angel essence. I've never been addicted to it, and I'm told it's difficult to do much about that. Iaris doesn't like you, but she doesn't lie, either. If she says no one has ever shaken off an addiction . . . She probably doesn't have much experience, but it's suggestive."

So she was doomed. Not that it came as much of a surprise. She'd have quite happily drugged herself into her grave, except that, because of Asmodeus's threats, the price for that was now so terribly high. So, so terribly high.

Her hands felt cold; her stomach empty, in spite of the meal she'd forced herself to eat earlier. "I don't understand what you're trying to say."

"That's because you're not listening." Clothilde's voice was only mildly harsh. "As I said, I don't know about that addiction. But there are other things you need to weather. Other losses that feel as though your world has been torn apart. That nothing and no one will ever protect you from the worst of what the House has to offer. I understand that."

Madeleine opened her mouth, and then thought better of that. She didn't really understand, but it sounded like territory she had no right prying into.

Clothilde rolled up both sleeves of her jacket. Underneath, her arms were bare—pale, spotted skin that was starting to edge into that of an old woman, and a constellation of whitish scars, crisscrossing one another, as if she had been repeatedly whipped.

No, not whipped. The world shifted and spun again, reminding her, again and again, that nowhere was safe. That there was no refuge against fear.

"The feeling of a knife against your skin." Clothilde's voice was low, mocking. She rolled down her sleeves again, and stood up. "There has to be something that works, Madeleine. Think on it. I don't want to be the one who passes your death sentence, but I have a mission. I have a duty to safeguard the House's future, and if that doesn't include you . . ." She shrugged. "I won't weep."

And then she was gone, leaving Madeleine alone, struggling to breathe. *There has to be something.*

She already knew, in her heart of hearts, that there wasn't.

THE delegation was larger than Madeleine had expected: in addition to the three of them, there were four bodyguards burdened by heavy luggage. They were gathering at the bottom of the stone steps of Hawthorn's main building, supervised by a snappish and utterly unamused Clothilde. Elphon wasn't there: Madeleine had caught a glimpse of him, closeted in last-minute talks with Asmodeus, and gladly turned away from them both.

Madeleine had expected to argue against the dress they would inevitably provide for her, but the clothes she'd found on rising were simple and functional: a gray shirt, a darker gray jacket, a set of trousers in the same shade, and a set of pins she'd used to tie her dark, graying hair into a makeshift bun. Only the wide shawl seemed out of place. Delicately embroidered with the hawthorn-and-crown arms of the House, it rested uneasily on her shoulders, and kept sliding off every time she shifted position.

On the other hand, it could be worse. She could have been dressed to match Clothilde: a long, flowing tunic with flowers picked out in golden thread, a matching shawl, and shoes so high-heeled it seemed a miracle she could keep upright instead of stumbling with every step.

Small mercies.

Clothilde, in spite of the clothes, moved as though something, or possibly everything, had personally offended her. She didn't seem to pay attention to Madeleine, but her eyes would, from time to time, effortlessly find her no matter where Madeleine moved. Asmodeus had, no doubt, had a word with her.

Madeleine felt hollow, empty, already craving the touch of angel essence. But if she took any, then he would find out. He would . . .

I know about fear. You live and breathe it.

There has to be something.

She wasn't even sure she could stay alive, to the end of this, but the alternative was worse.

Clothilde nodded at Elphon as he came out, and gestured for everyone to move. There was no farewell, no stirring speeches or anything grandiloquent. Instead, they merely walked through the gardens, to the waiting arms of the Seine.

The gardens of House Hawthorn were huge: the pride of the House, sprawling and verdant in an age of cracked pavements, blackened buildings, and noxious air. Legions of gardeners kept the hedges trimmed, the gravel immaculate; even though the trees were scrawny and wilted easily, and most of them didn't actually bear flowers or fruit for long; and the gravel crunched underfoot, spotted with debris and fragments of bone. As they got closer to the river, the link to the House in Madeleine's mind rose, a growing pressure against her thoughts, not an unpleasant feeling, merely something watchful. Another power lay within the river, and it wasn't one that could be controlled or tamed by Fallen.

When she looked up, Elphon had joined her. She half expected him to smile, but of course he didn't. Of course he didn't remember her, and didn't care. He was no longer a loyalist, no longer one of Uphir's old supporters. Whatever Asmodeus had raised from the grave had no memories, and just loyalty to his master.

"Here," Elphon said. "He wants you to have this."

He held out an engraved wooden disk. Madeleine took it before she could think. It was warm under her touch, and all too familiar. She'd had a similar one, engraved with the arms of House Silverspires—except that, when her fingers touched the silhouette of the hawthorn tree, something seemed to leap from the disk into her hands, run up her arm and straight into her chest like lightning earthing itself into her heart. She shook her arm. It felt as if it had gone numb. "What is it?"

"Tracker disk," Elphon said, with a shrug that was heartbreakingly familiar. "So we'll know where you are."

"They—" Madeleine took a deep breath. "They weren't like that in House Silverspires."

"This one is a bit special," Elphon said. "Lord Asmodeus wanted to make sure he couldn't lose you, not even in the dragon kingdom."

Of course. As if she'd run away from him: if she were Houseless, where would she go? It wasn't as if the dragons were any more welcoming.

"Don't look so glum," Elphon said. "Clothilde and I have one, too."

"And the others?" Madeleine said.

Elphon grimaced. "No time. This was hastily put together."

But not so hastily put together they'd forgotten about her. Madeleine bit back a curse, and continued walking, trying to ignore the growing pressure of the link to the House within her. At least it took her mind off the angel essence craving.

Ahead, Clothilde had stopped. They'd reached the edge of the gardens: the grass trailed off until it hit a low, cracked wall, and the stairs that went down to the river.

Someone was waiting for them there, by the low wall: an Annamite dressed in robes embroidered with the maws of monstrous animals, and a squared hat with two wings projecting out over each shoulder. She stood still and stiff, as if at attention. She was accompanied by attendants carrying three parasols and large red fans at the end of sticks. When she rose, they moved to hold the parasols over her. "My name is Thanh Phan. I am the grand chancellor of the Van Minh Palace, and a member of the Secret Institute," she said, bowing. Her face was wrinkled and brown, an old woman's, except for a patch of skin at her temple which was a pebbly gray, an odd, familiar color that Madeleine couldn't quite place.

And then she moved, slightly, and something shifted. Her left arm became bulkier and larger, and her hand became a pincer, and Madeleine realized that the gray was that of a crab's shell.

A very, very large crab, the kind that would cut you in half, given a chance. Her hand, instinctively, sought Elphon's. But he had stepped away from her, was looking at the woman with bright, curious eyes.

"Thanh Phan," Clothilde said, speculatively.

The woman looked at her, her face impassive. So much like Philippe, the Annamite who had been conscripted into Silverspires at one point. And, because she'd known Philippe, Madeleine could read the contempt in her eyes. "It will do," the woman said.

Clothilde raised an eyebrow. "My name is Clothilde Desclozeaux. This is Elphon, and the woman at the back is Madeleine d'Aubin."

"Come with me," Thanh Phan said.

As they walked toward her, she bent toward Madeleine and said, "Madeleine d'Aubin. The princess has not forgotten you."

Exactly the sort of reminder Madeleine could have done without. She forced herself to nod, and fortunately Thanh Phan appeared satisfied with this, and didn't say anything further.

Madeleine had expected the limestone steps leading down to the quay. What she hadn't expected was that they didn't stop when they reached the river. They went on, after a brief landing on the cobblestones, becoming slick and worn and covered with algae, the stones pitted in multiple places. The light, too, changed, as they descended, from the pale one of a winter sun to something deeper and bluer, shadows lengthening under their feet, and a rising smell of brine, of incense and mold, that made Madeleine's empty stomach turn.

At the bottom were the same steps she remembered from her time with Isabelle: thousands of dark, dull fish scales that crunched underfoot. Everything wavered and bent out of shape at odd intervals, as if the entire world were washed by a veil of rain: they were underwater, but it didn't seem to make any difference; they breathed as easily as if they had been back on the surface. The air was cool and cold, but something had changed. She remembered a serenity, a quietness that had set her teeth on edge, something that had sought to weave its way into her thoughts and into her dreams, soothing every trace of fear and every twinge of pain, like a hand smoothing the folds of a cloth. Now everything felt unbearably sharp, like shards of glass rubbing against her skin; the link to the House a burning flame in her mind.

God, how she hated the House.

An offer of marriage. My marriage. Asmodeus had lost his longtime lover, Samariel, a few months ago, but even then he'd hardly been affectionate. It was, to be sure, a diplomatic alliance, but to imagine him with an Annamite, with a dragon official . . . Her mind blanked out at the possibility. There was something else going on, some power play he'd be interested in, of course.

"You can't possibly believe they will accept his offer," she said to Elphon.

The Fallen she'd known, in the Hawthorn that was now dead, would have smiled. This one didn't even change expressions. "Later," he said.

They walked through hills dotted with paddies, where men and women in conical hats crouched. Was it truly rice they were harvesting, here? Madeleine threw a glance backward, and saw that they were now flanked by people in lacquered armor. "Elphon."

"I saw." He didn't appear particularly nervous. But Thanh Phan heard her. "It's for your own safety. Have no fear: we have no plans to anger Hawthorn today." She sounded as though all she really needed was an excuse to do so, but no one batted an eyelid.

The city in the heart of the dragon kingdom was the same as Madeleine remembered it: huge, its gates slowly creaking open to let them through, its streets filled by a flow of people who stopped to watch their passage—men and women with fish scales, with lobsters' pincers and crabs' stalked eyes; carrying coral, and algae; and necklaces of pearls, all tinged with the oily shimmer that lay on the waters of the Seine, all corrupted and polluted by the fallout from the war.

What could Asmodeus want with dragons? There were no riches here. Power, perhaps? But they would never relinquish that to him. Some artifact, something of little meaning to them, but that Asmodeus would crave to the point of striking such a serious alliance? She couldn't imagine anything that would be worth it for him.

Ahead of them loomed a gate with three arches, topped by a pavilion with a tiled roof; and behind, two rows of ancient statues framing a cobbled street that led to the palace itself: everything from elephants to horses to retainers, silently watching them as they drew forward.

Thanh Phan led them through, into a palace that had changed little from what Madeleine remembered: a maze of low buildings and vast court-yards, of lacquered pillars and glazed orange roofs, curving gracefully up-ward as if reaching toward the surface. Thanh Phan stopped, at last, in a courtyard where an octagonal pavilion overlooked a basin filled, not with water, but with a beautiful tracing of pebbles in shades of gray and blue, with the sharp pink of lotus flowers breaking its monotony.

"These will be your apartments," she said, gesturing to the buildings opening onto the courtyard. "We have provided refreshments, and everything else you might expect. Should you need anything, ask." Again, she didn't sound happy. "You have an appointment with Princess Ngoc Bich, may she live ten thousand years, at the noon hour. I will come and collect you."

Clothilde's face didn't move. She bowed, deeply and elegantly, moving with a smoothness more reminiscent of Fallen than mortals. "There was a previous envoy to this court." And, when Thanh Phan didn't reply: "Ghis-laine Le Guell."

The ambassador Asmodeus had sent to ease the way. What was wrong? Nothing had been mentioned within Madeleine's hearing.

Thanh Phan inclined her head. "Yes," she said.

"We would like to see her."

"She isn't my responsibility." Thanh Phan's face was serene, but Madeleine knew that expression: it wouldn't budge, and it wouldn't give anything it didn't have to. "Should you want to see her, I assume you have ways and means of getting in touch with her. With angel magic?" She let the words trail away in the silence. "If that is all, I will be back shortly before the noon hour."

After they'd left, Clothilde moved toward the largest of the buildings, and peered between two lacquered pillars. "That one has an antechamber, of sorts."

It was a room with a table and four high-backed wooden chairs. At the end, a door led to a bedroom. The bed was high, the bedroom small, almost an alcove, and it all looked almost too small to accommodate a normal person. The other buildings were much on the same plan, except with slightly different furniture that looked drawn from other time periods, more roughly hewn, and not inlaid with mother-of-pearl.

The bodyguards started unpacking the contents of the luggage. Clothilde had claimed the largest room for herself, and was now spreading papers on the antechamber's table, dislodging the basket of food that had been its centerpiece.

When Madeleine and Elphon came in, she was writing in the margins, her face creased in thought.

"Something is worrying you," Elphon said.

Clothilde made a face, but didn't answer. She finished annotating the current paper and turned it over.

"The audience with the princess?"

Madeleine pulled one of the chairs, wincing at the weight. They were engraved with an intricate network of sea creatures, everything from monstrous fish to long, snakelike creatures with manes and fangs, gobbling some kind of unidentifiable round fruit. The air was still tinged with that faint blue shadow. They could breathe, and move normally, but it was still hard to forget they were underwater.

Clothilde didn't answer Elphon. She got through the last of the papers, and put down her pen. "I can deal with the princess. No, the thing on my mind is that we haven't seen or heard from Ghislaine."

"We've barely arrived. Give her time, surely?"

"You mistake me." Clothilde pulled the same mirror infused with angel magic she'd shown Madeleine and stared at it, but made no move to inhale its contents. "No one has seen or heard from her in a while. It was in the mission brief." She made a graceful gesture with her hands, an unsettling copy of the one Asmodeus had made in Madeleine's room. A sketch of a face formed in the air: a woman of indeterminate age, with a striking combination of dark skin and pale, almost white blond hair. "As you can see, Ghislaine is quite distinctive. Hard to miss." She moved her hand. The sketch blurred, became a finely detailed tattoo of a dragonfly perched on a water lily. "And she has this above her left wrist. If you should see her . . ."

"Ghislaine is hard to forget," Elphon said, gravely.

Madeleine spoke up. It was almost reflex. "But it will also be hard for her to hide."

"Indeed," Clothilde said. "Unfortunately." She righted the papers until they formed a neat pile once more. "Anyway. Officially, we're here to discuss final terms. Unofficially, Lord Asmodeus is worried. Something has gone wrong."

Official envoys disappearing was . . . not good. Not good at all. What could have happened to Ghislaine? Had she overreached? And if so, how?

They would receive no help. They were down here with just four bodyguards, in the middle of whatever it was that had twisted out of control. Madeleine bit back a curse. No wonder her link to the House was going crazy. It wasn't quite immediate mortal danger, but it was the next best thing.

"Ghislaine will turn up," Elphon said. His voice lacked confidence; and by Clothilde's grimace, she didn't believe that, either.

FOUR
The Shadow of Heaven

PHILIPPE'S last patient of the day was Grandmother Khanh, a strong-willed old woman whose flat accommodated five different relatives and their children. All too commonplace, sadly: the Annamite community in la Goutte d'Or was a slum among slums, poor and destitute, surviving on scraps outside the House system.

Grandmother Khanh had caught what looked like a cold, but it was in fact pneumonia—when Philippe listened to the lungs, the noise of her breath was fast and nasty, and she kept shivering and shaking. Normally, there was nothing much that could be done for her. In the days after the Great Houses War—the cataclysm that had devastated Paris, reducing monuments to blackened rubble, turning the Seine dark with the dangerous residues of spells, and leaving booby traps that still hadn't vanished, sixty years later—drugs were in short supply, monopolized by the Houses for their own.

However . . . Philippe sent, gently, carefully, a burst of *khi* fire into Grandmother Khanh's lungs, drawing on the swirling *khi* currents outside the flat, the remnants of fiery war spells. He waited until it had gone deep within her, destroying the bacteria on its way in. "There. You should eat ginger," he said, rising.

Grandmother Khanh snorted. "That's never made much of a difference."

"Give it a try," Philippe said. He'd been careful not to use too much fire: she would be coughing and spitting up blood for a few days, before it all went away, leaving her wrung out and weak. As a recovery, it was painful, and just this side of plausible.

He hated it. Hated the lies and the evasion, and the pretense he had no magic. But he had to: in an environment where magic was the province of the Houses, the risks were just too high. He would get swept up again, be imprisoned again by one of the Houses seeking to use him as a weapon. And he would die before he allowed this to happen again.

Grandmother Khanh's daughter was waiting for him at the door: handed him, in silence, a tied-up cloth filled with white rice, the payment they'd painfully put together. "Thank you," Philippe said.

"It's not enough." Her voice was low, angry.

Philippe shrugged. "Plenty." He was a former Immortal, one who had risen to Heaven in Annam by starving himself to the knife's edge between life and death. He needed food, but not as much as they did. "Don't worry. I'll come by in a few days to check in on her."

Outside, it was late: not just past daylight, but late enough that the evening queues of people headed to the Houses to offer their services had trickled down. On the pavement, a few people wrapped up against the cold—or not, depending on what they had scavenged—watched him, warily.

He did what he could, practicing medicine on the strength of his knowledge (and a little magic, when he could afford it). It kept him alive. It kept him busy—but did not get him closer to his goal, to the accomplishment of the promise he'd made, back in the ruins of House Silverspires.

Fare you well, Isabelle. Wherever you are. I hope we meet again.

He had pledged to turn back time. To bring back Isabelle—the Fallen who had died because of him, because he'd taken too long to decide to help her, and found only a lifeless corpse with two holes in the chest, eyes wide-open in a bloodless, dusky face and staring at the ruined ceiling of the cathedral.

Death was not always the end, in a city where magic ruled.

There was a way. A spell, a ritual. He knew. He had seen it work, back in House Silverspires, bringing a dead body back to life. But no one would talk to him; or, if someone was willing, the price was too high.

It had been months, and he was still where he had started: being a doctor to the poor, the Houseless, the desperate, and trying to convince himself, every evening, that it was all worth it, that he was merely biding his time until he could find a clue; something, anything, that would get him closer to understanding what had happened, in the House.

With a sigh, he finally turned away, to walk back to his office and the cold comfort of his flat.

His road took him between the railways: once the pride of Paris, the two bundles of rails that led to Gare de l'Est and Gare du Nord were now rusted and fragmented, filled with broken trains that remained where they had fallen apart; a mined junkyard where children scavenged, running just fast enough to keep ahead of the booby traps left by the war. Not his favorite place: it was always deserted, always dark, and there was something sinister about the engines strewn over the tracks, glowing with a faint red light, as if they were merely waiting for a puppeteer's touch to set them alive again.

He turned right, into rue de Jessaint, a raised street that overlooked the tracks just ahead of Gare du Nord. He stopped, because someone was there.

There had been a streetlight, once. Now there was only a spike, a graceful column of metal broken off halfway in its rise toward Heaven. And a silhouette, highlighted in the perpetual twilight of nights in Paris, leaning with arms crossed against it—rising, as he walked closer.

The *khi* elements in la Goutte d'Or were chaotic and unformed, awash with the remnants of uncleaned spells; but nevertheless, Philippe called fire, held it in his hand, ready to do battle. "I'm armed," he said, quietly.

"Philippe." Something flickered on: a sphere of light high above the broken pillar, as if the lamp were back in its place, though its radiance didn't illuminate more than a narrow circle around him, a perfect shape at the edges of which light abruptly gave way to the darkness of nightmares.

And, in that light, he saw that it was Isabelle.

She looked just as she had when she'd died, with a faint light streaming from her, limning everything like fine porcelain held up to sunlight; not washing out the olive tones of her skin, but rather sharpening them, elevating them until she seemed a model in a painting, more real and more sharply defined than the original. She wore the white shirt she'd died in: two holes in the chest, with dried blood encrusted into the cotton, but no wounds that he could see, merely the radiant smoothness of her skin.

"You're dead," he said.

Isabelle smiled, and it was the carefree, innocent expression she'd had before the House corrupted her. "Of course. That doesn't change. Be careful, Philippe."

"Of what?"

"Darkness."

He had darkness with him, within him, always: the remnants of unleashing a curse on House Silverspires, wormed into the heart of his being like rot among the roots of a tree. "I know about darkness."

Isabelle shook her head. "No, you don't." Her image wavered and bent, as if in a great wind, and by her side was the second of the two people who kept haunting him, the visions and hallucinations that only he could see.

Lucifer Morningstar.

He wore the metal wings that had been his prerogative and distinguishing sign: the wings Isabelle had taken from him, and which Philippe had buried with her corpse, as sharp and as cutting as living blades, weapons of war rather than organs of flight. His hair was so fair it was almost white, his eyes the blazing, unbearable light blue of a dry-season sky at midday, his gaze a fire that had once made Philippe want to abase himself until his forehead touched the ground. "Beware, Philippe. You still know nothing about power." His voice was mildly amused, as if by the antics of a child.

"I know enough," Philippe said. He was stronger now, even stronger than the firstborn among Fallen. And Morningstar was nothing more than a hallucination, a trembling vision that a breath of wind would dispel.

Morningstar said nothing. His hands were in front of him, resting on the pommel of a half-translucent sword, a huge blade engraved with a tracery of spirals near the guard, which extended into a single, clean line along its length.

The light flickered and went out, and with it, Isabelle and Morningstar, except for the sound of her voice, echoing across the bridge, and something else. . . .

Philippe put his hand on the iron railings that separated him from the tracks, and found them ice-cold, sucking the warmth from his skin. But there was nothing more: merely the faint, lambent darkness of Paris with its pall of magical pollution.

Nothing, until the snow.

It had been snowing when he'd walked onto the street. But what fell around him now was a storm, a flurry of wet flakes, with a cold, biting wind, rising until he couldn't see anything but the cobblestones at his feet. And the cold from the railings seeped into the ground, until his teeth were chattering with it.

What—where? He flung the *khi* fire in his hands, and it lit up nothing beyond a small circle. The snowflakes had swallowed the space before and after the bridge. The *khi* elements around him were wild, swaying back like snakes in pain, cut off, abruptly, beyond that line of light.

He was alone. Isolated from anyone who could have offered help, though who would help him, among the Houseless?

The snow was falling inside the circle now. He looked at his feet, and found them white, colorless. Fading, as if something had painted over him. He wasn't in the world anymore. And it was creeping upward as he watched, slow and gentle touches that leached the black from his trousers.

He almost reached out to touch the snow, stopped himself just in time. It looked like *khi* water, ice and cold melded together, nothing that should have had this effect.

The cold filled his entire body. Not even *khi* fire could dispel it. It smothered everything, even the fast sound of his own breathing. He struck a foot against the cobblestone, once, twice—nothing, no noise, and even his foot felt increasingly distant, as if it weren't part of his own body anymore. Soon, he might not even be able to move it.

He shivered. Tried to stand up straight. He was moving through treacle, every movement costing him, bowing him farther toward the ground. It would be so easy to lie down, to give up and watch the cold and colorlessness creep up his legs. . . .

Beware darkness, Philippe.

He had tried dispelling the snowstorm, and that hadn't worked. But there was still light, beyond the bridge. There was still something he could come back to.

He grabbed the flailing *khi* elements, gently, slowly untangling the threads that were knotting one another in rootless panic, and, as carefully as he might have straightened out a ball of yarn—*Don't think of weariness; don't think of the way your entire body, hands and all, is fading, now utterly out of reach*—smoothed out two threads, of metal and water, the *khi* element of the evening and of winter and of the quiescent city, and then tried casting them like a fisherman throwing out a net.

They shot into the snowstorm, and he felt them go slack in his hands. Dead, or deadened, which amounted to the same. The lower half of his body was soaked, and cold was climbing up his chest, the bite of ten thousand teeth, jagged edges cutting into his skin.

He needed an anchor. Something real and tangible and powerful; and, above all, close by. But there was nothing—nothing—and he was going to be crushed here, or torn apart or worse—

And then, out beyond the snowstorm, a whisper; a movement, something standing out, a spike in the smoothness of rippling cloth. No time to think: Philippe took another three threads of *khi* elements and threw them again.

They connected.

A single jolt, in his body, like a hook digging under his ribs and neatly spearing the heart. And then he was on his knees again, shaking, staring at the cobblestones under him. When he could breathe enough to rise, he saw that the snowstorm was gone, on either end of the bridge: nothing now but the pall of pollution over the city, and the faint light of stars shining beyond it. Below him were the tracks, with the corpses of engines and carriages. He looked at his body: colors had come back, and he could feel his limbs once more.

He rose, steadying himself on the railings: they stood firm, immutable, the forged iron ice-cool under his touch. But, on the ground, there was a charred circle, the stones blackened and split, as if a giant hand had pushed them down.

Philippe was more than a thousand years old, and not a fool. This . . . whatever it was, it was no illusion. And it was bloody dangerous.

The Houseless areas of the city were dangerous, all the time. Life was cheap and short and nasty, with so many ways you could die, from starvation to a House deciding you didn't matter in their grand scheme of things. But this was different.

In fact, if he hadn't been lucky, if he hadn't found something to anchor himself . . .

Only then did he take a close look at his right hand. A thin line, water and metal intermingled like a leather braid, started from the base of his wrist, and went on, straight toward whatever he had anchored it to. It beat to the rhythm of his pulse, slippery and forceful at first, and then gradually steadying as the adrenaline wore off and the circulation of *khi* within his body slowed down.

What had he anchored himself to?

He started to walk back, following the thread to its destination. It led him to a building like so many others in the neighborhood: wedged on an acute-angled intersection between two streets, with more floors on one side than on the other. It was dotted with the sooty streaks of magical attacks, the windows patched in multiple places or boarded up altogether, and its missing entrance door filled with a large piece of wood.

It was fully dark by now, but the too-large door was open, and light filtered through it, dancing on the muddy pavement like fireflies, slight and grubby and so ordinary he could have wept. He pushed the door fully open, and found himself in a small, narrow courtyard, encased by four walls that gradually bent inward until nothing but a slit remained above, with no trace of moon or stars. Doors and windows opened in each wall, leading to a different part of the building where people would be living, crammed in whatever livable space they had managed to scavenge for themselves.

An Annamite woman was waiting at the entrance opposite him. She was wrapped in a thick fur coat and a woolen scarf that obscured everything but her eyes, which were white and lambent with a faint, familiar light.

Fallen magic.

How—? There were no magicians in la Goutte d'Or: they had long since been snapped up by the Houses, or sold to them.

She had black hair cut short, not quite boyish but close: cropped short at the back of her nape, and set in longer strands on either side of her sharp, foxlike face. His gaze went down. She was heavily pregnant, seven or eight months along at the least, and the same faint light played beneath her belly, outlining the curled shape of the baby within her.

"What a surprise," she said. Her smile was wide and unsettling, her Viet tinged with the accent of Saigon. "I wasn't sure what we'd caught, but you're certainly . . . unusual." And, before Philippe could ask or protest, she gestured to the stairs behind her. "Come in, Doctor."

THE palace had changed. Madeleine had a confused, hazy memory of being dragged through building after building, running after Isabelle, through grand courtyards and rooms, an alien, frightening splendor that had been trying to creep into her thoughts, offering her falsely comforting serenity.

Now there was nothing of that.

She felt empty, hollowed out, struggling to find words or thoughts. The link to House Hawthorn burned in her mind: the distant, mocking presence of Asmodeus, offering no comfort and no serenity. And the rooms they crossed were no longer alien or splendid, but as shabby as the inside of any House—their lacquered rafters chipped and worn through; rot spreading on the pillars, obscuring the faces of the monstrous animals—and the silk of the dignitaries they met was worn, the delicate embroideries tattered and frayed.

Had it always been like that? She remembered the rot, that feeling of something creeping into her thoughts, but nothing quite as pervasive or all-encompassing: nothing this small, this shabby. Did the protection of Hawthorn, of Asmodeus, make any difference to how she was seeing things?

Thanh Phan took them through courtyard after courtyard, until they reached a bridge over a moat, filled with pebbles and lotus flowers. Guards lined the bridge, their shapes flickering between man and dragon, man and crab, man and fish—patches of dull scales on their cheeks, their halberds tarnished. A wide, three-lobed arch then led to a courtyard, lined with more dignitaries; and, at the end, the largest pavilion Madeleine had yet seen in the underwater kingdom, its opening stretched the entire width of the courtyard. It was also packed with people; and in the center, waiting for them at the top of a flight of stairs, was Princess Ngoc Bich, crowned in black and gold, and sheltered by two dignitaries with a parasol.

She looked much the same. The palace might have changed, and the stones under Madeleine's feet might be worn and cracked, the shining luster of mother-of-pearl gone, but Ngoc Bich held herself tall, as if nothing were wrong. Her white makeup was impeccable, though Madeleine vividly remembered the places where her skin had sloughed off, and the bones hidden under makeup. Illusion? The antlers on either side of her head were chipped, yellowed, and translucent, like fragile porcelain, and the pearl under her chin was likewise dull, its luster completely extinguished.

"Clothilde Desclozeaux. Elphon. Madeleine d'Aubin." She didn't smile. "Be welcome to the dragon kingdom."

Clothilde made a sweeping bow, effortlessly inclining her entire body to almost touch the ground. Elphon also bowed, gracefully. Madeleine followed suit, awkwardly, feeling as though every seam of her clothes was going to burst.

"We are honored," Clothilde said. She rose, keeping her eyes away from Ngoc Bich.

"You come to us at a critical juncture," Ngoc Bich said.

Clothilde's voice was wry. "We are aware."

Madeleine's gaze roamed down the rows of dignitaries. Everywhere that same faded splendor, those old, patched silks, the magic that wouldn't quite hold, the skin that became shell, or scales, or dull fur. At the back was a group of people dressed in the French fashion, the swallowtail jacket and trousers looking almost incongruous on them.

"I sadly can't allow you the freedom of the palace," Ngoc Bich said, inclining her head. "There are many places where your presence would be inappropriate."

Clothilde nodded. "That is understood, of course. We have no desire to impose."

Ngoc Bich's face didn't move. "Indeed. Come," she said, and gestured for them to follow her inside, under the rafters of the pavilion.

Something was off. Madeleine had never been the world's foremost observer, but she knew about fear. Entirely too many people in that crowd seemed nervous. Afraid of a three-person delegation? That hardly made sense.

Inside, fish swam between lacquered pillars, skeletal and dull-scaled, their fins and tails encrusted with corrosion. Ngoc Bich walked past the ornate throne on its dais, to a room behind it, a smaller, quieter place decorated with faience, a continuous weaving of sinuous shapes and vivid colors that had chipped off in multiple places. The air smelled, faintly, of algae underlain by rot.

There was a table of faience: the surface showed two huge, entwining creatures that must have been dragons: serpentine shapes with four stubby, clawed legs, globular eyes, and large, fanged snouts. It, too, was chipped in multiple places: the pearls under their chins were all but gone, and the claws reduced to shreds. People awaited them, standing behind the high wooden chairs: dragon officials with those same curiously translucent antlers, and hair tied in topknots. One of them wore it long and unbound: it streamed in the water like the mane of a horse.

Ngoc Bich settled at the end. The attendants with parasols had vanished, replaced by two women carrying rectangular fans. A bevy of officials had also come with them; there was a moment of flux as everyone pulled a chair and sat down.

"You know Thanh Phan," Ngoc Bich said. She nodded to the official who wore his hair unbound. "This is Minh. He is the minister of public works." And then more names and titles, all said in French mingled with Annamite, which Madeleine couldn't follow but which Clothilde appeared enraptured by.

Clothilde set down a piece of paper, and slid it down toward the center of the table. "My letters of appointment." She smiled. "With Lord Asmodeus's personal seal, and the arms of the House."

This was passed down the table, with the closest thing to reverence that Madeleine had seen yet. Minh was the only one who appeared unimpressed. "Words," he said, with a frown. "Seals. Symbols." His irises were the muddy color of river silt, unfocused. Madeleine had seen that gaze before, in older people developing cataracts. But surely dragons couldn't, shouldn't, be sick?

"Words matter," Ngoc Bich said. "They are what we are here for."

"I have brought you the terms we offer," Clothilde said. She gestured, to the papers she'd given Ngoc Bich. "Under the credentials."

Ngoc Bich didn't make any move to lift the paper.

"House Hawthorn is eager to conclude this alliance," Clothilde said, in the face of a totally silent audience. They were all as impassive and inscrutable as the statues Madeleine had seen in the courtyards: faint smiles on their faces—it was impossible to read whatever they might be thinking, and they all looked young, too young. Philippe, ageless and Immortal, had looked in his late twenties; these officials seemed barely out of adolescence. And weren't friendly. "It will strengthen both of us to work together. A union of both worlds."

"Yes." Ngoc Bich inclined her head. "Thanh Phan, Minh, and Véronique have full authority to discuss terms. I will review your negotiations when they deem them ready for my appraisal."

"Of course," Clothilde said. She hesitated, then said, "I need to know, Your Highness. Forgive me for my bluntness, but if you happen not to be interested in this alliance, then we will leave. As I said, we have no desire to impose. We are not thieves or invaders."

Thanh Phan's frown of disapproval could have frozen water. "Fallen are always the invaders."

Ngoc Bich lifted a hand. "What gives you this impression?" she asked, to Clothilde.

"Ghislaine Le Guell." Clothilde bent forward, her hands resting on the table. She wore a dress with long, tight-fitting sleeves, but Madeleine could still remember the scars on her arms, still remember that terrible, wounding smile she'd given her.

There was silence, in the wake of her words.

"What of her?"

Clothilde shook her head. "We are negotiating in good faith." Not exactly likely, when Asmodeus was the one directing the negotiations. But still, she sounded like she believed it. How good a liar was she? Better than Madeleine, certainly. That wasn't hard. "I don't mind the small lies, the evasions. We all have our secrets. As you said"—she smiled—"there are places where our presence or prying would be inappropriate. The location of a previous ambassador, though, that is not negotiable, or inappropriate. I'd rather not share my predecessor's fate, if it can be avoided."

"Nothing happened to her," Véronique said. She was dressed in the French style, and her hair was cut in a short bob, looking almost incongruous on her. Her hands were fine, with two ruby rings, and a signet ring engraved with Chinese characters on the last finger of the left side. That last finger was skeletally thin, with hardly any skin to it. No, not skin. It was the thin, jointed blue-green shell of a crustacean appendage.

"Véronique." Minh's voice was a knife blade. He looked, unerringly, toward Ngoc Bich. "Empress?"

Ngoc Bich said nothing, for a while. She watched Minh, who said, "It is the time of sea and mulberry, Your Excellency. To have bamboo and plum trees grow together, you must be willing to plant them close to one another."

At last, Ngoc Bich inclined her head, her lips pressed together in reluctant approval, and Minh spoke up. "Ambassador Ghislaine was seen leaving the palace some three days ago. She hasn't returned, and we don't know where she is."

Silence, again. Clothilde brushed aside a small crab covered with lichen, which had started to climb over her hand. "I assume you've searched."

There was a glance, shared between Véronique and Minh. "We have searched the palace. Insofar as we can tell, she is not here. You are, of course, quite welcome to examine her room."

Madeleine bent toward Elphon, and whispered, "She had a tracker disk, didn't she?" And then she realized why they all carried a stronger version of it.

"Yes," Elphon said, in the same tone. "It's not responding."

But she wasn't dead, or Asmodeus and everyone linked to the House would have felt it like a bell toll in their heads, and anyone close enough to offer a rescue would have heard the magical equivalent of a scream for help.

"We will examine her room," Clothilde said. Her face had taken on the sharpness of a knife. "I would have thought an official envoy of Hawthorn would be safe in the heart of your kingdom."

"You are outsiders," Thanh Phan said, in much the same tone as she'd have said "barbarians." "You can be excused for not knowing what we pledged. Your envoy's credentials were recognized, and revered, but the person of an envoy isn't sacred."

"It is in France. Here."

"Here?" Thanh Phan's hand rose, showed the faience pillars, the table with its two broken-off dragons, the colored rafters of the ceiling, a strange and diminished alienness that was at once disconcerting and repelling. "This isn't France. This isn't a House. This isn't Hawthorn."

"If you would ally with Hawthorn, you would do well to show us respect," Clothilde said.

It was going to turn ugly, and fast. Madeleine laid a hand on Clothilde's arm before she could stop herself. "I thought we were going to negotiate terms?"

Clothilde looked at her—that sharpness, that sense of threat, turning her way—and then she exhaled, noisily. "Fine," she said. "My apologies for questioning your customs."

"Accepted," Thanh Phan said, as if it were a challenge.

Madeleine fought the urge to yell at them. Acting like spoiled children wasn't going to help anything or anyone.

"Thanh Phan," Ngoc Bich said. Her voice was gentle, but every word was wrapped in steel. "You know the stakes."

Thanh Phan inclined her head. "Your Highness. Of course."

"We all know them," Clothilde said, drily. "I was told you had settled the question of the bridegroom."

Ngoc Bich inclined her head. "With Envoy Ghislaine? It was agreed Prince Rong Minh Phuong Dinh would be satisfactory. If you would like to review—"

"I would like to meet him at some point, yes," Clothilde said. She didn't sound surprised that he wasn't in the room. And yes, it was a diplomatic alliance; yes, it was rather unlikely either of them was marrying for love, but . . . Madeleine hoped that Prince Rong, whoever he was, was fully aware of what he was getting into.

"I'll let him know. We will introduce him to you tomorrow," Ngoc Bich said. "Now, with Envoy Ghislaine we had discussed . . ."

The conversation became technical, dwelling on concessions and terms Ghislaine had negotiated on behalf of the House. Madeleine let her mind drift, trying to ignore the link to Hawthorn in her head, and the growing emptiness within her, the craving gnawing away at her stomach and lungs.

Noises came from outside. Then voices, raised in an argument in Annamite. Some kind of commotion?

Madeleine rose, heedless of the debate going on between Clothilde and the officials, and found herself face-to-face with one of the most forbidding dragons she'd ever seen. She had long hair that had almost twisted into a mane, and the lower half of her face lengthened into a snout, with glistening fangs. One of them was broken off, but it didn't make much difference. She had a pearl under her chin, like Ngoc Bich, but this one shone with fire, and the same fire was in the dragon's gaze as she looked at Madeleine. "Fallen," she spat. "Get out of my way."

"I'm not—," Madeleine started, but the dragon had already walked past her.

Outside, in the courtyard, the officials had gone, and the guards were clustering in unfamiliar patterns that nevertheless spoke to Madeleine. Wariness. Fear. What was going on in this palace?

The dragon was speaking to Ngoc Bich in a low, urgent voice. Thanh Phan had bent to overhear the words, her harsh face frozen in something akin to panic.

"My apologies," Ngoc Bich said, rising. "A matter of urgency has occurred. Thanh Phan will take you back to your rooms."

"We want to see Ghislaine's rooms first," Clothilde said.

"Of course," Ngoc Bich said. "We will arrange for it."

"Now." Clothilde looked as though she were going to breathe fire. She had a mirror in her hand, and the Fallen magic she'd inhaled from it filled her, made her skin shine like a sun or a bonfire, her eyes as white as the heart of stars—a faint outline behind her, lines so fine they were almost invisible, like spider's silk glistening in interrupted tracery: wings framing the dark shape of her head and making her seem taller than she was.

For a while, they faced each other: the dragon princess, with her broken antlers and her uncanny whitened face, and the eyes of snakes; and Clothilde,

Fallen magic streaming out of her, looking Ngoc Bich straight in the face. Madeleine remembered something, vaguely, about never looking at a higher rank of Annamite in the eyes. Wasn't it some kind of mortal offense, in the kingdom? Clothilde didn't seem to care.

Ngoc Bich didn't look away, but she nodded. "Escort them," Ngoc Bich said, to Thanh Phan.

Thanh Phan didn't look happy. "Your Highness," she said. "As you wish." It sounded like she'd swallowed something sour, and couldn't wait to spit it out.

FIVE
MISSING DREAMS

THE courtyard outside the audience room was now empty. But as their escort led them through a series of small, suffocating corridors that seemed to belong to another palace altogether, the sounds of men running filtered through, and so did slow booms, like a heavy gong being struck.

Clothilde appeared intently focused on their destination, but Elphon fell in with Madeleine. "What would you say is happening?" he asked.

"I—I—," Madeleine stuttered. "You're asking me?" Someday she was going to get used to having him close. He hadn't changed at all; he was a reminder of all she had left behind when Asmodeus took over Hawthorn; and she might *know* that he had been reborn, that he was now utterly faithful to Asmodeus, but in her mind she was still fifteen, and they were still racing each other to the bridge over the Seine.

"Obviously." Elphon shook his head. "I don't know what is going on between you and Lord Asmodeus. It's none of my business. You're with us because he thought you would be of use here."

Yes, to recharge artifacts for Clothilde and the bodyguards. As Asmodeus had said, a basic need that did not require advanced alchemical skills. She was down here because she was expendable, because he wouldn't lose anyone valuable if something did go wrong. And of course, she was also here because it was a test, to see how she handled herself, outside the House.

"I don't know," Madeleine said, at last. "They're scared. And . . . they've lived for hundreds of years in isolation. They've defended themselves against the encroachment of Houses and Fallen magic. Something must have changed." Asmodeus had said their time for secrecy had ended, but that wasn't enough to make them vulnerable, was it? "You don't strike an alliance with your worst enemy unless you're desperate."

"Or unless you have other ideas beyond the alliance," Elphon said.

That would be us. Hawthorn. "I don't think that's what is happening," Madeleine said, slowly. "They sound divided."

"Yes." Elphon looked at their guards, and then back at Clothilde. "I'm going to have a look around. Keep on walking, will you? Whatever happens, don't look back." He gave her a light squeeze on her shoulder. "And tell Clothilde I'll be back this evening. Hopefully that shouldn't make her too mad."

"Elphon?" Madeleine asked, but he had already fallen behind.

He had sounded deathly serious. What was he thinking of?

Don't look back.

Corridor after corridor, and the sound of booted feet behind them, and a rising smell, dust and blight, and patches of algae so thick on every surface they had hardened like mortar. The walls were no longer faience or wood, but what looked like lumps of coral, coaxed into forming pillars and roofs and whole buildings. Everything looking subtly wrong, until Madeleine realized it was because nothing had right angles, or perfect circles: every single shape slightly bent or twisted, a warped imitation of architecture done by someone who didn't really know how buildings worked.

She caught up with Clothilde as they reached their destination: a small room by another courtyard. The walls were green and blue, with the slight white sheen of unhealthy trees. The smell of decay was so strong that Madeleine struggled to breathe. She needed essence, something, anything, to stop her stomach churning. She took one step into the room, and was back out, kneeling in the courtyard to puke her guts out before she'd even realized what was happening.

A hand on her shoulder, steadying her. When she stood up, Clothilde was by her side, holding out the infused mirror she'd used. "It's almost empty, but that should help."

It wasn't essence, but Madeleine was past caring. She tipped the mirror open; found, by force of habit, the catch, and released the entire remaining contents into her nostrils. Something filled her mouth and her throat and her stomach, a slow, steady warmth like embers in a quiescent fireplace. It wasn't fire; wasn't that giddy feeling she could do anything, could defeat anyone, that her fears were only an illusion dispelled by the sun's scorching radiance. But it was enough that she could breathe again.

And enough so that, looking around, she could see that though their escort had positioned themselves across the courtyard, watching them both with incurious eyes, Elphon was now nowhere to be seen.

Clothilde frowned. "Where—," she started.

"Elphon said he wanted to have a look around," Madeleine said. "He thought you'd be mad."

Clothilde's expression was grimly amused. "You mean because when whatever spell he's used wears off, I'm going to be the one to explain to those guards why they've lost one of the people they were supposed to be protecting? 'Mad' is certainly an accurate description." She sighed. "Let's examine the room. I'll sort things out, somehow."

It was a small room, and it was clear that it had been, until recently, occupied. The smell—the stench—wasn't only rot; it was rot mingled with the remnants of incense and perfume. Small hermit crabs scuttled out of sight as they entered, making for the shadows under the furniture, and shoals of small fish turned tail and fled, a silvery, skeletal stream that passed right by Madeleine's face, too fast to be grasped.

Thanh Phan was waiting for them by the bed alcove, frowning. When they both entered, she said to Clothilde, "Weren't there more of you?"

Clothilde frowned. "Wears off fast," she said to herself. "Elphon is on a mission of his own. Without, I might add, my permission."

Thanh Phan looked as though she was going to have an apoplexy. "Left? Now, of all times?"

Ah well. When in doubt, be blunt. Madeleine asked, "Why? What's happening?"

"None of your concern," Thanh Phan said. "But we would advise you not to wander around unescorted."

"Because it's dangerous?" Madeleine asked.

"I don't know. Fallen magic." Thanh Phan snorted, and released a flow of little bubbles, a disturbing effect that reminded Madeleine they were still underwater. "We were doing fine for thousands of years, and within the span of a few decades you destroy everything. The princess is right. It's a cancer."

It was also the thing keeping Madeleine warm and upright, and clothed and fed and protected from the grimy, apocalyptic misery of the streets. "Easy for you to say."

"Look around you," Thanh Phan said, but it was spent and tired, as if she'd had this argument too many times. "It's not safe out there," she said. "No matter what fancy your companion may get into his head. And I don't want to have to tell House Hawthorn that we lost yet another envoy." She walked past them, calling out instructions to the guards in Annamite.

When she was gone, Clothilde poked at a burner left by the bed alcove, still filled with ashes. "Cinnamon and sandalwood," she said, curtly. "Might have been some use, before they burned themselves out."

Two large chests were piled one atop the other, each inscribed with a Chinese character. Madeleine wasn't sure why, as the Annamites used an alphabet, but either way she wouldn't have been able to decipher these. She opened the trunks, and found them full of clothes, from dresses to jackets to loose trousers. "She didn't pack much of anything." At the bottom was an empty container that gave a small, familiar jolt as Madeleine touched it. Angel magic, probably a severed finger or some fragment of skin. Ghislaine wouldn't have gone down into the dragon kingdom without resources.

"No," Clothilde said. She ran a hand on the small table in the center of the room, raised it to her face. "There were papers on that table, and they're gone."

"The room has been searched by the kingdom's soldiers, already."

"Yes," Clothilde said. "And God only knows what they thought worth taking."

"We took nothing," Thanh Phan said, from the doorway. "We're not thieves." She sounded offended.

Not, of course, that they had any way to check.

While Clothilde made her way to the clothes chest, Madeleine knelt by the bed. It was in a recessed alcove, with a low ceiling and a small size that must have made Ghislaine feel claustrophobic. Underneath the grime and the algae was a raised contour, with a faint whitish trace. She ran her fingers over it until something snagged, and pushed and pulled and prodded until the entire piece of furniture felt like it was coming apart in her hands.

It must not have been a hidden drawer at conception, but the layers and layers of hardened algae had turned it into one. Inside were a handful of badly disintegrated papers, and . . .

The smell was faint, and even fainter under the stench of the room, but she would have known it anywhere. The small container in front of her, lined with faded parchment, had once held angel essence.

Now there was nothing left but traces, but even traces would do, if they could assuage the emptiness within her. If they could . . . Her hands were shaking. She looked up: Clothilde was in an animated discussion with Thanh Phan, and was keeping only cursory attention on her.

She wasn't going to relapse. He would kill her if she did, would take her apart, smiling all the while, but she needed safety. Comfort. The promise of something she could go to when things became unbearable. She needed *this*.

Slowly, smoothly, she lifted the parchment from the container, and folded it as tight as she could, before sliding it into the pocket of her trousers. Clothilde would see her—Clothilde would know—but when she looked up, her heartbeat so loud she could hear it resonate through her entire body, Clothilde's gaze was still distracted and distant.

"Here," she said, forcing herself to speak in a slow, steady voice. "There was something." In fact, by the container was the imprint of a second container, as faint and as whitish as the opening to the drawer had been. "Angel essence."

Clothilde was by her side almost faster than she could draw breath, bending over the drawer with entirely too much concern. It didn't matter. She couldn't guess that Madeleine had already taken the parchment that lined it. "Mmm," Clothilde said. "Are you sure?"

"I'd recognize the smell anywhere." And that was easy, because it wasn't a lie.

Thanh Phan's face was frozen, in what Madeleine was coming to think of as the "inscrutable" expression, the dragons' variant of a poker face.

"And there was a second container, too," Madeleine said. "If they didn't take it—" She didn't dare look at Thanh Phan's expression, because she could guess.

"—Ghislaine did," Clothilde said. "So, in so much of a hurry that she didn't pack her clothes, but she did take angel essence. And used a fair bit of it beforehand." She lifted the container to the level of her eyes. "I assume this was full."

Madeleine shrugged. "I wouldn't know. But you wouldn't take two containers if one of them wasn't full." Her manic heartbeat was slowly coming down to normal, and she was breathing easily again. Natural. She had to act natural. That was the only way she was going to get away with what she had done. Because if Clothilde, at any point, suspected . . .

No no no. Don't think about this. Think about the essence, the feel of it in your hands, in your throat, the light that banishes the darkness, the fire that makes everything right.

"Fleeing," Madeleine said, before she could stop herself. "Frightened of something. Of someone here. Or elsewhere."

Clothilde was watching her, head cocked in a way that was all too reminiscent of Asmodeus. "Mmm. You assume everyone is afraid, don't you?"

Because she was. Because—damn him—Asmodeus was right, and fear filled her, night and day: the nightmares of Asmodeus's coup that she couldn't banish, the memories of crawling out of the House with broken ribs, every movement an agony, feeling blood draining out of her every time she managed to drag herself just a bit farther; that awful, rising certainty that she was going to die, right there, or worse, be taken back inside the House.

And it didn't change anything that her nightmare had come true. It made it all the worse.

She didn't answer. She couldn't.

At length, Clothilde shook her head, and moved back to the drawer. "She's left papers, too." She took them, gingerly, and folded them in half. "I can't make out what was on them, but I'll work on them this evening. Right after I've given Elphon an earful for his little stunt."

Except that, come evening, Elphon still hadn't turned up.

EVENING in the dragon kingdom was odd. The sun—which had been this rippling, inaccessible ball of light that looked nothing like the sun over Paris—vanished within the space of a few heartbeats, and darkness descended across the underwater kingdom as if someone had pulled a black veil over the entire landscape. Faint lights appeared from globes encased in the walls and lanterns spread on the pillars, but nothing like the wealth of radiance from chandeliers and lamps that filled House Silverspires or Hawthorn at night.

Dinner was subdued: Thanh Phan and Véronique, and the terrifying dragon official who had interrupted their audience, whose name was Anh Le, and a handful of others whose names Madeleine didn't catch or didn't remember. Conversation was a blur of subjects skillfully managed by Clothilde, while Madeleine stared obstinately at food. In deference to them, the table was laid in the Western manner, with plates and forks and knives, but the food was still unfamiliar, with a faint aftertaste of fish to everything that made Madeleine's stomach protest.

And still no Elphon, before, during, or after the meal.

After dinner, Madeleine asked Clothilde for the infused mirror she'd used. Clothilde handed it to her with barely a raised eyebrow. It was completely empty, its magic spent first by Clothilde, and then by Madeleine outside Ghislaine's rooms.

They might have lost Elphon, but two of the bodyguards were Fallen: it was but the work of a moment to ask one of them to breathe onto the mirror, and seal it safely shut after the polished surface turned black with trapped angel magic. While she was at it, Madeleine also refilled with breath the charged pendants the bodyguards had been using: they'd been draining a fair amount of magic to maintain the wards around themselves and the delegation's quarters, and there was no sense in their carrying around half-full artifacts.

When she came back into Clothilde's room with the charged mirror, Clothilde was ensconced with the papers. "Good," she said, curtly, tucking the mirror into a fold of her sleeve. "You can stay here now, and help me find ideas about what's going on."

Of course it wasn't really about ideas. It was about keeping an eye on Madeleine. She wasn't sure whether it was out of concern for her—too many people from Hawthorn had already disappeared—or because of Asmodeus's orders, or both.

No matter. Before dinner, she'd managed to move the angel essence from her trousers, and slipped it between the pages of the book she was reading, like an eccentric bookmark. Now she sat on the floor with her arms wrapped around her knees—the only way she felt comfortable around Clothilde.

"Those are Ghislaine's notes. There are factions within the dragon king-dom." Clothilde snorted. "Why did she feel she had to hide this? That's hardly secret knowledge." At length, she put the papers away. "Not much of interest, I'm afraid. There was another dragon kingdom called the Bièvre, some time before the war. It was . . . weakened."

"By the sewers." The river Bièvre had once run through Paris, but it had been driven underground to make way for the sewer system.

"Perhaps," Clothilde said. "I don't claim to understand why they do what they do. It's hard enough keeping up with all the Houses." Her face was harsh once more: Hawthorn's face to strangers, merciless and cruel. "At any rate, the Bièvre was absorbed within the kingdom of the Seine: the one we're standing in right now. It did not go smoothly."

"It's a kingdom. They had a king?" Madeleine asked, curious in spite of herself.

"It's unclear what happened to him," Clothilde said. "Whether someone from the Seine killed him, or whether he died of natural causes. What is sure is how much ill will is going around, and suspicion that the Bièvre refugees aren't treated the same as the native Seine people. They're stuck in menial jobs, and prevented from rising to high office unless their talents are extraordinary. Good to know it's the same the world over."

It was rather depressing, though Madeleine had never considered the dragon kingdom a viable refuge. Philippe might have, once, and perhaps Isabelle? But who knew what Isabelle had thought? She'd so seldom played by other people's rules.

Clothilde went on. "Thanh Phan was a high-ranking official in the court of the Bièvre. And so were a couple other people, whom we don't seem to have met yet. Someone named Yen Oanh is prominently mentioned. I'll have to see who they are."

That would explain Thanh Phan's animosity, not only to them, but to Ngoc Bich. "And that's all?"

"There are other notes about Fallen magic and the kingdom. Mostly baseless speculations. But all in all, not really fascinating or enlightening." She sighed.

Madeleine said, finally, "What are they asking for? From us?"

Clothilde shrugged. "Magic. Money. Weapons. Rifles that are better than the old, rusted ones they use. Support against any House or faction that might attack the kingdom, should it happen. The classic terms of an alliance."

Madeleine thought, for a while, of the flurry of activity, the armed guards. "They're already feeling threatened, aren't they?"

"Of course," Clothilde said. She sounded bored. "Nothing that need concern us for long. We didn't swear to fight their wars for them, and the treaty will limit the help we offer them."

"We—," Madeleine started. She couldn't imagine a consort was all that Asmodeus wanted of the venture. There were so many other places he could find a lover. "Why are we doing this?"

"Magic," Clothilde said. "Theirs. And"—she inhaled, sharply—"a permanent delegation of our dependents in the kingdom. Unfortunately one that will be subject to their laws and customs, instead of being exempted. Ghislaine didn't manage to get *that* past them."

It sounded small. Almost petty, and Asmodeus seldom did small, petty things. "Their magic? People to teach us? To serve us?" What could he want? A legitimization before a conquest? But the dragon kingdom was well defended and well armored against Fallen magic. When she'd gone into it the last time, she had come out of it only through the goodwill of Ngoc Bich. An army, even loaded with Fallen magic and the most powerful artifacts of the House, would flounder and drown before it even got to the capital.

Or did he want to use dragon magic in a power play against another House?

"Ghislaine wanted teachers," Clothilde said. "They're digging in their heels, though. We might have to be content with a few staff magicians." She sighed. "Better go to bed. It's going to be a long day tomorrow."

"Clothilde?"

"Yes?" She sounded annoyed now: too many questions from Madeleine. "Elphon had a tracker disk, didn't he?"

Silence. Then, "Oh. You're still worried about him." A smile that was pitying, like a slap in the face. "He's not in danger, Madeleine. Insofar as I can tell, he's somewhere in the city beyond the palace."

"They said it was dangerous. . . ." Madeleine could feel her face burn redder and redder, all the while: that distinct feeling of being chastised like a child was humiliating, and uncomfortable. Madeleine. Poor Madeleine, the world's poorest liar, sentimental and misguided. Of course she'd be too stupid to do anything but keep her word, be too caring to dismiss her jailers.

And in another, kinder universe, it wouldn't have been an insult.

"They said that because they didn't want us poking our noses where they don't belong." Clothilde exhaled, noisily. "Look. I appreciate your concern, but honestly, he's fine. We lost Ghislaine because tracker disks behave weirdly down here, but I can feel him clearly, and so can Asmodeus. If he's in any kind of danger, we'll all feel it. And you probably will, too. Now go to bed."

Dismissed, like a disobedient child.

Alone in her rooms, Madeleine pulled the folded parchment from the book, and stared at it for a while. The familiar, acrid odor wafted up to her, begging her to open it, to inhale just a fraction of what it had contained.

She would be safe. She would feel safe: not loved or cherished, but powerful enough not to care.

But she still had the bruises from the straps that had held her to the bed in Hawthorn, could still breathe in the smell of bergamot and orange blossom that always heralded Asmodeus's coming. The price was too high. It was too high.

She was about to put the parchment away, and take Iaris's medication for her cough, when she saw the faint blue lines on it. Handwriting. Ghislaine's?

She could, with care, unfold the parchment so that the pitifully small remnants of essence didn't fall out. She'd had years and years of practice in House Silverspires, scrounging all that she could from the bones she'd stolen in her tenure as House alchemist, before she got caught and thrown out. She could turn it around and around, memorizing everything that was on it—and, with the same care, transfer the lines to a sheet of blank paper.

She put the parchment away after she was done, because manipulating it had saturated her nostrils with the smell of angel essence, and she didn't trust herself to handle it anymore, because all she'd have to do was raise it to her nostrils, and then she'd lose the little she had.

Then she stared at the other paper, the one she'd filled in. It was a bit lopsided, especially around the folds, where she'd had to guess how the lines fitted together. She'd never been especially good with imagining things in three dimensions, and she couldn't pretend drawing was her forte. But, nevertheless, it was easy to read.

Prince Phuong Dinh is not unsympathetic. Find a way to talk to him, away from prying eyes.

Prince Phuong Dinh was the one they were supposed to bring home as part of the diplomatic alliance, wasn't he? Not unsympathetic to what? To the alliance? But why him specifically? It made no sense. What in heaven was going on here? No matter what Clothilde said, it was something pretty serious.

Outside, the slow booms had ceased, replaced by the faint sounds of the kingdom at night: crabs scuttling away, the passage of large fish by the doorway, and the low chatter of guards talking among themselves.

God, how she hated this place.

At length, Madeleine folded the paper. She wasn't going to show it to Clothilde. It made no sense, and if she did show it, she would have to explain where she had found it and why. But she could keep an eye out. She could try to understand what was happening. Because, no matter what Clothilde said, Elphon was in danger, and so were they.

SIX
THE LURE OF ANGELS

IN Thuan's dreams, he prowled the corridors of the Imperial Palace in the dragon kingdom, finding every room and courtyard empty, with cups of tea still steaming on tables, and incense sticks smoldering on the ancestral altars, the bowls of fruit still fresh and impeccably arranged as if they'd just been offered.

"Second Aunt?"

There was no answer.

In the ponds, the pebbles formed patterns, signs and symbols in a language he could no longer read. Small crabs scuttled away from him, and something crunched underfoot, coral or bones or both, and he couldn't even be sure what he was breaking.

"Second Aunt?"

In the mausoleum where his grandfather Emperor Rong Nghiem Chung Thuy lay buried, he found her at last.

She was sitting on the throne, by the emperor's golden effigy, her face turned away from him. The sign above her said, simply, PRINCESS RONG THUY NGOC BICH, with no other honorifics or achievements: plain and stark, and altogether heartbreaking, after all the trouble she'd gone through trying to hold the kingdom together.

"Second Aunt—"

"You're too late." She turned toward him, and her face was sloughed-off skin and cracked bones, and her eyes the mottled, grayish color of angel essence corruption, rotted from the inside out—and everything smelled sweet and sickly, a smell that rose and rose until he fell to his knees, gagging and struggling not to breathe, knowing that to breathe it would be his end, too. . . .

Thuan woke, gasping, and stared at the mold spreading over the ceiling of his room. *Oh, ancestors.* Her eyes. Nothing left of the beautiful gray-green of the river, of the irises that showed all the colors of mother-of-pearl. Just rot. The Fallen had won. They always did, in the end; always crept and oozed and wormed their way into every nook and cranny of Paris. Why should the kingdom be any different?

No. That was the nightmare speaking. He was going to find what he'd come here for: the source of the angel essence that was slowly destroying them. And then . . . Second Aunt hadn't been forthcoming about what she wanted to do, but if Thuan had his way, they would execute the traffickers, and leave the mangled bodies by the Seine as a message that the kingdom wasn't to be trifled with.

And if that could help them gain any hold in their negotiations with Hawthorn, it would be grabbed, too, held on to like a lifeline. No one in the kingdom really liked the idea of the alliance, or trusted Hawthorn to respect it, but there wasn't much choice. They were too hard-pressed.

He rose, and knelt by his small ancestral altar: four pictures of his parents and paternal grandparents, looking at him with the vacant expressions of the dead over the rim of a bowl with three tangerines.

"Please help me," he whispered, a quick, shameful prayer in a land where he barely managed to keep up the proper worship. Mother's death anniversary had coincided with an all-day exam at school, and by the time he came back to his room, utterly drained of coherent thought, the best he'd been capable of had been a small prayer.

The House was silent: it was still dark and freezing cold outside, with another hour or so to go to dawn, when the kitchen and laundry rooms would come alive, and the drudges would take their mops and brooms into the corridors, and light, one by one, the big chandeliers with candles on poles, to signal the beginning of the day.

Thuan had wandered it, at night, when only the bakers in the kitchens were up, kneading dough for the massive stone ovens: the main, cavernous edifice; the small, winding streets spreading out from beyond the gardens, their buildings cracked limestone confections with rusted wrought-iron balconies, and dependents in embroidered dresses and top hats leaning, languidly, against the pillars of blackened porches and patios. The broken ruins in the corners of the gardens: the abandoned buildings, with the trails of water running down glass panes like tears; the melted, pitted limestone overgrown with ivy and other creepers; the black debris mixed in with the gravel; and the broken-off hands on the statues in the fountains. All the traces of the war, in a House that hadn't been spared by it.

Second Aunt would have been pleased to see him given such free rein, but in truth there was little to see at night. Most of the rooms were closed and sealed, and most of the people who could have helped him were asleep.

Today Thuan had no particular destination in mind. He was just killing time until Sare woke up. Careful questioning of Nadine had established that angel essence was kept, not in the infirmary, but in the alchemist's laboratory, with the other by-products of Fallen magic. So it wasn't Iaris he wanted to see, but Sare, the House's alchemist.

He wandered corridor after corridor, losing himself in the labyrinth of the West Wing, running a hand on the wainscot of cracked wooden panels, his fingers brushing the engraved figures of game animals and trees. There was something addictive, alluring about standing outside the bedrooms of the House's elite, the leaders of each court, and their being none the wiser as to the danger he represented.

He stopped at a crossroads between two corridors, to look at a striking piece, a stag whose antlers blurred and merged into the thorns of a tree. Dogs were harrying it, yet the beast held itself tall and proud, as if it didn't even deign to notice them. The detail had chipped away, and there was dust around the design, a thickening layer like a gray outline.

On the right, the corridor curved sharply, flaring into something very much like an antechamber, at the end of which was a huge set of wooden doors. They were strangely plain: painted with a scattering of faded silver stars against a dark gray background. Two of those stars were falling from the firmament; their silver tinged with the scarlet of blood, a shade that never quite seemed to hold as the viewer moved.

It smelled, faintly, of bergamot and citrus, and he had no business being there. None at all. It was one thing to be outside the rooms of the courts' leaders, reveling in his freedom, but this was Asmodeus's bedroom, and Thuan had already stood out enough for a lifetime.

He was about to creep away as stealthily as he had come in. Then he stopped.

Because there was a light under the doors, quite visible in the darkness, and a rising sense of power coming from the room, a roiling magic like a storm tossing and snapping boats like kindling. Thuan was in the corridor before that antechamber corner, a good distance away from whatever was happening, and still it was terrible enough to send him to his knees, gasping to take a breath—a power that didn't feel like Asmodeus's or anyone's in the House. It was something infinitely old and cruel and merciless; and yet tinged, underneath, with a yearning for a lost home that hooked one curved finger under his heart, and pulled until a sharp, unbearable pain hollowed him out, stilling his breath in his lungs and leaving him thrashing on the floor like a fish with a broken spine.

What—? What . . . had he felt?

Thuan pulled himself upright, gingerly. The power was dwindling now, or perhaps he was merely getting used to it: a small hearth fire instead of a blaze. He couldn't stop himself from shaking, and he still felt that moment when it had reached out, carelessly taking everything from him.

Move. He had to move. He couldn't be sure. It could merely be a side effect, but if it had indeed reached out, if it had drawn something from him, then someone inside those rooms had received it. Someone would know he was there, which meant either Asmodeus or his closest associates. Either way, not what he wanted.

Move.

He forced himself to walk. His earlier insouciance was gone, and the carvings on the wainscoting leered at him, monstrous and distorted. The darkness was no longer his province, his joy, but something that muffled sounds and sights, that would hide his pursuers until it was too late. Nothing would save him if he was caught, no second aunt to shield him from the wrath of the House, and the cells that always waited for more bodies, like a hungry maw. . . .

One corner, and then another. No sounds coming from behind him. Nothing but the silence of the House, the distant sounds of servants getting up. He was—

He heard, clearly even from this distance, the distinct click of a door opening. And a voice, grave and melodious and instantly recognizable, calling words he couldn't quite make out.

The time for subtlety was gone then.

He ran. He took corridors in a blur of movement, two, three steps at a time, looking up merely to make sure he didn't slam into a wall, trying to make as little noise as possible, but he couldn't be fast or silent enough—with luck he might have turned enough corridors that Asmodeus wouldn't find him—he might have put enough distance between him and the magic, and found safety among others. . . .

Familiar doors around him now: the sounds of bells and alarm clocks, and moans and curses from people unwilling to get up. The wainscoting had given way to green wallpaper with the imprint of flowers, and the smell was no longer citruses or bergamot, but soap and leather, and the faint, sweet one of the coffee éclairs he and the others had shared around a tarot game, underlain with the sharp, familiar scent of mildew. He was back in the part of the House that he knew, where he had his rooms.

And doors were opening, farther away—*Slow down*. He had to slow down, lest he attract attention. If he could just breathe normally, make it not so blindingly obvious that he had just been running. If he could find again the carelessness with which he had wandered the House . . .

"Thuan? What are you doing up at this hour?"

His heart lurched within his chest, and then he realized it was only Nadine, accompanied by Leila, the other student she tutored. "Hello, Nadine. Couldn't sleep."

Nadine snorted. "That'd be a first. You're the world's worst morning person."

Second Aunt was up at dawn, or before. Thuan had never mastered that skill: whenever he attended to her, he would always find her ensconced with a pile of annotated state papers, and she would pointedly refrain from saying anything about his being hours late. He wasn't sure that really made it better. "I can get up early if I want to."

Leila hid a smile. "You were late for *exams*, Thuan. If they disqualified students for that—"

"Shut up," Thuan said, mock-punching her in the shoulder. "I passed, anyway." Not that it mattered much.

"Luck."

"Maybe. What are you doing up? I'll grant that you might be better than me"—he exaggerated the grimace—"but it's still very early."

Nadine made a face. "Infirmary duty, remember? You're not a real nurse, so you're excused, but we need someone there at all times."

"Oh." Thuan breathed in, out, trying to calm himself. It felt almost surreal to be speaking to Nadine, to reengage with the small concerns of everyday life inside the House. It should have made his experience with the magic feel unreal, too, but nothing would make that less vivid or nightmarish.

Nadine's eyes focused on him. "Are you all right, Thuan? You look like you've seen a ghost."

Restless spirits, for all their vindictiveness, would have been almost a relief in comparison. "I thought—" He took a deep, shaking breath. "I thought I heard—" He didn't have to try very hard to convey fear and surprise, and just a little hint of the stomach-churning dread he felt. "It's nothing. I'll be fine, when I've had time to breathe." Neither of them looked very convinced. "Did you have breakfast yet?"

Leila shrugged. "We're just going to grab something from the kitchen. Coming?"

He definitely could use something to steady his stomach. He didn't, daren't turn around to see if anyone was following him, if anyone had seen where he'd come from. In this House, he wouldn't have any warnings of what Asmodeus did or didn't know until guards showed up to drag him from his bed to the cells. There was no point in worrying about it.

That would have been the rational approach. Unfortunately, he was feeling less and less rational by the minute.

In the small, dingy kitchen for their floor, Nadine grabbed a chunk of bread from the assortment of food on the table and spread it with a thick layer of jam. Leila found some dried tea leaves, old and moldy, the kind Thuan wouldn't have drunk for all the jade in Annam, and set some water boiling, whistling a slow, rhythmic melody between her teeth. Thuan found a few scraps of dried ham, and ate these with his piece of bread. He'd never had much of a sweet tooth, and most definitely not in the morning. The salty, pungent meat slid into his stomach, where, as expected, it did absolutely nothing to quell the seething nausea and fear.

"This is horrible," Leila said, grimacing, as she stared into the teapot. "Are you sure we should be brewing this?"

"The tea?" Nadine shook her head. "Be thankful for what you have." She stared at the box of tea leaves. "No. You're right. I wouldn't drink this even if you paid me."

"It's prestigious," Leila said, deadpan. "A symbol of riches, and of all Hawthorn has that others don't."

Thuan suppressed a snort. The dragon kingdom had tea the color of cut grass, with a delicate taste that lingered on the palate. "Go ahead, poison yourself in the name of prestige."

"Enough." Nadine emptied the kettle into the sink. "No one is getting poisoned. For starters, the infirmary is full and I don't need any more patients."

Leila put a hand over her mouth, but her eyes were twinkling. "Anyone who drinks this tea is going to get a fungal infection from whatever gives it this horrible smell. Fungi are rather hard to deal with, too. Extra work."

"Leila! Anyway, you're not due in the infirmary this morning, Thuan," Nadine said. "As a helper, I mean."

"No," Thuan said. "I thought I'd wander around a bit." He put the ham back on the table. He really couldn't stomach the thought of more. "I'll be seeing you later?"

"For sure," Nadine said.

He could feel her gaze, and Leila's, following him all the way out of the kitchen. He was reasonably sure they had no suspicions, but also reasonably sure they were now worried about him. It was touching, but hardly what he needed.

One thing at a time. He needed to see Sare first.

THUAN found Sare in her usual spot in the laboratory: standing in the middle of the cavernous room, smelling faintly of various chemicals, with the familiar, faint odor of mildew that underlay everything in Hawthorn. She wore a white coat over her clothes and was utterly focused on the container on the large metal table. A couple of her assistants were busy among the shelves; and a half-dismembered Fallen body lay on one of the dissection tables, while other assistants busied themselves filling containers with body parts, saving what they could of the angel magic before it left the corpse altogether.

Sare looked up when he entered, round face shifting from a frown to a hint of a smile. "Thuan. How are you doing?"

He had an uneasy rapport with Sare. The Fallen was the one who had "found" him on the streets: to him, she had been a means of entry into the House, but he owed her a debt he could have done without. She insisted on mothering him: another thing he could have done without, as he was having more and more trouble sticking to the deception.

Duty to Second Aunt—who was the ruler of the kingdom, and his flesh and blood—outweighed any considerations of filial duty. But still . . . "I'm doing fine," he said.

"Not stellar at your courses, I hear."

Mostly because he had little motivation. "Yeah, I guess. I try my best."

"Do you?"

"I need to know," Thuan said. He put just the right amount of worried earnestness in his voice. "What happens if I'm not chosen, at the end of the year?"

"To be a dependent?" Sare set the container she was looking at aside, and looked him in the eye. "Oh, Thuan. Don't tell me you're having sleepless nights over this."

She sounded genuinely concerned, and she probably was. "No one taken by the Houses ever comes out," he said, stubbornly, as though he already suspected the answer to his question. "And the others have been talking. About the cells, and the cages . . ." He let his voice trail off, and he didn't have to fake the fear. As part of the mission briefing, he'd been shown, extensively, House Hawthorn's cells, and what Asmodeus did to those he thought disloyal to him. As a warning to tread carefully, or as a reminder he shouldn't get too attached to House Hawthorn, he wasn't sure.

Sare's face twisted. "Thuan. That's for traitors. You can't possibly think—" And then she stopped, and composed herself, visibly upset by his invented worries.

He felt terrible.

It's for the kingdom. For all the river people dying of essence addiction, the ones who would die unless he could confirm the source of the traffic. The alchemists of the kingdom weren't House ones: they didn't preserve the magic of angels, but rather analyzed and dissected it, trying to make sense of where everything fit in. They had looked at what found its way to them, and confirmed that all the new and deadly essence was distilled in the same place.

This place. It had to be. Essence weakened them, and being weak made them vulnerable to Hawthorn's predation: the House's unreasonable demands, and ancestors knew what other plans Asmodeus had for them, in the long run. It certainly wasn't an alliance of equals that they wanted.

They would never have dealt with Hawthorn in ordinary circumstances. But the kingdom was weak, the Houses brasher and brasher. An alliance was their only chance at survival, and no one was under any illusion Hawthorn's offers were going to be worse than any other House's.

At length, Sare spoke. "You were taught a rule, in class. Or will be taught—I don't know what they say when. If you do right by the House, the House will do right by you. You may not be a dependent, but you're still working for us. Or will be, one day. If you're not chosen?" She shrugged.

"Hundreds of people here aren't dependents. Before the war, they'd have come into the House every day. Now there are rather fewer day laborers, because the House needs to keep them safe. Most people are given a room here, but without the privileges that come with dependency."

"So I'd stay here?" A faint hint of hope, but not too much: he was meant to still be suspicious of what they were offering him.

"With a menial job. But better that than the streets?" Sare said.

Thuan nodded. He didn't need to fake that, either. He'd spent only one night on the streets, and he had no desire to relive any of it.

"Was that all that was troubling you?" Sare asked.

Not by a long shot, but it was a good excuse for him to barge into the laboratory at a ridiculously early hour. "I . . . guess," Thuan said. Again, not too much enthusiasm. Just the right amount. And he was going to feel better about all the lies he was telling her. Any moment now. "Thanks."

"Don't mention it." Sare glanced at the dissection table. "Don't forget to trim the nails," she said, sharply. And then, turning back toward him, "Sorry. Recent death. Father Arsène has finished with the last rites, which means we can finally start."

Thuan glanced at the walls, where icons of the Virgin Mary and the saints hung between the heavy wooden cupboards. Fallen tended to be arch-cynical, like Asmodeus (and from all stories his lover Samariel), or in earnest, like Sare, genuinely believing in God and trying to discern what was right to do on earth. How she reconciled this with the Houseless, or what was happening in the kingdom, he didn't know.

"Unexpected death?" Thuan asked, fascinated in spite of himself. The face, what little he could see of it, pale and with long, fair hair that was almost white, was utterly unfamiliar.

"Difficult assignment involving House Harrier," Sare said. "We can't prove anything, or else Lord Asmodeus would already be demanding reparations, but Harrier probably killed her, too."

Thuan grimaced. "You know, from the outside, we always think things are better inside the Houses. Not that you're at each other's throats like gangs fighting for territory." Or like factions of scholars in the kingdom, seating and unseating officials with memorials and gossip.

"If you believed that, you're a fool," Sare said. "A House is merely a bigger gang. We don't have moral superiority, though some do make that claim. We're merely more powerful, which gives us a duty toward the weak."

"Can I—" Thuan swallowed. "Can I take a look?" The mere thought of getting closer to that corpse—the corpse they were busy desecrating, mutilating with scarcely a second thought—was a knife's blade in his mind. But it was the conversation opener he needed. "I've never seen one up close."

"Fallen die outside Houses," Sare said, mildly, not disbelieving, not exactly.

"You have to be high up in the hierarchy to see a corpse before they cart it away," Thuan said. "Or really lucky." Accurate, if not applicable to him. Rather, no Fallen had ever died within the boundaries of the kingdom, and Thuan hadn't left the kingdom in decades.

"Feel free," Sare said. "It's not like anyone is going to protest." She sighed. "And we really could have done without the extra work." She went back to her container.

Close up, the corpse was less gruesome than he'd feared. It was hard to tell how she'd died, or even that she'd been Fallen. Her innards were opened up like a flower, her lungs already scooped out from between snapped-off ribs, and her diaphragm was being gently disengaged by one of the assistants. Thuan exhaled, carefully. He didn't have much in his stomach and would rather it remained there.

He kept his eyes open, but repeated, silently, the mantras the monks had taught him, back in the kingdom: the pathways to meditating, to freeing his mind and climbing higher on the hierarchy of awakened beings. It was hard, with the smell of raw meat around him, and that elusive sense of the magic brushing against him, as frail as a butterfly's wing, and growing fainter with every passing moment.

He waited, patiently, for the oldest of the assistants to snap off one of the ribs, and carry the fragile bones to the alembics in the corner of the laboratory. The smell here was acrid, fiery and roiling, the air as tight as before a storm. Then he settled down to watch the distillation, again very ostensibly. Sare glanced at him, but she appeared satisfied that all he was displaying was natural curiosity at the process.

What he was truly interested in happened some time after that, when the assistant came back to collect the gray dust that had collected at the bottom of the second container. He carefully poured it into a small box, and walked off with it toward one of the closed cupboards. Thuan followed, keeping his face smooth; mildly interested, but not desperate.

It was hard.

Because this was likely his only chance to see where they kept the essence, his only stab at getting some of it so he could compare it with the one in the kingdom. If he messed this up . . .

No, don't think about this. He couldn't afford to. He needed to be utterly focused, as he had been for his official examination, letting the words of the classics pour through him onto the page—his world reduced to the paper and the painting brush, and the soft grinding sound of the ink stick against stone.

The assistant reached for a box on a shelf, and opened it. Thuan caught only a glimpse of it, but it appeared mostly empty. Then he poured the dust into it, carefully, as if it were going to bite him, and left. Thuan let out a breath he was hardly aware of holding.

The shelf was inside a cupboard, which would normally be sealed, but because they were busy filling it with all sorts of magical containers, no one bothered to properly close it after they were done. What was the point, when they knew they'd be back in a moment?

On the shelf with the angel essence were two containers: one was the almost empty one Thuan had seen. The other was different: instead of being a small case, just big enough to hold a ring or a pendant, it was much larger; and it was made of wood instead of leather, with an intricate set of carvings that had seen better days. Most of them had been cracked, or outright torn off. The only distinguishing feature was a stylized star, not at all like the ones he had seen on Asmodeus's bedroom doors, but an elaborate set of unfamiliar engraved lines. It was closed, and Thuan couldn't see any way to open it without attracting attention.

Time for the backup plan.

"You don't seem to have much essence," he said, aloud. He'd known that, already: vast amounts were being moved by House Hawthorn, but what they were funneled into was a mystery.

Sare looked up, suspicious, but met only Thuan's bored, disinterested stare. "What, do you want to sell it on the black market?" The sarcasm hardly had any bite to it. "We've had an essence addict in the House. It's been a bit of a drain. And Clothilde insisted—" She sighed. "That woman will drive me crazy before we're done. Anyway, not much, no. We've had to buy most of our essence from elsewhere."

Thuan ran a hand on the box, negligently. "This one?" he asked. He flipped open the lid, ignoring the rapid beating of his heart. This was it. This was his chance. His only one.

There was, again, little inside, though it had once been full. Thank the ancestors the shelf it was on was relatively low; and that Hawthorn, lying close to the waters of the Seine, was saturated with strands of *khi* water. He gathered these to his fingers patiently, wove a tight net that got thicker and thicker, until nothing, no matter how small, could have passed through the interstices.

Sare's gaze rested on him, for a while. Thuan didn't move, forced himself to stand still, to hold his breath steady, his hands unmoving, his face impassive. "You're not an addict," she said.

"No!" Thuan said. The word was forced out of him before he could think.

Sare didn't take her gaze off him. "Why the interest, then?"

"Curiosity," Thuan said. He shuffled his feet.

"Really." She wasn't convinced.

"I was . . . I had a bet with someone," he said, at last, falling back on the last of his prepared excuses. "To look at some of it." As he spoke, his hand dipped, lightly, toward the top of the box—stopped, not touching it; but his fingers, spreading out, sent the *khi* net tumbling down into the box, a small scoop that trapped angel essence within. He withdrew then, making a pretense of being made uncomfortable by the heat; the invisible net coming with him—palmed swiftly, and shifted to his breast pocket in a well-practiced gesture. "To know how it felt."

Surely Sare had seen him. Surely she would know. . . . But her face was still filled with that distant, mild suspicion. She wanted to pin something on him, but couldn't.

Thuan closed the box, with an ostensible sigh. "Never mind."

Sare moved, came to stand by his side. She opened the box, peered at its depths.

Thuan *knew*, rationally, that he'd taken so little from it that it would hardly show: much, much less than the dose an addict would have needed, or what he could sell for a reasonable price. But the moments Sare spent looking into the box, silently, stretched to an eternity. She didn't speak, but she didn't need to. She'd seen . . .

At length, Sare shook her head. "I'll never understand you." She closed the box, and the cupboard, with a very pointed look. "You just like flirting with danger, don't you? You should be careful, Thuan. You'll get burned, one day."

In the very near future, if his disguise failed him. Or in the marginally less near future if he screwed up and had to report to Second Aunt. He winced at the thought. It was a nice distraction from worrying about whether Sare was going to insist on searching him. The *khi* net would be invisible and intangible to her, like all *khi* elements were to Fallen, unless their wielder chose to make a dramatic spell. But still . . .

Still, he didn't relax fully until he was out of the laboratory, well out of earshot of Sare; and back in the safety of his rooms, where he transferred the essence he'd stolen from the net to a folded piece of paper.

Thuan stared at it, for a while. It felt almost innocuous, in such small amounts. Not a promise of power, or anything—not that it would tempt him, in any case. He could use Fallen magic because he'd been taught the rudiments of it, but he was not interested. The power he wanted would be given by Second Aunt's favor; or, possibly, in the far distant future and if things changed drastically at court, by the council of officials that would confirm the designation of an heir. Not that it would happen: Thuan was realistic enough to know he was only a minor relation; the youngest son of a youngest sister, born in genteel poverty and called back to court only because Second Aunt had found a use for him.

His life had been spent waiting, and he certainly had no time for something that corrupted and shortened life spans.

But he did have a mission, and now he was one step closer to accomplishing it.

He slid a hand under the ancestral altar, and got out a small, lacquered box with a picture of a plum tree and bamboo. If pressed, he would have said it was the ashes of his grandmother: an absurd, ludicrous fabrication, but there was no one in the House capable of gainsaying him. When he flipped the lid open, a fraction of the warmth he'd felt in the laboratory brushed against his fingers: there was more essence in that box than the small pinch he'd been able to steal from Sare; and he already knew how dangerous it was, because he'd seen the effects on others.

Thuan shivered again, thinking of broken-off antlers, and rot.

Then he drew on the *khi* currents in the room—water, there was so much water in Hawthorn, the breath of the Seine at the bottom of the gardens, the element that came easily, smoothly into his hands: the power of the river, ready to be harnessed. His hands shimmered, sharpened into claws, and a thin tracery of scales shone beneath his skin. He'd closed and locked the door, for otherwise, anyone who might have seen him would know he was not what he pretended to be. A touch of *khi* earth, taken from the wasted gardens: the center, the fulcrum around which everything was balanced, and the element of loyalty and faithfulness . . .

A thin, pulsing line rose between the essence in the box and that on the piece of paper, gaining body and heft with each passing moment, water and earth mingled in unbreakable strands, the silhouette of a thin, elongated dragon leaping from one to the other, its body rising from the parquet floor of Thuan's room like steam from an invisible vessel of boiling water.

Thuan brought his hands together, and snuffed out the spell. The line remained for a brief moment, like the aftereffect of a great light blown out; and then it, too, faded.

There was no doubt. The essence was not *quite* the same—the Fallen bones from which it had been refined must have come from different dead bodies—but it bore, quite clearly, the mark of the same alchemist. The same maker.

Except, of course, that Sare had said it came from another House.

His gut feeling told him that, different House or not, that essence was the one that ended up in the dragon kingdom. It was too much of a coincidence already: the two had to be linked.

He had no proof. Asmodeus, if pressed, would simply place the blame on that other House. He would say that they were the ones involved in the traffic, not his people. Never mind that he was the one who found an advantage in weakening the kingdom, the one who needed the dragons subservient so they would accept the alliance he offered them with only a bare minimum of negotiations, desperate for any lifeline that could save the kingdom. And why should Asmodeus not bring in another House, or several others, if his own couldn't sustain the high amounts of essence to be smuggled into the dragon kingdom?

It made terrible sense. But it wasn't enough.

Now what?

They had something to hide, which meant that they would be on the watch for anyone who might be getting close to it. Sare was suspicious now: the laboratory might as well be closed to him, because she would watch him like a hawk whenever he set foot in it. Not to mention the open question of whether anyone had seen him run away from Asmodeus's rooms, a distinctly unpleasant prospect.

He needed more evidence, but he would have to tread very, very carefully; or he would see the inside of Hawthorn's cells rather too closely for comfort.

SEVEN
HEART'S DESIRE

THE room was exactly what Philippe had expected: cramped, with cracks in the warped walls, smelling of smoke and cooked shallots—a small burner over a fire the only kitchen, and the metal frame of a bed rusted through and through. The window was cracked, too, and had been patched over with what looked like an old, faded counterpane.

The pregnant woman had let him climb the muddy, narrow steps ahead of her. She closed the door as she entered; and, on that sound, the person seated in the plush blue armchair turned to face Philippe.

She was small, unremarkable, thin and starved, with bruised eyes, and cheekbones peaking sharply under the skin of her face. Her dark hair fell to her waist, shot through with so many white streaks it appeared paler than it was. Mortal, Philippe would have said, and then she shifted, and the pale light of Fallen magic shone beneath her skin.

"Fallen," Philippe whispered. She was the source of the magic that permeated the pregnant woman. Had to be, in spite of the fact that she barely looked the part: no skin made translucent by the light of magic, no burning gaze, no hint of coiled power or unearthly grace. Just a faint smell of myrrh, as she bent to get a better look at Philippe.

"Welcome," the Fallen said. "My name is Berith, and this is Le Thi Anh

Tuyet, though she prefers Françoise." Her Viet was surprisingly good, slow and deliberate but properly accented.

"I'm Philippe. Pham Van Minh Khiet."

Berith looked . . . frail, old, something unheard of in Fallen, who enjoyed insolent, ageless good health. "Philippe." Her eyes narrowed, and focused on him.

They were brown, quite ordinary, until something shifted, and he saw that they were flecked with silver, with a dozen—a hundred—shards caught in the irises, as if someone had thrown a handful of metal slivers into her face. The world wobbled and shifted, and her gaze was the only thing holding him steady.

"Pham Van Minh Khiet." Her voice was a song, a soaring, uplifting harmony. The room around them widened; no longer small or cramped, but filled with the shadow of wooden bookshelves: nothing cracked or moldy or burned, but a smooth, dark, and rich color that had never known fire or magic, or even the touch of time. The armchair had grown and stretched, becoming a straight-backed throne on a dais; and instead of a gray shirt over a long skirt, she was now draped in an ermine-lined coat the deep blue of the sky, embroidered with lilies and apple flowers. Her face, transfigured, was a blur of light that hardened her features into a different cast, with only the eyes unchanged, her gaze still holding him, now burning with the intensity of a wildfire.

"You . . ." He forced himself to breathe, to speak. "That's what I felt. On the bridge, rue de Jessaint. I would have died if you hadn't anchored me."

The Fallen spread her hands, gracefully, to encompass the throne and the bookshelves and the impossibly blue sky above, the deep color of approaching evening at summer's end. "This is my dominion."

"How—how are you alive? How—" Philippe sought words. A Fallen. She was just a Fallen, as careless, as arrogant as the rest of them. But he could feel wind on his face, and smell the musty smell of old books, reminiscent of a grander, less damaged Silverspires library.

"People have sought to kill her," a voice said, behind her. "She's hardly defenseless."

Françoise was leaning against one of the bookcases—her face no longer the pinched, starved one he saw everywhere on the streets, but smoother, transfigured, too, into something rich and strange and oddly wonderful.

No. It was Fallen magic. It was Fallen that had torn him from his home, kidnapped him on the streets, and sought to make use of his powers for their own ends, and Berith was no better than any of them. He had to—he had to remember that—but it was hard, standing under that gaze.

"Your dominion," he said, each word feeling as heavy as a stone. "Other Fallen congregate into Houses. You don't."

"My dominion is always with me, wherever I go. You've met others of my kind. Lucifer Morningstar. Guy. Asmodeus." Berith's voice lingered on that last name. Philippe wished it hadn't, because all he could remember about Asmodeus was pain, and broken fingers, and crawling under the merciless light of the stars.

"I've met some of them," he said, cautiously.

"Then you'll know we are different. Morningstar only understood usefulness. Guy divides the world in terms of superiority. And Asmodeus, of course, only thinks of ownership."

"And you?"

"Let's say what I understand is desire."

She was worse than Morningstar, in so many ways. He had been raw power, careless, heedless dominance, easily asserted, and expected the entire world to bring him his due. Berith didn't expect anything. Didn't want anything. Someone who simply . . . offered? But no. Everyone wanted something; Fallen more than anyone else, reaching and grasping and taking all they could from a world that they only lightly touched.

They'd reached and grasped once, before the war: rolling into Annam with their rifles and their magic, taking what they wanted from the land, their magic spreading to cover everything. The guardian spirits and the Immortals like Philippe had died in their assaults, or retreated into mountain fastnesses to recover, banning all contact with the mortal lands that were now under the sway of Fallen, where the *khi* elements were now weak and almost inexistent, subdued and made powerless by the wash of alien magic.

And, of course, when the war had gone badly, when they had needed all the bodies they could spare, they had taken people from Annam—like Françoise's parents, like Philippe—to be more cannon fodder in their endless internecine fights, and left them to fend for themselves in the devastated city after the war had ground to a halt.

"I don't want anything." He tasted ashes, and bitter dregs, on his tongue. "I'm the one who owes you. For the bridge."

"An honest man." Her voice was light, ironic, Fallen through and through.

"I—" He turned, to look at Françoise. "I owe you. I can deliver the child, for you, when the time comes."

"Not long now. A month," Berith said. "But we have a midwife already." She looked at Françoise, who shook her head.

"You'll forgive me, but doctors tend not to be very effective when it comes to childbirth." Some of Berith's light, ironic tone had crept into Françoise's voice. "About one in ten women in Hospital Lariboisière's maternity wards comes out in a coffin."

"I'm not just any doctor," Philippe snapped, and stopped. He'd just admitted he was using magic. But then again . . . she already knew.

"The magic?" Berith asked, and smiled. "You hide it very well, normally. But I felt it on the bridge. I know what you are. You radiate power as easily as you breathe, when you set your mind to it."

"What magic?" Françoise asked.

"Enough to change the world, isn't it?" Berith's voice was light, sarcastic. "Something Fallen neither understand nor care for."

As if she was different from her kind. As if she understood. "You only care if you think it's of use."

"Of course," Berith said.

"Magic or not, I'd rather have someone I trust deliver the child," Françoise said. She was looking at him thoughtfully as if trying to work out something, the darkness of her skin washed away by the magic that suffused the room. "But, if you have magic that's not Fallen . . . there is something else you could do for us."

On her throne, Berith frowned. "Françoise—"

Françoise walked up to her, laid a hand on her wrist, and gently squeezed, with the familiarity of a lover rather than a friend. "Please."

Berith lowered her gaze to stare at Françoise, an odd hunger etched on every line of that perfect face. "He won't do it. Too many risks."

"Won't do what?" Philippe asked.

"Then we won't be worse off than we are now, will we?" Françoise shook her head. "It's worth asking. Please."

Berith was silent. The bookshelves wavered and vanished, and Philippe was standing once more in the cramped apartment, watching that frail, skeletal body ensconced in the chair, with Françoise still clinging to Berith's arm. "Sometimes," Berith said, "angels Fall together. It's extremely rare. A bit like live twins, among mortals, and like twins, these Fallen remain close all their lives. Which are much longer than mortals'."

"Thanks," Philippe said, not bothering to keep the sarcasm out of his voice. "I think I know one thing or two about Fallen by now."

Berith didn't smile. "I had a Fall-brother. Once. We quarreled, a century or so ago. Perhaps more." Françoise's hand on her wrist had tensed. "I found my way here, eventually. Found this life. Found Françoise."

Much longer than mortals'. Françoise was—what?—thirty years or so? Hardly more, and Berith much, much older. What would they do, when she grew old? Though by the looks of it, Berith might actually die before Françoise. Philippe had never seen a Fallen look so ill.

"That's a sad story, but I'm not too sure where you want me to fit in."

"It's been a long time," Berith said. "And I'm dying." She said it simply, matter-of-factly. So much for Philippe wondering. She grimaced, an expression which made her skin stretch over the bones of her face, until a death's-head grinned back at Philippe. He stood his ground. "Wounds sustained during the Great Houses War, because I was Houseless and an easier target than the House-bound. I've lingered long, but everything has its end."

"You'll heal." Françoise's voice was low, tired. They'd had this argument before, and she clearly didn't believe it anymore.

"No," Berith said. "I might live long enough to see our grandchildren born." She smiled, wearily. She looked so mortal. So vulnerable; it was hard to remember what she was, where she had come from. "Anyway. I have regrets. I want—" She paused. "Reconciliation, before it's too late."

Philippe still didn't see where he fitted in, but he held his tongue.

Berith shifted again. "I won't move from here."

Not because she didn't want to, but because she couldn't, Philippe realized. Because whatever had happened to her during the war, it had made her the Fallen equivalent of an invalid. "Tell me what you want."

"Françoise can go plead in my stead. But I won't send her alone. I want you to escort her."

Into a House? "No," he said. It was gut reflex. He'd been almost killed the last time he'd gone into a House: taken and used and discarded, with his lungs pierced and every bone in his body shattered. He forced himself to breathe.

"It's not as dangerous as it sounds. An audience comes with a safe-conduct," Berith said.

"Because Houses respect that kind of thing?"

Her face told him all he needed to know. "He . . . does keep his word, usually."

"'Usually,' unless it suits him otherwise." Like all Fallen, for whom rules were only tools of the oppression of others. "I'm sorry, but no. I owe you, but not that much."

Silence stretched on, long and weighty and uncomfortable. At length, Berith said, "I can offer you something else in exchange."

"There is nothing you can offer that would—"

Berith stretched, and shifted; and for a moment, the shadows of bookshelves were at her back again, and the outline of great, golden wings, and a smell of myrrh as if in a church. "Is there? As I said, my dominion is desire, and magic. And what you want burns within you like a wildfire, Philippe."

"You know nothing."

"Don't I?" Her voice was mocking, an echo, for a moment, of Asmodeus's facile nonchalance. "You want things to branch differently, in a long-ago past. For a dead friend to come back to life, and walk once more upon the earth."

Isabelle. "No one can—"

"*I* can."

Philippe wasn't sure what Berith did; he couldn't see. But the books flapped in an invisible breeze, and, as they shifted and moved and stretched, like a living thing, he saw fragments of words, in French and Viet and Chinese; fragments that came together in his mind for a moment. And, for a moment—a mere moment only—he stood on the edge of a circle etched in the stone floor of a broken-down cathedral, and he *knew* what he had to do, from beginning to end; knew the writing to carve around the circle; the spell that he needed to speak, the *khi* elements to weave together, the precise location and timing of the wounds he would need to inflict on himself; and how his blood, dripping down within the confines of the circle, would stretch and coalesce into the shape of a Fallen, dark-haired and with olive skin, not the corpse he had buried, but one who would open her eyes, and look at him with the confusion of the newly born.

And then the moment snapped away from him. The books were just books, and the words they contained incomprehensible, and the memory in his mind, so sharp just a few minutes before, blurred away into meaninglessness.

"This is my dominion," Berith said, again. "Magic, and rituals, and your heart's deepest desire."

"I—" He struggled to breathe. Illusion. It had to be illusion, like all Fallen promises, like all their vaunted magic: useless in the end, a canker that had already destroyed the city. But. But the memory of that spell lay in his mind like a sword. It had felt real. More real than anything he had achieved, after months of running into dead end after dead end.

I know enough.

Enough to bring her back?

Morningstar's voice in his mind was grave: not mocking, as he remembered it, but that of a teacher asking a question of a presumptuous student.

And he knew—if he was honest with himself, which he strove to be—what the answer was, what the answer had always been. "And you're offering me this in exchange for walking into a House."

"You don't like the Houses." Berith didn't sound surprised.

"Who does?"

"Not I." Berith shrugged. "The House is Hawthorn. And my Fall-brother is easy enough to find. He heads it."

The head of the House. The head of House Hawthorn. Asmodeus.

No.

Light glinting on glasses in a room with beige wallpaper, and the smell of blood everywhere, and someone screaming and it was him—it had always been him—"You're . . ." Philippe ought to have been flippant, or nonchalant, or sarcastic, but he couldn't even breathe. "You're his sister?"

"Brother, once." Berith shrugged again. "Things have changed. I Fell into the wrong body, but I fixed this long before the war. No matter. You've already had dealings with him."

He'd have been tortured to death by Asmodeus, if Isabelle and the head of House Silverspires hadn't intervened, if he hadn't run away on shaking legs, his breath rattling in his chest—crawling, in the end, into the dragon kingdom to die of his wounds, only to find himself miraculously healed. But even miracles had their limits, and none of them could erase those sharp, terrible memories.

Françoise's voice was low, and toneless. "He won't do it."

It wasn't that he wouldn't do it. It was that he couldn't walk into Hawthorn, couldn't face that green-eyed gaze again, that smell of orange blossom and bergamot, overlain with that of a charnel house. . . . "You don't understand," he said, struggling to breathe. "Asmodeus almost killed me. Not even in Hawthorn, in another House altogether. I—I can't protect Françoise against *him*."

"Asmodeus tried to kill you?" Berith's voice was mildly curious. "Why?"

Shadows, smoothly gliding on the walls of House Silverspires; Morningstar's shade by the four-poster bed, his massive sword in his hand, the light of his golden hair falling on the bed, throwing every bloodstain into sharp contrast . . . "I was in the room where his lover died. Samariel."

He met Berith's gaze: she didn't need to voice her doubts to make them clear. "I didn't kill him!" he snapped, unsure of why he was so ashamed of himself. The darkness within him—the curse of House Silverspires, the source of the two ghostly presences in his life—had been the cause of Samariel's death, but he wasn't about to mourn for a Fallen.

"You didn't." Berith watched him, for a while. "You hated him, but you didn't kill him." She made a gesture, with her hand, and the air within the room went slack, as if a storm, rising, had suddenly burst.

"Find someone else," Philippe said. He tried very hard not to think about the ritual in his head, about the tantalizing possibility that there might be a way to resurrect Isabelle.

It was Françoise who spoke up. "You're not defenseless. Even without Fallen magic."

"He fought Asmodeus." Berith's voice was speculative. "And he's still alive."

"And I'd like to keep it that way," Philippe said. And not so much "fought" as was pummeled.

"Mmm," Berith said. Something stroked Philippe's wrist, a touch like warm embers that dredged up the fragments of the threads that had brought him here, water and metal beating on the rhythm of his heart.

"Stop."

Berith raised a hand. "Listen to me. Asmodeus is head of the House. No one can stand against him in his own domain, not even the most powerful of magicians. But you—"

"I told you he almost killed me."

"But you didn't have my magic," Berith said.

Her magic. Philippe clamped his lips on the reflexive "no." He didn't want Fallen magic within him, but of course he was going to end up wielding it, no matter what happened. What else did he expect Berith's spell of resurrection to be?

"I'm his Fall-sister," Berith said. "Even outside my dominion, my magic is strong. Not strong enough to hold him at bay, but, combined with your own powers . . ."

The thread on his wrist became unbearably tight: Philippe snapped it into harmless scraps before he could think. He raised his gaze, met Berith's mocking one. But she didn't ask more questions about his magic, or how it worked. "So you pump me full of your magic, and send me to do your dirty work in Hawthorn," he said.

"I prefer to think of it as the work I'm not capable of doing," Berith said, calmly, utterly unriled by his insults. "And in return, I can give you your heart's desire, Philippe. Well? What do you say?"

He opened his mouth to say it was the height of foolishness, and no thinking person would ever say yes, and then he saw Isabelle again: leaning against the lamppost on rue de Jessaint, haloed in light, with the two bloody wounds in her chest. He saw her corpse again, framed by two metal wings, looking like an angel finally come to rest—the corpse he had buried near the Grands Magasins, making her the promise that he would find a way to resurrect her.

He wanted no part of House politics. He wanted no Fallen magic. And, above all, he wanted to stay away from Hawthorn and Asmodeus. But in the end, he owed Isabelle something he could never return, and all his unbending principles had ever brought her was death.

Berith was Fallen, but not House; and that, perhaps, was all the grace he was ever going to be granted, in the end, by a God who wasn't his and whom he had no interest in worshipping.

"I—" He took a deep, shaking breath. "I'll do it."

EIGHT
MASKS AND ESSENCE

MADELEINE had expected the introduction to Prince Phuong Dinh to be a private audience, but it turned out to be an informal lunch. For given values of "informal": they set a large circular table in one of the pavilions, filled it with all manner of dishes, and sat Clothilde and Madeleine with Ngoc Bich and a number of dignitaries—Thanh Phan and Véronique, and another few that seemed to be new, or whose faces Madeleine couldn't make out. Clothilde made effortless small talk with Ngoc Bich. Madeleine found herself wedged between Thanh Phan and the prince.

Phuong Dinh was a large, pleasant man with a lean face, and even Thanh Phan seemed to like him. It wasn't anything like the prickly respect she showed Ngoc Bich, but rather the fondness one had for a friend's child.

He, in turn, watched Madeleine struggle with the food: some kind of pungent mixed meat, smelling like rotten fish; something chewy that had to be innards, but so salty it was almost inedible; and cucumber that turned out to have a sharp, bitter taste. "You don't look like you're appreciating the food, Lady Madeleine," he said, with a hint of a smile in his eyes.

Madeleine stopped herself before she could say what was really on her mind. "I'm not used to your customs."

"That is certainly . . . visible." Phuong Dinh pointed to one of the serving bowls in the center of the table. "These buns are sweet. You would probably enjoy them more. And do feel free to use the spoon. It's not polite, but then, neither is waving your chopsticks as though you're going to stab someone with them."

Madeleine tried to hold her chopsticks more delicately, and then gave up and reached for the spoon. The bun piece, when she bit into it, proved insipid, almost without seasoning. Elphon hadn't come back in more than a day, and Clothilde might not seem worried, but that was unduly optimistic. Anything could happen in a place like this. "I'm not a lady," she said. Just Asmodeus's pet experiment, and where that placed her in Hawthorn's hierarchy God only knew.

"I know," Phuong Dinh said, but Thanh Phan cut him.

"You are an envoy of Lord Asmodeus." Her face was severe. "As such, we owe you respect."

Phuong Dinh looked as though he was going to tell her to lighten up, but said nothing.

Madeleine wasn't about to be stared down by a crab, especially one that looked like a walking skeleton, and whose idea of their interests included hiding danger from them. "Someone owed Ghislaine respect, and it didn't prevent her from disappearing."

Thanh Phan closed up immediately. "You impugn us. We had nothing to do with her disappearance."

"Didn't you? She was scared," Madeleine said. "As all of you are. What is going on here?"

Clothilde looked up sharply, and made a gesture with her hands that Madeleine knew only too well: *Don't make waves, and please for the love of God shut up.* But it was too late to take the words back.

"Lady Madeleine." Phuong Dinh's face had quirked into an amused smile. "This is an old, old place, and it has its share of half-remembered myths and histories. And some of them . . . bite."

Great. Madeleine nodded, and tried to focus on the food. If only every dish hadn't been such an unpleasant surprise. She stared, instead, at the table under the tray, at the greenish mold that had crept across the inlaid nacre palaces and bridges.

Phuong Dinh went on. "You say you're unfamiliar with our customs, but you know more than the others, don't you? You don't seem as surprised as you should be."

She was the one whose expressions were written all over her face. "The others aren't surprised."

"Aren't they?" Phuong Dinh's expression was unreadable. "Being rather louder than they should, rather more aggressive. I should think they're hiding it better than you, which is a different thing."

Madeleine said nothing, and silence dragged on. At length, because it made her uncomfortable, she said, "I knew someone, once. An Annamite. You're not that different from him."

"A mortal?" Thanh Phan's contempt was obvious. No solidarity between countrymen, then. But why had she thought there might be?

"I'm not sure," Madeleine said. She'd never worked out, or been allowed to know, what Philippe was exactly. "A magician."

Thanh Phan snorted; clearly, being a magician wasn't much of a recommmendation, either. "You'll find they don't have much in common with us. The mortal Annamites."

Madeleine disagreed, but she really wasn't feeling like arguing over it. "I wouldn't know."

After the meal was over, Madeleine made to join Clothilde, but a hand on her shoulder stopped her. It was Véronique, the official dressed in French garb, smiling at her with blackened teeth. "Prince Phuong Dinh asks if you will walk with him."

One of those invitations, wrapped in velvet, that could hardly be refused. Madeleine glanced at Clothilde, who was deep in conversation with Ngoc Bich. "I think we're supposed to look at some papers in our rooms."

The hand rested, lightly, on her shoulder; steered her, gently but firmly, toward the other end of the pavilion: fingers that were too thin, phalanges too long, too hard, to be human. "They can wait, I should imagine." Her eyes under the bonnet were slightly too round, slightly too much away from the face, as if something within the orbits was pushing them out. "Come."

Madeleine looked at Clothilde, who still wasn't looking in her direction. "You'll tell her where we're going?"

Véronique gestured. Another official in French garb, top hat and all, appeared as if from nowhere. "Tell Lady Clothilde that Lady Madeleine is with the prince." He nodded, and made toward Ngoc Bich and Clothilde, while Véronique continued steering Madeleine toward the exit.

As they approached the building where Prince Phuong Dinh was waiting for her, Madeleine cast another glance backward. Clothilde and Ngoc Bich appeared locked in conversation; just as she and Véronique passed under the building's doorframe, the official Véronique had sent managed to signal his presence to Ngoc Bich, who waved him over.

And then the shadows of the building closed over her, and she couldn't see any of them anymore.

Véronique steered her between red-lacquered pillars with paint peeling off, through a courtyard with two large bronze urns, and then a maze of buildings that all started to blur into one another, until they reached a wide, open expanse overlooking a cliff planted with coral and gray anemones, their nests of tentacles streaming in invisible currents. Shoals of gray, sickly fish swam over the crags. Every so often, one would flop down, and not swim back up again.

Prince Phuong Dinh was waiting for her on the stone path that led to the cliff. "This isn't a trap," he said, in an amused voice. "Merely a chance to talk without the diplomatic masks."

As if Madeleine knew what a diplomatic mask was. She forced a smile. The entire palace made her feel ill at ease, but this area was creepier than the others.

Isolated, she realized. There were no courtiers here, no officials going on errands with parasol-holding servants, no lacquered trays or heaps of papers being carried. Rather, an odd, contemplative, terrifying silence, with only the slow sounds of the river; and, high above, clouds drifting, covering the rippling, blinding sun and throwing the entire hill into darkness. "Come," Phuong Dinh said, and started toward the hill, slow and stately.

Madeleine walked to him, trying to project a confidence she didn't feel. "You want to talk about Ghislaine," she said, finally. She didn't think he did.

"Perhaps. But first you can tell me about Asmodeus."

"You're joking," Madeleine said. A cold current rose, buffeting her against the side of the path. Ahead was only the prince, with his thin, translucent antlers, his yellow silk clothes, threadbare and patched, a mouth that had lengthened, slightly, in the beginning of a snout. "Why . . . ?"

"Arranged marriage doesn't mean blindness," Phuong Dinh said. "To all intents and purposes he will be my husband. My . . . consort." He inflected the word as though he really meant "master."

So he did know, or appreciate, what he was getting into: Hawthorn, the casual cruelty of the House, and whatever plans Asmodeus had for him. Abruptly he looked small, and forlorn, and vulnerable, nothing Madeleine would have imagined moments earlier.

"I'm sorry," she said.

"No masks." His voice was slightly mocking. "What is the use of them, in a time and place like this?" His hands were curled into claws, their fingers tapered and short. Something in his pose, in his face, was familiar, in a way Madeleine couldn't place. What was going on here?

She dragged her voice from an infinitely faraway place. "He will own you. He will consider you his possession, to use or discard as he sees fit." Or to frighten into submission, or brutally shape into the steel that he needed. She thought of Samariel, Asmodeus's dead lover—tried to remember what they had been like, the two of them. "He's a widower. His lover died, a few months ago. I expect he's not doing this to find love." She didn't know why Asmodeus was doing it at all. A few dragon magicians and a permanent delegation hardly sounded worth bothering with. There had to be something bigger, larger, at stake.

"Oh, Lady Madeleine." Phuong Dinh snorted, gently, blowing bubbles into the never-ending stream of fish around the hill. "Do you think *I'm* doing this for love?"

"I don't know you. I can't tell."

"Necessity. Duty. Family. We do not expect love to feature very highly in our marriages. But I thank you for your candor."

If only it didn't sound like an insult, or a source of amusement to him. She was badly out of place here, had known it since the beginning. The disk against her chest, the physical reminder of Hawthorn's presence, was warm, like a living heart. "You knew Ghislaine," she said.

"Did I?" Phuong Dinh looked up. They were halfway to the foot of the cliff: from close up, she could see some kind of building atop it. An altar, or a shrine?

"She left a message."

Phuong Dinh said nothing for a while. At last, he set his foot forward again, toward the cliff. "Favor for favor, Lady Madeleine. Envoy Ghislaine . . . meant well, but she played with fire."

Here, in this kingdom where everything was damp and miserable? Madeleine clamped down on the words before they could escape her. "How so?"

"There are factions here, as there are everywhere," Phuong Dinh said. "You will have heard of the Bièvre."

"Credit us with a little knowledge," Madeleine said. A bad lie, and he would know it in a heartbeat.

"Envoy Ghislaine grew frustrated with things my aunt wouldn't budge on, and frightened, I think, at how different things were down here, at a kingdom which was neither as weak nor as vulnerable as what had been sold to her." Phuong Dinh smiled: the teeth in his mouth curved like a predator's fangs. "And she made the mistake of listening to Yen Oanh."

Yen Oanh. The name was familiar. Clothilde had mentioned it, hadn't she? One of the Bièvre's ex-partisans, but she'd had no inkling of what role she played at court. "I've heard the name."

Phuong Dinh didn't answer for a while. They had reached the foot of the cliff: the path went on, leaping over groupings of rock strewn with the shriveled, tainted corpses of fish—as if made for something that could fly. He stepped straight out over the first drop, and floated upward.

Of course. Water. They were still underwater. Madeleine followed, and tried not to gasp as her feet left the solidity of the path, and her entire body rose.

For a while, they didn't speak, as they crossed ridge after ridge, always with that odd, heart-wrenching moment when the path faltered under her, and she had this sensation that wasn't flying or swimming, of hanging in the void somewhere in Heaven. Or Hell.

Phuong Dinh paused halfway through the climb, waiting for her on one of the larger ridges. The rock's surface was mottled with gray algae: it looked solid, but crumbled under Madeleine's fingers, riddled through with a thousand invisible cracks. Fish still swam around them; one stopped, so close she could have touched it, the flesh of its head all but gone, looking at her with empty orbits, its teeth stained black and unpleasantly sharp.

"You won't have heard much about Yen Oanh." Phuong Dinh looked down, at the diminishing shape of the palace building. "Second Aunt won't be pleased that you have even heard her name, but I guess you would have found out, eventually."

"Found out what?"

"Every change has its detractors." A bitter, unamused smile. "Thanh Phan and her faction disapprove of the alliance with Hawthorn, but measure its necessity. Yen Oanh was different. She said, in a memorial meant to be nailed at the gates of the palace, that the dynasty had lost the mandate of Heaven. That any emperor or princess who would choose to ally with the canker eating at us was no worthy ruler, and not worthy of the people's respect. And then she resigned, and left."

Madeleine rather doubted this marked the end of Yen Oanh's involvement with the court. "What did she do?"

Phuong Dinh's eyes shone white in the oval of his face, lit as if from within. "She rebelled against the throne. Mustered an army that she hopes will one day topple the capital."

The soldiers that had escorted them from Hawthorn. The solicitousness. The insistence on not wandering around, the fear and worry etched on every face at the welcoming ceremony. That odd incident that had caused Ngoc Bich to dismiss the guards. "They're winning, aren't they?"

Phuong Dinh's face was a study in blankness. "Yes, and no. Their reach extends into the city. It's not a siege yet: they don't have the manpower for it. And the throne is safe."

His definition of "safe" was clearly something Madeleine didn't really agree with. "So you want our help because it will help you put down your rebellion." It probably wasn't why they'd started negotiating with Hawthorn in the first place, but now . . .

"Among other things, yes." Phuong Dinh looked away, toward the top of the cliff and its distant shrine. What was it about him that was familiar? She had never met him in her life.

"And Ghislaine?"

"Envoy Ghislaine thought she could use one power against another. To gain the concessions she could not obtain otherwise. Not a novel idea. But a dangerous one. Yen Oanh respects nothing, and certainly not the envoys of Fallen."

"You think they frightened her?"

"I know she learned something while speaking with Yen Oanh," Phuong Dinh said. "Something that convinced her that she needed to return to Hawthorn, urgently."

"That's not something small," Madeleine said. Defying orders and returning to Asmodeus? It would have to be more than negotiations gone wrong.

"No," Phuong Dinh said. "I think . . ." His voice was thoughtful. "I think she was worried about Hawthorn. And that in turn led her to leave the safety of the palace, and try to return home."

"That's impossible. Nothing that happens down here should affect the House," Madeleine said, surprised at her own vehemence. She didn't care for Hawthorn. Why should she start defending the House?

"Perhaps. Perhaps not. I think I've told you enough. Too much, some would say."

But it was to tell her this, wasn't it, that he had called her here? This, and to find out more about Asmodeus.

As if she'd ever be in a position to feel other than fearful and sick when it came to him.

"Véronique and Charles will walk you back to your rooms," Phuong Dinh said. "I have no doubt you and your friends will have much to discuss."

Friends. Elphon. Elphon, who was out somewhere in the city, within easy reach of an armed band with no liking for Fallen. She needed to tell Clothilde.

So principled. So softhearted. The voice in her mind was Asmodeus's, low and mocking. Elphon was her jailer, not her friend. She shouldn't have cared one jot about what happened to him. She should have been concerned that his disappearance would leave her alone with Clothilde in the kingdom, not worried over him like a mother hen gathering her chicks.

But that wasn't how she thought. It had never been.

Véronique was waiting at the foot of the hill, her dress billowing in invisible currents, some of the dye washing away in little whorls of blue and red ink. By her side was Charles, the official who had been sent to tell Ngoc Bich about Madeleine's absence.

They walked, for a while, in silence.

"I am sorry about Ghislaine," Véronique said. "She was kind, and I admired her a great deal."

"I hardly knew her," Madeleine said.

Véronique smiled. "We are not all Yen Oanh. We know that the future lies with the Fallen. That the House is our only salvation. Ghislaine understood this, more than anyone in the kingdom."

They were crossing a corridor Madeleine did not recognize: an empty, deserted affair with the usual cracked, red-lacquered pillars. The pavilion ahead had collapsed under the weight of its roof, and now lay in ruins; and the courtyard to her right was little more than drooping weeds, with no garden of algae or pebbles. A wall, rather than another building, closed it off, and Madeleine could hear a distant, indecorous bustle from beyond it—access to the outside?

"Ghislaine understood you," Madeleine said, slowly.

"Fallen magic . . ." Véronique's face contorted. ". . . Fallen magic is not dead, or stricken, or ailing. It's alive. It makes us feel alive, and powerful. We need that power." Her face was transfigured, awash as if with an inner radiance. And suddenly, the world shifted and contracted, and Madeleine saw.

The hands, which Véronique was holding still only with an effort of will. That peculiar translucency of her face, the angel magic roiling beneath the skin. The voice, with the fervor of a convert, but more important, the slight slur on the words, which covered—barely—the growing hoarseness.

"Essence." Madeleine kept her voice flat, expressionless. "She gave you essence."

"She didn't. But she did teach us how to use it," Charles said.

Madeleine would have laughed if it hadn't been so tragic. "You're essence addicts. You—" She thought back to the hill, and Phuong Dinh's expression. "You and the prince and God knows who else." It would eat at their lungs, slowly at first, and then faster and faster as time passed, as it stopped having an effect and they needed ever more of it. Perhaps it wouldn't kill them. They were crustaceans and fish and dragons, and who knew what effect it would have on them? But she doubted it.

"Madeleine." Véronique's voice was low, urgent.

What was Asmodeus going to say, when it turned out his bridegroom was no better than Madeleine: a wreck on his slow way to the grave? "What did you think we were going to do when we found out?"

"Madeleine. Please." Too late, she realized that everything had fallen silent. And that whatever she should be looking at was behind her.

Turning, she saw something large and gray floating over the wall, like the body of a whale, and silhouettes leaping or swimming down from it toward them.

And then something hit her in the chest, and there was only darkness.

NINE
THE HOUSELESS

FRANÇOISE was woken up by a flurry of kicks within her. She tried to turn over, before she remembered her belly; and then gave up, and flopped on her back, staring at the ceiling until it stopped. Her back pulled at her, reminding her that she was going to pay for this when she did get up.

"You'll pass out again," Berith said. She'd pulled herself out of the chair, and was cooking breakfast over the brazier. The smell of flatbreads crisping in the battered pan wafted up to Françoise, painfully reminding her she'd eaten nothing for a day and a half. "Remember how the baby presses down on the vena cava?"

"Hmmf. I've only done it once." Françoise turned on her side, edged herself out of the mattress on the floor; and slowly, carefully started the process of pulling herself upright.

"Here. Let me." Berith's frail arms passed under her own, and lifted her, effortlessly. A tingle of magic passed between Berith and her, a little jolt that sent the baby kicking again. Every time Berith did this, every time her strength seemed limitless, her magic boundless, Françoise thought, again, that it was a lie. That she wasn't wounded, or dying. That she would be there to watch the children of that child grow into adulthood and old age and have children of their own. There was a comfort in that, in the knowledge the world would go on, regardless.

It was unfair. Mortals who became the lovers of Fallen expected to die first. They didn't have to worry about a time when the Fallen wouldn't be there anymore.

"You're thinking morbid thoughts again. I'm fine," Berith said. "I'm not going to abruptly go away."

Françoise clamped on the words that came to her mouth. Berith had heard them all. She stopped, briefly, by her ancestral altar, wedged into a corner of the room: faded pictures of her grandparents, who had died young, of sickness and broken bodies, the fates of the Houseless. And a picture of Etienne: she'd only slept with him to get pregnant, and he'd been rather too fond of absinthe, heedless of what the stuff did to his body, but he hadn't deserved the sepsis that had shriveled him in mere days. Françoise had left them all a single tangerine, a gift brought by Grandmother Olympe the last time she'd dropped by, but it was now looking worse for wear.

Nothing much left, in the flat. The air was cold, but then it was freezing outside, the city in the grip of a chilling, biting winter. She laid some fresh bread by the tangerine, whispered a quick prayer. No incense; they'd burned it already. *Watch over me. Watch over the baby, so that one day they will come and worship you here.*

Berith waited until she had finished to speak up. "Come and eat something. It'll do you good."

The bread was warm, comforting. It wasn't the pristine white loaves that came out of the Houses' ovens, and the grit in the flour crunched a little on her palate, but it didn't matter.

"No jam, I'm afraid," Berith said. "That time of the month again."

Meaning their cupboards were bare. Françoise glanced at the pile of clothes in the corner. "I'll drop these off at Grandmother Olympe's. It should bring some money in." Olympe didn't run a clothes workshop, but she had an arrangement with the House factories to the east, by the devastated stations: the Annamites of the community brought their sewing, and got more and fairer money than they'd have if they'd negotiated on their own.

Berith had magic: the power she'd invested into the flat, the roots that went deep into the place, locking her within it, but also sustaining and healing her. The part of it that wasn't rooted went into keeping them safe: keeping Françoise from being mugged in the streets, and gangs from besieging them by providing the odd spell or service. It should have been worth ten times what they earned sewing and mending clothes, but only if someone were willing to pay for it, instead of threatening and coercing and killing.

The baby moved again, an odd feeling, as if he or she had grabbed some internal organ and pulled. "In some ways, I'll be glad to give birth." A month away. Like a cliff's edge, always coming closer.

"I have news." Berith's face was grave. "You don't actually sleep better *after* the birth."

"Oh, shut up."

"Just thought you'd want the benefit of my great experience."

"Still doesn't make you a better parent."

"No." Berith's lips quirked up in a smile, which faltered only a bit. "You realize parenthood is a terrifying and unknown prospect."

Like death, Françoise thought, and berated herself for the unwelcome thought. "And here I thought nothing ever frightened the Fallen. I'm glad that for a change, I won't be the one who's terrified."

"Liar."

Françoise shrugged. "We'll see who is most scared in a month's time, shall we?"

Berith made a face. She couldn't leave the flat, which meant she would be taking on the bulk of the care for the child while Françoise ran errands outside. So far it hadn't seemed to faze her, but Berith had very little experience with children. Most Annamites were too scared to come to see her. Whereas Françoise was used to babies, as Grandmother Olympe's house always seemed to have four or five, screaming at the top of their lungs and then almost magically quieting when their mothers or nurses breastfed them.

Truth was, the birth and the child were less scary than some of the other things coming up. "You think he'll do it?" Françoise asked.

"Philippe?"

It wasn't his name, at least not the one he'd been born with, but then, neither was "Françoise." "He didn't seem happy."

"I know his type." Berith turned down the flames on the brazier, and set the frying pan on a cracked wooden board. "He'll be happy when the sun crosses the sky backward, or the gates of Hell release their dead."

"Which is what you promised him."

"*A* dead person," Berith said. "Not the same. A dead Fallen. It's been done before."

They were both skirting around the subject. Françoise, tired of the unsaid, tackled it head-on. "And walking into Hawthorn has been done before, too."

Berith moved back to sit in the chair, but didn't summon the bookshelves again. "Do you want to know the worst that can happen?"

"I've got a pretty good idea, thanks." She'd grown up with Houses in the background, with their raids, the corpses they would leave splayed on spikes as a warning—their processions, seen from afar, bright and beautiful and terrible, as inaccessible as the idea of Heaven. She'd grown up with the smoke of Hawthorn's pyres—and it wasn't just dead leaves and branches they burned there—with Lazarus's brutal charity, which killed those who strayed from the right path; with the metal cages outside Harrier's front doors, where they left their handiwork displayed for all to see.

Berith was silent, for a while. "You don't have to go. I'll find another way. Philippe can deliver the letter."

"The letter is my credentials," Françoise said. "That's its only worth. He'll only answer to a personal plea." It really should have been Berith, but Berith couldn't leave the flat. Failing Berith . . . well, that left her, didn't it? Berith's lover, and the mother of their child, the only one who had a chance of convincing Asmodeus to come to the flat and speak to Berith.

"I'm sure he prefers abject abasement." Berith sounded wearily amused.

"I guess." It didn't make Françoise happy, but it was the only way. She moved closer to Berith, passed both arms around her neck, let them dangle there, close to the familiar, electrifying feel of Fallen magic. "What's he like?"

"Asmodeus?" Berith's voice was low. "I don't know, not anymore. He wanted to change things, but he was scared."

"Scared" was not a word Françoise would ever have applied to the head of House Hawthorn. "Centuries ago."

"He was young." Berith sighed, and took Françoise's hands in hers, lifting them to her mouth for a long, lingering kiss that sent a thrill of desire up her spine. "And so was I. So many things . . . He wanted to join a House. Said it was the only way he and his would ever be safe. And I couldn't. I said I knew the price and wouldn't pay it. We had . . . words." She kept her grip on Françoise's hands, as if it was the only thing linking her to the real world, to their dingy flat and the smell of cooking and the chittering of cockroaches. "He won't harm you."

"For old times' sake? Because he respects pregnant women?" She didn't believe either. That kind of outward respect might have been the norm, once, before the war. But nothing that had been true then applied now.

"For my sake, perhaps. But also because you're not a threat."

"Great," Françoise said. "Remind me never to ask you for reassurance."

"Would you rather I lied?"

Françoise didn't answer. Her arms were starting to ache, and so was her pelvis: currently, standing up for too long always had that effect. "I don't know what I want," she said, at last.

A better world. A future for them and the child, where they didn't have to fight for every scrap, where there was even a future, and she didn't die giving birth; or, worse, survive and lose the child.

"Heart's desire," Berith whispered.

"You could—," Françoise said. They'd had this conversation already. It was well-worn tracks, on a road to nowhere.

"Offer you that? Yes, I could," Berith said, wearily. "But there's a price, Françoise. There is always a price."

"I would be willing to pay it." If it meant her child was born and survived, what wouldn't she give?

"The price might be the health of our child," Berith said. "Desires are seldom granted in the way that you want. It might be a healthy child now, and die in five years—an eyeblink. Or born with wasted lungs, or a tumor in the brain. I . . ." She kissed Françoise's lips. "I'm sorry, Françoise. But I can't do it."

Neither could she, and they both knew it.

Françoise glanced at the table, where their latest chess game was on display—not the Western one with its kings and queens, but the Annamite one with generals and armies, which many old people in the community still played. "Aunt Ha might come by later," she said. "You should clear that."

Berith shrugged. "I'll clear it if she does come and wants to play, and anyway I'll set it back afterward. Don't think you're getting out that easily. I still think I can beat you."

Françoise snorted. "That's not hard." She currently seemed to have no brain to focus on anything strategic, and spent most of her evenings embroidering the baby's clothes.

"If it was easy, I'd have managed it by now. Western chess is easy. This . . . this doesn't cooperate." She looked as though she wanted to incinerate the board with a glance.

"You can look at the book again," Françoise said. The book was small and tattered, and was meant to cover the basic strategies of the game. Olympe had found it for them, rather surprisingly, since Olympe didn't approve of Berith. Perhaps she was simply making the best of a bad situation, though that didn't sound like Olympe at all.

Berith made a face. "I can, but I would like a break from damaging my eyes and my brain simultaneously. I'm not too sure who thought manually adding diacritics over words was a great idea." The book was in Viet, but like many such books, it had been printed on a press that covered only the Western alphabet. The diacritics on the words, the distinguishing features between similar spellings, had been manually added over the page, making it hard to read, especially for Berith, whose grasp of Viet was still poor.

Françoise smiled in spite of herself. "True wisdom: not so easily gained."

"Chess strategy?" Berith snorted. "Interesting, but not what I'd call wisdom. And it's mostly a language problem. For the moment."

"Think of it as motivation to learn better Viet."

"I'm not too sure who's going to be interested in the technical names for openings or tactics." Berith snorted again. "Some days, I think I should ask Olympe for a recipe book. At least I'd have some subjects of conversation with people."

Françoise tried to picture Berith and Olympe chatting over cooking matters, and gave up. "I . . . don't think that'd be a good idea."

Berith said, "You always pour scorn on my ideas. Ah well. You might as well bring me my work. Those shirts aren't going to sew themselves, and at least I'd be making my contribution to this household budget. Let's save the delights of chess for later."

She was, unfortunately, right.

Françoise disengaged herself from Berith, gently; went to pick up the pile of clothes to hand her: the ones her hands were too thick, too clumsy to deal with. Berith was the better seamstress. "Here. And then I'll get the rest of it back to Olympe's, and get paid."

AS it turned out, she never made it there. She wrapped herself in her coat and scarf, ponderously descending the stairs, and found Grandmother Olympe waiting for her at the bottom. "Françoise!"

Olympe wasn't Françoise's real grandmother. She was, in a way, everyone's grandmother, knowing everyone in the tightly knit Annamite community, and making sure that everyone's business was her business. Which verged, sometimes, on the annoying, especially when said business was disapproving of Françoise's choice of partner. She was wearing her usual clothes: a long-sleeved shirt of rough silk with two long flaps over the hips, and matching pants. Both were a dull brown: peasants' garments, Françoise's parents had whispered, with a hint of admiration for keeping to the old ways, even away from Annam. Françoise did admire the way Olympe always dressed the same way, no matter the temperature: with the cold, she needed two extra layers, but Olympe didn't have a coat, or gloves, or anything that would have been a concession to winter.

"Grandmother? What brings you here?" Françoise said, wedging her basket of clothes on her hip, as best as she could. The baby was moving again within her, little fists and legs hammering into her belly. "My parents—"

"—are fine," Olympe said. "No thanks to you, I should add. When was the last time you visited?" She waved her canvas bag, which she always carried with her, stuffed with food or clothes or both.

Too long ago; but then, it was so difficult, to sit still while they dropped more or less pointed hints that she should find a nice father or mother for the child: a mortal, and preferably an Annamite. "You know exactly when," Françoise said. She felt exhausted already, and they had barely started.

Olympe's wrinkled face stretched in a grimace. She was small, and wiry, but she still could tower over anyone who didn't show the proper respect. "Filial duty isn't optional, child. Especially these days, when everything else is going to waste."

Françoise made an attempt to shorten the conversation. "You didn't come all the way here for a lecture. Did you?"

She half expected Olympe to nod and continue said lecture, at which point she wasn't altogether sure she could have prevented herself from hurling the basket of clothes in sheer frustration—not at Olympe, because she'd never hear the end of it, but at a wall, or somewhere that would make a satisfying thud and crash. But instead, Olympe nodded, briskly. "I've come because I have a body for you. An unconscious woman."

"A . . ." Françoise paused. She must have misheard.

"An unconscious woman." Olympe's voice was grim. "You know people have been disappearing from the docks."

"Yes," Françoise said. She'd tried to warn Philippe about this, but she wasn't sure how much attention he'd paid: she might be living on the edges of the community, but he seemed to be on a different planet altogether.

"You'll want to be careful," Olympe said. "Jérôme went missing yesterday. Disappeared late at night on his way home. Nothing but a dark circle to mark where he'd been."

Late at night. Just before or just after Philippe had come to them. "That still doesn't explain the woman."

"Bénédicte and Sébastien found her among the crates. Half-starved, and beaten almost to death by the looks of her." She hesitated, a fraction of a second only, and said, "There was the beginning of a black circle around her. As if someone had tried to snatch her and was interrupted."

Françoise rubbed her belly, feeling the mound of the baby within her. It wasn't kicking or shifting, but she already felt tired all the same. "So she escaped. I still don't see why your first thought was to bring her here."

Olympe gestured toward the courtyard. "Because she's one of yours. If anyone can help, it's your partner." Whom she pointedly didn't name.

"One of—" A Fallen? Françoise started to protest she, too, was Annamite and mortal, envisioned the rest of the conversation, and stopped. She had no desire to go there. She considered protesting that their flat was barely large enough for the two of them, not to mention the baby, and discarded that, too. "You could take her elsewhere."

"I could," Olympe said. She smiled, sweetly. "But it's best if she's with her own kind, isn't it? You know what they say about not mixing oil with water."

One day. One day Françoise would be old enough that she could enjoy the same casual respect Olympe expected and effortlessly commanded. Right now, it seemed all that kept her going.

An unconscious woman. Olympe wasn't carrying her; therefore she was heavy. Berith couldn't move from the flat, and Françoise certainly wasn't about to attempt carrying someone up two flights of stairs. Which meant allowing people into the flat, however briefly.

"I'll tell Berith." She needed to: the wards on the flat were strong enough that most people would stop halfway up, unless Berith let them in.

TO her credit, Olympe didn't overstay her welcome: her two helpers—two young Annamites, dockworkers by the look of them—dropped the woman on the bed, and withdrew, leaving Olympe framed in the door opening. "That should keep her safe and sound. Send for me if you need anything," she said, before leaving, too. "And you can tell me what she has to say about the dark circles, if she ever wakes up."

"Wait—," Françoise said, but the stairs were already creaking under Olympe's weight, and it was amazing how fast little old Cochin Chinese ladies could go, when they wanted to. Certainly faster than Françoise, whose best speed was waddling at the moment.

Olympe had left a package, too, even though it wasn't the end of the month: brown paper wrapped around a small bottle. Françoise opened it, expecting some of the personal stuff Bénédicte and Sébastien had found with the woman, but instead the familiar smell of fish sauce rose in the room, making her eyes fill with tears. Even in childhood she'd tasted so little of it: a precious rarity her parents would open with reverence. This one, like all the bottles in la Goutte d'Or, was diluted and adulterated, cut to be cheaper; but it wasn't soy sauce, salted water, or any of the substitutes that got foisted on poor Annamites.

"I don't need a reward to do the right thing," she said, sharply.

"No, but you do need cheering up," Berith pointed out. "Keep it. It'll go well with the rice."

Berith rose from the chair, and knelt to look at the woman. Faint traces of Fallen magic still clung to her skin, and she was mortal. Olympe must have meant a magic user rather than a Fallen. The woman didn't even look of French descent, or if she was, at some point in the line of ancestors she'd had people from the Middle East or the Maghreb, giving her skin a dark tint, all the more striking because her hair was blond, so pale it was almost white.

"She's pretty badly hurt," Berith said. Her hands rested, lightly, on the chest. "I don't think she's likely to name her assailant anytime soon, and I should hope Olympe is intelligent enough to know this."

"Olympe isn't a fool." She'd said "if she ever wakes up," and she'd known exactly how unlikely that was.

Even from where she was, Françoise could see the string of bruises on the face and the arms, and the way the hands rested, folded against each other, knuckles lightly touching. The legs oddly extended, rotated inward. Not a natural position. "What's wrong with her?"

"I'm not sure. Hypothermia." Berith shook her head. "She was warmly dressed, but I don't know how long she lay in the cold. And two broken ribs, certainly. I'm not sure what Olympe thinks I can do. Magic can't heal, at least not wounds that serious. Most healing spells—"

"I know," Françoise said, wearily. They'd already established that no magic would prevent her from dying in childbirth. She moved, started the slow, excruciating process of squatting by the mattress's side.

Up close, the woman looked worse: her pulse was barely palpable. She still breathed, though. Her clothes must have been rich once: a dress of dyed cotton with mutton sleeves and a high waist, which was now so torn the petticoats—also torn and bloodied—showed. Above her wrist was a dark stain. No, not a stain; a tattoo. Françoise knelt, pushed back the sleeve. It was a dragonfly perched on a water lily, a fine, painstaking pattern that must have taken weeks of work.

"She must be House," Françoise said. She let her hand trail on the chest; drew, for a moment, on the magic that always filled the flat, feeling the way it spread into her body like waves, gently taking her where she needed to be. Her spell sent a small burst of it in the chest, toward the heart.

There was no answering echo. "No House link."

"No," Berith said. "I didn't think so. Else a House would already have come for her. But there are ways to cut it off."

"There are? I wasn't aware."

Her voice was dark. "You don't want to meet those who can do it."

Françoise was about to withdraw her hand, when she saw the burn. It was slightly above and between the breasts. "That's strange," Françoise said. "I wonder what caused it." Every other injury looked like the result of a beating: this one stood out—a distinct shape, an oval or a half circle. The skin was raw and inflamed, whorls and patches of red, burned flesh that traced a pattern Françoise couldn't name. "It looks like someone tried to brand her." Which was silly, because no one branded anything or anyone, even in Paris. Cattle in the countryside maybe, but certainly not mortals. "I don't know what with."

"Maybe an accident," Berith said. "Something got burning hot against her skin, and it was engraved or embossed?" She was lifting, carefully, the right hand, unclenching the knuckles, exposing it, palm up, to the pale light filtering through the boarded windows. "She fought off someone with a knife."

Multiple cuts on the fingers and palm, crossing and crisscrossing the lines of the hand. But . . .

"It was an odd kind of knife." Françoise traced one cut, carefully. "They're very long cuts. Most knives have shorter blades. And . . ." A tingle of magic crept up her arm when she withdrew, something that wasn't Fallen magic, but utterly unfamiliar. Something hard and unyielding, pressing against her until all the air went out of her lungs, and she felt like she was breathing nothing but dust and ashes.

Finger by finger, Berith unclenched the left hand. More cuts, and—

"Glass?" she asked.

Françoise shook her head. She'd never seen it in such a state—broken pieces, with edges as sharp as glass—but she knew exactly what it was. "Jade." The stone chips were green, translucent, with a thin line of darker green running through their heart. "It must have been a beautiful piece, before it broke." Was it the pendant that had burned her between the breasts? Hard to tell—the chips were so completely smashed.

She picked one of the largest pieces, and almost dropped it, because the feeling of something that just waited to crush and choke her was sharp and almost unbearable. But it was just pain, and fear, and neither was the master of her. "I think—" She angled it to the light, noting a sharp, thin edge that wasn't jagged or broken. "I think this is the knife. What's left of it." It didn't look like a knife: more like a sword, with the beginnings of a sharp curve. But there was no mistaking it: *this* edge was deliberate, not the result of breakage. "The edge was crescent-shaped."

"Odd weapon," Berith said. "It was bound to break."

"Mmm. Give me a bowl, will you? One of the really badly broken ones. Might as well put them to good use." It was either that or break them completely and start using their shards as defensive weapons. Which would have been entertaining, if not actually useful.

"Too small," Berith said. "Fortunately, we've got two broken ones."

Françoise carefully put the piece down, and then started collecting all the other fragments from the hand. When Berith laid the bowls by her side, she dropped the pieces, one by one, into them—and breathed a sigh of relief when that odd feeling of choking finally left her, as if someone had filled the room with fresh air. "It's enchanted. I'm assuming it wasn't meant to break."

Berith picked up one of the pieces, looked at it. "I feel nothing."

"I don't think it's Fallen magic," Françoise said.

Berith made a face.

"There are other things. Were." She'd heard tales, when she was growing up: flower fairies and spirits and ghosts, except, of course, that all were long since dead, ground into insignificance by the Fallen.

Berith smiled, displaying sharp, white teeth. "You saw Philippe. I'd say the past tense is probably inadequate."

"I still don't understand why we have her." And then she thought back to what Olympe had said. A half dark circle. Someone had tried to snatch her, and failed. "Safekeeping."

Berith rose again, waited for Françoise to start struggling to her feet. When that didn't happen, she went back to her chair and sat, watching the woman. "Protection? It makes sense. If there's anywhere in la Goutte d'Or that would keep someone safe . . ."

"So they're still looking for her." Whoever "they" was—whoever thought it made sense to steal Annamites and other immigrants. No, the issue wasn't whether it made sense. If you needed people, for whatever twisted reason, taking them from the Houseless areas was the best idea. Few defensive spells, and no recourse, even if the communities worried.

Berith shrugged. "They're welcome to try and get her. I don't think they'll make it past the door."

"I don't know," Françoise said. She knew the rules of la Goutte d'Or: it might not have the distant, unattainable safety of a House, but nevertheless . . . The worst they faced was famine, and illness, and poverty. The disappearances of dockworkers and other Annamites were something else altogether. "There's something out there, isn't there? Something that just takes and takes." Something that wasn't subject to the unspoken rules of the Houses, or the ever-changing ones of the gangs. Something different.

Berith grimaced. "My dominion is over this flat. It would take some effort to move it elsewhere. I can tell you if we're under siege. I can't tell you what might be happening several hundred meters from here, on the docks or rue de Jessaint or elsewhere."

"You helped Philippe on rue de Jessaint. Or so he said."

Berith's silver-flecked gaze grew distant. "He was in a place that wasn't here. A little pocket of space that had been cut off from the city. And there was . . ." She paused, collecting her thoughts. "Something coming. Something rising from forgotten places."

Françoise withdrew her hand from the bowl. "It's still out there."

"Yes. But as I said, I can protect you against it, but not much more. And only if you're not reckless. I don't know what it is, but . . ." She looked at the body again. "If I didn't know better—"

"Yes?"

"I've seen someone beaten up like this, once. Except not as badly. A child who fell into a lock, just as it was filling up with water. Bruises and cuts made when their body was thrown against the walls."

Françoise shivered. "There are locks, behind la Villette Basin."

"Yes. I haven't been to them since the war. I imagine they're much diminished. That much less safe."

"The knife wounds—" Françoise shook her head. "She was attacked and someone pushed her in?"

"I assume so."

"We . . . we can't tell if she's going to be fine," Françoise said. "You said there were two broken ribs in the chest, but we don't know if any major organs have been pierced. She needs a doctor." They couldn't afford one. And whatever had happened to the woman, it was probably already too late for medical attention. She would either pull through on her own or die.

Berith said nothing. Magic swirled, lazily, around the chair, circled it like flames. Her eyes, when she spoke, were the golden shade of wheat in summer, in an impossibly faraway land. "Let's ask Philippe."

"We can't pay him."

"And we can't let her die, either," Berith said. "Can we?"

Françoise shivered. She already knew the answer. There was only a single possible one. "No. I'll ask him, when he comes."

They both knew that when he next came—soon, too soon—it would be to escort her into House Hawthorn.

TEN
HAWTHORN'S OWN

MADELEINE woke up, and wished she hadn't.

She was lying on something hard and cold, and the smell of mold was all around her—in her hair, in her nostrils, in her chest, as if she'd been entombed within a damp cave for centuries. And, within her, the link to the House was seething so strongly she thought, for an agonizing, heart-stopping moment, that Asmodeus was standing by her side.

She sat up, gingerly. Her chest ached when she moved: there was a nascent bruise all across her torso, by the looks of it.

Where—

The air rippled around her, slowly, lazily. The dim light allowed her to see only the walls of the room she was in. Even covered in algae and mold, they were vaguely familiar. The link to the House was still pressing against her mind, sharpening her thoughts to unbearable clarity: Asmodeus's presence so vivid she could imagine his voice. *Run away.*

He knew where she was, didn't he? She patted her clothes. Her clothes had taken a rather thorough battering. The tracker disk was still in the inner pocket of the jacket where she'd left it. Instead of pulsing like a living heart, it was cold, its beating almost completely stilled. She pulled it into the light, stared at it. It had charred at the edges, and the insignia of Hawthorn was blurred, the hawthorn tree reduced to a straight line, the crown all but smoothed away. At a guess, even with her appalling talent for magic, this was not good. Not good at all.

Run away.

Yeah. As if she could right now.

There was another person in the room. She crawled over there, ignoring the twinges of pain in her chest, and laid a hand on the wrist. Her finger met, not flesh, but the scabbed, barnacled surface of shell.

It was the other Annamite: the man who had been with Véronique. What had been his name? "Charles," she whispered. There was no answer. His clothes were torn, his chest bloodied; the eyes slightly too far apart, and the flesh shadowed with gray scales. They flaked off under her touch, leaving the imprint of her fingers in red, glistening flesh on his cheeks.

No. She was going to do more damage, despite trying to help him. She withdrew her fingers, trying to keep them still. Where were they?

At length, she got up on unsteady feet, and tottered, as best as she could, to the opposite wall. There was a door, but it was locked, and the sole, minuscule window in the wall, a circular oeil-de-boeuf, was plastered over with something hard, like mortared stone. No, not stone: barnacles, wedged so close together they had fused in a lumpy, whitish mass.

Still in the dragon kingdom, then. But then, anything else would have been unlikely.

Run away. The link to the House was insistent, like a knife cutting, again and again, at her flesh.

She knelt, again, by Charles's side. Her fingers brushed against something hard in the pocket of his jacket: she withdrew a small snuffbox, the kind a gentleman would keep his tobacco or aniseed sweets in. But the warmth of it, the weight of it, in her hand were all too familiar.

Essence.

All she had to do was open it, to breathe it in. She'd have enough power to blast the door open; enough recklessness to attempt an escape, to have the voice of Hawthorn fall to a bearable level in her thoughts.

All she had to do . . .

But the only thing she could think of was Asmodeus's face; and the way he had unfolded, one by one, the fingers of his right hand, like a doctor putting on a glove before an operation. All she could hear was his voice, amused, lightly ironic. *You might as well be of some use, after all, even if it's only for a few hours of my own enjoyment.*

No. Not that.

She took the box, and slid it in the same pocket as the tracker disk. Then she settled by Charles's side, and waited.

When the door opened, she jerked awake with a start. Two guards in dark orange tunics with conical hats came in, carrying peculiar weapons: a cross between a halberd and a knife, a long pole topped by a short, narrow blade tapering to a point. The blades were a dark brown with thin green streaks. They pointed them toward her, penning her as though she were an animal, an arm's length away from the person who entered through the door.

She was Annamite: a dragon, with the antlers Madeleine was coming to recognize as characteristic. But where Prince Phuong Dinh's antlers had been translucent, as fine and as delicate as porcelain, these were thick: an opaque, off-white color that gave the impression the owner wouldn't mind using them to fight.

The woman looked from Charles to Madeleine, her face not exactly emotionless, but close. "Well. What do we have here?"

As if she didn't know, exactly, what it was she had captured. Madeleine bit back on an answer.

"An essence addict, and . . ." She lifted a hand, and a cold, slimy current wrapped itself around Madeleine's wrists, like invisible bonds that slowly started to rub against her flesh. The link to the House flared so strongly it was all she could do to remain standing, to not run, blindly, heedlessly, toward the open door and a rather dubious safety. "And a Fallen-bound. And also an addict."

"I haven't touched angel essence in months," Madeleine snapped.

"Of course. And you could hold some in the palm of your hand and not be tempted to partake." She sounded amused. "Not that it would matter. This room is proof against any magic you can conjure."

"There's no power on earth that is capable of that."

"Is there? You're not on earth." The woman smiled. "My name is Yen Oanh. But you already guessed this." She gestured, gracefully, at the guards. "Come. Let me show you my little corner of the dragon kingdom."

Two extra guards carried Charles with them. He hung, limp, between them, on the thin line between unconscious and corpse. "You shouldn't move him," Madeleine said, before she could stop herself.

Yen Oanh's gaze was pitying. She didn't bother answering.

They emerged into the same odd, rippling sunlight of the dragon kingdom, on some kind of narrow platform overlooking a vast expanse of sand. Directly below them was a small encampment, and buildings of coral and diseased mother-of-pearl, crooked and distorted, like quick, hurried sketches instead of a real construction. In the distance was what looked like a half-built wall of dark brown stones. People the size of dolls carried tools and clear green stones to it. There were several piles already, and masons reaching for them. Barely visible behind the wall was a set of stone stairs. It took an impossibly long, almost absurd time for Madeleine to realize that the stairs were identical to the ones they'd descended, to get into the dragon kingdom.

Were they walling themselves off? The wall hadn't been there when they'd left Hawthorn. It had to be another set of stairs, another part of Paris's quays they were cutting off. As if that would change anything; like trying to plug a colander by blocking off one hole. Asmodeus, much as she disliked him, was right: the time for secrecy had ended, and they were now vulnerable.

The guards still held her at arm's length with their halberds, as they walked down the planks. Madeleine looked down. It was iron, corroded and blotched, and slippery, with the sheen of spilled oil. The door to the cell was set in a wall that must have run the entire length of the platform; but half of it was now nothing more than algae-encrusted rubble, with crabs and fish settled in the nooks and crannies, and protrusions of coral distorting every available surface like a hundred tumors. Inside, a corroded, smashed iron structure, and large basins, their surfaces covered in verdigris. It was both . . . familiar and creepy at the same time, the remnants of things Madeleine could name, made meaningless by their sojourn in the water.

There was a cage, the edge of the platform: the guards opened it, and set Charles down inside, before closing the door. They hadn't bothered to get rid of the previous occupant: a shrunken, barnacled corpse with a blistered, greenish black face, gazing at them with empty eye sockets, and large chunks of the lips missing.

"You can't—," Madeleine started, and then found her voice again. "He needs a doctor."

"He's dying." Yen Oanh's voice was harsh. "And, because of people like him, of their embrace and promotion of Fallen ways, other people, far more defenseless than him, are dying, too. Don't expect me to pity him. Come." Her face still hadn't moved.

When they reached the edge of the platform, the guards merely pushed her off. Madeleine had a stomach-clenching moment of terror as she floated free, before the water caught her, and carried her down. Of course. One couldn't even trust gravity here.

Yen Oanh and the guards were already waiting for her. Madeleine walked toward them, knowing she would be pushed and prodded if she didn't follow. As she left the shadow of the platform, she turned, briefly, to stare at the cage where Charles lay dying, and saw, at last, what she'd been imprisoned in.

It was the wreck of a boat. And now the copper basins and the structure made sense, because this was not a merchant boat or a seagoing vessel, but one of the old laundry barges, the ones that had dotted the Seine before the war; before the river turned dark and angry and made barges like these unsustainable. It looked as though its hull had been staved in, and then crushed by something. The hole was colonized by algae and coral formation, almost completely plugged, but its outline was clearly delineated; and the same for the cracks.

Crushed by dragons.

She saw, for a brief moment, a large, serpentine shape breaking the surface of the Seine, its antlers driving deep into the fragile wood, its coils wrapping around the shape of the hull and the cabins, and tightening until the entire thing snapped like twigs in a storm—and shivered. She'd thought the dragons unfamiliar, and alien, but not outright terrifying. A good thing, after all, that they were weak: who knew what they could do when they were strong?

The cage with Charles inside was dangling down the remnants of the hull, a dark extrusion that had to be visible from a large distance. From the walls they were building, perhaps? Yen Oanh clearly meant to set an example.

And, equally clearly, Madeleine—House-bound, essence-addicted—was the other part of the example.

She shivered, again.

Yen Oanh and the guards herded her toward one of the ramshackle buildings: the largest one, its walls crooked and bulging out of shape, the coral turning an unhealthy gray-blue in large patches, and the bars on the windows already crumbling into dust.

Inside, it was dark, cool, and silent. Then, as her eyes adjusted to the shadows, she saw that the building was full. Bunk beds, three to a single space, held bodies, packed so tightly one could hardly move between them. No one spoke for a while: Madeleine watched the people moving between beds, changing sheets, taking pulses, and giving out medicines and injections.

It was . . . a hospital? The people moving between beds looked and acted like nurses and doctors, but it didn't sound like any healing was being done. Some people, convulsing, were strapped to the beds. Others didn't move. Most of them were fish or crabs or other crustaceans. Some were dragons, their antlers thin and translucent, except that their clothes weren't faded, patched silk, but rough, unadorned cotton in an even worse state of wear.

And there was a smell, a sweet, sickly one that was somehow familiar.

"I don't understand . . . ," Madeleine started.

A stretcher was moving toward them, carrying a body. No, not a body; a corpse. Because no one could survive with half the flesh of their face sloughed off, the bones glistening below the slack, jellied red of corrupted muscles. Because no one's eyes were that color, mottled and grayish and with the sheen of decomposing oil, or that size, revulsed and shrunken in their orbits like shriveled grapes. The same smell rose, sweet and sickly and so strong nausea welled up in her mouth—corruption, decay, mingled with something else, the acridity and warmth she knew all too well.

Angel essence.

Yen Oanh laid a hand down on the face, on the lips, on the chopstick held between the corpse's teeth. She touched, gently, the antlers on either side of the face. One of them snapped off in her hand, with a crunching sound, not like bones breaking, but like cracked eggshell, coming apart with just a touch. Dust came up. It was almost the familiar taste and fire of essence, except that everything was swamped by that unbearable sweetness, traveling up Madeleine's nostrils and her mouth and making her stomach somersault.

Madeleine gave up, and fell to her knees, vomiting. Once, and then again and again, until she brought up nothing but bile, which swirled around her, borne by the invisible currents. But the sickening taste didn't go away.

"This is your handiwork," Yen Oanh said, softly, somewhere above her. "The easy lure of magic, and the decay that overtakes us when we yield to temptation. And, as always, it's the poor, the hunters, the peasants, the workers, who bear the brunt of it."

Madeleine struggled to stand up, to breathe—let alone to speak. "We don't—"

"You encroach on us. You weaken us." Yen Oanh's voice was almost expressionless, stating a fact. She should have been angry? Sad? Something, anything that would have made sense. "And now the princess thinks she will make an alliance with you. All for what? So we can have more and more people follow this way of life?"

Madeleine dragged her voice from where it had fled. "Not everyone is an addict."

"And not everyone in your House is a Fallen. But you do enough damage, as it is."

"We didn't ask you to consume angel essence!"

Yen Oanh laughed. It was dark, and utterly without joy. "You offer rice to a man dying of hunger. Do you think he will not take it? Essence is the promise of pleasure, of power. When everything is crumbling around us, do you truly think we will walk away from it?"

"You took Ghislaine." Madeleine pulled herself to her feet, shaking. "And Elphon."

Yen Oanh smiled.

"What—what do you want?"

Yen Oanh didn't even blink. "If I had my way? Your death. Publicly, messily, slowly. To show the kingdom, and the city, that Fallen magic has no power over us."

Like Charles, dying in his cage, with no one to comfort him and nothing to ease the pain. She hoped to God he would never wake up, never realize what was happening. "I'm not Fallen."

"No, but you're the next best thing, as they say. Fortunately for you, you have value beyond this."

"What value?"

"As you say, you're not Fallen. And much as I would like to clean the kingdom of every trace of House presence . . . I would rather have your master."

Ghislaine had been worried about the House, Prince Phuong Dinh had said, worried enough to leave and try to warn them. And now Madeleine knew why. Because it was a trap for Asmodeus.

In other circumstances, she would have said Yen Oanh and Asmodeus were welcome to each other, but now she only felt small, and scared, with only a worthless link to the House reminding her that she was in mortal danger. "I don't understand."

Yen Oanh reached out, running a clawed hand on Madeleine's face. Something pushed against the link to Hawthorn in her mind, again and again; like a snake's tongue, probing for weaknesses in all the wrong places, rasping at her skin until she bled. The presence of Asmodeus flared, a brief image of a tree of thorns, and a fire, and the touch on her mind withdrew.

"I would poison you if I could." Yen Oanh's voice was emotionless, as if she were merely talking about the weather. "I would break into your mind as you lay dying in agony, and use the link to your House to slip past its wards. I would shatter Hawthorn from within, into ten thousand pieces that could never be picked up."

There was . . . there was a confused legend of Echaroth doing this once, back when she'd founded Hawthorn. House Montenay. A vague, frightening memory, a tale told to children in the dark. "That's—"

"No longer possible, sadly. The House has changed, in the centuries since Hawthorn's founding. I'll have to find another way. He sent you here. Presumably you have value to him."

"He's . . ." She thought of Ghislaine, and Elphon. "He's lost people here already. To the kingdom." Had Yen Oanh already taken both of them, and sent her message to Hawthorn? Had Asmodeus known, when he had sent the three of them into the kingdom nevertheless—had he picked ambassadors he could spare, those who could die with no consequence to Hawthorn?

"I know." Yen Oanh's expression was sharp, unpleasant. "He will have to risk himself, one way or another, for his subjects."

Dependents. "He's not a fool. He won't come."

"We shall see," Yen Oanh said. "If he doesn't come, I can always start making an example of you."

Of course he wasn't going to come. He hadn't risen to be head of Hawthorn by being a fool, and running after every dependent he lost.

She was on her own in the middle of nowhere, with no help to expect, at the mercy of someone who thought of her as a pawn to be martyred. The link to Hawthorn flamed in her mind, scattering all her thoughts into cinders. She managed to remain standing, but it was a close thing.

Madeleine. Run away.

She couldn't.

ELEVEN
No Easy Things

TIME passed, slow and jagged and unbearable. They'd shut her back in the small cell where she'd woken up, and from time to time they would give her a bowl of rice with that omnipresent fish sauce. They might have meant well, but the smell of it alone turned her stomach. Light filtered through the door: she couldn't be sure, but there were fewer meals than there ought to have been. They were starving her, so she couldn't escape.

Her cough, now unchecked by Iaris's medications, came back, doubling her over whenever she shifted, whenever she tried to get up, her lungs once more feeling wrung out and bloodied, without any of the comfort of essence to make it bearable. And prayers came back, too, the half-remembered entreaties of her childhood, fragments of songs and hymns beseeching God for help on paths of darkness and valleys of death, begging Christ to have mercy on them. But there was no one there to answer, in the darkness. There was no God, because this was Hell, where all the Fallen were consigned, and they were all damned, too.

The tracker disk was cold against her flesh. Was Elphon trapped here, too? She didn't know. They wouldn't speak to her; merely delivered the food, and took away the bucket in which she relieved herself.

Madeleine managed, through sheer stubbornness, to chip a small hole in the barnacles that covered the oeil-de-boeuf window. Through it, she could see a pane of hardened, yellowed glass so thick she couldn't even dent it, but she could get a glimpse outside. Of the wall, rising; of the stairs leading back to Paris, so far away she might be in another universe.

Run away.

The link to the House grew and grew within her, unfolding like a tree of thorns, every branch and every spur shoot prickling into her thoughts. She couldn't keep anything together, couldn't focus—could only hear the cool, assured voice in her mind telling her to escape, again and again until she thought she would go mad with its echo.

Run away.

One day, there was a commotion on the bridge of the wreck, a glimpse of coarse cotton tunics and the dark orange clothes of guards, and a familiar rippling in the air, like a memory of something she'd lost long ago. Fallen magic? Here? No, it was just angel essence, another addict Yen Oanh was dangling in a cage to die of exposure.

Words filtered down to her: barks in Annamite, and then someone speaking French calmly, evenly. For a moment, a brief, impossible moment, she thought it was Hawthorn. That it was the House, coming for her, but the voice was unfamiliar.

No one entered her cell.

The noise eventually died down, and darkness fell again, on the crawl of her days and nights. The smell of fish, mingled with that sweet sickly odor of essence, had turned even sourer. She hadn't thought it was possible, but it felt like it was stuck in her throat and nostrils, clogging her breath, gumming her eyes. She was going to be sick again, but if she did bend over the bucket, the smell of urine would be enough to make her vomit, anyway.

She had to . . .

She had to hold on to something. To remember—to—what was the point, anyway? No one was coming for her.

She pulled out the tracker disk, held it to the light, fighting back a fit of coughing that bent her double, leaving the salty taste of blood in her mouth. The insignia of the House was faded and charred, unreadable; its beat all but invisible, as if it, too, were dying. It was cold against her fingers, like the touch of a drowned man.

Clothilde had said she could feel Elphon. That she knew where he was. Madeleine closed her hands around the disk, willing it back to life, clinging to it with the stubbornness of a prayer.

I'm here. I'm alive. Please. Find me.

I'm here. I'm—

There was no change in the disk, nothing to tell her it worked. Ghislaine had had one, too, and they'd lost her anyway. Madeleine needed magic, but she had no artifacts, no charged mirrors with angel breath she could have used.

Nothing.

Except . . .

They hadn't bothered to take away the box of angel essence. Probably they hoped she would inhale it all, and save them a struggle when they dragged her out for her execution. Yen Oanh had said it would make no difference, that the cell was proof against any Fallen magic she could think of.

Madeleine took the box, weighed it in the palm of her hand. The smell of it rose, strong and acrid enough to banish the other, sickly, corrupted one. It promised power. Relief. Oblivion.

He would kill her if she relapsed.

If she did nothing, she would die here.

Her hands were shaking. If she stopped to think about this, she would simply throw it all away; or, worse, inhale it all. She was an addict: as Iaris had said, no one had ever shaken the addiction. People just died of it, like the dragons in Yen Oanh's makeshift hospital, which was nothing more than a house of death, a place to slowly slide away from the world. She knew all about those; she, who had hidden in House Silverspires for twenty years, waiting for essence to take her all the way into her grave.

Madeleine set the box on the floor, well away from her. Then, slowly, carefully—*Don't think on what you're doing, not now*—she took a pinch from it, laid it in the palm of her right hand, and withdrew, fast. A fit of coughing made the world swim, but she ignored it.

She stared, for a while, at the essence. The smell of it was rising, sharp, familiar, irresistible. If she closed her eyes, she'd be back in her old laboratory in House Silverspires, waiting for Oris or Isabelle to finish sealing flesh into containers. She'd be safe under Morningstar's protection, where no one and nothing could touch her.

And you could hold some in the palm of your hand and not be tempted to partake.

No, of course not. She knew exactly what she was, and how she had come to this.

She raised unsteady hands, cupped together, to the level of her nostrils; and, tipping them, breathed the entire pinch of essence in.

Living fire, coursing through her, down her throat, all the way into her lungs and stomach—filling her up, overwhelming the smell of decay. She was held, cradled in arms of light. She could do anything, go anywhere, face whatever was coming with a wave of her hands that would summon enough power to blast away her enemies. For the first time in what felt like forever, she was safe. Not loved or cared for, but armed against the world, against nightmares.

Here, now, for this suspended, blessed moment, she was not afraid.

She needed to do something else. *Focus. Focus.* Her hands, now utterly calm and steady, picked up the tracker disk, wrapped themselves around it. Magic coursed from them, from her heart into the charred wood, sending a burst of magic like a clarion call.

I am here.

The wood beat, once, twice, under her fingers; and for a moment only, the hawthorn tree and the crown were limned in traceries of light. *I am here,* she whispered again, and every word seemed to shake the barge's wreck to its foundations.

She waited, but no answer came, and the disk grew quiescent again. No guards came, either, to burst in and ask what she thought she was doing. At least that was something, but Yen Oanh was right. The cell was proof against whatever she might attempt.

The pinch of essence she'd taken slowly left her system; and the room became drab and corroded once more, every smell sharp and overwhelming, the rippling, dim light alien and frightening, a reminder she was far away from any kind of home, from any kind of help.

The smell of angel essence still filled the room: she had forgotten to close the box after opening it. If she reached out, she could take the rest of it in one glorious rush. It was a small amount: not enough to kill her, but it would corrode her lungs further. It might make her insensate, sparing her what was to come.

Yes, Asmodeus would kill her, but only if he found her. If he bothered to come, and she already knew he wouldn't come. Whereas Yen Oanh's threats . . . they would materialize. Yen Oanh didn't need Madeleine, not even as bait; certainly not whole, not unharmed.

Be sensible, Madeleine. That was the only thing that made sense. The only thing she could do.

Her hands were shaking again, reaching out, almost against her will, toward the box, dipping into it and feeling the touch of magic like warm embers on her skin.

Once an addict, always an addict.

PHILIPPE had braced himself for a number of things once Françoise had sent word that Hawthorn's safe-conduct had come through, but an unconscious woman certainly wasn't among them.

"We'll pay," Françoise said behind him, stiff and formal. She and Berith had been playing chess when Philippe had come in, the board precariously balanced on Berith's knees. While Françoise showed him the mattress, Berith had carefully put the board back on the table, tidying up the dislodged pieces with quiet certainty, as if she'd memorized the entire configuration.

"Don't worry," Philippe said. He couldn't ignore a woman in such a bad state. Ah well—it wasn't as though he needed to eat much, or to pay for a roof over his head. World's worst doctor when it came to actually profiting from his abilities.

Philippe knelt by the woman's side. She was mortal, not Fallen, but she'd been, at some point, boosted by Fallen magic; otherwise she would not have survived the battering she'd taken. Even so . . .

Her posture was rigid, the arms bent inward, and the legs rotated and unresponsive, the soles of the feet flexed. Her hands were clenched into odd fists, fingers flexed as well, knuckles resting against each other on the chest.

Not good.

He sent a burst of *khi* fire into the body, tracking its progress toward the liver and heart, along the meridians. It dispersed after a scant handful of seconds, and the same burst sent into the eyes didn't elicit a response. The pupils were dilated, failing to constrict. The pulse was barely palpable, but that wasn't a surprise.

He laid his hands around her head, slowly, carefully; sent the same burst of fire into her brain. It didn't vanish, so much as echo hollowly within the confines of her skull, sinking down into a gradual silence.

Françoise watched him with burning eyes.

"Her brain is badly damaged," Philippe said. He could try to operate, to reduce the swelling, but—he thought, again, of his burst of *khi* fire, fading—it would bring her scant comfort.

"And"—a deep, noisy breath from Françoise—"there is nothing to do?"

He shrugged. "Make her comfortable. Wait."

"Not for a miracle," Berith said, from the chair.

"Unless you can grant her heart's desire," Philippe said, not bothering to hide his sarcasm. The woman was probably a House dependent, probably used to Fallen, the only thing that had kept her alive this long. He should not have had one ounce of sympathy for her.

But you're getting old, he thought, not without irony, because he didn't, couldn't age. More likely it was Berith getting on his nerves.

"I need a ritual," Berith said. "Consent, you might call it, though it's a little more complex than that. Certainly nothing that could be performed on an unconscious woman. I'm sorry." She didn't sound sorry, more like frustrated and annoyed. Powerlessness, things not going her way? How very Fallen.

Philippe rose. "Well, as I said, you can wait." He said, because he knew Berith was going to doggedly come back to the subject, "You don't need to pay me. That's not what I'd call a very effective diagnosis."

He felt . . . a little queasy, as if whatever he had eaten lay heavily in his stomach—a little irritable, but after all, he was going to walk into the House of Hawthorn with only Fallen magic to protect him and Françoise—and then he turned.

Françoise was holding a bowl to him, with shards of something: a particular smell, a mixture of damp, moldy earth with the barest tinge of wood, the two *khi* elements entwined, and overlaid with a thin veneer of Fallen magic—a . . . a monstrosity so unnatural he could barely breathe. "What—"

"She was holding it," Françoise said, with a shrug. "I thought you would know what it was."

Not exactly, no, other than something that shouldn't have existed. Philippe forced himself to look into the bowl. It looked like shards of jade: of a blade of jade, enchanted with that spell. And the smells of brine and the *khi* water were faint, but distinctive. "Dragon kingdom," he said, aloud, before he could stop himself.

Françoise stared at him. *"Rong,"* she said in Viet. "That's a myth. Tales told to children, to distract them from the devastation of the war."

Things of Annam, which was long gone, long inaccessible, to her and to him? Six months ago he would have said the same thing with the same fervor. Now he just shrugged, remembering the smell of decay, and Ngoc Bich's bitter smile. "There's something under the Seine."

"Another power?" Berith asked.

Not one that would ever be conquered or understood by Fallen. "Nothing you can tame."

Berith raised an eyebrow. "I didn't intend to. I assume this closes the subject?" She gestured to the table. "Have something before you go. Françoise made these especially."

It was a plate of buns, not brioche or cake, but the steamed buns that Philippe remembered so well, with a faint smell of cooked pork and vegetables. They'd been closed awkwardly, some of their pleats bursting open during the cooking, revealing the dull gray of their filling, and they weren't pure white, but the cream color of flour, with darker specks of grits.

He bit into one. It was mostly bun. The filling, as expected, was small, salty and concentrated, with only the barest hint of fish sauce, but it was still a taste of home. He could have wept. "Thank you."

Françoise looked as though she didn't want to let the subject of dragons go, but, with an effort, she laid the bowl down, and waddled to the table, where she helped herself to one of the buns. "You should visit Grandmother Olympe more often. She always has food."

Olympe, insofar as Philippe could tell, was undisputed queen of her little kingdom. No wonder she would get the best of everything the community had to offer.

She had also told him to stay away from Berith in no uncertain terms, muttering a Viet proverb about unpleasant consequences, "For every seed, a matching fruit," which was, as far as Olympe went, fairly transparent.

Not, of course, that Philippe intended to listen to her advice.

Berith was sitting in her blue armchair, watching him. "Come here," she said.

He crossed the room without a word, to stand before her.

"I'm afraid sharing breath is more effective," Berith said.

Philippe shrugged. Fallen magic was bad enough. Touching lips meant nothing to him.

She smelled of myrrh; as he bent toward her, her dominion shimmered into existence again, the bookshelves and the impossible blue of that summer sky, and the smell of dry paper, the rustle of wind through pages. Something rose within him, like the storm of crows in his rib cage that had been the curse of House Silverspires: a warmth that spread to his hands and feet, that sizzled in his arms until he felt that his slightest move would crack open the floorboards and send thunder up into the heavens. Was this how magicians felt, all the time?

He pulled away, with an effort, met Berith's knowing gaze. "All I can spare," she said. "It will wear off, never fear."

It had better. He had no intention of spending his life tainted by Fallen magic.

"Ready?" he asked Françoise.

She was wearing a silk dress and a matching shawl with faded embroidery: it must have been very fine, once, and very costly, but now the many holes in it had not all been patched, and the embroidery had unraveled, leaving the animals looking like half-baked monsters from a nightmare. "I suppose so." She gripped Berith's hand, so hard her dark skin went pale. "I suppose so."

They both knew neither of them could really ever be ready for this.

THEY took the omnibus to Hawthorn. As it left la Goutte d'Or and the Houseless areas around Lazarus, the crowds thinned. The hard-faced, thin workers in frayed clothes were replaced by middle-class shopkeepers and artisans; and then finally by day laborers attached to Houses, thin, haggard faces giving way to plumper ones, and patched clothes to the faded splendor of uniforms in House colors.

Françoise stared straight ahead, and didn't speak. She and Berith had had a long, agitated conversation before she left, and she had come out of it looking neither reassured nor happy.

Philippe thought of Isabelle, of that elusive, blissful feeling he'd had, that he knew how to resurrect her, that each word he spoke would be one more thread, spun tight against the previous ones, until there was a rope, an anchor she could follow back to the world of the living.

He thought of her surprised, delighted smile; of the way it would transfigure her, from Fallen to young, impulsive teenager.

Soon.

They walked the last part of the way, to the great wrought-iron gates of Hawthorn's entrance. Behind the gates was a garden: given the state of the rest of Paris, it might have been small and run-down and stilled by the cold winter, but it still looked like a luxuriant jungle. On the lawn on the left of the path, a group of four people in Hawthorn's dark gray and silver uniform seemed to be practicing military maneuvers, casting spells at a shriveled tree that looked as though it couldn't take much extra abuse. It brought back unpleasant memories of the training Philippe had undergone in House Draken during the Great War, when he'd been dragged from Annam and conscripted in their army, when all he'd focused on was the desperate need to survive. He looked away, at the gates.

Vines twined around the hinges: the leaves a deep green color, except that close up they were speckled with small, pale traces of mold; and the iron of the gates was corrugated. A welcome reminder: the House hadn't come out of the Great Houses War unscathed, either.

Still, even standing at the boundary, Philippe could feel Hawthorn's presence: not that of Silverspires, the last House he had been in, not a genteel, quiet, decaying thing, but a brash statement of power.

His fingers ached. He flexed them, trying to forget what he'd felt as they'd broken, one by one, but he could still remember crawling in agony under the light of unfamiliar stars. He had Berith's power within him, a rising, searing wave, but it brought him no comfort.

Hawthorn. Asmodeus.

For you, he whispered to Isabelle's unseen ghost, not expecting any answer.

THEIR guide, a teenager of Maghrebi origin with a face serious beyond her years, left them in a wide, airy antechamber with two sofas upholstered with faded tapestry, and a single tree bearing bloodred oranges. Their scent filled the air until Philippe thought he would choke.

He looked upward, saw the faint traces of mold on the ornate ceiling. There had been buildings in the gardens that looked abandoned altogether, the glass panes of their windows opaque with dust and traces of rain; and outright charred ruins on the gravel strewn with debris. The House might look grand and magnificent, but it was like the rest of the city: barely hanging on to normality, struggling to maintain itself against decay.

He had to believe that. Had to remember that, else he would run away screaming, and never come back.

They barely had time to get settled when the door to the main chamber opened. Françoise looked at Philippe, and in her eyes he saw some of the same fear he felt squeezing his innards. "It'll be fine," he mouthed, against all evidence. And walked in, slowly, to face the master of Hawthorn.

The room was brightly lit, with a wallpaper of colorful birds perched on a variety of trees in flower. The carpet under their feet was Persian, lush and thick, interlocking patterns of red and brown flowers and intertwined branches, the frayed threads barely visible at its edges. On the right side were a low rattan glass table and matching chairs, in the colonial style that had been all the rage before the war.

Asmodeus was sitting behind a large mahogany desk, reading a book. The desk itself was empty, with no papers or anything that made it look as though it was in daily use. He looked up when they entered, his gaze behind the horn-rimmed glasses ironic and amused, until he saw Philippe, and something swirled in those gray-green eyes, like a prelude to a storm. He said nothing, though, until Françoise came to stand before him; her whole body quivering, as though what she really meant to do was flee. For which Philippe couldn't blame her, really.

"Le Thi Anh Tuyet." His Viet was atrocious, but then, few Fallen could speak it properly. "Honored to make your acquaintance. Do forgive the disarray. I have other pressing obligations to attend to, shortly. Your companion can wait outside." The look he flashed Philippe was not friendly.

Asmodeus does keep his word, usually.

A pity he'd also sworn to make Philippe pay for the death of his lover Samariel.

Something was rising, within the room, a sharp, unpleasant magic that pressed against Philippe's skin like the prickling touch of ten thousand knives. Françoise's face was distorted by a rictus, and her hands had clenched into fists, light seeping from beneath her fingernails. She felt it, too.

It met the roiling edge of Berith's magic within Philippe and shattered, leaving the air in the room taut and not one bit less threatening. Asmodeus raised an eyebrow, but made no comment.

The only *khi* currents within the room were water, because of the presence of the Seine nearby. Philippe pulled on them, slowly, gathered them close to him, ready to cast a spell if need be.

"I'd rather my companion stayed," Françoise said. She'd unclenched her fists, was standing watching him, her gaze clear and steady.

"As you wish." It didn't seem to faze Asmodeus, but Philippe doubted that would be the end of it.

There was a single chair in front of the desk, high-backed and without any padding. Françoise pulled it out, and sat down, hands on her knees. "I won't be long."

A short, sharp smile. "I'm sure you won't. I didn't know you were pregnant."

"It's hardly relevant."

"Mmm." Asmodeus closed the book, and leaned back in his own armchair. "Perhaps. Perhaps not. You're aware, aren't you, that I remain linked to Bereus, or whatever else he calls himself, these days?"

"Berith." Françoise's voice shook, but she steadied it. "She. She calls herself Berith now." She reached inside her dress, and withdrew an envelope: cream parchment paper with a red wax seal. From where he was, Philippe couldn't see what it depicted. She laid it on the desk, carefully. "And this is from her, to you."

"Berith." Asmodeus rolled the two syllables on his tongue, as if they were cuts of juicy meat. "Sister mine." He picked up the envelope, and slit it open with a fingernail as sharp as a claw. He barely glanced at its contents. "Trite matters. I already know you're her partner and lover."

"And that I come in her stead?" Françoise asked. "You have it in writing."

Asmodeus shrugged. "I don't need to. As I said—once linked, always linked. Not much, to be sure. The dying embers of a fire, one might say, if indulging in poetic excesses."

"I don't see what you're driving at."

"You don't?" Again that sharp, unpleasant smile of a predator. Philippe found his hands clenched into fists. "If Berith truly, deeply desires to see me . . . I don't need a letter, or a safe-conduct, or any of the rigmarole we're currently indulging in."

"You—" Françoise took in a deep, shaking breath. She rubbed her belly as if for reassurance. "You can feel her dying."

The eyes behind the horn-rimmed glasses rested on her. Something seemed to pass between them. Silence stretched, slow, thick, unbearable. "Always." Asmodeus's voice was light, toneless.

Françoise said nothing. She had her hands crossed on the mound of her belly, and was watching him, gaze for gaze, refusing to be cowed. This was madness. Or something Philippe couldn't properly name.

He glanced at the rattan chairs. Sure enough, there were two cushions on each of them. He turned and walked toward them—something, anything rather than endure that silence. The cushions were silk, smooth and sliding under his touch, reassuringly solid and mundane. As he walked back, Françoise said, "Then you know." She took a breath, slow, deep, noisy. "Please. She asks if you'll come to the flat. To talk."

"Because she won't leave her pitiful dominion?" Asmodeus's smile was wide, mocking.

"Please. She's your Fall-sister." Françoise's voice was shaking. "And she'll be gone forever soon. You—" Another, softer magic in the room, a touch that lingered on the skin, insistently probing for weaknesses. With Berith's magic, Philippe could see it: a thin network of luminous threads, slowly converging toward Françoise, hardening into unbreakable bonds that would pin her to the chair.

Philippe dropped the cushions, and drew on *khi* water to fashion twin blades. He flicked his wrists, slicing at the threads of Asmodeus's magic— again and again, until nothing but faint scraps remained. He knelt then, picked up the cushions again, but not before he'd seen the anger in Asmodeus's eyes.

"Enough. He—" Asmodeus stopped, shook his head. "She sent you to me. To make a point."

"No," Françoise said. "To plead with you."

As if that would ever work.

"The child," Asmodeus said, slowly, "isn't hers. Fallen are sterile."

Françoise shrugged. "There's more to parenthood than blood and seed." Philippe reached the chair, and handed Françoise the cushion. She took it and slid it behind the lower half of her back, with a curt nod, but didn't break eye contact with Asmodeus.

"And more to love?" Asmodeus shook his head. "I see." He folded the letter, held it in his hands, utterly steady. "I'll give you my answer, then, though she already knows it. Berith may visit at her convenience. As for you . . ." Françoise tensed then. Philippe saw her force herself to remain still. "I will offer the protection of the House, to you and your unborn child."

"I don't need the protection of the House." Françoise's voice was calm, but it must have cost her.

Philippe thought Asmodeus would get angry, but his face didn't move, not even the slightest sign of surprise. "Do you not? You may find it's no easy thing, to raise the child with a Fallen." He shifted, and the letter in his hands burst into blue, thin flames; he held it, unmoving, heedless of the way the fire licked at his fingers, until all that remained was a small, charred thing that he dropped on the desk.

"My child isn't your toy, or your property."

"How adorable. You're not the first to whom I would say this—but in this world, we're all owned by something or someone. The best you can hope for is to choose your own masters."

"Then consider my choices made." Françoise rose, slowly, ponderously. "I don't owe you or anyone else anything."

"Of course not. The offer remains open. I would urge you to think on it. Leila will see you back to the gates of the House."

Philippe fell in behind Françoise, walking toward the open doors, toward the brightly lit antechamber where their guide would be waiting for them. Almost there, almost out of the House, his promises all kept, his bargain fulfilled . . .

"Philippe." Asmodeus's voice was the lash of a whip. "Stay a moment."

Ahead of him, Françoise was the one who turned, her eyes bright and feverish, still riding the high of her confrontation. "You said we'd both be safe if we came into Hawthorn."

"Did I?"

Philippe stood rooted to the floor, remembering that light, ironic voice; the bonds tying him to the chair; the sharp, unbearable, unending pain as bone after bone cracked. Within him, what remained of Berith's magic twisted and pushed, trying to fashion wards, protection, anything that would get him out of here in one piece. . . .

At length, after what seemed like an eternity, Asmodeus laughed. "Have no fear. I keep my word. You'll get him back, at some point."

"Whole and unharmed," Françoise said, stubbornly. "And not 'at some point.' After this interview."

"That can be arranged." Asmodeus gave him a look—light glinting on the frame of his glasses, the fires of the Christian Hell dancing in his gray-green eyes—the memory that still woke Philippe up, sweating, on particularly bad nights. . . . "Come. What do you think I can do in a quarter of an hour?"

"Enough, I would say." Françoise's gaze was on Philippe. He opened his mouth to say something reassuring, something flippant, nonchalant, platitudes, but the House seemed to have shriveled his tongue against his palate.

"I'll—" He shuddered, struggling. "I'll be fine. Honestly."

She threw him a sharp glance that wasn't entirely hers. There was something of Berith's steel in her gaze. "I'll be outside. Call, if you need me," she said; and turned, and waddled out, leaving Philippe alone with Asmodeus.

He didn't want to move. But if he didn't, Asmodeus was going to win this round. So, centimeter by painful centimeter, he forced himself to turn, and found himself face-to-face with the Fallen, who had left his desk and was standing by his side.

He wore dark gray and silver, a perfectly cut, elegant swallowtail suit, with blue brocade at his throat, and the smell of orange blossom and bergamot wafted in the air, hanging like a miasma. "Of all the places I didn't expect you would dare to walk into . . ." His voice wasn't light or amused anymore.

"People will do anything, for the right price."

"Will they? Mind you, I am surprised to find you still alive."

"Through no effort of yours." It welled up out of him like blood out of a wound.

"Of course not." The eyes behind the horn-rimmed glasses were jewel hard. "You know that Samariel died."

He knew that nothing could have survived what Samariel had endured—the curse Philippe had unwittingly unleashed within House Silverspires, which had turned muscles to jelly and collapsed lungs and bones like melted candle wax. "Yes," Philippe said. He could have said he was sorry, but he wouldn't have meant it. It wasn't that he had wanted Samariel to die in agony, but he had had no particular affection for either him or

Asmodeus, and to apologize would be to admit guilt—which, in this time, in this place, was about the most suicidal thing he could have done.

"For the right price." Asmodeus didn't move. He was standing close, entirely too close for comfort; the smell of him was suffocating. "I wonder what kind of price would entice a man like you to walk into such risk."

When he didn't speak, Asmodeus moved back a fraction, though it didn't make anything easier. Defiance, then, because he couldn't see anything else to do.

"If you're going to do something to me, just go ahead. It's not like I can prevent it." Not quite true, that. He still had some of Berith's magic, and the twin blades of *khi* water that he'd wielded in his hands, though they were both diminished by his sparring with Asmodeus. . . .

A hand with long, elegant fingernails tousled his hair. Berith's magic sent a spike of power upward, a jolt through Philippe's entire body. Asmodeus didn't even flinch. "I am merely curious. But of course I already know the answer. Berith always had a knack for making people dance to her tune."

"As opposed to torturing people to death to get what you want?" He was flippant, and insolent; bad idea, but he couldn't stop himself.

"Because of you, Samariel died. I wouldn't be so keen to offend here if I were you." Asmodeus withdrew his hand, and said nothing for a while. Then, at length, "I did give my word," he said, slowly. "So, for what it's worth, this is a warning."

"*You're* warning me? Whatever for?"

"Be silent." Asmodeus raised a hand, and the air in the room tightened around Philippe's throat. Philippe struggled to break the hold, but couldn't. Berith's magic was spent now, and the *khi* water in the room had sunk to almost nothing. "You'll know that Berith and I fell out, a long time ago. Or if you don't, I highly suggest you do some basic research, before you go meddling in affairs you don't understand." He paused, but the noose around Philippe's neck didn't loosen, didn't allow him to speak. "I wanted to safeguard what was mine. Berith wanted to help others."

It hardly sounded like a warning, unless you thought like a House-bound, and saw plots and intrigue everywhere. Asmodeus said, simply, "She's

Fallen. She distorts whatever she touches—like a child, even though she doesn't mean to. Sometimes it's benign; sometimes it's not." He smiled, again. "Ask her what happened to those she helped. It should be entertaining."

The noose withdrew. Philippe massaged his bruised throat, and said, "You're not warning me. You're merely toying with me."

Asmodeus smiled. "Did you think I would grant you favors? By all means ask."

As if he could trust anything Asmodeus said. "I see," Philippe said. "Was that all?"

"For the time being." Asmodeus smiled, again. "If you don't pull away from Berith's orbit, I should hope to see you very soon, Philippe. And you might actually be thankful for that."

No. Never.

FRANÇOISE was waiting for him outside. She took one look at his face, and gestured toward the exit to the antechamber. "Let's go."

Philippe nodded, numbly.

Ask her what happened, to those she helped.

Western mythology was replete with tales of bargains with demons: a concept that had once been alien to him, for one didn't negotiate with the messengers of the King of Hell. But now that he had been in Paris for long enough . . .

He shivered, and pulled the shawl tighter around his body.

As they followed Leila out of the House, Philippe caught a glimpse of something in one of the empty, decaying rooms: the ghost of Isabelle, standing with her back to him, leaning on a pale green conversation chair. She wore a white tunic—the color of death, of mourning—and she didn't turn as he passed. Beside her, as translucent as she was, was Morningstar's ghost, also with his back to Philippe, exposing only the sharp, serrated wings. He held his large sword in one hand. The other was on her shoulder, holding her close as a father might hold a beloved daughter.

Nausea rose, sharp, biting; he kept walking, staring straight ahead—just as she stared straight ahead, not looking at him.

*   *   *

IN the flat, Berith was sitting in her usual armchair, reading a book with a frown, a dictionary wedged open on her knees. The dying woman in the bed looked to be in the same position Philippe had left her in, her unmoving face staring at the ceiling with the vacant expression of the unconscious.

Berith rose when Françoise came in, hands outstretched, heedless of the books clattering to the floor. "I'm sorry," she said, and wrapped her in an embrace of swirling cloth and myrrh. Fallen magic rose in the room, a warm monsoon wind. "It went badly."

Françoise's eyes looked bruised, her face pale, slowly taking on color and translucency as she absorbed Berith's magic. "I was telling him nothing he didn't know," she said, finally. "He said you could come to Hawthorn, but he wouldn't come to you. And Philippe—"

Philippe cut her off before she could give Berith anything to hold on to. "Don't worry. It's my own business with House Hawthorn." He coughed ostensibly. "I should leave, anyway. I can come back later."

Berith shook her head. "I pay my debts." She looked at Françoise, who shrugged and moved away from her, leaning on the small, rickety table with the remnants of the buns. "Do you want my blessing, Philippe?"

He thought of the ghost of Isabelle, standing in that empty room in Hawthorn; of Asmodeus, smiling and saying they would meet again soon. *Ask her what happened to the others.*

You're not the master of me.

There'd be a price to pay. Of course, there was always a price to pay. But to get Isabelle back—her quick, easy smile; her awkward attempts to fold dough into bread that never quite seemed to rise in the oven; the tin of biscuits she'd kept in her room, for their evenings together . . . What did it matter?

He'd failed her so many times already. He wasn't going to fail her again.

"Show me," he said.

Berith sat in the armchair again, and watched him for a while. Then she gestured, and the scene shifted: the shadows of bookshelves, the throne on a dais, the ermine cloak the color of the sky. "Come," she said.

There were three steps, leading up to the throne. He took them, to stand before her. Demons take him before he'd kneel to a Fallen, even if it would get what he wanted from her.

Berith's eyes were now luminous: the fragments of silver in the irises shining like molten metal. Her face—it was not a blur of light, but every gaunt, hollow feature was now unbearably sharp, the kind of beauty that killed one to behold. The air was filled with the musty smell of paper, and something else, a faint residue of ash like the memory of a fire. "You ask for your heart's desire," she whispered, and every word seemed to grab Philippe's heart and squeeze it into bloody shards.

She raised a hand, which was dripping with blood. He hadn't seen her cut herself, but then he saw that every line of her palm was an open wound.

"Your desire shakes the foundations of the earth," Berith said. "It leaves bloody footprints upon buried bones, and cracks open the wall between life and death." She laid her hand on Philippe's forehead. He almost pulled away, almost did the sensible thing and ran from the flat, but it was too late. Her touch was warm, cloying, smelling of charnel houses, like much, much more blood than the wounds on her hand.

Everything blurred, like a landscape under a red rain. The bookshelves receded into meaninglessness, and a freezing wind rose, bringing stinging rain into the room. For a while there was nothing around them but the soft patter of water on parquet; and nothing he could see, either, beyond a cold, silvery curtain. Then the noise of rain became something else, every drip, drip lengthening until it became words, spoken in a hundred voices that never seemed to stop or care for one another—fragments of French and Viet and Chinese and other languages he didn't speak, harsh and sibilant.

Heaven or Hell . . . Fallen . . . where . . . call back . . . bond . . .

Only the reaper . . . a harvest of rib cages . . . hearts and minds . . .

And one voice—which he would have known above all else—speaking over every other one: Berith's voice, ringing like a bell call to enlightenment.

The wall of death is thick and strong, and corpses are its foundations. . . .

The flecks of silver in her eyes peeled away one by one, a cloud of fireflies—and, stretching, expanding, became the eyes of ghosts.

He couldn't recognize them all—no, not any of them, just white, elongated faces with sharp teeth and gazes that scooped all the warmth from his body, hanging in the air just a stone's throw from him, a veil of feature-less, hungry masks all watching him.

Philippe . . . Philippe . . .

"You have my blessing," Berith said, and the rain faded, and the throne, and the dais; but the ghosts remained, their gazes transfixing him like spears, driven, again and again, into his flesh.

TWELVE
THRESHOLDS

FRANÇOISE was at Olympe's, helping with the children.

There was always a gaggle of children in Olympe's cramped flat—mothers dropping by with nursing babies, boys and girls jostling one another, fighting to be the first to help with the rice pancakes and the fried rolls. And, with the biting cold outside, perhaps it was no bad thing: it kept them all warm in spite of the poor insulation.

Currently, Françoise and a little boy named Nicolas were attempting to seal some rolls. Not that difficult a task, with the small amount of filling available, and even that had been bulked up with potatoes and fat.

"See, Auntie?" Nicolas said, holding up the last one he'd made. "It's all rolled up tight!"

Françoise smiled, then hid a wince of pain as the baby shifted within her. "It looks very nice. Can you make more like this one?"

Nicolas took a dubious look at the bowl of filling. "I'll ask Auntie Ha for more meat!" he said, and ran off toward the kitchen space.

Françoise finished her own roll before it went too soft to be of use, and stared at the windowpane. It had been broken twice, and patched up with glue and pieces of other windows of slightly different colors, giving it a faint resemblance to a stained-glass church window.

Not, of course, that she ever went to church. To the pagoda, maybe, once in a while; but the serenity of the Buddha's teachings seemed at odds with her own life, and reminded her of her parents, and the spoken and unspoken reproaches.

"Up, up up!" A chubby-cheeked baby was crawling under her feet, holding both arms imperiously. Françoise stifled a laugh, and bent down. The baby smelled of soap, though her hair was already stained with flecks of meat and potato.

"Child?" It was Aunt Ha, holding Nicolas's hand. Françoise liked her. She didn't seem to mind Berith—she dropped by several times a week for a game of chess, and the two of them would sit for hours, arguing over moves and half-filled cups of tea.

"Yes?"

"Grandmother Olympe asks if you can come down to the courtyard?"

Françoise divested herself of the baby, kissing her on the crown of her dark head and ignoring her disappointed crying. Then she picked up her pullover and coat from a chair, and her scarf from the floor—a slow, laborious process involving far too much bending down and kneeling, not to mention the uphill climb of straightening up. She was sure she'd put it on the chair, but one of the children had probably disturbed it. Ah well. She'd better get used to screaming children.

Olympe's flat was in the same kind of building as hers: everything crunched up around a small courtyard that was barely large enough for four or five people to stand together, littered with soot and debris, and the torn ends of clothes and tablecloths.

Olympe was in the courtyard, as regal as ever, in the rough silk shirt and slim black trousers she always wore, even when outside. She'd laid her canvas bag on the ground, and she wasn't alone. The courtyard was full.

And not just of any people: sleek, well-fed, pale-faced, they could only be House-bound. They wore red and gold, unfamiliar House colors, and a small insignia on their chests, at the level of the heart: a circle with seven points that formed the broad shape of a star from which grew a golden rose.

"We're looking for Le Thi Anh Tuyet," the leader said. She was Fallen:

small, comfortably plump, and she looked as though she'd punch a hole through the walls of the courtyard if something didn't go her way.

Why would they—how would they even know she existed?

Berith.

"That's me," Françoise said, slowly, carefully. "You can call me Françoise, though." It'd save them butchering her name again.

"My name is Nemnestra," the Fallen said. "We're from House Astragale."

Beside Françoise, Olympe sucked in a sharp breath. A warning to tread carefully, as though Françoise needed that. If they didn't get what they wanted, they could, like any House, level the building and the people inside with scarcely a second thought. "I'm not familiar with it."

"It's in Saint-Ouen," someone else said: a tall, gaunt human with curved fingers.

"Célestin," Nemnestra said, shushing him.

Saint-Ouen. Not that far, as the crow flew. Or impossibly far, if you were Houseless in la Goutte d'Or: another universe that scarcely ever touched you.

For some reason, she thought of Asmodeus again, leaning back against the rich leather of his armchair; and felt the same stark, naked anger she'd felt then, at the unfairness of it all. "I'm not too sure what you want with me."

"Olympe mentioned you were . . . out of touch with the community," Nemnestra said. She had pale, fair hair, and hands caked with a whitish substance—essence, or merely dust? "Astragale was founded in the days before the war, by day laborers attached to major Houses in Paris. We felt that workers should have someone to speak up for them."

They didn't look much like blue-collar workers, or day laborers, anymore. Françoise kept her face smooth, emotionless. "That's all very laudable, but I still don't see what it has to do with me."

"We have to find someone in la Goutte d'Or," Nemnestra said. "A woman who stole something very important from Astragale." She extended a hand, and drew in the air as though on a canvas. Françoise wasn't surprised to see a fuller, healthier version of the woman dying in their flat.

She'd had years to hone her skills at lying, keeping the magic she got from Berith bottled up within her, not making herself an easy, tempting target for thieves. She kept her face utterly expressionless, as if the woman were a stranger to her. "You've talked with other people."

"Of course," Nemnestra said. "But I was given to understand you could offer us . . . substantial help."

Did they know about the woman? How could they? They had just come into la Goutte d'Or, and they would have needed to find the right people to know this. "What kind of help?" Françoise asked.

"Your partner's magic," Nemnestra said, with a cold smile.

Berith. So they were well-informed, and knowledgeable enough about Berith's powers not to lightly threaten her. The last people who'd made a kidnapping attempt on her had been struck with burns, as if from acid splashes, and not all of them had survived. "And you'll offer a substantial reward in exchange?" she said, slowly.

"For anything that allows us to locate her," Nemnestra said, with a cold, unamused smile. She didn't like Françoise: that much was obvious. But she was smart enough not to let that get in the way of her job. "Our favor—our protection—will be valuable to you soon."

As much value to her as Hawthorn's promises, though it was tempting, to imagine herself away from the cold, from the perpetual hunger that stretched her too thinly, in a place of safety where no one would question her and Berith . . . "I see," Françoise said again. "I'll think on it."

"Don't think too long." Nemnestra's expression was unfriendly. "You've been surviving on your partner's magic, and on Hawthorn's goodwill. Neither of those will last long."

Hawthorn? "Hawthorn never gave us anything," Françoise said. She felt cold, as if winter had reached within her and twisted out her guts.

"We're not idiots. Everyone knows what would happen if Asmodeus's Fall-sister were to die. They might be estranged, but he would declare war on any fools who harmed her."

It was . . . not surprising, she supposed. But the threat was so bold, assertive.

"I'll think on it," she said, stubbornly. And held Nemnestra's gaze, unwavering, thinking of warm drawing rooms, and the smell of sandalwood, and unaffordable luxuries. For all their talk about saving workers, they were no better than the Houses they professed to be so different from.

It was the Fallen who looked away, but casually, as if Françoise were a stubborn child. "As you wish. You have been warned."

Françoise waited until they left, and were well out of earshot, before turning to Olympe. "How much do they know?"

Olympe sucked in a deep breath. "Nothing, I think," she said. "Not yet."

Of course. If they had known, they wouldn't have had this roundabout conversation with Françoise.

"Would—" Françoise hated herself for asking the question, but she had to know. "Would they keep their promises?" She didn't ask about their threats.

Again, that sharp, noisy breath. "They're a House. They might have been workers, once, but you know how it goes. Power is power. Those who hold it seldom remember where they came from." She frowned. "Perhaps they did mean well. Or still do. But to play the games of Houses and remain alive . . . you need to be ruthless, and certainly not indulge the Houseless." Her voice was deeply ironic. "It doesn't much matter."

It should. But Olympe was right: founding another House just meant playing the same games as the others, by the same rules. "So you're saying I shouldn't believe them."

Olympe shook her head. "All Houses take the Houseless. If they see value in them."

And in Berith? Françoise shivered. She didn't want to be drawn into that—moth to a flame. Nothing good could ever come of being noticed by Houses. Only blood and guts and flayed skin.

"They don't make promises lightly. Not House Astragale."

"How would you know?"

"They're around," Olympe said. "On the docks, most days, to trade the wealth that comes to them on the river. It's all before the locks, before the Seine."

Before the Seine, the river that was wild, and dark, and unpredictable. Before the waters that killed. Philippe's words came back to her. *Rong. Dragon kingdom.* Myths. Legends. Tales to make life bearable for children. "So people see them. And hope." She wasn't sure how she felt about that.

"They're friends with workers. They pay them with drinks and food, and they get gossip from them. Sometimes take some of them as day laborers. As I said, they're a House." Olympe sounded frustrated. "What matters is that, yes, I think they would keep their promises, and yes, the offer they're making is uncommon. And valuable."

Françoise said nothing, for a while, digesting this. Not making promises lightly. Therefore, not making threats lightly, either. "You said 'not yet.'"

Olympe didn't even attempt to argue with her. She must have been extremely worried. "They'll ask around. For that kind of price, other people in the community might well talk. And it's common enough knowledge. We weren't trying to be discreet."

So they'd be back. They . . .

You've been surviving on your partner's magic, and on Hawthorn's goodwill.

No House had ever tried to take Berith head-on. And it was all because of Hawthorn? Because of the delicate network of threats and counterbalances that she'd never felt a part of, yet it had always protected them?

She needed to think. She needed to talk to Berith.

"Let them ask around, then. We'll be waiting," she said, with a lightness she didn't feel.

Olympe said nothing.

"You disapprove?" Françoise asked.

"Not of that," Olympe said. "But I'll spare you the lecture, this time. I didn't give you that woman so you could give her up at the lightest threat. I'll have a word with people."

Which probably meant glowering at them and using the weight of her age and authority to convince them. "You shouldn't set yourself against Astragale," Françoise said, slowly. "If they find out—"

"They won't," Olympe said. Her voice was freezing. "The affairs of Houses shouldn't be our own."

"Thank you," Françoise said. "Do you still . . ." She hesitated, because she was involved in too many things as it was. "Do you still have dockworkers disappearing?"

"Yes," Olympe said. "You've at least heeded my warnings and stayed away from the docks."

Mostly from lack of time, because she'd been busy worrying about Hawthorn and Asmodeus; and in the end, all for nothing. "I guess," Françoise said. "Do you know what's happening?"

"No. They just vanish. In a dark circle of cobblestones. Almost a dozen in the last three weeks." She sighed. "No one is going to care, here."

"You do," Françoise pointed out. Nemnestra was right: she held herself apart from the community, because it didn't approve of her relationship with Berith, because it thought that Fallen and mortals weren't meant to mingle and that she was breaking some unspoken taboo of nature, sleeping with a being old enough to be her ancestor.

"Yes," Olympe said. "But they need to earn a living. I can't tell them to avoid the docks."

No. Françoise thought about what Philippe had said. "They say dragons live in the Seine."

She'd expected Olympe to laugh, to tell her that was children's stories and fairy tales, that there was no such thing. Instead, Olympe went deathly still, her wrinkled face frozen in something that might have been anger, or longing. "Do they? Who told you this?"

"Philippe," Françoise said, slowly. Who was, she knew, more than he seemed, able to draw on *khi* currents the same way magicians drew on Fallen magic. "But surely . . ."

"Vo Thi Dieu Huyen," Olympe whispered.

The name meant nothing to Françoise. "I don't know her."

"You wouldn't. She died three years ago. But she said, when she was dying . . . she said that a woman dressed in mourning clothes brought her back the three incense sticks that she offered to the spirits of the river. She said that the woman gave her the blessing of the Seine." Olympe shook her head. "It's impossible. Dragons are spirits who watch over us. Why would they take people?"

Françoise thought of the black, oily surface of the Seine, the water writhing as if in the grip of a storm. "Perhaps we haven't been very effective at placating them. But they already take their toll, don't they?" They didn't need circles, or spells, or anything like that. The Seine was already dragging people from bridges and quays, spitting out drowned, mottled bodies.

It made no sense. If the woman woke up, in their flat . . . but Philippe had said that was unlikely. The woman. Nemnestra. Her thoughts went back to House Astragale, and the threats they'd made. Focus. She needed to focus on the more pressing problem. She needed to be back at the flat. She needed to talk to Berith. "We can talk about this later. I'll be back."

SHE'D expected Berith to shrug off the threats made by House Astragale, as she'd shrugged off those made by the gangs. But Berith listened intently, and then said nothing for a while.

Françoise had thought her stomach couldn't plummet any further, but it did. The baby writhed and kicked within her. She had to sit down to catch her breath. "You're . . . afraid of them?"

Berith sighed. "They're a *House*, Françoise. I can't set myself against them."

"You—" Françoise had always thought—she'd always believed that, for as long as they were alive, Berith would protect her. That this, at least, was something she didn't need to worry about. "I thought we were safe," she said, finally. She couldn't keep the reproach out of her voice.

"No one is ever safe." Berith went back to her armchair, wincing. "I made a choice to live outside the Houses, years ago, in full knowledge. I'm sorry. I assumed you knew."

"I—" Françoise tried to think of something, of anything, to say—all the words pressing themselves against the dryness of her palate, and they all came tumbling out like water from a broken dam. "I'm not House, Berith. I'm not Fallen. You might live and breathe politics like the rest of them, but I don't! Whatever made you think I did?"

"You never asked!" Berith's face was taut. "And I'm not like the rest of them."

"Aren't you?" There wasn't much space in the flat, with the dying woman on the bed. "She said all that stood between us and oblivion was the fear of what Asmodeus would do if you were attacked." The glint of light on glasses, and that insufferable sense of superiority, offering the protection of the House, when he had to know—he had always known—that some of it was already extended to her. "Is she right?"

"Françoise." Berith extended both hands to her.

"No," Françoise said. "Tell me. Now."

"I haven't had anything to do with him in years," Berith said. "But yes, it would make sense."

"And you counted on that?"

"No," Berith said. "But it happened, regardless."

"It doesn't change anything!"

Berith was silent, for a while. "I'm still linked to him. Family bonds don't break just because I don't care for them. If either of us ever has a burning need, the other will feel it. A bit like the link to a House. And yes: he learned, early on, that power and defending what was yours was the only thing that mattered in this city." There was almost affection in her voice. Françoise felt sick.

"You're not supposed to care for him anymore." Even before she'd finished saying it, she knew how petty, how small it sounded.

Berith rose, came to stroke her hair, gently. "We can't exist without Houses." Her touch was like fire, a warmth that grew in Françoise's belly and spread to her lungs, to her heart. "They hold all the power in the city. It's naive to think that we can stand apart from that."

Just as illusory as the idea she could stand apart from the rest of the community? "No," Françoise said, stiffly. "And we're not giving up our guest, either." She wouldn't survive for long, but Houses had a way of making people pay for the slightest offense, even the dying.

Berith didn't move. At last, she said, "No. I wasn't suggesting that, either." She sounded regretful. "But I wasn't expecting this would set us against a House. I can uproot and relocate to a new flat, but it's costly, and would leave me defenseless."

"I'm not asking you to." The words rang hollow in Françoise's mouth.

"I know. But we might need to brace ourselves for incursions."

From House Astragale. From Nemnestra. Françoise took another deep, shaking breath. "I love you," she said, and it sounded trite, and slight, and insufficient.

Berith kissed her, gently, deeply. "I love you, too. We'll find a way. Come on. Dinner is almost ready, and you can help me translate something."

The game again. Françoise sighed. She'd tried to think of her next move all day, but her brain seemed to have turned to mush. At least translating was going to be easier than actually moving a chariot or an elephant across the board. "Where are you?" She waddled toward the board, shifted it so that they'd have space to eat. The book was closed, with no bookmark.

"End of chapter one," Berith said, scooping dirt-flecked rice from the pan on the stove. "I'm starting to wonder if I should write a translation to refer to. Would be easier."

"You can if that helps. Maybe Aunt Ha—"

"Françoise." Berith's voice was gentle. "We picked this because we needed something to do together. I play enough games with Aunt Ha already."

"I can't keep up," Françoise said, forcing a smile. It came more easily than she'd thought, the tension of the day slowly receding to bearable levels. She flicked through the book, staring at the small drawings of the board demonstrating the values of different openings. Oh yes. The chariot sortie, and here was the diagonal move of the adviser in answer to avoid checkmate. "And you said you needed easier adversaries, after all."

"Hahaha." Berith was busy mixing fish sauce with a dash of vinegar to make a dipping sauce for the rice. She nearly always got the taste right. It had to be magic, given their dearth of ingredients, but Berith didn't ever seem to use anything but her hands. "You really think Aunt Ha is a worse player than you?"

"I don't know," Françoise said. "Evenly balanced, I think. But we don't think the same way. Which bit didn't you understand?"

"Last paragraph," Berith said. "Every word makes sense, but the whole doesn't." She grimaced. "At least I think so, assuming I got the separation of syllables right."

Françoise snorted. "Your Viet isn't that bad."

"It is with unfamiliar words."

Françoise moved to the last paragraph, stared at it for a while. She'd learned from a similar book, once, but hadn't actually read one in a long time. Some of the older people in the community enjoyed passing around chess problems, but she'd never taken part in puzzling them out. "It's a saying," she said. "A Chinese one, so no wonder you're having issues with it. It would translate to . . ." She thought for a while. "'You're a poor player if you don't use a chariot within your first three moves.'"

Berith laid out chopsticks by the side of the chipped bowls. "Ah. Makes sense. The chariot is a powerful piece. Long attack range."

"Mmm," Françoise said. She looked to the next page. "The next chapter walks you through some of the less common openings, but there are plenty of drawings. Should be easier."

"Except for the part where my brain twists into knots trying to work out the logic," Berith said. "All right. We can eat now. Thank you."

"Sure." Françoise closed the book, and moved toward the table, but stopped. "Hang on. I just want to check in on her."

"It's not as though dinner can grow colder," Berith said, with a deliberately impassive face.

"Oh, shut up. I won't be long."

Françoise went to kneel by the woman's side. Her face was paler, her breathing shallower. She probably wouldn't last the night, if that long. Berith, for all her protestations, had also left the table. She ran her hands over the burn between the woman's breasts, marking its contours with the tips of her fingers. It started, faintly, to glow, raised ridges brought into sharp relief by the light. "It was a tracker disk," she said, finally. "You can still see the edges of the engraving."

"So she is House." Françoise shook her head. It wasn't as though that was a surprise. "I wonder what she stole, that they'd want her back so badly."

Berith shrugged. "Trifles, for all you know. Houses aren't forgiving, or inclined to let go of what's theirs."

"Nemnestra said . . ." Françoise closed her eyes. ". . . that House Hawthorn's goodwill might not last. Why not?"

"I don't know," Berith said. "You can't trust anything they say. Hawthorn is on the rise, and Asmodeus isn't a fool. House Astragale, for all their posturing, is a newcomer at this."

"Of course." Françoise wished she had Berith's confidence. And that she knew where that left them—possessions of House Hawthorn? Stakes in House Astragale's plots?

She wished she had an answer.

*   *   *

IN the middle of the night, Françoise woke up soaked. The baby must have kicked her bladder while she slept—again—and her throat felt as parched as a desert. "Sssh, ssh," she whispered, getting up and rubbing her belly as the baby stretched, bumping into some organ and leaving an odd, twisting feeling within her. Berith was sleeping in the armchair, her head drooped on her chest. Her breath was slow, regular.

"Let's get you some water," Françoise said to the baby, rubbing her hands against the fullness of her belly.

She stopped.

Because, on the bed, the woman was awake, her pale, glistening eyes open, though she hadn't sat up or moved. She merely lay, staring at the ceiling. More slowly than she'd have liked, Françoise made her way to the woman's side, and crouched down. It was going to be hell to get up, but no one ought to be alone in moments like these.

"You're safe," she said. "It'll be fine." A blatant lie, but it wouldn't matter for long.

The woman's eyes rested on her, and moved away as if she were part of the furniture. Françoise exhaled, and removed the wards that kept Berith's magic contained. A surge of magic filled her body, swift, exhilarating, that misguided feeling that she could do anything, take on anyone.

She raised a glowing hand, laid it on the woman's forehead. It was ice-cold, and even the magic didn't warm it. Not long, then. "You're safe." And, because she had to try, "Who harmed you?"

The woman's eyes held hers. At last she said, "I stayed too long. That was a mistake." Françoise had expected her voice to be thin, or incoherent, but it had the firmness of someone giving a lecture to recalcitrant children.

Stayed too long. "In the House? In Astragale?"

"She's smart," the woman whispered. "Patient, weaving her cloth of lies and betrayal piece by piece." She shuddered.

"Who?" Françoise asked. She let out a little magic into the woman, but there was only a gaping emptiness on the other side: she might as well have tried to fill an abyss with a glass of water.

"I tried to—but I couldn't return to the House. The rot is inside, you see. Like a worm, gnawing away at the foundations. The seeds of twenty years, poison distilled in alembics and drawing rooms. The heir." The woman laughed. It was high, unfocused; and utterly, completely bone-chilling. "Building a field of ruins, a wall of dreams. It won't work. Nothing has ever worked."

"You're . . ." Françoise started to say she wasn't making any sense, and then gave up. It would have been churlish, and unconstructive.

"In the grove there's a harvest of hanging corpses in place of fruit." The woman laughed again. "That's what she wants, the heart of the matter, the history she carries with her. To add one more body to that parade—to hoist it up, like a strung puppet, to dance to her tune, flayed skin and eyes pecked out by crows . . . The body that will make everything right."

If it hadn't been the flat—if it had just been a street, and the dark around them—Françoise would have started backing away from her, death or no death.

The woman shuddered again, and then her eyes opened again, and she saw Françoise. Really saw her this time. "It's all right," Françoise started to say, but the woman's hand went upward, and gently pulled her hand from her forehead, and held it like a lifeline.

"It's dark," she whispered. "I always thought . . . there would be light, at the end. Light . . ."

Françoise was still holding that hand come morning; but it had gone limp within hers, and she had no need of Berith's calmly kneeling by the woman's side to know that she would never wake up again.

THIRTEEN
QUESTION AND ANSWER

THE world had shrunk.

Help me, please—the words running, over and over, in her mind, to Hawthorn or God or whoever else was listening, but there was no answer.

There was only the sweet, sickening odor of essence; the bouts of coughing, which left her spread on the floor, struggling to breathe, the taste of blood in her mouth; and, on the edge of her field of vision, bright, pulsing colors, merging and melding into one another, expanding until they filled her.

A door opening, in some faraway universe. No footsteps, that she could hear, but someone knelt by her side, and, for a moment only, the smell of bergamot and orange blossom overwhelmed everything else—no, not him, not him; she tried to crawl away as far as possible, but none of her limbs would answer her. And then the smell of essence fell again, obliterating everything else.

"You're a mess." Asmodeus's voice held the sharpness of a blade. Magic pulsed on her skin: an insistent, warm touch that clawed at the caked essence on her clothes and her hands, whittling away at it until nothing was left.

Madeleine took a deep, shaking breath, held it. Nothing in the air now but citruses, the trembling, stomach-clenching smell of Hawthorn. "I—I didn't—" A fit of coughing wracked her. She struggled for purchase on the slats of the boat's floor, even as splinters dug into her skin.

Hands—his hands—pulled her up, into a sitting position, forced her upright, to stare at him. Asmodeus wore his usual swallowtail jacket in the colors of the House, with a silver scarf at his throat, and looked as comfortable as if he were sitting in his own office.

"I—didn't—," she tried again, had to stop again. She had taken just the pinch of essence she needed for the spell, and no more—had just lain on the floor, her life seeping away, rather than face him drunk on essence.

"Oh, Madeleine." Asmodeus shook his head. "Do you really think that's the main concern, as things are?"

"You—you came. You—" Words seemed to have scattered in her brain, to come out mangled no matter what she tried to say. "You knew it was a trap."

Asmodeus raised an eyebrow. "I didn't get to be head of House Hawthorn by being a fool. Can you walk?"

Madeleine drew a shaking breath. "I . . . think so."

His face didn't move when she rose and tottered to the door, but he stopped her with a raised hand. "This is not going to work. May I?"

The words in his mouth made no sense. "May you what?"

"Give you magic. It's either that or essence, and magic won't corrode your lungs any further." He didn't say anything about the addiction, she noticed.

And then her thoughts finally gathered themselves from where they'd fled, and she understood what he was asking for.

A touch or a breath, but a breath was so much more effective, and so much more potent. He was offering her the choice. "You could leave me here."

His smile was dark and amused. "Do you really think whatever they have in store for you is any kinder than what I will do if you relapse? Besides, I made you a promise. The point of those isn't that you abandon them when they're inconvenient."

"But—" She closed her eyes, sought words that failed her. He was waiting for her answer. She guessed he could have done what he wanted without it. A small kindness. She ought to have been grateful. "Do it."

He bent, and his lips brushed hers. To call it a kiss would have been obscene. Something passed between them: warmth, fire, the living, breathing power she'd get drunk on at night, pretending that it was hers for the taking. But what filled her, slowly spreading from her mouth to her heart, and from her heart into every limb, felt like fingers stretching to fill the holes of a glove, pushing the cloth taut until only a thin, almost debased layer of it remained.

"There." Asmodeus pulled away. "Now let's get back to the palace."

Madeleine finally found her voice, dragging it from the back of her throat. The words tasted sour in her mouth. "Elphon—Ghislaine . . ."

Asmodeus didn't even flinch. "You're the only Hawthorn dependent here."

How could he know? With Ghislaine, he'd lost the link, hadn't he? And even the disk on her chest, the one that was tied to her, the same one he'd given Elphon, had barely worked until she'd boosted its powers. "You can't know that."

"Yen Oanh isn't subtle. If she had any of them, she would have dangled them in front of me as a further inducement to lure me here. Besides, I know where Elphon is. It's an odd location, but it's nowhere near here."

"Where?" Madeleine asked, but Asmodeus had already walked out as if nothing were amiss. Madeleine followed, a puppet tied to his strings.

Outside, at the foot of the boat, Yen Oanh was waiting for them, in the middle of a tight knot that included two dozen guards, and a Fallen wearing Annamite clothes, whose face Madeleine didn't recognize. Facing her were four bodyguards in the colors of Hawthorn, carrying slung rifles with bayonets.

"I've kept my word," Asmodeus said, curtly.

"And I mine." Yen Oanh's voice was light, ironic. "Your dependent is alive and unharmed."

"I disagree with your ideas of 'harm.'"

"Whole, then."

Madeleine looked up. The cage where Charles had lain was still dangling from the side of the boat; a shrunken body within, holding antlers and long, serpentine limbs, the alienness of dragons laid bare in death.

Whole. Alive. She shivered.

"You certainly have my attention," Asmodeus was saying.

"And I didn't before?"

"I wasn't here, was I?"

"No. Not here, and not as vulnerable as you'll ever be." Yen Oanh's face was harsh. She gestured to the guards by her side. "Take him."

The currents on either side became cold fingers, grasping at Madeleine's skin, weighing her down, dragging her inexorably toward the smooth riverbed. But within her, the puppeteer's hand stretched, dragged her upward. The cold vanished.

Asmodeus moved, impossibly smoothly. Before Madeleine could catch her breath, he'd grabbed one of the halberds from the guards, and, reversing it in one elegant movement, dragged it across Yen Oanh's midriff. Silk parted, and skin, and scales. Yen Oanh grunted and fell, hands doubled over the wound as if she could prevent it from widening any farther. Asmodeus withdrew the halberd and, still in that frozen, impossible moment when nobody could react, stabbed the Fallen with the point.

One of the bodyguards grabbed Madeleine, and shoved her away from the battle. "Run," she said.

Madeleine ran. Slow and ponderous at first, struggling to breathe, fighting the cough. From behind her came the noises of battle: the resonant sound of metal against metal, and a noise like breaking glass, contracting the waters around her. Her legs felt like lead. One step, and then another and another . . .

Blood in her mouth, in her lungs. A stitch in her ribs, right under the heart. And, within her, rising like an unstoppable force, the House: Asmodeus's light, ironic presence, the thorn tree flowering in place of her spine, a maelstrom that swallowed every thought, every word, and remade her into sharp steel.

Run away.

Run.

One step, then another and another. Up a small hill where fish scales crunched under her feet; past an old, ruined pagoda with a tumbled-down roof. Her feet, leaving the ground as she passed from ridge to ridge, climbing a cliff of white, oily coral—everything crumbling under her, into clouds of dust that the river carried away.

Up. Up. Away.

When she finally stopped to catch her breath, the link to the House sinking to lukewarm embers in her mind, Asmodeus's presence receding to a mere omnipresent whisper, she was at the top of a small hill. A shrine crowned it: a delicate concoction of coral so fine it was like translucent porcelain, with six yellow fruits she couldn't recognize aligned before a pitted marble statue. A smell of incense wafted from three sticks, planted in a greenish sponge flecked with mold.

She flopped down, the rush of energy that had sustained her leaving: a puppet with cut strings, lying on that odd, mossy carpet of brown algae.

She couldn't see anyone. Above her, the sun shimmered through that impossible sky, bending and wavering with the shifts of the mass of water that separated her from the surface. Behind her, distant shouts and cries, a pursuit that wouldn't be so easily deterred.

Time must have passed. The sun's light darkened and shifted, casting long, dancing shadows over her. She had to get back to the palace, but she didn't know which direction to travel in. She didn't even know where she was.

Run.

Great advice.

Voices, cresting the hill. Madeleine pulled herself up, every muscle in her body protesting. She didn't have the energy to run anymore. What was she going to do—face them down? As if she could even fight.

It was Asmodeus, and two of his bodyguards. Asmodeus looked odd, his jacket in disarray, with three deep, bloody gashes across the shirt. Red oozed into the water around him like splashed paint. The bodyguards didn't look much better—one of them distinctly pale, stumbling rather than walking, leaning on one of the dragons' halberds, probably the one Asmodeus had used to down Yen Oanh. The last one, the woman who had pushed

Madeleine to run, was carrying a rifle, and the prone body of the Fallen Asmodeus had stabbed.

Asmodeus smiled when he saw her: sharp, predatory; no better than Yen Oanh, after all. Run, she needed to run, except that she had nowhere else to go. "Ah, Madeleine."

The tracking disk pulsed against her skin, slowly, lazily, like a second, diseased heart. Of course he would find her, wherever she went. Of course she would always belong to Hawthorn, now and until the hour of her death—at his hands, most likely, when she ceased to amuse him. "Asmodeus." Her voice scraped her throat raw, every word still tinged with his smell.

"The palace is that way, about two days' march, if the geography of the place doesn't decide to give up on us. Come."

And she followed, because she no longer had any choice.

WHEN darkness fell, they were in the hollow of yet another hill, within a landscape of endless rolling hills, all in various states of decay: the fish scales brittle and dull, the algae rotten, the coral bleached, or overrun with large black and brown pockmarks. Everything smelled of mold, though at least it wasn't the sickly smell of dragons on angel essence.

Madeleine sat with her back to a small, shriveled coral outcropping, too winded to talk. She watched shoals of fish bank, high above them, giving them all a wide berth. Asmodeus was conferring with the two remaining bodyguards. The female one, Valchior, had handed her a chunk of bread, which she nibbled on despite not feeling really hungry, or thirsty. Merely emptied. Like a tree hollowed from the inside out.

It felt unreal. A dream she was having while high on essence, while dying in the cage where Charles had died. It—

If she stopped to think, if it ever became real, she would feel its claws digging deep into her heart, and she wasn't ready for that. For any of it.

At length, Asmodeus came to sit by her side. A cloud of broken coral rose as he wedged himself against the same outcropping. "You're holding up reasonably well, considering."

Considering she'd been dying.

"Here," Asmodeus said. He held out a small package wrapped in paper. Essence? Of course it couldn't be.

Madeleine unwrapped it. Within were four of Iaris's pills, the ones she took against the cough.

"Valchior should have some water," Asmodeus said. "Considering the state of the Seine, I'm not overly keen to investigate drinking the atmosphere, even if we could."

"I—" Madeleine stared at the pills. He'd come for her. She kept running, again and again, against this one inescapable fact. "You're wounded."

Asmodeus glanced at the three gashes on his chest. "These? Not much you need worry about."

She wasn't worrying about them. Or maybe she was. He was her only chance of making it back to the palace now. And she couldn't help but notice that although they weren't deep, they were still bleeding. Which, considering Fallen healed fast, was . . . Well, perhaps worrying was the right word. "You should bind them," she said.

He said nothing, merely waited. For her to minister to him? Something finally rebelled within her, a core of steel buried under the layers of numbness.

"I'm not a doctor. Or a nurse."

Asmodeus's gaze held hers—gray-green, the color of a stormy sea in bygone times. She'd gone too far. He was going to turn on her, relapse or no relapse.

At length, after what felt like an eternity, he nodded, and shrugged off his jacket and shirt, carefully peeling the cloth back from his wounds. Red pooled, lazily, against his skin.

Asmodeus tore the shirt into strips and, wedging one of them under his shoulders, tied a knot into a crude bandage. The muscles of his torso were taut, and a thin white line ran from his heart to his hips, a scar from something that hadn't healed well. Madeleine was—had been—an alchemist, dissecting Fallen for their magic. She knew the only wounds that didn't heal well were those that removed body parts.

He must have noticed her staring. "Yes. I have no heart. Well-known fact."

He was making a dark, twisted joke at her expense, speaking metaphorically rather than literally: he had to have a heart in his chest, for not even a Fallen would have survived with the heart taken away. But ribs? Around that telltale line of the torso, you could remove one or two, and it wouldn't bother him much, would it? Had this happened under Uphir?

Asmodeus put on his jacket again, and buttoned it up, all the way to the straight, embroidered collar. "Don't get maudlin," he said, with a cold, easy smile. "Everyone has scars. I ran into some bad company when I was young, that's all; before I knew how to protect myself, and what was mine. And I didn't come for you out of sentimentality. I do need to know, after all, what is going on in the dragon kingdom, to be capable of making my move."

Not out of sentimentality. Well, that made things easier, didn't it? Greed and plots, and self-interest, except she didn't know, anymore, what was truth and what wasn't. "You killed Yen Oanh," she said.

"Did I? You'll find that dragons are extremely hard to kill. I doubt I've done more than mildly inconvenience her." Asmodeus took off his horn-rimmed glasses, and rubbed them clean on the lapel of his jacket.

Was that what had led him to ask for the alliance? But the kingdom was weak and in disarray; surely, even so close to Hawthorn, it wouldn't be much of a threat? She wasn't good at politics, had never been, and even less at the cutthroat games of Houses. But he seemed to be in a good mood, insofar as he ever could be. She gathered her courage, and said, "You said—you said you had always known they were there. The dragon kingdoms. Why has no House tried to deal with them before? Morningstar knew, too." He had gone into the dragon kingdom looking for help Ngoc Bich had been unable to give him.

Asmodeus watched her for a while. At length, he shrugged, as if what he was going to say mattered little. "Morningstar knew because I told him."

"You—?"

"Remember our little chat in the gardens?" The one when he'd pierced her hand, when he'd threatened her, when he'd told her he had always intended her to come back to the House, that twenty years were as nothing to him. "I said I had business in House Silverspires, the night Uphir fell. When I brought you to their doors and left you there."

"Yes," Madeleine said, through speaking was a struggle. "I remember."

"You would. I struck a bargain with Morningstar, that night. He was desperate to safeguard his House, at any cost." He sounded . . . disapproving? He didn't like Morningstar, for reasons Madeleine couldn't fathom. He treated all other heads of Houses with amused contempt, but Morningstar seemed to have touched a nerve. "And, of course, I knew that the location of the dragon kingdom would interest him. Such raw, alien power right beneath his nose. He would seek it like a man dying of thirst."

"You—"

"Hawthorn is close to the river. We've had to deal with the kingdom for a while, but they were strong then. There was little interest in telling other Houses we were beholden to them."

"But you told Morningstar."

"For a price," Asmodeus said. "For a *prize*. Something to make every spell or magic of mine pale in comparison. An investment for the future, you might call it."

A spell. An artifact, something infused with Morningstar's magic—the magic of the first and most powerful of all Fallen, a burning sun compared with pale, faraway stars, enough magic to reshape the world to his will. "What—?" Madeleine started, but Asmodeus shook his head.

"I have my own schemes," he said. "That's all you really need to know."

Madeleine lowered her gaze, staring at the sand at her feet. It was more information than she'd expected, truth be told. And still none of her business: probably connected to Asmodeus's plans for his consort and the kingdom; plans not even Clothilde would discuss. Perhaps she didn't know.

"They'll be after us," Madeleine said, finally, to change the subject.

"Of course. But first they have to find us. And they also need to sleep, when night falls. Nothing I've seen or heard indicates that they can see in the dark better than we do." He smiled, sharp, lazy. "Get some sleep. Valchior will keep watch. She's good at that." He rose. Something glinted in his hand: the unsheathed blade of a knife.

"What—?" she asked, but she already knew what he'd say.

"I'm going to get some answers, and I'm sure you'd rather not hear what happens before that Fallen talks. Although . . ." He shrugged. "Who knows? He might break early. Some do."

He was right: she didn't want to know. She didn't want to hear, and the only thing she could think of, over and over, was that she was glad it wasn't her he was going to use the knife on. Such bravery. Such naive, conceited morality.

She swallowed one of the pills; she'd been doing this for so long she hardly needed water. Then she turned her face away from them all, and closed her eyes, and slid, almost without noticing, into a dark, tumultuous sleep shot through with the screams of the living.

SOMEONE knocked at the door.

Françoise expected Laurent and Alexandra, teenagers who hung out in the streets and had agreed to dump the woman's body by the docks, well away from the flat and any evidence either of them had ever been implicated in this. "Come in," she said.

"Françoise." Berith's voice was a hiss. "No."

Françoise got up, ponderously. Opened the door, and found Nemnestra, and the gaunt man with long fingers—Célestin?—staring at her with the unpleasant smile of tigers who had just found their prey.

A fist of ice tightened around her stomach. "Nemnestra."

"We were told to see you," Nemnestra said. "About a runaway woman."

"Who—?" Françoise started, and then shook her head. It didn't matter. Too many people had seen Olympe and the dockers with the body.

Berith rose from the blue armchair. Something had shifted: her eyes became flecked with silver, and her entire frame seemed to expand. She went toward the bed, and picked up the body of the woman. "This is what you are here for, I trust?"

Nemnestra said nothing. Célestin's gaze was cold, and hungry.

"Here." Berith hoisted the body on her shoulders, without apparent effort, and carried it to the doorway. "Stay out of the flat, and out of my affairs. We have no interest in your House quarrels, Nemnestra. Neither of us do."

"But you still took her in."

"We took in a dying woman," Françoise said. "And she never woke up." She left out the delirium. Far better for them to think they had nothing.

She went to the cupboard, and took out one of the bowls they'd collected the jade shards into. "She was holding this."

Célestin knelt by the body, but it was perfunctory: taking the pulse and making sure she was dead. Nemnestra held out her hands to receive the bowl, which Françoise passed to her through the doorway—careful, Françoise noted, to remain on the side of the stairs. "Do you know what this is?" she asked.

Even if she had, Françoise wouldn't have admitted it. "No. Berith is right. We have no interest in your plots."

Nemnestra smiled, and Françoise fought the urge to flee. House-bound. House dependents. The unthinking arrogance of the powerful, taking what they wanted from others. They could never hold out against that. "Even that won't be enough to save you."

"Is that a threat?" Françoise asked, with a nonchalance she didn't feel. This was someone powerful enough to worry *Berith*.

"Merely a promise," Nemnestra said. "Staying out of fights isn't your path to salvation."

"You think we should take a stand against you?" Berith asked, coldly. She'd come by Françoise's side, one hand resting on her shoulder.

"You could," Nemnestra said. "If you want to lose." Her hands were limned with cold, blue light. She laid them against the surface of the door-frame, pushing gently, carefully. Pain—sharp, unexpected—rose within Françoise, every bone aching under the pressure.

Berith grimaced, but didn't move. "You'll find I'm no easy prey," she said.

Nemnestra continued probing for what felt like an eternity, while Françoise braced herself for what she could do, if they managed to break in. At length, Nemnestra shook her head. "Not yet."

"Not ever." Berith's voice was conversational.

"You're very sure of yourself," Françoise said through clenched teeth.

"And you're poorly informed," Nemnestra said. "But no matter."

Nemnestra withdrew her hands. The pain ebbed away, though Françoise was shaking, and Nemnestra could clearly see it.

Berith's voice was soft. "You set yourself against Hawthorn?"

"Why not? You'll find the time of dominance of many Houses has passed. Silverspires, Hawthorn . . ."

"And House Astragale's star is on the rise?" Françoise asked. Get her talking, if nothing else. Get her to say where the storm that she threatened was going to come from. "You're very assured."

"With good reason. We have strength and numbers on our side. And allies."

Allies? Another House, no doubt. An alliance against Hawthorn. Françoise didn't care, except that it left them exposed. And—a little treacherous voice within her—except that Berith would care, too. "I've been into House Hawthorn. You'd need quite something to bring Asmodeus down."

For a fraction of a second, it looked as though she'd managed to needle Nemnestra, but then she shook her head. "Well tried. But no. Let me assure you, though, that the day is coming when that pitiful door will no longer defend you." She lifted both hands again. Françoise couldn't help but flinch. "And when that happens, it will be my pleasure to take you down. Both of you," she said, with a nod toward Berith.

Berith's face didn't move. "I think you should leave, Nemnestra."

Nemnestra bowed, deeply, ironically. "Until later, then." Célestin carried the corpse of the woman, and she still held the bowl.

It was only when they were finally out of sight that the shaking truly hit Françoise. "Come away from that door," Berith said, firmly. "Please."

"I'm sorry."

"Don't even mention it," Berith said. "Sit down." She all but pushed Françoise into the blue armchair. "House business is scary stuff."

Françoise lay back, feeling the warmth of Berith's magic slowly suffuse her again. "It shouldn't be our business."

"It always is." Berith's voice was sad. "And it's not the first time someone has thought Hawthorn weak, either. Because Asmodeus has only been heading it for twenty years . . ."

Twenty years. An eternity for mortals, nothing compared with a Fallen life span. "So you think he'll weather this one, too?"

"I'm sure he will." She sounded unsure. Worried. "I'll ask Laurent or

Alexandra to carry a message to him, to let him know House Astragale is planning something."

Françoise opened her mouth to protest, and then closed it again. House Astragale had made it abundantly clear they wanted to kill them, and also that Hawthorn was their only protection against House Astragale. They had to make sure Hawthorn stood. There was no other choice.

"I could go . . . ," Françoise started, and then let it trail away. The mere thought of entering Hawthorn again, of facing Asmodeus, struggling all the while to show no anger, no feeling that he could latch onto . . .

"I risked you once," Berith said. "I'm not counting on anyone's goodwill a second time." Her hands lingered on Françoise's shoulders, slowly massaging her back. A spike of desire arched even through Françoise's weariness. "If worse comes to worst, we can always run away. Somewhere they'll never find us."

"And leave you weak?"

"Weak is better than dead," Berith said. "We'll be fine, I promise."

If only things were that simple.

FOURTEEN
BLOOD AND GHOSTS

PHILIPPE dreamed of the dead.

They were always with him, always close enough to touch, and yet he would reach out and find their flesh parting like water on his own skin, leaving only a cold feeling like a drowned man's last, fleeting hold.

They spoke, too: snatches of languages that he could *almost* understand, the path to bringing them back from the Christian Heaven, or their slow, tortured path through Hell, to rebirth—the knowledge they had acquired or remembered, as they tore free of the body. It was French and Viet and Chinese and a hundred other tongues that he neither spoke nor understood: constant whispers in his thoughts as he slept, as he woke.

At the edge of his field of vision was Isabelle's ghost, and Morningstar's: more sharply defined, but almost drowned beneath gauzy silhouettes; masked faces, sharp teeth; mouths shaping words he couldn't make out.

He was going to drown, but he needed to understand what they were saying.

Blood . . . Vermilion dreams . . .

A door opened, in some faraway land, slammed with a sound like a crack of thunder. The dead wavered, withdrew, as he woke.

"Child?" someone said.

Philippe tried to speak, tasted only blood on his tongue. The words he could think of were small, inadequate, encompassing nothing of meaning.

"I warned you. I told you, time and time again."

"Olympe," he said, finally.

She pulled him up. The basket of food she'd brought lay on the floor; and the smell of steamed rice and fried fish rose from it, a fragrance so strong and so familiar that, for a moment, it dragged him back to the real world.

His clothes were torn, and hundreds of cuts had opened on his arms and hands. The blood was spilled on the floor, in complex, unrecognizable patterns that had dragged *khi* currents out of shape around them. It had all made sense at some point, he could have sworn. He was transcribing what they said. Building a ritual that would make sense, that would pull Isabelle from their midst.

"'Physician, heal thyself,'" Olympe said, darkly. "What did she do to you, child?"

It was abundantly clear whom she meant. "Nothing." The taste of blood and salt in his mouth wouldn't go away, and his voice felt as raw as if he'd screamed for hours. "Nothing I didn't ask for. Why are you here?"

"Because no one has seen you for two days," Olympe said, sharply. "You haven't opened the door to any of your patients. Or anyone. Your friend"— she said the words in a way that made it clear she didn't approve—"Ninon was here, too. She was worried."

Ninon was flippant, sarcastic, and rather unlikely to admit to worry. She'd consider Philippe an asset to her gang first, a friend second. "Friend," he said, tasting the word like a dry, bitter gourd on his tongue.

Olympe looked him up and down, and pursed her lips. "And, insofar as I can see, you didn't eat for two days, either."

Philippe didn't need to eat. Or, rather, he'd fasted once already, driven himself to the knife's edge between life and death through starvation. He could do it again. He wanted to say that, but it shriveled in the face of Olympe's disapproval. She wasn't *older* than him—born in the years of the war or shortly afterward, whereas his childhood had been so long ago every remnant from that era was dust, or broken. But she acted, effortlessly, with the authority of the old, the matriarchs who ruled entire households and fractious families.

He found himself, somehow, pulling out a chair—the one his patients sat in, not the one behind his desk—and sitting in it. Olympe set a bowl of rice flecked with dirt in his hands. He stared at it, breathing in the smell, unwilling to break the moment by actually tasting it. It seemed to be all that kept the dead at bay, though he could still hear, faintly, the words they whispered to him, and still guess at faint silhouettes awaiting him.

"What is happening?" Asmodeus's mocking warning; his hands tightening of their own accord as he remembered pain and crawling under the stars.

"I don't know," Olympe said. "You can't trust Fallen, Philippe. Not the House-bound, and not the others, either."

"I—" He swallowed, seeing Isabelle leaning against the crooked doorway, translucent and indistinct, overshadowed by the blinding ghost of Morningstar. "I know this. I trust in their power."

"The kind that will eat you from within?" Olympe's voice was withering. She leaned against the desk, and watched him for a while. "I don't know where you come from, child. I've never *inquired*." She made it sound like a favor, rather than a right. "But you should know better."

Better. Better wouldn't bring Isabelle back. Wouldn't lighten the weight of his failures. But Olympe didn't, couldn't know about that. The taste in Philippe's mouth was almost gone. "What do you want, Grandmother?"

Olympe sighed. "Some trust would be nice," she said. "Failing that, some connection with us, child. You can't live in isolation from the community."

He could. He had. He opened his mouth to speak, but Olympe cut him off. "Who will catch you when you fall?"

Philippe shook his head. "No one catches Fallen angels," he said. Only gangs, waiting to take them apart for magic. Only . . . Isabelle's ghost raised her right hand, showing him the two fingers missing from it, the two fingers he had taken, when he was still running with a gang.

"Fallen angels, perhaps not. But you're not one of them."

"Then perhaps I don't need to be caught," Philippe said, softly. *Or deserve to.*

"Everyone needs someone," Olympe said. "Tell me about dragons."

It was so completely unrelated to anything else that Philippe didn't process it at first. "Dragons?" he said. He used the Viet word, the one that, in context, could mean only the spirits of rain and river.

Olympe's face was grim. "Françoise told me."

He tried to remember what he'd told Françoise. All he could remember was staggering out of their flat with the dead clustering close to him in a cold wind, and before that, Isabelle and Morningstar standing in the drawing room of Hawthorn—a way to avoid thinking what had happened before that, the noose tightening around his neck when Asmodeus had raised his hand. . . . "The Seine," he said. "Under the waters. There is a kingdom there, struggling to maintain itself in the face of Fallen magic. Don't you leave incense sticks, to appease them?"

Olympe's face tightened. "Perhaps not enough anymore. Thank you, child."

"Wait . . . ," Philippe said. She was already halfway to the door. "What is this about?"

She didn't even turn. "Trust goes both ways, Philippe. Let me know when you're ready."

The rice had gone cold; the smell of it was faint, intangible. The ghosts pressed themselves close to him, and Isabelle was drowned again, out of sight, unreachable. Shadows moved, across the oiled paper that closed the eastern wall, like fish caught in a thin layer of water; they should have vanished as soon as he focused on them, but they were still here, hidden behind voices and faces and masks, a constant reminder of why Isabelle had died.

A trail of blood upon the floor: he was kneeling, tracing words with his fingers and trying to complete a pattern that would make sense, that would make everything right.

A startled face on the stairs: Hai, the cook with the sprained wrist, a wrapped package wedged under her good arm. She had an appointment with him, didn't she?

"Doctor—"

"Come back later. I'm sorry," Philippe said, but the dead choked out his voice.

He was downstairs, and in the cold, watching the lights of the flats, entranced by the way they prolonged one another, fed off one another, winking on and off, with silhouettes moving behind broken windows, people jostling him: a slow, secret dance that was the voice of the city, that was the voice of the living.

And the dead, crowding by his side, clamped on his arms and legs, blood running down his skin, staining the muddy cobblestones a deep, crimson red: patterns again, words whispered in the dark, the beginning of a spell that he could find, given enough time . . .

He was hardly aware of leaving the street, of going deeper and deeper into the Houseless areas, the crowds going thinner as he went, trying to find an answer in the keening whistle of the cold wind, and the voices of ghosts; staggering away from the flat, into a world where nothing human made sense anymore.

THUAN used his spare time to go to the library.

It was almost restful compared with the rest of what he was doing: the books weren't bound by bamboo strips, or adorned with the elegant calligraphy of masters, but the smell of paper and glue was familiar. He'd found refuge in Second Aunt's private library more than once, thumbing through pristine poetry volumes and losing himself in the words on the page.

To be fair, no one would call Hawthorn's accounts poetry, unless by "poetry" one meant sprawling, and cryptic.

The shelves at the back were not accessible unless one could sweet-talk an archivist into getting at them: the wind from the gardens had blown in some sort of spell that covered the books in a dark, creeping fungus, one that obstinately clung to skin and fingernails. No one was sure it was contagious, but the archivists didn't want to take the risk, either. But the account books that interested Thuan weren't at the back, with the other arcane texts on the history of the House. They were at the front, and frequently used, if seldom by the sufferance students.

"You all right?" Sylvain asked. The archivist had been amused when

Thuan had asked for last year's account books for a private project. "They're not easy to read."

To say the least. Thuan forced a smile he didn't feel. "I'll be fine. Just getting used to it."

"Fine. Call me if there's anything else you need."

A spell that magically made sense of everything would have been nice, but failing that . . . Thuan sighed, and forced himself to look at the pages again.

The essence problem in the kingdom was thorough, and deep-rooted, impacting all levels of society from officials to farmers. In short, there was a lot of essence being transported into the Seine, and something like that always left tracks somewhere, especially if Sare was right and they'd had to buy it elsewhere. If Hawthorn was doing it, somewhere in this book was the trace of whoever had authorized it.

Two hours later, his head was aching, his vision swimming. The account books had been tallied by different people, and one of them had absolutely atrocious handwriting.

He closed the book, and brought it back to the desk. Sylvain had left, and the archivist in charge gave him a harried smile as she took the heavy volume from Thuan's hands.

The account books had an extensive tally of essence, earmarked for use by Clothilde, the House magician who was currently conspicuous by her absence. But there was something else, too: something well hidden, buried within layers of other attributions, other lines. Thuan had grown up with books, and the hunting down of obscure classical references. A feeble attempt to disguise something in account books wasn't going to stop him for long.

It was still earmarked for Clothilde, but the handwriting was different, and there was rather more of it. Substantially more. In fact, he daren't take a piece of paper and do calculations, because there was a risk that it'd be found, but he'd have said easily six to seven times the amount that was "officially" acknowledged.

Payment had been made to a Nemnestra of House Astragale, neither name meaning much to him. The double accounting, though . . .

The double accounting suggested that whoever was doing it—the person who wasn't entering essence into the accounts as a matter of fact—didn't want to be caught. Plausible deniability, in case the kingdom asked to inspect the books?

Thuan walked back to his rooms in a thoughtful mood. He had grown up away from the thick of court intrigues, but that didn't mean he was a stranger to them. And House Hawthorn, in that respect, was very familiar. It was possible this was an attempt to ensure there was no paper trail, that Asmodeus couldn't be accused of ruining the fortunes of the kingdom; couldn't be impugned and forced to costly concessions in the game of diplomacy.

But the likelihood of that was small. The more likely explanation was less attractive.

Every court, every large congregation of powerful people, had its factions and its disputes and its attempts, more or less blatant, to carve out individual little domains. So the more likely explanation? That there was a faction within Hawthorn that wanted to traffic with the dragon kingdom. *Why* was an open question, but if he was to hazard a guess . . . the other thing that was conspicuously missing from those account books was the money: the vast amounts of coin that should come back to Hawthorn for the sale of the essence.

Someone within the House needed cash, and a lot of it. Clothilde, perhaps?

He raised the subject of Nemnestra and Clothilde with Nadine at their next meal together. Leila had insisted on taking their dinner in the gardens, in spite of the rather wintry weather, with a bright, pale sun that warmed nothing, and cold that seemed to rise from the ground like an exhaled breath.

"Nemnestra? Can't say I'm familiar with the name," Nadine said. "Astragale is one of the minor Houses, outside the city." She frowned, not looking pleased. "Why are you asking about Clothilde?"

"You're the one who was worried about her," Thuan said, with a casual shrug. "And you don't sound like you're less worried now."

Nadine shook her head. "I'll be fine. Adult stuff," she said. "Though you two are almost adults, in truth. And you don't want to get tangled up with Clothilde."

"Why not?" Leila asked, her mouth full of bread. "Because she's too important for us?"

"That's not it," Nadine said, severely. "Didn't you pay attention in class? High birth and low birth don't apply in Hawthorn. You rise on merit."

Or on ruthlessness. "Then why?" Thuan asked.

Nadine picked up a piece of bread and spread some pâté on it, carefully. "Because of who she was. There's . . . Look, sometimes Fallen will pick mortal favorites."

"Oh." Leila's eyes were wide. "You mean Lord Asmodeus slept with her."

Thuan managed not to choke on the pâté, but it was a close thing.

"No!" Nadine said. She looked up. The gardens were deserted, but you never knew who might be listening. "Lord Asmodeus doesn't sleep with anyone. Not since Samariel . . ." She closed her eyes, and started again. "Samariel was the one who picked Clothilde. Twenty years ago."

Twenty years ago. Thuan was starting to guess what the problem was. "Loyalist?" he asked. The ones who had supported Uphir, the previous lord of the House, and then, in increasing desperation, his heiress, Ciseis, before it became clear that Ciseis wouldn't come back, wouldn't challenge Asmodeus's hold on the House.

"Yes," Nadine said. "He found Clothilde in a cell. I don't know what he promised Lord Asmodeus to spare her life. I don't want to know. But she was . . . his pet, I guess. His little project. His student."

Explaining why she was a magician. Taught by a Fallen, shaped and molded by him. "A very good magician, then."

"I wouldn't know. I don't know what she thinks, either. But Samariel is dead."

And Asmodeus presumably, with the long, long memory of a Fallen who never forgot grudges, especially if they involved disloyalty, wasn't inordinately fond of her. A woman who had been close to his lover; a former loyalist, and who knew if she was still one? "There are no loyalists left, are there?" he asked, aloud.

Nadine looked startled. "Of course not," she said. But he could have sworn she was going to say something else and had changed her mind. So: probably yes. And ancestors knew what their goal was now. Undermining Asmodeus's rule, presumably.

Though, if they were working with Ciseis, and Ciseis was in turn working with someone else . . . It was a possibility, but he had not one shred of evidence for it. And it didn't change anything.

The House wasn't like the kingdom, being slowly nibbled away by essence. It was younger, brasher, its foundations more solid. There was opposition to Asmodeus, yes—there had always been, would always be. Fallen had long memories, and that didn't just apply to Asmodeus's side.

What it meant was just that the House had no vulnerability that he could find. That, presumably, Asmodeus was up to something else with the kingdom, but he had no idea what.

He tried to imagine Second Aunt's face if he made her that report. It wasn't a happy thought.

"You're looking thoughtful," Leila said.

"Or passing out in the cold," Thuan said, shaking his head. "I wasn't made for these climes!"

"Me neither." Leila reached out for a slice of apple tart, and put it in her mouth. "I'll never get used to these."

Out in the streets, the flour wouldn't be so fine, the fruit so fresh. Thuan knew this, intellectually, but he'd never really been out on the streets. In the kingdom, the issue would have been that the closest thing to apples was jujubes, assuming the harvest didn't rot on the trees like the two previous ones. "It's not bad," he said.

Leila looked around the gardens. "You know, we've been all around here, and we've never seen a hawthorn. Why is the House called Hawthorn?"

Nadine looked as though she was going to berate them again for not paying attention in their classes. Thuan said, "Because it was a village here, once, with a commons. And there were hedges of hawthorn trees separating it from the rest of the village. That's where the House is. On the remnants of the common."

"That's boring," Leila said. "You know there are better stories."

"The poison berries?" Nadine asked. She smiled. "I've heard some of them. They're interesting."

"Tell us," Leila said, never one to miss an opportunity for a scare.

Nadine sighed. "I'm pretty sure my role as a tutor doesn't include ghost stories."

"No, but we've finished our homework," Leila pointed out.

"Have you?"

Thuan shrugged. No exams coming up for a while, and the dissertation on the uses of breath-infused containers wasn't a particular difficulty if you had enough magical theory. Which he had, because Second Aunt's unspoken policy was *Know your enemy.* "For the time being." There was the other matter, too: that of the accounts book and the report he'd have to make to her, but that could wait until he untangled his own thoughts. "Why not?"

"You're too serious," Nadine said, with a frown. "Sorry." She shook her head. "It's probably no laughing matter, being on the streets."

"You laugh while you can." Leila was suddenly grave beyond her years. "Else you never do. Come on, Nadine."

"All right." Nadine smiled. "The ones I've heard . . . There was a copse of hawthorn trees here, where the House stands now, or very close to it. And you know that you must create wards to found a House? Well, when Echaroth decided to make Hawthorn, she sacrificed herself to create the wards, and they hung her body from the largest of the hawthorn trees. It was her blood upon the earth that bound the first dependents to the House."

How very uncivilized. Thuan bit back a sarcastic comment. "Except no one knows where the trees are."

"They are not in this world," Nadine said. "Not anymore. Though on dark, moonless nights, in the gardens, you may find a path that doesn't belong anywhere, and follow it to a copse where Echaroth's body still hangs, dripping blood like fire. And if you're foolish enough to go wandering in, she'll grab you, and pull you up among the thorns, to take your blood for the good of the House, to keep the wards strong. . . ." A cold, cold wind had risen in the garden, and the trees around them seemed to shimmer and recede in the distance, to grow small and stunted, and with berries the color of blood. . . .

In spite of himself, Thuan shivered. "Tales for children," he said. He'd seen some of the magic of the House too close for comfort, but this was overdramatic.

"Of course," Nadine said, and forbore to point out that, insofar as the House was concerned, they were both children. "As I said, there's all sorts of stories. Leila mentioned the poisoned berries. It's less fanciful but equally gruesome."

Leila was obviously enraptured; she nodded and waited for Nadine to continue.

"It's not the trees that the House refers to, but their fruit—their small, red berries. Back when Hawthorn was founded, there was a House already on this ground that Echaroth wanted to claim for herself. I forget its name. Montenay, maybe?"

"So she declared war on them?" Thuan asked.

"In a manner of speaking," Nadine said. "The House was strong and powerful, and Echaroth had few Fallen and fewer magicians in her service. But she did have one asset: a magician named Camille Decors, who found a way to turn hawthorn berries into a liquor that killed magic."

"What do you mean by 'killed'?" Thuan asked.

"Inhibited, if you prefer. Completely removed the ability to practice it: it's not clear whether that was for a day or forever. But for a Fallen . . ."

For Fallen—whose very existence depended on magic, whose bones were too light to sustain their bodies without it—even an hour without magic was too long. Their own organs would kill them, caving in to gravity, after their bones snapped and left them on the floor, gasping for breath through lungs that had melted. . . .

Equally gruesome. "So she poisoned them all?" Leila asked.

"Not quite." Nadine's voice was wry. "She invited five of their dependents to visit her. Not the head of House, of course, but some who were high in the hierarchy of the House: convinced they had the upper hand with her. Echaroth served them wine, which was an unusual, vivid red. And—"

Thuan closed his eyes. "I'm not sure I want to hear the end of this."

"Squeamish?" Leila said.

"You're the one who complains about the smell in the infirmary," Thuan pointed out.

"Yeah, but ghost stories are different. They're just stuff to scare ourselves."

As if they didn't have enough sources of fright, as things were.

"The liquor was poison, too, for mortals. Not the most pleasant way to die. And, as they lay dying and vulnerable in the banquet hall, Echaroth seized the link to House Montenay through them and shattered its wards."

Thuan snorted. "It's a nice story." Wards were meant to last, and if any dependent was that great a liability to the House, no one would be allowed to leave, ever.

"It was the past," Nadine said. "Or it's a myth. Take your pick. I don't say it has to make sense. Or that things haven't changed, in the meantime. Houses aren't static."

To Thuan, they seemed ever the same, before or after the war: diminished, perhaps, but still bloated and greedy.

Nadine shrugged. "Anyway, she destroyed the House through her wine, and her magic. That's why Hawthorn is here. Go to the reception hall sometime, and stand under the dais. You can still see something sitting in the high chair, a translucent ghost. That's her. Sitting. Watching while they drain their cups, and preparing her ritual to invade House Montenay."

"And she built her own wards on the blood of those dead dependents?" Thuan guessed. He didn't expect Nadine to answer: how a House made their wards was possibly their most well-guarded secret, for why make public the making of what protected them?

"Probably. It's always blood, isn't it?" Nadine said. "And carving out territory through atrocities."

Standard things, in the existence of Houses. But then Thuan thought of the Bièvre, and the invasion, and of the countless dead to strengthen his grandfather's rule. Was it so different? "The world belongs to the ruthless."

Nadine sighed. "I wish it didn't." She picked up the discarded napkins and plates from the tablecloth. "Come on. It's getting really cold, and dark. Time to head back."

They hadn't yet lit the lamps in the corridors when they got back; the

House hovered at that uncertain stage between daylight and candlelight: the hour between dog and wolf, they called it, when you couldn't be certain if the shape on the road was going to lick your face or chew it off. Thuan wasn't one for fancies, but . . .

"Remind me not to do ghost stories," he said. "Or drink red wine."

Leila merely laughed. They left her at the entrance of her own room, and Nadine walked a little farther with Thuan. Her quarters were in the other wing of the House, with those of full dependents.

"You all right?" she asked.

Thuan shrugged. "Fine. I should ask you the same." Even in the dim light she looked awful, with drawn circles under her eyes, and pale skin that seemed as though all the color had been shocked from it.

Nadine grimaced. "Mother has been unbearable. Lord Asmodeus has left the House to do God knows what, and she's been riding us all hard."

If he'd left the House, then that meant there was a chance to dig deeper. "He's coming back soon, though, isn't he?"

Nadine shook her head. "No idea. I hear you've been haunting the library in your spare time."

Thuan tried to look casual. "I want to know more about the House," he said, which was entirely true.

"About Clothilde?" Nadine sounded skeptical.

"Her name came up."

Nadine sighed, and shook her head. "Thuan. Curiosity is all well and good, but trust me: too much will get you killed. Especially with Clothilde."

"I think I got the message," he said, drily.

Nadine grimaced. "I'm just trying to help."

"I know." She meant well. She liked him, as a student, as a teenager. None of this would survive the revelation that he was trying to undo the House's careful work, or that he was much, much older than he seemed. "Thank you. Now go get some sleep."

"Don't you try to mother me," Nadine said, but she sounded more amused than angry. "I'll remember this. Good night, Thuan."

"Good night."

He'd braced himself to leave the light on. It was a night for ghosts and nightmares, and he was pretty sure he'd find Echaroth haunting the dragon kingdom of his dreams in one form or another.

But, when he came in, he immediately knew someone had been in his room.

It was small things: the slight disarray on the ancestral altar; a faint after-smell that didn't quite belong, like a tang to the air. Someone—

Who?

Someone from the Court of Persuasion? They couldn't suspect him already, and he'd burned the essence he'd stolen from Sare immediately after using it.

There was something on the altar. Thuan moved closer. It kept wavering out of focus, removing itself from the field of vision. He let out a breath he hadn't even been aware of holding: he knew that spell, and it wasn't a Fallen one.

Under the bowl of fruit he'd left for his ascendants, someone had wedged a slim, translucent piece of rice paper. When he pulled it out, he smelled brine, and the sharpness of ink, and a faint touch of *khi* water like the memory of a storm. A message from the kingdom. He unfolded it, and stared at the vermilion seal at the bottom of the page, elegant characters forming the word "Jade" in Ancient Viet. Ngoc Bich. Second Aunt.

The message was short, and to the point, so short that the seal was its only signature.

Child. Things have changed drastically, not for the better. I find myself forced to cancel your assignment.

We need to talk of the future. Of your future. Come back to the kingdom, now.

FIFTEEN
STUMBLING, FALLING

MADELEINE had the impression she'd barely slept when Valchior shook her awake. "We have to move," the bodyguard said. "Again."

Madeleine rose, brushing tiny crabs from her trousers. She wasn't sure how much time had elapsed since they'd left Yen Oanh's jail, wasn't even sure whether time as it passed in the dragon kingdom had any meaning. Last time she'd been down here with Philippe and Isabelle, a few hours had become an entire day.

They'd left the small shrine behind, and the corpse of the Fallen Asmodeus had tortured, spread out on the hill with his throat cut. Asmodeus had shrugged when Madeleine, gathering her courage, had asked him. "The ravings of a lunatic. Something about a wall that will separate us once and for all."

"They *are* building a wall," Madeleine said, remembering what she'd seen from the deck of the boat.

"I saw," Asmodeus said. "But they can't build a wall around the entire dragon kingdom."

"Around the capital?" Madeleine asked, but knew that wasn't it. The location was all wrong.

"Not where it's placed, no. It's at the boundary between the kingdom and the edge of Hawthorn. To close everything off, they would need power beyond imagining, beyond what even Morningstar was capable of, at his height. Which means they're up to something else." He'd not elaborated, and the brief conversation had ended there.

They crawled across a landscape of cliffs and hills, watching the shapes of their hunters growing ever closer: slim shapes when she'd woken up that first morning, now close enough that she could guess at their faces. There were too many of them: a dozen, against the four of them.

Asmodeus was kneeling by the second bodyguard, whose condition had worsened, and who had spent the end of the previous afternoon being carried by Valchior and Asmodeus in turn. He looked up at Valchior, and shook his head. "Not anymore."

Valchior's face was set. She knelt, and laid a hand against the wrist. "No pulse." She whispered something, the beginning of a prayer Madeleine found herself voicing alongside her.

"Give him eternal rest, O Lord, and may your light shine on him forever . . ."

She'd expected Asmodeus to be sarcastic, but he merely listened, his face grave.

Who knew whether God was listening, in a kingdom even more heathen than a city of Fallen? But . . . but, if he was . . .

Watch over him, and lead him toward life eternal.

"The wounds never healed," Madeleine said, after the prayer. Her voice was hoarse. She was weak, light-headed, neither the drugs nor the bread making much of a difference.

Asmodeus's face didn't move. "No," he said. He got up, leaning on the halberd. Madeleine, who was looking for it, saw the slight stumble. *His* wounds weren't healing, either. All of which wasn't normal. Fallen wounds healed. Not necessarily instantly, but always in time, unless strong magic was involved to prevent it.

Ahead lay the capital, and the palace: a day's march, maybe? It had seemed to get no closer in the previous day.

Asmodeus drove the halberd into the ground: a cloud of sand and silt rose to wrap itself around his feet. "Enough is enough. We're not getting closer to the city because they've been making us go in circles. Waiting for us to exhaust ourselves, so they could pick us off one by one. This stops, now." He stepped back from it, and closed his eyes. Light streamed out of him, the shape of great, black wings slowly coalescing at his back. Magic filled the air, cold, cruel, amused, the same feeling within Madeleine, the link to the House, to Asmodeus. It reached out, like a clawed hand seeking purchase. Something stirred within Madeleine in answer: the puppeteer's fingers, wearing her like a glove again—for a moment she was one with him—for a moment, she understood what it meant, to tumble down from Heaven and to have no memories, and no resources beyond magic and the fear it inspired. Then the moment passed.

Ahead, something shimmered: a veil, shot through with gray-blue reflections. The city and the palace were beyond it, obscured, blurred. Asmodeus brought his hands together, and clenched them, and Madeleine felt the fabric of the world twisting and tearing. The veil fell into tatters, slowly crumbling like a burned curtain of gauze. The city was now a sharp presence, looming over them.

Asmodeus readjusted his glasses on his nose, and grabbed the halberd. "There. Let's go," he said. Again, that slight stumble, which you wouldn't see unless you were watching for it. "I've had enough of the affairs of dragons, for the time being."

The city grew larger and larger, from a shape on the horizon to individual buildings. They left the cliffs and the coral reefs behind, and walked in the midst of algae fields with off-white speckles and a smell of brine overlaid by rot.

And behind them were the hunters. The riverbed was vibrating now with their advance, their voices growing more and more distinct, and they couldn't seem to shake them off or get ahead of them.

One step, and another, and another. Asmodeus and Valchior were in front of her now. Asmodeus was striding ahead as if nothing were wrong, his swallowtail jacket impeccable, his shoes leaving little clouds of sand on the riverbed. Nevertheless . . . as the day wore on, he slowed down. Hard to tell, because she wasn't doing much better, just trying to put one foot in front of the other and not falter, because who knew what they'd do if she couldn't keep up?

He was going to falter. They were all going to falter, and then Yen Oanh's men would catch up. She sneaked a glance behind, as the landscape became rice paddies, all deserted, with the odd rusted bicycle or rickshaw against the terraces. Their pursuers' silhouettes were distinct, and she could almost see their faces. Not long now.

The only thing that kept her going was the link to the House, and the memory of Charles's body in the cage—running from one thing into an uncertain future, a monster in front of her, a monster behind her, with nothing worth choosing or reaching for. She wanted essence. Oblivion. So, so badly it was a tightening in her chest, a vise that made every breath burn in her throat.

There should have been a smell of churned mud; but what rose, as they went deeper into the rice paddies—and as, finally, they saw crabs and lobsters and small, slight dragons tilling the fields—was the cloying smell of corrupted essence, as if her wish had been granted by an uncaring, cruel God. The paddies became dotted with small villages, and tumbledown temples, and still no one seemed to pay them anything but the slightest of attention. She knew that expression: had seen it, all too often. It was that of the Houseless when the fighting between Houses started, the prayer they all learned, outside the only safety in Paris. *Please let it pass me by.*

Madeleine would have prayed with them, if she had any idea what to pray for.

Asmodeus turned as they crested a rise, sheltering his eyes with the flat of his hand. None of the farmers appeared to do more than stare at them. And why would they get involved, in a fight that wasn't theirs? "They're very close. Valchior?"

Valchior shrugged. "No more bullets. But the bayonet . . ."

Asmodeus nodded, curtly. As Madeleine stumbled past him, he grabbed her. For a single, terrifying moment she thought he was going to throw her down the hill, and then he brought her close to him, so close she could smell orange blossom, and bergamot, except that it was all slightly off, tinged with the slight tang of mildew.

You're not healing, she wanted to say, but the look in his eyes stopped her. "You're a useless fighter," he said. "But you need this to lean against. Give it back to me before the fighting starts." He gave her the halberd.

There was a slight tingle like magic, something shifting within her, as if the weapon wanted to choke the life out of her. "It's enchanted," she said, as she stumbled down the hill. Asmodeus, for a moment, drew level with her, his face impassive, his horn-rimmed glasses glinting in the sunlight.

"If I had a guess," he said, "to kill Fallen, and dragons."

"So Yen Oanh—"

"Wouldn't make a weapon that would kill her with a single stroke," Asmodeus said. "Though perhaps having her innards ripped out was more than a minor inconvenience. I imagine she's annoyed." He sounded amused again. "Try to keep up. We can't afford to carry you."

And what would they do if she fell behind, if the hunters caught up with her? Just abandon her as so much chaff? No.

No: he had come for her. For Hawthorn's sake, he had said, for the information she had, which was pitifully small. Her thoughts went back, again and again, to his kneeling by her side, to his lips on hers, his magic filling her—that inescapable reef on which they shattered.

Ahead, before the end of the road, was a gate, a small arch topped by a tiled roof, a much diminished version of the one she and Clothilde had gone under, with the outskirts of the city behind it, a scattering of skewed coral buildings. The gate was manned by three soldiers, small figures in blue and yellow uniforms, carrying bayonets, who didn't seem to become larger, or at least not as large as the hunters behind them. As they walked toward it, some kind of commotion seemed to take it over. One of the soldiers ran toward the houses behind the gate, and came back with more people, gesturing wildly, and speaking words that the currents smothered.

Madeleine turned again. She couldn't help it—it was like staring into the abyss. The hunters were almost upon them. "Asmodeus . . . ," she said, choking on sand and silt.

She expected him to move smoothly, impossibly so, as he had when wounding Yen Oanh. But instead, the three of them came to a slow stop, and Valchior was the one who took the halberd from her. It was all she could do to stand once its support was removed.

"My lord." Valchior gave the halberd to Asmodeus, who hadn't moved since he'd stopped, staring at the dozen soldiers coming at them. Faint, lambent light came from his skin, but it was weak, tinged with darker shadows, and what came from him was the smell of soured citruses, and decaying flowers.

Madeleine, exhausted, gave up; and fell on her knees on the road. Over. It was over. She hadn't thought there could be anything stronger than Hawthorn, but . . .

Asmodeus didn't move, or cast any spells. Behind them, from the gate, came the sound of booted feet, and cries in Annamite. Ahead of them, gathering, were the hunters, the same kind of soldiers that had picked Madeleine up in her cell, wearing orange clothes and carrying the tall halberds with their brown, knife-shaped blades. Enchanted to kill Fallen. She could barely feel any magic, but then, she wasn't an Annamite practitioner.

"Go ahead," Asmodeus said. "You know what happens, to traitors and the disloyal. I should imagine it's not much different from Hawthorn."

The leader—a woman with a pronounced snout, and a burning pearl, who reminded Madeleine of Anh Le, the unpleasantly brusque dragon at court—spoke up. "We could kill you all. Easily."

"Could you?" Asmodeus's smile was sharp. "We don't die so easily, us House-bound. And then you'd have to deal with the men behind us."

They stared at each other. Behind them, the voices were getting closer and closer.

Madeleine forced herself to roll up, every muscle protesting, every ache of the journey vividly outlined in traceries of pain. Two dozen soldiers had marched from the gate, armed with rifles and swords. They were perhaps fifty or a hundred meters away. Cold currents swirled around them, so strong she could feel them, even from a slight distance.

"You're running out of time," she said, turning around, slightly, so that she could see both the approaching soldiers and Yen Oanh's men. Two of them had dropped to their knees, balancing rifles on their shoulders.

"Do they have cages, to expose rebels?" Asmodeus said. "I wonder." His voice was light, amused. "I was told of so many entertaining customs—death by a thousand cuts, over several days. Entire families beheaded for the sins of their fathers and brothers. Broken and flayed bodies displayed as examples, and eyes and fingernails eaten by fish and shrimp . . ."

The leader moved then, lunging toward him, but she was the only one, her followers hesitating for one fatal moment. Asmodeus grabbed the handle of her halberd, and used it to throw her on the ground. "Run," he said to her hunters, his smile the fiery one of demons.

The crack of a gunshot shattered the air, and another and another, and then the soldiers arrived. The path became a muddy confusion, a short, desperate battle that Madeleine couldn't follow—metal against metal, and the sound of something breaking, and screams—and she fell to the ground, curling into a ball and trying to make herself as small as possible.

Hands pulled her up, steadied her. It was a young dragon, her face barely old enough to have made it out of adolescence, and only a few flecks of iridescence on her cheeks to remind Madeleine that she wasn't human. "Elder Aunt, are you all right? We'll get you back to the palace."

Madeleine struggled to breathe. The world was contracting and blurring, and standing upright *hurt*, and she wasn't sure what had happened—could only see the hunters running away, with soldiers in pursuit, and a cloud of dust where they had all been. "What—?" she said, trying to line up words, and failing. "What—"

Asmodeus and Valchior were speaking to two soldiers, while two others carried the prone body of the leader. She could hear only snatches of sound, things about blood and ravings and punishments. Of course.

I was told of entertaining customs—death by a thousand cuts, over several days.

She shivered.

The halberd Asmodeus was leaning on was now broken: not where Madeleine expected it to be, which would have been anywhere along the handle, but halfway through the blade, a clean break that had shaved off part of its edge. It was no longer a dark brown, but a translucent, soft green color reminiscent of the tea with the cut-grass smell they'd been served in the palace.

"Let's get you back," the soldier said, pulling at her sleeve insistently. "Come on, Elder Aunt."

AFTERWARD, she wasn't sure what happened, exactly. They must have got back into the city somehow, but entire moments disappeared into a growing maw of darkness. There were only bright snatches, like lantern fish swimming out of the depths.

A food seller setting skewers on her cart and stopping as they walked by, eyes wide, face frozen in surprise. The large, three-lobed gate with its red pillars, and the statues behind bending and twisting as if in some unseen wind. Asmodeus, walking ahead of her as if nothing were wrong; and then the slight stumble as he passed the gate.

A gathering of guards and officials in the courtyard—parasols and feather fans, and frayed brocade, and Clothilde, running ahead of them all, her face twisted in something close to panic. "My lord," she said. "My lord!"

Asmodeus's laughter, low and good-humored. "Worried for my well-being, Clothilde? I should think we're finally safe." And then another stumble, and his grunting, falling to one knee, catching himself on the cobblestones of the courtyard, his face pale, his bandages stained with the vivid red of blood.

And the expression on Clothilde's face, fear and adoration and the outright horror of one who sees her entire world overturned. "My lord. Please. Please please please . . ." As she knelt by his side and pulled away the clothes and the bandages, her eyes were wet with tears.

No. No.

Fear tightened a fist of ice around Madeleine's lungs, each breath a struggle.

Because it was her future.

Because, once Asmodeus was done with her—once he had broken her, once and for all—that was all she would be, a puppet subsumed in mindless devotion, the only thing that he valued. Loyalty. Allegiance. Abject obedience.

The link to the House burned within her like a naked blade, and she heard, once more, the screams of the Fallen Asmodeus had tortured, following her into the dark.

THERE was a grove in the gardens of Hawthorn. It lay, not anywhere near the main buildings of the House, or on the remnants of the commons that had once been surrounded by hawthorn hedges, but at the back of the gardens, near the banks of the Seine—with a broken, algae-encrusted staircase leading down to a disused quay.

Within the grove were hawthorn trees, as far as the eye could see, a profusion of white flowers so bright they hurt the eye. And, on each tree, hung a body.

They hung limp in the embrace of branches, thorns driven deep into their flesh, a spattering of scarlet blood falling upon the parched earth every time the wind grasped and shook the trees. Their flesh was tight over wasted muscles, mummies rather than corpses, desiccated until they hardly seemed human or Fallen anymore. The air smelled, not of blood, not of flowers, but of that peculiar sharp, acrid scent of magic, a tang on the palate that promised power, and dominion, and double-edged miracles.

Someone walked in the grove. And, where they walked, the wind died down, and the bodies stopped shaking and bleeding, and opened up large, white eyes to stare at them.

They reached, at length, a tree deep inside the grove. The body that hung upon it was not an emaciated skeleton with a thin layer of flesh, but something whole and plump. It could have been resting, if not for the three thin, sharp branches that impaled it. Its eyes, when it opened them, were cornflower blue; and its smile bitter, almost that of the living.

"Is it time?" it whispered, and the visitor smiled, though the smile was joyless, and harsh, and tinged with tears.

"Almost," they said. "Almost, my lord Uphir."

SIXTEEN
Painful Awakenings

FRANÇOISE came back from her weekly run to the marketplace to find Berith entertaining a visitor. She didn't worry at first: the visitor was Aunt Ha, one of the numerous mothers who hung out at Olympe's flat, and Berith's other chess partner. Except that neither Berith nor Aunt Ha appeared to be playing chess: the board was spread out on the table, but it was still displaying Françoise's and Berith's game, and neither Berith nor Aunt Ha was so much as moving a piece.

Aunt Ha's toddler, Colette, was diverting herself by jumping up and down on the mattress, saying, "Mommy, jump, jump," over and over. Françoise had to stop herself from snatching her. The mattress was clean, or as clean as it was ever going to be after a woman had died on it.

Françoise took off her coat and scarf, and dropped the basket of root vegetables in a corner of the flat. "It's a pleasure to see you, Elder Aunt," she said to Aunt Ha.

Aunt Ha's face, when she turned to Françoise, was lined with worry. "It's you I wanted to see, child."

"Me?" Françoise pulled a chair and sat in it, while Berith put away the cups of tea and the dough fritters. "I'm not sure—"

"Grandmother Olympe has disappeared."

"What?" She must have misheard. But Aunt Ha's face was grave, and Berith didn't make any comment. "That's impossible. Where—"

"She was at the docks by the basin," Aunt Ha said. "Looking for something in the water, or so the workers tell me. They left her there when a ship came in with flour barrels, and when they came back, there was only a dark, empty circle."

"I— She—" Françoise tried several sentences, gave up. Olympe was indestructible, with that particular stubbornness of those who had survived anything. Yes, other Annamites had disappeared; other people in la Goutte d'Or had been taken, day after day, a slow, endless toll that—to be honest— had not concerned her much, because she'd known herself to be protected by Berith's magic, and because her own ties to the dockworkers were distant.

"How long ago did this happen?"

Aunt Ha looked on the verge of tears. "I don't know. Three, four hours ago?"

As if less time would change anything. As if . . .

Her mind was still struggling to wrap around the enormity of it all. Olympe had been infuriating, and bossy, and likely to stick her nose in business that wasn't hers, but without her, Françoise's life would have been very different.

Françoise looked at Berith, who shook her head.

"The docks are too far away." She closed her eyes, and magic limned her, for a brief moment. "Something is rising."

"From the river?" Dragons. *Rong*. Stories to comfort children at night. Except, of course, that now there was no comfort left.

"Through the river," Berith said, reluctantly. She moved away from the stove, and kissed Françoise on the lips. The familiar warmth of power spread through Françoise; held her, unmoving, while it rose, a wave that seemed to have no end. Berith's eyes were flecked with silver, and for a moment Françoise saw her as she must have been in Heaven, bright and beautiful and terrible enough to drive people blind, or mad, or both.

"I love you," she whispered, her lips moving on Berith's warm, scented flesh.

The wave crested, and broke. Berith pulled away. "I, too," she said. Her eyes still shone with that otherworldly light. "And, much as I want to, I can't keep you cooped up in the flat forever."

Françoise shifted. The baby stretched and kicked within her, an odd feeling above her right hip, as if it had grabbed something that bothered it. The world felt unbearably sharp and distinct, every scent magnified, the tea growing cold in the cups, the rot and mold in the wall, Berith's skin, beaded with sweat.

She didn't have to go. She didn't have to get involved, with a community that barely tolerated her, that waited, calmly, patiently, for what they saw as a disastrous affair to run its course.

She'd never forgive herself if she didn't do anything. "I'm not planning on risking myself."

"Of course not." Berith went back to the armchair, and leaned against the worn plush back. "But you never know."

Françoise reached out for her coat, and her scarf. "Let's go," she said to Aunt Ha.

IT was early afternoon, and the activity on the docks was slowing down. Workers moved crates from quays to warehouses, and sat down behind the broken doors, just out of the way of the wind, to nibble on buns or bread or a little something that made up their lunch. By the boats, guards in House colors supervised, making sure that nothing was stolen.

Aunt Ha headed straight for the end of the docks, the part where la Villette Basin gave way to the Saint-Martin Canal. There were no ships there, and no quays, either: the warehouses went straight up to the water's edge, with cranes that had been broken since the war, never repaired. Sometimes, boats would use the ground floor to unload their merchandise; but the basin never worked at full capacity, so there was little point in going this far.

In the shadow of one such crane was a circle, and, a little farther away, Olympe's canvas bag, torn and bitten through as though it had been savaged.

Françoise tried to crouch, and gave up, sitting by the side of the circle instead. She was going to need Aunt Ha's help to get up.

It looked like sunken cobblestones: as if something heavy had touched the quay, time and time again—blurred, successive imprints, like a child's attempt to draw. When she ran her fingers across it, she felt a slight tingle of magic, and an answering spark from within, even as the baby stretched within her womb. Fallen magic? Not, not only. There was something else, something she could barely touch or encompass, the same choking feeling she'd felt from the halberd.

"Show me," she whispered. She inhaled and, splaying her fingers across the boundary of the circle—nothing there but wet, slick cobblestones—thought of Olympe: of the smell of jasmine rice in her apartment, the rough silk tunic that she always wore, the way she'd walk through a courtyard or a street as if she owned it, expecting everyone and everything to defer to her, Françoise's continued exasperation with her reminders to be more filial, more respectful. . . .

Within her, magic bucked and surged. The cobblestones writhed like something alive, trying to throw her off-balance.

As if that'd work, when she was firmly planted on the ground, with all the weight of her pregnancy. She drew on more magic, feeling Berith come alive within her, flecks of silver in her brown eyes, the impossible blue of a summer sky.

Everything grew still, as if the entire world were holding its breath. The circle didn't move, but a thin line shimmered into existence, the same deep red color as the New Year's Eve lanterns. It led, unerringly straight, from the circle into the water of the basin, and continued *through the water*, toward the lock that closed off the basin. Françoise got up with Aunt Ha's help, biting her lip as her feet skidded on wet stone, trying not to fall. She wasn't very tall, and the lusterless light of the winter sun didn't allow her to see very far, but insofar as she could tell, the thread went on, through the Saint-Martin Canal, and straight toward the Seine.

She remembered Philippe's conversation with Berith.

There's something under the Seine.

Another power?

Nothing you can tame.

"Show me," she whispered again, and poured more magic into the spell.

Where it met the water, the thread buckled and reared, splitting, slowly stretching, as if some invisible hand were drawing a delicate tracery in the air. The temperature dropped around Françoise. The wind rose again, but it was tinged with the sharp, biting coldness of snowflakes, coming fast and strong, so that the canal, and the lock, and the ships on the other side of the basin, vanished.

The light was still moving, still reshaping itself. A long, lithe body with stubby legs—indistinct, then sharpening into five-clawed paws—a scaly tail, dipping into the water, and, towering over Françoise, a maned head with a snout, the ghosts of antlers, huge, glistening eyes, their gaze transfixing her where she stood.

"*Rong,*" she whispered, because there was no French word that would do this justice.

Its long, serpentine body lay coiled around the circle. Françoise realized, suddenly, that it wasn't finger smudges that had formed that sunken imprint, but rather the mark of huge scales pressing their way into the ground.

The dragon inclined its head, held its shape for a long, agonizing breath, and then vanished like a burst bubble. The air smelled of wet, warm wind, an electrifying, impossible feeling. Françoise felt so full she could have wept.

"Child." Aunt Ha's voice was shaking. "Child."

She didn't want to listen. Legends had come to life in this city, in this place. Tales that had always been distant dreams.

"Françoise."

The wet smell grew stronger. She looked down. Around her and Aunt Ha, a second circle was growing, like stains of ink spreading on rice paper. It was almost closed, and beyond it was nothing but snow, falling so hard and so dense that it drowned everything.

"You have to do something," Aunt Ha said, but her voice sounded oddly muffled, and even her body was pale, the translucency of snow, of jade. Vanishing. Taken away.

Where? No. That wasn't the issue. That—she tried to speak, but her gaze was drawn by the curtain of snow—it wasn't just snowflakes, was it? There were things, moving within the dense whiteness, silhouettes like cardboard cutouts, serpentine shapes, swimming through the snow as if they were underwater. And, rising from the depths, the fragile, heartbreaking shape of a city: pagodas and large avenues lined with statues of elephants; a covered bridge, arcing over a canal; and lanterns dangling from coral trees—if she could reach out, she would touch them, feel their warmth in her hands, gather blossoms to her, and breathe in a fragrance that had fled the city a long time ago. If she could—

Something flared within her: a sharp, stabbing pain in her belly. The baby. She was on her knees, with both hands doubled over her midriff, feeling the fetus within her kick and move and kick and move, and Berith's magic flared up like a spike driven into her spine.

Her hands were white, leached of color, as if she'd plunged them into the blizzard outside. Her fingers felt like something that didn't belong to her anymore. And she was almost at the edge of the circle, her face centimeters from the wall of snow. She didn't remember taking those three steps.

"Elder Aunt!" She grabbed the other woman as she was about to step over the edge of the circle, and shoved her down, mercilessly, held her down, trying to keep her belly out of the way of the thrashing legs. Aunt Ha's eyes were white and translucent, the color of fine jade or porcelain, shining with a light that was too pale and cold to be Fallen magic. Her face was . . . It was as if someone had thrown a gauze veil over it, every feature becoming blurred, insignificant—nothing but that white, lambent gaze looking *through* Françoise.

Focus. Focus. Getting creeped out wasn't going to help.

Philippe.

Philippe had said . . . Her eyes drifted, again, to the wall of snow. She saw mountains and hills, and the growing shape of a shrine. No no no. She pulled away, gasping, just as her feet were about to clear the circle. Her hands still held Aunt Ha. She couldn't hold on for long; she was going to get kicked in the belly, or kicked down, or both. She had to do something.

Philippe had said that when he'd been attacked on rue de Jessaint, he'd been helped by Berith. Anchored. How?

Not much time, not much time, and she was running out of it, her breath running in sharp, short gasps, hanging in the air before her. The cold was going to get her, if she didn't vanish first.

Focus.

Berith's flat was her fortress. It was virtually inviolable, but she couldn't leave it without sundering its protection and needing to start the long, painful process of building another refuge. And Berith had never said so, not in so many words, but Françoise suspected that was part of how she kept herself alive: by bolstering herself in her own dominion, rewriting the laws of magic if she needed to. It was, in many ways, a House of one.

It had been there for decades, ever since the war, before Françoise met Berith. It had heft. Solidity. And all the magic swirling within her came from the flat, from Berith herself. There was a link between them. A hint that the universe wasn't all snow and ghostly cities, and vanishing bodies crumpling under the assault of the cold.

Berith. Françoise leaned, with all her weight, on Aunt Ha—sent a brief prayer to whatever ancestors and spirits might be listening, to watch over the baby—and called up everything she had within her.

It felt as if she'd caught fire. Air burned in her lungs. Her heartbeat magnified a thousand times, joined by the second, weaker heartbeat of the baby. She was kneeling by Aunt Ha's side, but Berith was by her side. Françoise couldn't see her, touch her, but the sense of the Fallen's presence was so strong it was overwhelming, like a hand on her shoulder, bolstering her, steadying her.

She reached within her, fanned that fire, again and again, drawing on the magic Berith had given her, slowly, carefully unspooling a thread that started within her and went to the flat—no snow, no impediments, just a walk down the docks, into la Goutte d'Or, past the broken door, into that small, cramped courtyard crammed with debris, and up the rickety stairs, into the stale, familiar space that was theirs, the smell of rice and bread and of magic, and the plush blue armchair, transfiguring itself into the throne and the dais, and the bright, frightening figure sitting within it, lips shaping around the syllables of her name. . . .

A sharp pain went through her like a jolt. It didn't leave. It spread to all of her, centering finally in her belly, twisting as if a fist of flames were tearing at her guts. Screams, her screams. The circle, going up in flames with a sharp smell of brimstone. The veil of snow, receding, slowly, until she could see once more the ships on the other side of the basin. Workers, running toward them. She was still screaming; she couldn't stop.

"Child. Child."

She was on her side, vomiting, staring at people's feet, her hands curled on her belly. Aunt Ha kept saying her name, over and over. The pain passed, leaving her wrung dry. "I'm fine," she said, slowly.

Water pooled between her legs. No, she realized. It was warm, and it came from within her, and it wouldn't stop dripping. Amniotic fluid. She'd just lost her waters. Too early. Too early, and with nothing and no one to help her. She was going to be fine. No, she was lying to herself: she knew neither she nor the baby was safe. Ancestors, please . . .

"Can you stand?" Aunt Ha asked.

Focus. Focus. "I—I need to get back to the flat. Now." Before the contractions started in earnest, and she couldn't move anymore. "Need—to find the midwife."

Arms, picking her up, carrying her to a makeshift stretcher. The amniotic fluid, still running out of her like an unstoppable river; the baby completely still within her. Voices talking in Viet, overrunning one another until she could no longer keep them apart. "Too early," she whispered, but nobody seemed to hear her.

"We'll get you back. You'll be fine," Aunt Ha said, and they both knew she was lying.

THUAN found the palace in complete disarray. Attendants with trays of food and bundles of clothes ran through the corridors, barely stopping by to greet him, and the few officials that he could find looked at him with something close to panic, before waving him on. Even the two cousins he met, who were usually effusive in their affections, wore grim faces and only sent him on to Second Aunt's private rooms.

Things have changed drastically, not for the better.

What had happened?

He couldn't see any Fallen, so probably not a House invasion. He couldn't see any rebels, either, and the walls hadn't looked breached—at least, not any more than they had been before, crumbling into dust all on their own. He'd crossed the city on foot without any problems, stopping only to buy a steamed bun from a food seller at a crossroads. She'd been fearful and reserved, but he'd assumed it was because his accent and vocabulary were those of the court.

If it was the rebels, it wasn't anything as straightforward as an incursion, either.

No use speculating. He needed facts, and it looked like Second Aunt was the only one who had them.

She was not in her rooms; the attendants directed him to the ancestral temple, a little away from her private quarters.

He found her burning incense before the effigy of her father, her back to him. "Second Aunt," he said, bowing. For one long, stomach-wrenching moment, he thought she was going to turn toward him and show him eyes gnawed away by rot, and the decomposing face of his nightmares. But then, when she did turn, she looked much like herself, except that the makeup couldn't quite disguise the exhaustion.

"Child. It's good to see you."

They embraced, her nose briefly rubbing against his, and a smell of sandalwood and brine enfolding him, a reminder of a childhood that was getting more and more distant by the minute. "I don't have much for you," Thuan said. He'd come out of Hawthorn much as he'd entered it, empty-handed and at night. He'd left a message to Nadine and Leila: as much as he'd wanted to say good-bye, he wouldn't have been able to avoid the awkward questions that followed. The only things he'd packed had been the pictures on his ancestral altar, and the tangerines he'd set in front of them. It was those he handed to her now. "Here."

"Keep them," Second Aunt said. She moved away from the altar, pulled one of the wooden chairs to her. Crabs scuttled under it.

"Tell me what's happened," Thuan said.

Second Aunt didn't speak for a while. "I need to know," she said, finally, "where you stand on the subject of women."

"I—" Thuan gaped at her. "I have no idea what you mean."

Second Aunt's voice was matter-of-fact. "Your previous two lovers were a second-rank court official and a newly raised member of the Grand Secretariat. Both female."

"Yes," Thuan said, slowly. It couldn't be the lovers. The affairs had been short, torrid, and ultimately unsatisfying for both parties. No animosity that he could think of, unless one of them had changed her mind?

"And before that, the minister of personnel, who was male at the time."

"Yes," Thuan said, because he didn't know what else he could say. "It's not a crime."

"No," Second Aunt said. "You'll understand I'm only asking out of courtesy. I could order you, as both your elderly aunt and your ruler, but it would be messy and protracted. But, nevertheless . . . Are you over the passions of the cut sleeve?"

Thuan was starting to have an idea of where the conversation was going, and not liking it one bit. He toyed with the idea of lying, and then gave up. The cost would be too high for the kingdom. "If I see an attractive man, and the feeling is mutual, I won't say no," he said with a shrug. "Same for women."

"Good." Second Aunt leaned back in the chair, and watched him.

"I know what you're thinking," Thuan said. "But you said Cousin Dinh would—"

"Your cousin was gravely wounded," Second Aunt said. "It will be months before he can rise from his bed, if he gets up at all."

Thuan closed his eyes. Cousin Dinh, who'd always come up with the most idiotic plans, like when they'd sneaked over the wall to hear a famous courtesan recite poetry, and had almost fallen facedown into a bed of pebbles. Or hiding fireworks in their cousins' quarters, a joke they'd paid dearly for. "What happened? Rebels?"

"Yen Oanh's men attacked the palace. They made off with prisoners. Your cousin was trapped under collapsing rubble, and by the time we found him, he'd suffered extensive burns, and broken what the doctors assure me is almost every bone in his arm." Second Aunt's voice was dry, emotionless, as if she'd spent all her tears already. "You'll understand this seriously jeopardizes the alliance, unless I can offer an alternative."

Extensive burns. Thuan closed his eyes. Forced himself to focus. Cousin

Dinh's health wasn't the issue at the moment. Second Aunt had talked of an alternative. That all sounded sensible, until they got to who the alternative was. "I . . . ," Thuan said. "I've been spying in his House for months. Do you—" He stopped, before he openly criticized an elder, but it was close. He knew exactly the fate of traitors in Hawthorn, and he would have only the faintest of protections once he was handed over to them. To Asmodeus.

"I haven't said I liked it," Second Aunt said. "But I have no other choice. It has to be a prince of imperial blood—"

And as Thuan well knew, his many cousins were almost all women, and there was only one such candidate besides Cousin Dinh: Thuan himself.

Second Aunt went on, slowly. "I know you're worried about the spying. But it's commonplace. Part of the game we all play. Asmodeus has his spies in my kingdom, and I have mine in his. He knows the rules. And yes, he'll probably recognize you when I introduce you as his new prospective consort. But he certainly won't harm you at a negotiating table in the presence of half the high officials of the kingdom, not to mention my own."

"You mean he'll wait until we're back in Hawthorn," Thuan said, sharply.

"No," Second Aunt said. "He won't go through all that trouble. He'll merely find an excuse to reject the alliance if your being in the House is such an unforgivable offense. I doubt it, to be honest, but . . ." She paused, shook her head. "As I said—he knows the rules. He'll pretend he's known all along, when he brings you back to Hawthorn. That you spied with his full knowledge, if not his outright blessing, because that's the way things work. He'll save face, rather than admit he was weak."

"I know," Thuan said, more sharply than he'd intended. "I still—" He paused, bit his tongue again.

"You don't like it," Second Aunt said. "Believe me, I don't like it, either, child. But the stakes are too high. We *need* this alliance." And Thuan knew it perfectly well.

Asmodeus. Thuan closed his eyes, and thought of the power that had hooked claws under his ribs and pulled; of those eyes behind horn-rimmed glasses, dry and amused. "Do you know what he wants? It's not merely marriage, is it?"

"I was rather counting on you for that," Second Aunt said. "Something big and large and splashy." Her face didn't move. Her mouth, thin and red, was set in an unamused smile. "And no, I don't think that's merely an alliance. That's not the House's style."

"I . . ." Thuan hesitated. "I don't think he's the one behind the angel essence traffic."

"So someone else wants to weaken us."

"Or to grow rich," Thuan said. "It may be a simple matter of greed."

Second Aunt shook her head. "Perhaps. But whatever Hawthorn wants, it's not as simple as money, I'm afraid. We have something that interests Asmodeus. Magic, perhaps? He wanted us to send him teachers."

Thuan thought, again, of that power in Asmodeus's bedroom. "He already has that in abundance. Something else," he said. "A prelude to a conquest?"

"How? We're weak, but not that weak." But Second Aunt sounded thoughtful now. "We'll have to look into it some other way."

Pillow talk. Thuan tried to imagine himself doing that, and gave up. He could lie and smile, but while in bed . . .

"Anyway." Second Aunt sighed. "He's in the palace now. Resting, after his adventures with the rebels."

"I think," Thuan said, softly, "that you'd better tell me everything from the beginning."

AFTERWARD, Thuan walked through the corridors of the palace, to the bedroom where Cousin Dinh slept fitfully, with a tired-looking dragon doctor keeping an eye on him. He was covered in thick bandages, and one arm was immobilized in a sling. Thuan could barely see his eyes, swollen and bruised, and the sound of his breathing was slow, labored.

"How is he?" he asked, and the doctor shook her head.

"I don't know," she said. Dragons had healing powers stronger than any Fallen or mortals, but there were limits to what the flesh would bear. "He will heal. But it will not be tomorrow, or next week. And there might be scars. Extensive ones."

Thuan sat, for a while, watching his cousin. He remembered Cousin

Dinh, standing in front of a mirror and turning around, to watch the swirl of yellow silk on his new robes. He'd always been a bit vain, a bit of a rooster in love with his own reflection. Always a bit flighty, chafing at the strictures of palace life and wishing he could change things.

Things would change, for him. Thuan couldn't be sure what Cousin Dinh would have wanted. But it was certainly not months of coma, and disfiguring scars, or the memory of being trapped under rubble and unable to reach anyone else for help. "I'm sorry," he said. It felt small, and slight, and utterly inadequate. "I hope you heal fast, and well." *Ancestors, watch over him.*

The doctor said nothing. Wise of her, not to commit. And Cousin Dinh, of course, couldn't say anything. Second Aunt had said he hadn't regained consciousness since the attack. He probably couldn't hear a word Thuan was saying.

Thuan was supposed to be joining Second Aunt and the delegates, to sign the alliance contract—which, for him, would be the binding marriage, ceremony or no ceremony. He could put it off, for a time. He could not think about it, or about what it all meant to him.

He had read the memorials, and all the materials that were remotely relevant. He *knew*, intellectually, that Second Aunt was right, that they needed a replacement for Cousin Dinh, and he was the only other suitable person. He just . . . He'd always known marriage wouldn't be a matter of love or preference, but he'd at least hoped for some respect.

For something more than being bartered away to ensure the increasingly fragile safety of the kingdom. And even that would have been fine if he'd believed anything he did or said could influence Asmodeus, but it wasn't going to happen. From all of Second Aunt's accounts, from all the official reports, the Fallen came as conquerors, demanding what they could not take by force. And if a marriage was involved? That, too, must encompass something Asmodeus wanted.

He was probably only going to learn what when it happened to him, and he very much doubted it would be pleasant. He thought again, of the legends Nadine had talked about in the gardens—saw bodies, hanging in the branches of ghostly trees and forever writhing in agony, and imagined one of these was his—imagined being stretched out on branches with all his bones shattered, all his muscles a mass of pain, and his life force leaching into the wards, to feed the power of the House. . . . *Ancestors, watch over me.*

It would have been nice if he could believe the ancestors' reach extended anywhere inside Hawthorn.

SEVENTEEN
IN THE NAME OF ALLIANCES

MADELEINE was trying to put together the shards of the halberd. It was a puzzle she could focus on, something that didn't require thinking about Yen Oanh, or the grueling walk back to the palace, or the nightmares that flashed across the insides of her eyelids every time she tried to rest. The worst of it wasn't Asmodeus, or the memories of the cell on the laundry barge, but Clothilde. She'd always been effortlessly sarcastic and calm in the face of everything the dragon kingdom had thrown at her; and as Asmodeus stumbled, she'd crumpled like crushed paper.

From Clothilde's room came the low murmur of voices. They'd both been closeted in there for a while. Madeleine hadn't been invited, and didn't want to be. Neither of them seemed to be overly concerned about Elphon's continued disappearance, or their continued failure to find Ghislaine.

The table in front of her was mother-of-pearl, tinged with those same oil-spill colors of Seine waters. She'd laid the salvaged shards on them, and pivoted them to reconstitute almost the entire blade. It was almost a short sword, or a knife. The only thing missing was a small, triangle-shaped piece near the tip. The blade hadn't turned dark again, and that odd, oppressive feeling she'd had when handling it whole hadn't come back. When she touched it, she only felt the slight, familiar tingle of Fallen magic.

This was no alchemical artifact, but it worked on some of the same principles. The container that it had been infused into was the blade, and when that had shattered, the magic had seeped away like water from a broken cup.

"Madeleine?"

She looked up, and saw Véronique. She looked much as she had before, with thin-jointed fingers, patches of grayish blue shell on her cheeks, and that incongruous Western dress worn like a costume rather than a suit. "I—" Madeleine struggled for words. "I thought you were dead."

"Badly hurt." Véronique smiled. There was no joy in it. "But we heal fast, as your lord has reason to know."

Asmodeus, from what Madeleine understood, had let himself be looked over and bandaged by dragon doctors. He had not spoken all the while, and had refused the rituals of healing that had been offered to him. "Charles died. I'm sorry."

"I know." Véronique's face shifted, slightly, as if she'd already been told numerous times, and numbed to grief already. "I won't forget. One day . . ."

"And the prince?"

Véronique said nothing.

Oh. She hadn't liked Phuong Dinh, per se—it was hard to like someone she'd met for only a few moments—but there'd been so much blood, and waste. And if she'd understood anything about the way Hawthorn worked, this was only the beginning. For the death of his dependents, Asmodeus would exact payment in blood and pain, and remind the world that no one trifled with Hawthorn.

It was her House. The one to which her fortunes were inextricably tied, the one who might swallow her whole and torture her to death, but would leave no one else that privilege. She had to remember that.

"May I?" Véronique said. She ran a finger on the edge of the blade, and sniffed. "The rumors are true, then."

"What rumors?"

Véronique's smile was edged with a hint of plated, rust-colored segments around her mouth. "You can't feel it, but there are *khi* elements on this blade. Someone merged Fallen and dragon magic to create this weapon."

"Why?" Madeleine started, and then remembered what Asmodeus had said. To kill Fallen, and dragons. "Magical blades. To have an advantage over Fallen and Houses?" Fallen wounds healed almost instantaneously when they didn't remove organs, and if they weren't outright fatal: it was extremely hard to incapacitate one of the Fallen. Madeleine had seen many corpses in her laboratory, back when she was working as an alchemist. All of them had been gravely wounded, with injuries that had proved fatal within a short amount of time, or outright drained of life by magic. Isabelle had been killed with two bloody holes the size of fists through her chest.

"You're hard to kill," Véronique said, without rancor. "And the rebels aren't that numerous."

Asmodeus had said that dragons were hard to kill, too, and healed themselves. But that didn't change the sheer number of Fallen, and what would happen if even a fraction of House Hawthorn arrayed themselves against them.

"But you can't root the rebels out on your own."

Véronique shook her head. "We're not that numerous, either." She didn't sound ashamed of admitting to weakness. Ngoc Bich probably wouldn't have approved. "And a lot of us, on both sides, are taking care of the dying."

The hospital. The dying dragons. Madeleine fought back the taste of corruption in her mouth. "You didn't tell us about the angel essence problem."

"Of course not," Véronique said. "Since you're the ones causing it."

"We're not!" Madeleine started, and then stopped. Where else would they get Fallen bodies? And how else would they weaken the kingdom enough for negotiations? She opened her mouth again, remembered Clothilde telling her to remain silent. "I can't say anything," she said, finally. Because she didn't know, anymore, what was going on and what the stakes were, and what she might jeopardize.

"Not allowed?" Véronique shrugged. "It's fine. Honestly. We're not *friends*." She slid a piece of the blade toward her, tilted it toward the ceiling. "It's very fine jade. Almost too fine. No inclusions, and the color is too uniform, too perfect." She bit her lip. "I'm not sure this was quarried any-where in the kingdom."

"I don't know what you mean," Madeleine said.

"This was made by magic. Except I don't know of any spells which could do this."

"It was dark," Madeleine said. "With green streaks, until it shattered."

Véronique nodded, distantly. "That wall you saw . . ."

Madeleine looked up, startled. "How do you know—" Oh, of course. Asmodeus or Valchior, or possibly the prisoner, would have mentioned it.

"We're not friends, but we *are* allies. The wall—would you say it was the same color as this?"

It hadn't occurred to Madeleine. "I only saw it from afar, and it was only half-built." She thought, for a while, trying to remember. The stone had looked odd. "I think so. I'm not sure." And then she remembered the workers. "The workers were carrying clear green bricks. But they were dark on the wall. Why?"

"Things can change, when they become part of a spell," Véronique said. "But the princess was wondering. Jade is fragile. It's an odd choice for building anything. For weapons or for walls."

"This one shattered," Madeleine said.

"It should have shattered the first time it hit something hard. Like glass." Véronique looked at the halberd, for a while. "Fallen magic," she said at last. "Crammed into it until the *khi* elements were forced out. Making this more resistant. It is, after all, always dominant." She slid the piece back toward Madeleine. Her face was expressionless. Something, long delayed, finally worked its way to the surface of Madeleine's thoughts.

"You're not just essence addicts, are you? You—you believe in us. You think we're your salvation. That the House is your salvation." She wasn't sure how that made her feel.

"We're weak," Véronique said, simply. "Dying out. The king of the Bièvre didn't die because the Seine invaded him. He died like our previous emperor, choked by the residue of spells and pollution. Fallen magic will be like fresh blood. An infusion of power that will revitalize us."

And yet Fallen magic—the aftermath of the magical war, and the angel essence—was what was killing them. "There have to be other ways."

"Your lord would think otherwise," Véronique said. "And, to remain on the victors' good side, here is a little token of our goodwill." She laid something on the table, beside the broken blade: a piece of paper folded in four.

It was addressed to Madeleine: the handwriting hurriedly crammed together on the paper. When she touched it, magic rose, a faint, insistent touch she would have known anywhere.

Elphon.

She unfolded it. Something tugged at her, merging, for a moment, with the tracking disk she still wore, and then letters formed on the blank paper as if an invisible quill were writing them.

> *Madeleine. You're the only one who can read this. Come to the docks of la Villette Basin. There is something you need to see. But, for the love of all that is holy, do not bring Clothilde with you, or tell her about this message.*

"I don't understand," Madeleine said.

Véronique shook her head. "If you don't, I don't, either. I'm just carrying the message. Not its meaning. We should go, or we're going to be late."

"Late for what?" Madeleine asked, and then, looking up, saw Clothilde and Asmodeus waiting in the courtyard.

IN the pavilion by the great courtyard, Ngoc Bich was waiting for them in full court regalia: a robe of yellow silk with the sprawling figure of a dragon amidst waves—almost new, with barely a trace of decay—and her crown of black cloth and beaded tassels. She was followed by four attendants with a parasol, another three with fans, and three carrying incense burners. Behind her was a large group of officials: Thanh Phan, Minh, and others Madeleine couldn't recognize. And, by her side, a young Annamite with long hair tied into a topknot, who looked barely out of childhood—though they always looked younger than they really were—wearing red robes that were so vivid and striking that he seemed to throw everyone else into insignificance.

"This is Rong Minh Thanh Thuan," Ngoc Bich said, gravely, to Asmodeus. "I trust you find him acceptable."

Asmodeus bowed, a fraction. His smile was sharp, wolfish, as if he had remembered some hold he had over them all.

They all sat down around the large table. Valchior's movements were stiff and a little awkward, but nothing whatsoever indicated that Asmodeus had been wounded less than a day ago.

There was a stack of papers in front of Clothilde, who fanned them out slowly, and handed them to Ngoc Bich. "This is what we agreed on," she said. "Rifles and magical artifacts, and a complement of soldiers to help you train yours."

And essence. Madeleine couldn't get Véronique's face out of her mind. In her hand, Elphon's message was warm, a touch of reassuring magic that wasn't the link to the House.

Asmodeus was watching Thuan intently. The prince, in turn, had to have noticed, but pretended to be unaffected. "You neglected to mention how bad your rebel problem was," he said to Ngoc Bich.

Ngoc Bich raised an eyebrow. "Did you think we would negotiate with you if we were strong?"

"I know you're not." His eyes were still on Thuan. If Madeleine had been the focus of that much attention, she would have been sick by now. "Madeleine told me they're building a wall. Not to mention being able to reach inside your city and palace."

Ngoc Bich's voice was freezing. "They're our problem."

"Hawthorn's, too," Asmodeus said, with a mocking smile. "Since we're now allied. I would hate to have to change interlocutors."

"You're quite free to open negotiations with them if you wish." Ngoc Bich's smile was almost malicious.

"I've already had words with their leader," Asmodeus said, with a shrug. He took off his glasses, and toyed with them for a while, his gaze still on Thuan. "I fear not ones which were conducive to an agreement. Also, she's killed three of my dependents, and harmed two others." His left hand rested, elegantly, on the chipped claws of one of the dragons on the table. His voice was low, even, as if they were having a pleasant chat about the weather. "In those circumstances, I find it hard to argue for anything less than destruction."

His dependents. What belonged to him, the possessions of the House. It wasn't a promise, or affection, that had made him come for her, but simply anger, and greed, and pride.

Asmodeus went on. "But I would like to know what they're doing. Yen Oanh has to know she can't invade your city, or do more than harry you. And yet she was confident enough to attempt to draw Hawthorn into the fight."

"How nice," Ngoc Bich said, drily, "to know that the world revolves around you."

"You mistake me. I know where we stand today, and what power we wield. That's the only superiority I claim." Asmodeus's smile was sharp and unpleasant. "Nothing more, but nothing less, either."

Ngoc Bich was silent, for a while, as if weighing options. "I can hazard a guess," she said, "from the halberd you brought back, and Madeleine's observations that the same stone was being used to build the wall. You will be familiar with symbolic magic."

"Intimately," Asmodeus said, amused. "I didn't know dragons were."

"Always know your enemy." Ngoc Bich didn't even blink. "There was earth, in that halberd. And metal. The *khi* elements that choke, that bind, that bury. And a hospital for the dying, nearby, wasn't there?" She'd turned to Madeleine, who, shocked, simply nodded.

"Few things are as absolute as the boundary between life and death. Even ageless Fallen die, eventually. Even dragons." Ngoc Bich's voice was mirthless. "That wall partakes of some of this."

"You mean Heaven and Hell lie beyond it?" Asmodeus's voice was scornful. "That's hardly—"

"You're not listening. It's a symbol. It draws its strength from that near-unbreakable boundary, but it's not the path to the land of the dead. Of course not."

Madeleine found her voice, spoke in the silence. "It was half-built."

"Of course. The kingdom is as vast as the Seine. You can only build something like this across a small distance."

Asmodeus's face was creased in thought; serious, for once. "So they want to cut off a small part of the kingdom. Seceding from you?"

"It's possible." Ngoc Bich's hands rested on the broken mosaic of the table. "But it is not something we will tolerate for long."

"Thanks to our help," Asmodeus said. "Which reminds me. What did you do with the prisoner?"

Ngoc Bich's face was serene. "She'll talk. You're not the only one to have a Court of Persuasion, though I am given to understand that you were never its head. What were you head of? I forget. Oh, yes. The Court of Birth. A charming way to pass your time—finder of newborn Fallen, and midwife to the children of essence addicts."

Asmodeus watched her, for a while. Then he smiled. "Princess of the dragon kingdom. The title ill suits you. You deserve higher."

"I'm glad you think so." Ngoc Bich was imperturbable. She pulled the pile of documents toward her—didn't read them, but looked at Thanh Phan, who nodded. Though she didn't look happy at all. "And glad you decided not to press for further concessions in the light of what happened to your dependent." She inclined her head toward Madeleine, who suddenly felt the sole, uncomfortable center of attention of the entire table. She'd have dived behind a pillar if she could.

"My dependents, you mean?"

Ghislaine. Elphon looked to be safe, even though Madeleine didn't understand what he was embroiled in. But Ghislaine had never turned up, and if Yen Oanh didn't have her, where was she?

"Envoy Ghislaine?" Ngoc Bich shrugged. "Insofar as I can tell, she left the safety of the palace of her own will. I am sorry that she came to grief, but you can't expect us to protect people who are determined to venture into danger."

Something swam out of the morass of Madeleine's thoughts: a memory, sharp and unwelcome, of Prince Phuong Dinh warning her. He'd told her Ghislaine had learned something about Yen Oanh. Something bad enough, and worrying enough, that she'd thought she needed to get back to Hawthorn, without waiting for Clothilde's delegation.

And now Elphon was warning her against Clothilde.

"I should think blame in this matter is . . . ah. A shared thing," Asmodeus said. He'd looked, briefly, at Madeleine, and then back at Thuan. "But since you're offering me such a delightful morsel . . ." His hands moved, on the chipped table, as if drawing the shape of a noose.

Thuan didn't flinch. He was comforting, unremarkable—not an addict to angel essence, not cool and competent and alien like Ngoc Bich—the kind of person she could imagine behind a desk, or buried amidst books.

"I would remind you the alliance is contingent on his well-being," Ngoc Bich said, a little too sharply.

Asmodeus shrugged. "I shall keep that in mind."

"As to the rebels . . ." Ngoc Bich shook her head. "The alliance aims to defeat them, among other things. Then you won't have the grief of changing interlocutors."

"I know." Asmodeus's face went grave, for a fraction of a second. "Which is why the delegation will remain here, to help you with them."

Ngoc Bich's face didn't move. "Of course." The treaty gave her a permanent delegation from Hawthorn, Madeleine remembered, though Ngoc Bich probably didn't expect it to start so soon, or to be so clearly invasive.

"Shall we?" Asmodeus asked.

"We might as well." Ngoc Bich took up a brush, and, dipping it in vermilion ink, signed every page of the contract. One of the attendants brought her a large golden square seal, topped by an engraving of a dragon, which she stamped on the last page. Then she slid the documents across to Asmodeus, who, reaching inside his jacket pocket, produced a marbled red fountain pen and a knife, the same knife he'd used on the Fallen he'd killed. Unlike Ngoc Bich, he scanned every page before scrawling his initials on it. He finished by prickling his fingers on the knife, and laying three of them at the bottom of the paper, by Ngoc Bich's seal. When he withdrew his hand, they revealed the bloody shape of the House's arms, the branches of the hawthorn tree pushing into Ngoc Bich's seal like daggers.

"Here," he said, and handed them to Thuan, who pressed his own seal at the very end.

Something tightened in the room, not Fallen magic but a coldness, as if a dozen currents had suddenly converged on the table. Thuan's hands clenched into fists. Ngoc Bich's face remained serene and distant, as she gathered the papers and handed them to Thanh Phan. "We will expect your goodwill soon."

"Of course." He waited, watching her. "And the ceremony?"

"As you fully know, your presence here was unexpected," Ngoc Bich said.

Asmodeus raised an eyebrow. "Not my fault."

"It was always assumed Clothilde would escort Prince Thuan to Hawthorn, where the wedding ceremony would take place. Though, technically speaking, you have both signed the marriage contracts already."

Asmodeus inclined his head. "It was planned that way, yes."

"But, since you're both here, you can be introduced to the ancestors as Thuan's husband, as would be proper."

Asmodeus shrugged. "As you wish. Hawthorn won't renege on its obligations, though it might be a little while before we can organize everything."

"Of course." Ngoc Bich inclined her head. "I'll await your invitation, then."

Madeleine tried to imagine the ceremony: a full-fledged, formal affair with a seated dinner, and people in swallowtail suits and mutton-sleeve dresses mingling by a buffet, having polite and inconsequential conversation around canapés and wineglasses. Tried to imagine the sheer alienness of dragons and crabs and other sea creatures among them, and gave up. In House Silverspires, she'd seen Philippe, the captive Annamite, looking awkward and ill at ease in his suit. But Ngoc Bich and her train wouldn't bother with suits, or looking ill at ease. They'd move around House representatives like birds of prey among tigers, two different kinds of predators with no intention of giving any ground.

No wonder Asmodeus looked amused, if that was indeed his intention.

THE ceremony, whatever it was, didn't include the delegates, or the officials: just Ngoc Bich, Thuan, and Asmodeus. Clothilde paced, all the while they were gone, and finally settled by Madeleine's side. "We're staying on," she said. "It's not over yet."

Madeleine hadn't thought it was. She kept her fingers wrapped around the message from Elphon. "The rebels?" she asked.

"Whatever they're up to." Clothilde's voice was dark. "There was a Fallen with Yen Oanh. That means House involvement. This means something larger than a small civil war in a land we don't really care about."

For the love of all that is holy, do not bring Clothilde with you, or tell her about this message.

She didn't know anything about Clothilde. Or about Elphon, in the new House of Hawthorn, or why he would suddenly stop trusting Clothilde. It made no sense, but the only person who might have the answers in the vicinity was Asmodeus, and she couldn't take the problem to him. Even if he deigned to explain, she couldn't control what he decided to do. And, with no idea of the stakes . . .

"A House. Which one?"

"I don't know," Clothilde said. "It's not like anything is solved. The dragon kingdom is still under siege. Yen Oanh is still . . . I don't know what she's up to."

Building a wall. Healing addicted dragons. Putting together weapons that damaged Fallen past healing. Snatching delegates from a heavily guarded palace, in the heart of Ngoc Bich's power. Making Ghislaine flee to Hawthorn, for a safety she'd never reached. It didn't sound altogether promising.

"She's a threat," Clothilde said. "And Lord Asmodeus will want her dealt with."

As a message. As revenge. Madeleine said, slowly, "She wanted Asmodeus, specifically. To throw the House into disarray?"

"To send a message," Clothilde replied. "But yes, that, too. Historically, it's been chaos when the head of a House died." Her gaze became distant. "It was bad enough when Uphir was deposed."

Madeleine shivered, touching the wound on her calf, the one that had never properly healed. "It was a bad time for everyone."

"You were lucky," Clothilde said. "You left."

Left wounded and dying after Elphon had died; and crawled to House Silverspires, to endure twenty years of trying to drug herself into an early grave. "I guess," Madeleine said. Clothilde would have been an adult by then—how had she lived through it?

She could find no good way of asking the question, and gave up on it after a while. She wouldn't get her answers that way. But, equally, she wouldn't get to Elphon if she had to stay on with Clothilde.

Which left only one way of dealing with the problem; and she so, so wished there were another.

AND then it was over, and Asmodeus was back at the table, just long enough to announce his intention of leaving the kingdom, consort in tow like a prize prisoner.

It was now or never.

Easy to say, far less easy to do. It took Madeleine three tries to gather enough courage to approach him. "You know where Elphon is," she said, hoarsely.

He looked at her with curiosity, as he might at an insect who had learned to speak. "Of course."

"I—" She swallowed, her hand wrapped around Elphon's message. "I need to speak to him."

"And you want me to tell you where he is? Clothilde could tell you as well as I."

For the love of God, don't tell Clothilde. She had so little idea what was going on, or why. "I—" She swallowed again. "I want your permission to join him."

"How . . . delightful." Asmodeus rolled the word on his tongue as though it were red, bloody meat. "Behaving like a proper House dependent. I'm almost touched."

He wasn't, and they both knew it.

"Joining Elphon?" He was silent, for a while. He was going to ask her the obvious question—why she didn't go through Clothilde for any of this—and she was going to have to answer, and she didn't know what she could say or do that wouldn't lead to either her or Clothilde in the cells. Instead, what he said was, "You pledged your loyalty to me."

"Of course," Madeleine said. "Because I had no other choice." Honest and suicidal. Beside Asmodeus, Prince Thuan winced.

Asmodeus laughed. It wasn't cruel or malicious, but merely amused, a parent by the antics of a child. "Still disastrously naive and forthright, I see. Will you renege on that pledge?"

She couldn't afford to, even if she'd wanted to. What would she do? Rebel alone and singly against him, and be crushed as he had crushed the loyalists to Uphir, twenty years before? "You know I won't." The words tasted like ashes in her mouth. "Too principled." If there was a choice, any choice that left her free, that took her away from him, but there was none.

Asmodeus took a handkerchief from his jacket pocket, and carefully wiped his fingertips. Three dots of red spread across the white cotton. "You are quite free to intrigue as you wish," he said. "As long as it's not against me, and doesn't weaken the House. A word of advice, for what it's worth: you're not, to put it bluntly, very good at intrigue." His eyes rested on her, gray-green, the color of the sea before the storm—expressionless, as they would be when he chose to take the knife blade to her. . . .

She shivered. "No," she said. "I don't have to be."

"You might have to, if you want to survive." He looked back, to where Clothilde was still talking with Thanh Phan and Ngoc Bich. "Though I could argue Clothilde's intrigues aren't that subtle, either."

Elphon. She needed to think of Elphon, of seeing him again, alive and well. Of getting away from the suffocating alienness of the dragon kingdom, and back into a House she feared and hated, but was familiar with.

Prince Thuan looked at her, curiously. He didn't seem worried, or fearful, but then, Ngoc Bich probably hadn't had time to explain the situation she was dropping him into.

"Elphon is on the docks, by la Villette Basin," Asmodeus said. He buttoned up his jacket, fluffing up the pleated silver stock at his collar. "I'll have a word with Clothilde. She can stay here and work with Ngoc Bich on how to destroy that wall and the rebels. And you, of course, will return. I would be displeased if you didn't."

He knew exactly where she was, just as he did with Elphon; and he also knew there was no other House that would take her, and no Houseless that would dare shelter her. "Of course. Thank you," Madeleine said. The words tasted bitter on her tongue.

"Don't thank me." Asmodeus was amused again. "That's all you have from me. If anything does go wrong . . ."

Then he wouldn't back her. It would be her against Clothilde. "Of course," Madeleine said, the words sharp and acrid against her tongue. "I understand."

EIGHTEEN
A ROOM OF THORNS

THUAN didn't remember the presentation to the ancestors, or the long, long climb away from the kingdom into House Hawthorn. The only sharp thing in the blur of his world was bowing in front of the altar to his grandfather and grandmother, lighting three sticks of incense that barely disguised the smell of rot, and desperately praying for their blessing, and good fortune.

If they gave any answer, he didn't hear it.

The gardens were choked with snow, a grayish sludge mixed with debris from spell residue, almost obscuring the burned trees and the ashes scattered through the gravel. As he crossed from the stairs to the quay into the grounds of the House, Thuan felt a slight resistance, as if the House itself knew what he was, and wanted to keep him out. It was cold, more than the winter winds, deep-seated and biting, a feeling that hadn't left him since he'd put his seal at the bottom of the contract.

Husband. Consort. It felt unreal, to be coming back to the House walking a step behind Asmodeus, who hadn't spoken a word to him, only watched him with a gaze that threatened to devour him whole.

He'd said nothing when Second Aunt had introduced Thuan. Merely smiled, sharp and amused. He knew. He had to know. Save face, Second Aunt had said. He had accepted the alliance: to harm Thuan would end it, and why would he want to jeopardize everything he'd pushed for? He would have to pretend he had known all along.

But, regardless of what Second Aunt had promised, he'd find ways to make Thuan pay that didn't involve spilling blood. There were so many intricate forms of punishment, and Thuan didn't need much imagination to understand how Asmodeus worked.

They headed down the corridors to the West Wing. Thuan ran his hand over the wainscot, remembering wandering the House at night.

The bodyguards showed him into a large, airy room. The attendants unpacked his meager possessions, and left him alone. The bed was a four-poster one, smelling faintly of mildew, and a pale red conversation chair occupied most of the remaining space. On the walls, a series of large white panels with a green contour, and the occasional mirror, which reflected Thuan's pale, exhausted face; and a huge filigreed chandelier over the bed, ablaze with lights and looking like a small sun from underneath.

On the secretary desk, someone had left paper and paint, and a delicate sketch of pomegranates and oranges so vividly done it seemed to leap from the page. It was signed with a single "S" at the bottom, twisted into the shape of a snake, and Thuan knew, abruptly, who had painted it.

Samariel.

Was this a message, a subtle reminder that he would never take Samariel's place? It wasn't as if he'd ever wanted to.

There was also a suit, draped over the chair: a dark gray swallowtail jacket and trousers, and a subdued shirt that was more silver than gray—the colors of the House he now belonged to. They appeared to have been cut for a larger man than him: Cousin Dinh quite probably. Thuan gave the matter some thought. He had worn Western fashion in the House before, but he hadn't so badly needed a bit of comfort, something that would remind him of home. Better to keep his own clothes. He could always tell them the fit was wrong.

He sat down on the bed, closed his eyes, and attempted, unsuccessfully, to meditate. When the door opened—a heartbeat, a lifetime later—he was no closer to feeling serene than he had been when leaving the kingdom.

They took him down a familiar corridor: one that curved, sharply, flaring into the antechamber with the huge set of wooden doors, and the two bloody stars falling from the firmament. They opened now, into a room that could have been the twin of the one where he was accommodated: same conversation chair, same four-poster bed, and a red armchair in which Asmodeus sat with steepled fingers, watching him. He'd taken off his suit, and was now wearing a dark blue dressing gown, embroidered with birds caught among ivy vines.

The room also contained—pale and wan and frightened—both Nadine and Leila.

Nadine's mouth shaped around his name, stopped.

"This is Prince Rong Minh Thanh Thuan, from the dragon kingdom of the Seine," Asmodeus said, as the bodyguards closed the doors behind Thuan. "My new consort, though I gather you've already met him."

Neither Nadine nor Leila would look at Thuan. Leila's hands were clenched. Thuan knew what was running through her mind. She wasn't House, she was there only on sufferance, with only one chance at becoming a dependent, and now she'd drawn the attention of the head of the House by associating with a spy and a traitor.

He found his voice. "They didn't know. Not them, not Sare, not any of the others." It shook less than he'd thought it would. "I give you my word they didn't know."

"Your word," Asmodeus said, thoughtfully, readjusting his glasses on his nose, "would seem to be rather worthless." He looked at Nadine and Leila—Leila fearful, Nadine holding herself straight—she wasn't afraid; she was angry, so angry that she shook. At Thuan, quite probably, and quite rightly. "You may go, though keep silent about this. I'll have a word with Sare later."

They both slipped out so fast they might as well have been running. Nadine threw Thuan a glance that he couldn't interpret on her way out, as if she wanted to say something and didn't dare.

The doors closed again, and now it was just Thuan, and Asmodeus. Something was tightening around him: magic drawn from the room, the same thing he'd felt outside it, a hook drawn into his heart, old and merciless, pulling and hollowing him out until it was all he could do to stand without falling to his knees.

Asmodeus unfolded his body from the chair, slowly, lazily, like a tiger shifting from its rest. As he stalked closer to Thuan, the shadow of dark, ethereal wings unfolded behind him, and a reddish light glinted on the frame of his horn-rimmed glasses. The magic that was holding Thuan tightened. He breathed deeply, rapidly, but none of it reached his burning lungs. The *khi* currents in the room were stunted and exhausted: no water he could draw on, nothing that would save him. . . .

"You're lucky," Asmodeus said, softly, "that I need a consort, for the time being." He ran a hand across Thuan's right cheek, a touch of warmth that became sharp as his long, elegant fingers raked the skin from eye to chin. "We would be having quite a different conversation, otherwise. One that you wouldn't find so comfortable."

Thuan tried to speak, but no words would come. If this was Asmodeus's idea of "comfortable" . . .

"You're also lucky that the marriage contract is binding regardless of what happens between us." Asmodeus withdrew his hand, and tipped Thuan's head up; his lips inches from Thuan's own, until the smell of bergamot and orange blossom filled him to bursting. "Consummation isn't required, though I'm tempted. You're not unpleasant to the eye." He moved away, releasing Thuan, and the magic that had seized him abruptly vanished, leaving him gasping.

He wasn't going to fall to his knees. He wasn't going to give Asmodeus the satisfaction of seeing him weak. He said, slowly, hoarsely, "You mock the princess for the rebels in her kingdom. Perhaps you should be paying attention to your own House."

"And to the spies in its midst?"

It wasn't as though he could make the situation worse by admitting what he knew. "Someone is running angel essence traffic with the dragon kingdom," Thuan said. He thought of his tutor Old Bao, made his face expressionless and his voice ring with the tone of one who quoted from the classics, and took his strength from them. All for show, of course. "Through Hawthorn."

Asmodeus turned to look at him; a brief pause, and in that moment Thuan could have sworn he looked genuinely surprised. Then it passed, and the usual sardonic mask was back in place. "Not I, as you already know. Though it's an interesting idea. Weaken you enough you'll agree to anything—"

"You already did that," Thuan said, more forcefully than he'd meant to. "That's why I'm here." Why he was standing, breathing in magic and perfume—intoxicated and weakened by it in equal measures.

"Yes." Asmodeus watched him, unmoving. "But, as I said, this wasn't my doing."

"And you don't think you should know what is happening inside Hawthorn? One of your dependents is obviously not reporting everything to you." They were unwise words, but he'd had enough of catering to others' whims. "I'd call that a slight loyalty problem."

Asmodeus's voice was silken soft. "You think to tell me how to run my own House?"

"I'm your consort." The words were torn out of Thuan's mouth before he could stop to consider. "Perhaps it should count for something."

"Or perhaps I don't need that kind of consort."

But he did need Thuan. He'd said as much, earlier: "for the time being." What did that mean? Thuan had thought the angel essence traffic was the issue, but something else, something larger, was going on. He shrugged. "Then feel free to silence me, in any way you want. I had the feeling you needed me."

Silence. Then, unbearably close, bergamot and orange blossom; and Asmodeus's lips on his, a brief, electrifying contact that sent a spike of desire arching through him. Unwise. Unwise.

Asmodeus pulled away and watched him, for a while. His glasses hung slightly askew, fogged with Thuan's breath. "A morsel," he said. His voice was toneless, but Thuan was starting to understand that he would never display emotions, unless they overwhelmed him.

"You—" Thuan swallowed. "I didn't give you permission."

"Did you not? Then I'll apologize, if you deem it necessary."

His entire face felt on fire. This was not only unwise; it was idiotic.

Asmodeus didn't care for him, didn't have his well-being at heart, was just toying with him. "No," he said, struggling to gather words. "It won't be necessary. You left the sketches, in my room. Samariel's."

"Samariel is dead," Asmodeus said. He was leaning against one of the bedposts, his dressing gown slightly parted to reveal the pale skin of his torso. Thuan closed his eyes, trying to breathe normally. "But not unmourned."

"I didn't say that."

They watched each other for a while. Thuan wasn't sure, afterward, why he said, "It was all earmarked for Clothilde's use. The angel essence. It's in your account books. Well hidden, but not impossible to find. The handwriting that entered it is probably recognizable, too."

"I see." Asmodeus didn't move. He took off his glasses, and cleaned them on the lapel of his dressing gown. He looked oddly young without them, oddly vulnerable. How much of his life was a constant act, a constant projection of strength, of sarcasm, lest he be construed as weak? "This is unwise," Asmodeus said.

"The kiss?"

"The confidences." He smiled, and it was grave, and unamused. "But thank you."

"Tell me something, then," Thuan said.

"What will happen to you? I'm afraid that's my business." He sounded almost regretful.

"No." Thuan exhaled. Pillow talk. Well, that was as close as it was going to get. "What do you want from us?"

Asmodeus moved then, came to stand close to him once more. Thuan breathed in citruses, and bergamot, trembling on the tip of his tongue. He thought it was going to be another kiss, but Asmodeus didn't even touch him.

"What does anyone want, from another House or kingdom? It's always the same thing. You're weak, and ripe for a conquest," he said. Thuan saw, shining in the gray-green irises, the light of magic, like the beginning of a storm. "If not I, it would have been someone else."

"Are you making excuses?"

"Of course not. Merely seeking power, to defend what is mine."

"And I—" Thuan swallowed, tasted bitterness in his throat. "I'm not yours."

"You're not a dependent but a consort. A living link to the dragon kingdom in Hawthorn. A necessity." And then, moving away once more: "You'll understand that I won't give you the freedom of the House, given the circumstances."

Thuan didn't answer. He wasn't even sure what he could have said.

"Ask, should you need anything. It need not be an unpleasant imprisonment."

Except at the point where it ended, but the words remained stuck in Thuan's throat. "A gilded cage, until my death becomes more valuable than my life?"

Asmodeus laughed. "I like you, dragon prince. More than I should. But you fail to understand: in this House, in this city, death is always more valuable than life." He laid a finger on Thuan's lips, held it, unmoving, for a while. "And love, or desire, always less valuable."

AFTER the encounter, Thuan lay on the four-poster bed in his own room, staring at the ceiling. There was mold, in one corner, and patches of rusty dampness on the wallpaper. He still could feel desire, trembling in the air. One kiss. One disastrous kiss.

You're not unpleasant to the eye.

This is unwise.

The kiss?

The confidences.

What had he—why had he even—?

Then again, why had Asmodeus felt the need to kiss him at all?

Great. Thuan was hundreds of years old, and he felt like a teenager dealing with a crush on a schoolmate. Except that he had greater problems. How he'd get out of this room, to start with.

You're weak, and ripe for a conquest. Not that weak. Not that ripe. But Asmodeus had sounded utterly convinced it was the case. What had he been thinking about? Somehow it was tied to Thuan, or the contract. Or to the soldiers that Hawthorn was sending? But there would be a few dozen of them, not nearly enough to take over the palace, even if they were armed with rifles and Fallen magic.

A knock at the door. Thuan was startled awake, before he remembered it was locked.

A key turned, and the door opened. Much to Thuan's surprise, it was Nadine, carrying a tray with bread and soup, which she set on the table, before going back to the door and closing it.

"You don't work in the kitchens," Thuan said, the only thing that would come to mind.

"No, but a few people owe me a few favors," Nadine said.

Thuan sighed. "Go ahead. I know you're angry with me."

"You could have trusted me." Nadine looked as though she was going to backhand him.

"To keep silent about this? You're *House*. Your mother is close to Asmodeus."

"I'm not my mother." Nadine sat down on the bed, next to him. She sighed. "And I know the cost of speaking up, Thuan. Don't take me for a fool."

"I'm not one, either," Thuan said, stiffly. "And it's not like I planned to return, once I'd left." Except, of course, that it had all gone disastrously wrong.

"You mean after the rather terse message telling us you were leaving?" Nadine shook her head. "I suppose we should be grateful for it, since it was the only evidence we had that you were still alive."

"As opposed to . . . ?"

"Being disappeared."

"Sare said—"

"Sare doesn't know everything that goes on in this House," Nadine said.

"And you do?"

"More than you, I would guess."

"That's not hard." Thuan shook his head. "I don't know what I'm supposed to do now."

"In Asmodeus's world?" Nadine stretched, staring at her hands. "Keep silent until he decides that cutting your throat is in his best interests."

Thuan ran a hand on his lips, remembering the touch of Asmodeus's fingers on his mouth—the kiss, running through his spine like a shock. "I had worked that much out, thanks."

"How old are you?" Nadine asked. "Truly. You're not a teenager, are you?"

Thuan laughed. "Close to three hundred years old. Dragons don't age as fast as humans. Though we do age."

"Wise and knowledgeable." Nadine's voice was sharp. "You didn't need any of the lessons, did you? And the infirmary stuff—you'd probably seen it hundreds of times already."

Meaning that she was angry her time had been wasted, that she'd bothered to teach Thuan things that he'd pretended not to know. "I wish," Thuan said. "I'm a scholar, and the books I know are in Viet. I'm not a physician. I knew a little about the history of Hawthorn, but not that much. And as to the infirmary . . ." He shook his head. "Trust me, I learned things there. When you managed to knock them into my head." Whether he'd reuse them was debatable, but that was another problem.

Nadine grimaced, half-placated. "You were a quick study."

"Mmm," Thuan said. "How is Leila?"

"She'll be fine," Nadine said. "Had the fright of her life, but ultimately there'll be nothing held against her. Sare, though . . ."

Thuan drew in a short, sharp breath. "He must know that I was planted by the kingdom. Carefully fabricated to infiltrate the House. That Sare didn't see through me is no failure on her part."

Nadine grimaced, again. "Try telling him that."

"I did," Thuan said, darkly. "Whether it did any good . . ."

"Probably not. Asmodeus doesn't listen to the disloyal. Except to their screams in the cells."

Thuan shivered. "Let's not talk about this."

Tell me something, then.

What will happen to you? I'm afraid that's my business.

Nadine was watching him. There was something, in the way she held herself, in the set of her shoulders and the tightness of her jaw.

"You want to ask me something, and you're not sure if I'll like it," Thuan said.

"No," Nadine said. "I'm not sure how far I can trust you. You're not Hawthorn. What makes you tick, Thuan?"

What did? He wished he did know. "I'm here because I was asked to be. Because the kingdom signed an alliance with Hawthorn. My first loyalty is with them. Not to the House."

Nadine hesitated. Then: "Things will change, in this House. Soon."

It didn't sound like she meant the conquest of the kingdom, or whatever plan Asmodeus had in mind. Thuan said nothing, well aware that the least word could silence her.

"They could change for you, too," Nadine said, softly. "We have no interest in the dragon kingdom, except as a means to an end."

It didn't make sense. "All right," Thuan said, slowly. "Though I'm not sure what you think I can do." He was still dissecting the previous sentences.

"Nothing, for the time being." Nadine shook her head. "I can't get you out of this room. I can't even stay long, else it will be noted. Just . . . you're not alone, Thuan. Be ready."

And she left, not looking back.

Thuan went back to lying on the bed, his hands pillowed behind his head. Nadine. Of all people. He wasn't even sure how to interpret what had happened, or how he felt.

He'd known for a while now that there were different factions in the House: the various courts were endlessly bickering and jockeying for status and power. That one of these factions would turn out to be working against Asmodeus was not a surprise, either, especially when said faction had been very, very careful to keep their accounts out of the House's official ones. But that Nadine would be involved with them . . .

We have no interest in the dragon kingdom, except as a means to an end. Which meant there were more of them—whoever "they" were—than just Nadine. And also that they were already in contact with the dragon kingdom. With Yen Oanh? He couldn't imagine it was anyone else: the court's contacts with Hawthorn had been thoroughly restricted by Second Aunt.

Things will change in this House, soon. How? When? And what had he changed, by telling Asmodeus about the accounts?

And more important, whom should he support, and why did he feel as though he genuinely didn't know? His fortunes should have been tied to Asmodeus's, except that Asmodeus had made his intentions of conquering the dragon kingdom quite clear.

He closed his eyes and tried to sleep, knowing already that he wouldn't manage even that, not with the taste of bergamot and orange blossom still on his lips.

NINETEEN
WEIGHT OF THE PAST

MADELEINE sat on the parapet of Pont Saint-Michel, watching House Silverspires.

It wasn't, strictly speaking, necessary, or even on the way to joining Elphon. But it was her first moment of something that looked like freedom since she'd been dragged back into Hawthorn, and she had to go back.

The House had changed: the ruins of Notre-Dame were now capped by the crown of a banyan tree, its roots extending over the walls of adjacent buildings. In a city of ruins and wreckages, it looked even worse, on the verge of being erased altogether. But it was still alive. Still, a steady stream of people in the House's red and silver uniforms carried baskets and supplies, going over the Petit Pont, crossing the parvis. There were fewer of them on Pont Saint-Michel, and those few all gave Madeleine a wide berth, seeing the uniform of another House.

It was disquieting, but if she was honest with herself, she had never been very social, in Silverspires. She had spent twenty years cloistered in her laboratory, putting together artifacts and drugging herself on angel essence, waiting for the death she'd been running away from to claim her.

"Madeleine?"

It was Aragon, the House's chief doctor, and Emmanuelle, its archivist, walking back over the bridge side by side. They'd been in some kind of animated conversation. Emmanuelle was, as usual, half-hidden by a stack of books, which she laid on the blackened parapet.

They both looked unchanged, Aragon prim in a suit that sat awkwardly on his large frame, Emmanuelle tall, elegant as always, her dark skin contrasting sharply with the straight white cotton dress she wore—the only indication of her allegiance a small embroidered insignia of the House on her right shoulder. Both unchanged, while Madeleine's world twisted and turned, and dragged her utterly beyond the safe or familiar.

She could have wept.

"Sorry," she said, getting up. "I shouldn't have—"

"Stay," Emmanuelle said. "Please."

"Selene . . . ," Madeleine said. Emmanuelle's lover was head of the House; and it was she who had cast Madeleine out, months ago, when she'd discovered her alchemist was also an essence addict.

"I'll handle Selene." Emmanuelle's gaze was hard. "If anything arises."

An awkward silence followed, while they all looked at one another. Aragon broke it with his usual bluntness. "How are you? You don't look as though the House is treating you well."

Madeleine stared at the House behind them, wondering what it would be like to walk its corridors once more. "All right, I suppose. I—" And because, in spite of everything else, she was still honest: "It's not—I mean. It's a scrape I got myself into. I can't really blame the House for that." Especially not after Asmodeus had rescued her.

She was going to get used to that idea. She was. One day.

"How is Silverspires?"

Emmanuelle shrugged. "Rebuilding. Selene is cautiously reaching out to other Houses. And we're removing branches and roots from about every damn room in the place."

The roots of the tree had choked Silverspires, drawing out its magic until Selene had ended the curse. Madeleine hadn't been to Silverspires since then. She hadn't been allowed out of Hawthorn, except under close supervision.

"Is . . ." Madeleine hesitated. ". . . the hospital still understaffed?"

Aragon snorted. Emmanuelle hid a smile. It was a subject that was sure to draw his ire. "Not so much understaffed as incompetently staffed. Seriously, some of those nurses . . . We take what we can get, I guess. But if this year's class is anything like the previous one . . ."

Abruptly, Madeleine thought of Iaris, of that desk in the lonely room, and orderlies holding her, strapping her to the bed. Her hands were shaking. She stared at them, stilled their tremor.

"Are you all right?" Aragon asked.

"Aragon," Emmanuelle said, gently. "You know—"

"Interference can go rot," Aragon said. "I'm not House." He sat down on the parapet by her side. "It's the essence, isn't it?"

The smell of it; the feel of it, caked on her hands and arms. Asmodeus's lips on hers, with no trace of desire or lust, the magic rising within her, filling her. And, further away, that night in House Hawthorn, the inescapable memory of standing still while everything she had ever known erupted in blood-slicked slaughter . . . She struggled to speak, but no words would come.

"I think he's right," she said, numbly. "I've never left the House."

Aragon was quick on the uptake. "Hawthorn? You've returned to it. That doesn't mean your time here was meaningless."

Oris. Isabelle. Elphon. The dead, all lost to her.

"He is right, though," Emmanuelle said, gently. "You need to walk away."

From Silverspires? From Hawthorn, twenty years ago? She didn't know. She looked, again, at the buildings that had been her life for decades. At two friends who now—for all their desire to help—were strangers with whom she wasn't meant to speak.

"All Houses are the same," Aragon said. He shook his head. "Hawthorn or Silverspires or Harrier. None are gentler or kinder."

She was going to say something about Asmodeus, about Selene, and then she remembered that Selene had cast her out without a single regret.

"You can't afford to be kind," Aragon said. "Selene understands ruthlessness."

Emmanuelle looked as though she was going to say something, but changed her mind. "She's had to learn," she said, at last.

And Madeleine, of course, would never learn, but was it such a bad thing? In her mind, the link to Hawthorn burned, slower and quieter than it had been, or was it simply that she was used to it now? "I have to go," she said. "Thank you."

Aragon snorted. "Don't even mention it."

"I'm sorry," Emmanuelle said.

What was there to be sorry for, other than for herself? As she left, Madeleine looked at the banyan tree that now choked Notre-Dame; at the buildings, ruined by fire and war spells and constricted by roots.

She'd never left the House. The House of Hawthorn; because she knew, now, that House Silverspires was forever behind her.

MADELEINE found Elphon in one of the bars that bordered the docks. He was sitting alone at one of the rough wooden tables, watching the dockers chat among themselves in Annamite. He smiled when he saw her, but it was a wan expression, utterly devoid of joy.

"Managed to get away?"

Madeleine's tracker disk pulsed on her skin; and the link to the House—Asmodeus's presence—was still as strong as ever. "In a fashion," she said, hating the hoarseness in her voice.

"I worried about you."

Elphon shrugged. He wore a worker's faded blue *bourgeron* and a cap, and coarse cotton trousers; he looked much as he always did, oval face, sharp cheekbones, eyebrows creased in mild concern. It was Madeleine who felt stretched and hollowed out, somehow made different by her imprisonment in the dragon kingdom. "I followed Ghislaine," he said.

"Here?"

Elphon rose, grabbing his coat from the chair. "Come."

They walked in silence to a building at the end of the docks, a makeshift assemblage of corroded sheet metal and patched-up wood. The dockers and the House guards thinned: no ships there, no stacks of crates or unstable cranes unloading barges. If it was a warehouse, it was one of the run-down, broken, or booby-trapped ones.

The single, bored Senegalese at the entrance of the building nodded at Elphon. "You again," she said.

Elphon bowed, an intricate and terribly old-fashioned gesture that brought an amused smile to the woman's face. "Mind if I show my friend?"

The woman shrugged. "It's not like she's going anywhere."

The building wasn't heated. Madeleine imagined many Houseless ones weren't, but in this case it was clearly deliberate, because all it contained was bunk beds with bodies on their lower beds. For a moment she was back in Yen Oanh's house of death, gagging on the putrid smell of angel essence and dying dragons. And then it passed, and she saw that the beds all held corpses. The smell in the air was the normal one of decay: familiar and comforting, the same background to her days as House Silverspires' alchemist, stripping corpses for magic and spells.

"The morgue?" she asked.

Behind her, the Senegalese said, in the accents of the street, "The docks are a dangerous place to be. People drown, or are blown up on protective spells. Or something else. If no one comes to claim them . . ."

Elphon was already headed to a bunk at the back of the room. "Here," he said.

It was a woman of indeterminate age, with long, fair hair, and swarthy skin. Death hadn't been kind to her; or rather, what had happened before death had not been kind. Bruises, and—Madeleine reached out for gloves, stopped herself—where would she find gloves, here?—and simply laid her hand on the chest, in the odd concavity above the midriff. "Broken ribs," she said.

Elphon nodded.

"That's Ghislaine." The wrist was bare, with the dragonfly and water lily tattoo Clothilde had shown them. There was a circular, charred imprint on her chest. Madeleine pulled out the tracker disk she had on her, laid it against the imprint. No wonder Asmodeus or Clothilde hadn't been able to track her. If the imprint was any indication, the disk was ashes by now, its spell incinerated.

"As you can see." Elphon sat on one of the empty bunks, unaware or uncaring that it had, in all probability, held a corpse in the recent past.

"How did you find her?"

Elphon's smile was tired. "I asked questions. Of a lot of people. Dragons. Houseless. Dockers. She was trying to hide, but I fear she made quite an impression, all the same."

"And someone found her, in the end." Madeleine's fingers itched for a sheet; for something they could draw over the wreck of the body, to preserve whatever little dignity was left. She hadn't known Ghislaine at all, but it didn't seem fair that she'd lie unclaimed and unmourned, without the House being even aware that she had died.

"You . . ." Madeleine struggled to speak. "You told me not to bring Clothilde."

"And you didn't."

"Why?"

Elphon sighed. "Because a House dumped the body here."

"A House—?"

"Astragale."

House Astragale? It meant nothing to Madeleine: one of the large suburban Houses, making its fortune on the small shipping traffic they could manage to get through to Paris.

"It's been a busy week on the docks," Elphon said. "Dependents of House Astragale have been hanging around, both here and in la Goutte d'Or. Ostensibly looking for a dependent who stole from them. Except that the description they gave was Ghislaine's."

And they'd found her. And dumped her again? "They wanted her dead."

Elphon's smile was bitter. "Yes. Once they were sure of that . . . they didn't burden themselves with a body."

"I still don't understand what this has to do with Clothilde."

"No," Elphon said. "You haven't been in the House long enough." He sighed, an expression that tugged at Madeleine's heart, so, so familiar, a remnant of a time long gone by. "Do you remember Ciseis?"

"Lord Uphir's heir."

"Yes. She was meant to die in the coup that took Hawthorn from him, but she escaped."

It was ancient history, the coup that had torn her life apart. But she'd never paused to consider its politics, and hadn't been in Hawthorn in the aftermath: she'd already found refuge in House Silverspires. "And was hunted down and killed?"

Elphon's face was grim. "We wouldn't be talking if that were the case. No. She fled, and asked for asylum within another House, where Lord Asmodeus couldn't hope to touch her without reigniting a war."

"Astragale," Madeleine breathed, slowly. "I still don't see what Clothilde has to do with any of this."

"Clothilde was a loyalist."

"So were you!"

His expression was unamused. "Yes. And I died. I don't remember anything."

Not that long, endless night where thugs with orange scarves had roamed the House, killing all those who opposed them; bursting into the servants' quarters, slashing and stabbing while Madeleine stood shock-still, trying to make sense of it all. Not Madeleine, or anything they'd shared, or the moment of his death, when the light had fled his body, and Madeleine had known that she had lost him forever. "No," Madeleine said. Her heart felt as though it were going to burst in her chest. She wanted angel essence; just a whiff of it, something, anything, to keep the pain at bay. "You don't remember."

Elphon's face didn't move. "Sometimes, it's best to forget." His voice was almost gentle. "The past is past, and there is no salvation to be found in rehashing old grievances."

Asmodeus's mocking voice, a long time ago. *You never left, Madeleine, did you? Always crawling away from the wreck of the House, never leaving the shadow of the past.*

And where did that leave her now, trying to protect a House that had changed beyond recognition, a House now run by the Fallen who had turned every good memory of it into ashes?

She didn't have answers.

"You . . ." Madeleine shook her head. "You think Ciseis is up to something. And Clothilde is helping her." She looked, again, at the corpse, at the bruises, the broken bones, the burn on the chest. How much pain had Ghislaine been in, at the end?

Justice. That was something she could understand; and the rest, all the weight of it, all the unappraised consequences, could wait.

"I don't know," Elphon said. "Samariel plucked her from the cells, twenty years ago. Insisted to Lord Asmodeus that she would be loyal. As I said, I was dead, so I don't really know what happened. But Samariel is dead now, and something or someone prevented Ghislaine from returning to House Hawthorn."

The prospect of being caught by Clothilde?

More than that. "Someone beat Ghislaine up. To silence her? House Astragale said they stole something from them."

"Yes," Elphon said. "But it might have been a convenient excuse. I don't know."

Madeleine touched Ghislaine's body again. How long had it been in the morgue? It was cold outside, and she'd hardly decayed. One, two days? "I can find out where she died," she said, slowly. "Maybe there'll be something there that can help us."

Elphon nodded. "Do you need anything from me?"

"I brought some things." Madeleine no longer carried the large leather bag that had held her alchemical supplies—Asmodeus had taken it from her, before he took her back into Hawthorn—but her small green bag held a charged mirror. She broke the clasp, inhaled the magic within. Thank God, it wasn't Asmodeus who had infused it. The warmth that ran through her had no trace or characteristic of him, no distant amusement, nor that feeling of being taken over by a puppet master. But, equally, no searing warmth spreading to her entire body; no familiar comfort, no giddy rush from angel essence.

Her vision swam, showed her the world with new underpinnings. Or would have, if there had been any magic to see. But here, among the House-less, there was nothing to find: not even Ghislaine's link to the House, long since scattered and gone.

She knelt down, and traced a circle around Ghislaine, marking each cardinal direction with the flat of her hand and whispering the words of a spell. The magic within her sloshed, gently, showing her every wound on the body, every bruise, every bone that had cracked. Ghislaine had not died easily, or fast.

Then, bracing herself, Madeleine rose and came to stand by the body again, and said the final words of the spell.

There was pain, a low, diffuse thing that was almost background, and a gaping maw of emptiness within her, the place where the link to the House had been, before it was burned from her—before she tried to cross the wall, to walk into the grove and straight back into Hawthorn—and found herself facing only death, and ghosts, and a burning feeling as they reached for her, feeding on everything magical until nothing remained.

There was darkness, and cold, and the smell of jasmine rice. A woman's voice, softly speaking, asking insistent questions, oblivious to the rising numbness in her midriff, and the darkness getting deeper and deeper, and the rising fear, the sharp realization that oblivion beckoned, without any kind of recourse . . .

Madeleine came to with tears streaming from her face, struggling to breathe, her hands gripping the edge of the bed. So alone. Ghislaine had been so alone, at the end, so aware that her House was as unattainable as a promise of Heaven.

Madeleine had lost a link to a House once, but she hadn't been wounded and dying.

Elphon was waiting patiently for her. She raised a hand, touched the body. A thin thread of light shimmered into existence for a split second, streaking out of the warehouse, and straight into la Goutte d'Or, and into a building, and a flat, the images burning themselves into Madeleine's mind.

"Let's go," Madeleine said. She felt full. Bursting with nightmares and agony, and things that weren't hers, and God knew she had enough un-pleasant memories as it was.

They came out of the warehouse under the bored eye of the guard. There appeared to be some kind of a commotion: the dockworkers were all gathered by the edge of the basin, staring at the water.

What—?

"Madeleine." Elphon's voice was grave. "Look."

On the surface of the basin, drawing a long, curved line toward the Saint-Martin Canal and the Seine, were dozens—hundreds—of sodden white flowers, all wilted and bruised, and flecked with dirt—no, not dirt, but the same grayish blue mold that had overtaken everything in the dragon kingdom.

"Hawthorn," she whispered, trying to make sense of it all. "They're hawthorn flowers. And they're all dying."

PAIN came and went, in waves that seemed to grow no closer. At first Françoise managed to pace up and down in the small space, while Berith sat in the armchair watching her with burning eyes. Then she stopped every few steps, riding a wave of stillness that seemed to cut the breath from both her and the baby. And then she was the one in the armchair, breathing in searing air, struggling to speak.

She didn't need to see Berith's pale face, or Aunt Ha's, to know that it wasn't going well.

"Midwife Thuy—"

"We've sent for her," Aunt Ha said. She and the other mothers had fanned around the armchair, their meager score of advice long since exhausted. The flat was overcrowded, but for once, Françoise didn't mind.

"She's coming," Berith said, but her face said otherwise.

Françoise waited for the contraction to pass, and said, stubbornly, "Tell me."

"There's another delivery," Aunt Ha said. "And it's not going well at all. She said she's doing all she can."

"I see," Françoise said. She knew the meaning of that: knew better than to hope.

"I've sent for Philippe. I didn't know what else to do," Berith said. "But—"

But it hadn't been their bargain. He didn't have to come, didn't have any interest in helping her, now that Berith had given him what he wanted. . . .

Françoise leaned against the back of the armchair. There had to be a position that was comfortable. There had to be something to stave off the pain, which had been growing until it was unbearable, except that it kept changing and growing again. And, each time, between each contraction, a long, drawn-out moment when she forgot, briefly, how bad the pain had been when it had seized her.

No words for it, anymore.

It could last hours, Aunt Ha had said, and one of the other mothers—whose name Françoise couldn't remember—had nodded, speaking of two days' labor.

Berith's hands were clenched, so tightly the thin, skeletal fingers had gone white. "We'll find someone. We have to."

Great. "It'll be fine," Françoise said, with a confidence she didn't feel.

Aunt Ha knelt by her other side. "It's not breech," she said. "Can I?"

Françoise nodded. At length, Aunt Ha stepped back. "You're barely open."

"It's her first," Nicolas's mother—Aunt Linh—said.

Aunt Ha's grimace was eloquent. It had been hours already, hadn't it?

Françoise gritted her teeth, and thought of the baby. She'd lit some incense on the makeshift altar, the smell of it like a prayer. "Heart's desires," she said, stifling a bitter laugh. "Useless." She sucked in a breath as another contraction hit; waited for the pain to recede, if there was such a thing, anymore.

"Of course," Berith said. "Otherwise we wouldn't be here, would we?"

Still no midwife and no Philippe. But even if anyone were there, could they have made a difference?

It hurt—it hurt so much, to stay awake. If she could move, but no, moving wouldn't make a difference, either, not to what was constricting her breath, turning her entire body as hard as stone. She . . . she needed it to be over, one way or the other.

The door opened. Another one of the mothers, arriving late?

Berith's hand slipped from hers. The Fallen rose, slowly, deliberately, silence filling the room in her wake. Philippe?

But, when Françoise managed to turn enough to look at the open door, it wasn't Philippe she saw, but Asmodeus, his lean form filling the narrow frame of the door, light glinting on the temples of his glasses.

"You." Berith's voice was shaking. "You . . ."

Asmodeus glanced at the mothers spread around the armchair. "Out," he said. "Everyone."

"You can't—," Aunt Ha started. Magic, cold and merciless, rose in the room like a winter wind.

"You're of no use here," Asmodeus said. "Now, do I have to ask again?"

They scattered like scared children, and now it was just the three of them. Couldn't blame them. Françoise was surprised they'd come at all, standing by her in spite of their disapproval. Probably worried that Olympe would glare at them, if Olympe did come back from wherever she had vanished. No. That was uncharitable, and unworthy.

Another contraction. She dug her fingers deeper into the armchair, waiting for it to pass. Asmodeus and Berith were still staring at each other.

"You forgot," Asmodeus said. "It's still there." His voice was toneless.

"The link?" Berith shook her head. "I hadn't forgotten. I thought . . ."

"That I couldn't feel it anymore?"

"That you didn't care anymore." Berith's voice was sharp.

Asmodeus didn't speak for a while. At length, he said, rubbing a hand against his chest as if he expected it to hurt, "I was badly wounded. Almost died, in fact. That made me . . . reconsider." He walked into the flat, knelt by the armchair. The sweetness of orange blossom filled Françoise's nostrils, and for a brief moment, she was back in the House of Hawthorn, watching him burn Berith's letter and never flinch. "How close are they?"

Françoise stared at him, trying to make sense of what he said.

"The contractions," Asmodeus said. His voice didn't change tone.

"You . . . ?" Berith closed the door. "How much do you know about childbirth?"

His smile was sharp, ironic. "How much do *you* know?"

"Asmodeus. That works on other people. Not on me. Can we drop the pretense, please?"

"I led the Court of Birth in Hawthorn, once. I've helped in the hospital. And I know how bodies work." He smiled, again.

"From taking them apart? I'd feel a lot better if you'd brought an actual doctor," Berith said.

"Not . . . very reassuring," Françoise managed, between gritted teeth.

"You forget," Asmodeus said. "I had no way of knowing what was going on. Just that you were in some distress."

"And you just decided to leave the House on your own?"

"I have a squad of bodyguards downstairs." Asmodeus sounded amused. "I'm not that careless."

"Just unwise."

His expression wavered, became younger and more vulnerable, and Françoise knew with certainty that the people who had seen that expression were either trustworthy or dead. "It wouldn't be the first unwise thing I've done today."

"You're slipping." Berith's hand reached for Françoise's, held it.

"And you're wandering." He turned, again, to Françoise. "How far apart?"

"Three minutes or so." Françoise grimaced. "Aunt Ha—said—it wasn't progressing."

"No." Asmodeus shook his head, and spoke to Berith again. "She's been saturated with your magic throughout her pregnancy. Have you never dealt with the children of magicians or essence addicts? Births like that have to be helped along. That's what the Court of Birth is for."

"It's premature," Berith said.

His face didn't move. "Doesn't change a thing. Except for the risk of infection. And . . ." He looked at Françoise for a while.

"Not—a fool," she said through clenched teeth. "The baby's not ready." Neither the baby nor her. She was going to give birth without a doctor or a midwife in attendance, in a grimy cold room that was far from sterile; pushing out a premature baby, in a labor that didn't seem to progress. Exhaustion was going to fell her; and if it didn't, infection or blood loss would. And all she had, to make sure she and the baby survived, were two Fallen—two powerful Fallen, but Fallen magic couldn't heal, couldn't even stave off death. . . .

Ancestors, it was going to take a miracle, or several, for this to end well.

"Eight months." Berith's voice was flat.

"Good enough. Come here." Asmodeus was talking to Berith in a low voice. She couldn't hear anything they were saying, but Berith nodded, from time to time. Another contraction, another wave of pain, the baby stilling within her, everything becoming unbearably sharp, her breath cut off, her belly as hard as rock.

At length—a minute, a quarter hour, an eternity—Berith came back, and knelt by Françoise's side. She was pale, exhausted, looking even more unhealthy than usual. "There's a spell," she said. "I'll spare you the technical details."

Another contraction climbed up Françoise's spine. "Do."

"We'll . . . force it out."

"We?"

"It requires a powerful magic user, usually," Asmodeus said. "In a hospital, with doctors and nurses in attendance. But moving you now is out of the question."

So two magic users, for safety. Berith was fine, but the thought of Asmodeus helping . . . What was she doing, quibbling over gifts? "All right." She took a deep breath. Tried to; all she could feel was the weight of the baby within her, lodged so deep it couldn't be excised.

"You'll need to move," Berith said. "Lie down on the mattress, if you can." She held out a hand.

The mattress the woman had died on. No. She wasn't going to be morbid, not now.

Françoise pulled herself out of the chair—everything was happening in slow, short bursts, with pauses when the pain gripped her, stilling everything—leaned on Berith's arm, tottering toward the mattress. The room smelled, faintly, of myrrh and citrus.

She lay down, sinking into the bed's worn softness—that smell again, overwhelming, the mattress rising around her, a suffocating hold she couldn't get out of. She thrashed, making a soft, keening sound.

"It'll be all right," Berith said, gently, holding her down. Her arms were as hard as hewn stone; nothing of weakness or of ill health in her now. Light streamed from her, driving the shadows of early evening from the room; and an answering light, too, from Asmodeus, as he knelt on the other side, with the faint, translucent shadow of wings at his back, their pinions touching Berith's brown, luminous hair.

Françoise tried to speak, but pain gripped her again, inescapable. "Please," she whispered.

"It'll be fine," Berith said, her hands pulling away layers of cloth. Cold on her skin, and then Berith's fingers on her belly, driving it all away.

"It will hurt. Births are always painful." Asmodeus's hands rested on her chest, above the heart. She tried to move, found she couldn't. Just pain now, and fire in her lungs, everything too close together for her to breathe.

Ancestors . . .

The door opened again—Asmodeus's voice, raised in something close to anger: "I told you to go away."

Françoise struggled to raise her head, caught a glimpse of Aunt Ha, standing unmoving in the narrow entrance. "I may not be a magician, but I've helped at births. You're not doctors, or midwives. What will you do if something goes wrong?"

"Asmodeus." Berith's voice was sharp. "Come on in, Elder Aunt. I'm sorry about the unpleasantness."

A silence. Their hands, pressing her down, holding her against the bed, holding the baby down as she gasped for breath.

"Now?" Berith asked.

"Now."

Fallen magic was supposed to be like fire, like a drug coursing through your entire body. It was . . . She was supposed to believe she could do anything, take on anyone. It wasn't supposed to *hurt*. Wasn't supposed to— everything in her body spasmed and buckled, and the pain of contractions spread from her belly and back to her arms, to her hands.

Again, and again—it was becoming the rhythm of her birthing pains. Pushing further, harder. Her throat was raw from screaming. Her hands— she tried to move, but she couldn't seem to control anything.

The ceiling swam and blurred in her field of vision; not for long, because someone—Berith—slapped her. "Stay awake, Françoise. Please."

"If you sleep, the baby dies."

"Has anybody told you you're the least reassuring presence to have around?" Berith's voice, drifting in and out of focus; her touch on Françoise's belly, and the magic coming in endless, relentless waves, everything distant and receding further and further.

"She doesn't need lies. Not now. Stay awake."

More pain. More . . . She had blood in her mouth. Must have bitten her tongue. Must have—

She slid, inexorably, into a world of blurred interstices, of fiery hands, of gasping breaths, flopping limbs. Pain after pain after pain. Wave after wave after wave. Magic and orange blossom, and myrrh. Darkness stealing across the flat, and cold, and an unbearable warmth within her that she couldn't expel.

"Françoise. You have to push. Now."

She was a puppet in the puppeteers' hands, except it shouldn't have hurt so much. She tried to push, but nothing was moving; she could feel nothing. . . .

"Again."

Their touch on her, holding her down again. She was tired; so tired, wrung out from pain, and she hadn't even given birth yet.

"Again." And then something tore out of her, an absence she could feel, even as she lay back and let the mattress enfold her—the pain didn't stop, or the magic.

Aunt Ha said something, but she couldn't hear it. The hands let her go, and for a brief, blessed moment, she was alone in her own skin, and there was no magic, no warmth of spells keeping her energized, just a familiar, almost comforting pain.

"Here," Aunt Ha said, holding out something blue and limp, a splayed doll that looked unreal—and then Aunt Ha's hands moved, and it seemed to inflate like a balloon, opening its mouth, its scream tearing at Françoise. "It's a girl."

Let me hold her, she wanted to say. *Let me . . .*

But darkness hovered at the edge of her field of vision, and rose to swallow her whole.

TWENTY
HOUSE ASTRAGALE

LATER, much later, she must have woken up, woozy and delirious, with an unpleasant taste in her mouth—she had a confused memory of Aunt Ha holding the cold rim of a glass against her lips, telling her she had to drink; and of hands on her belly, pushing hard, but everything was uncertain and fuzzy.

The baby was wedged against her, suckling at her breast. A girl. Camille, the name she and Berith had picked before the birth.

Camille.

Berith and Asmodeus were talking in low tones, their silhouettes wavering in and out of focus. Slowly, painfully, Françoise managed to raise a hand, stroking Camille's back.

"She might have bled to death."

"I know. If Aunt Ha hadn't been here for the afterbirth . . ." A heaviness in Berith's voice. Françoise wanted to hug her, but she was too far away and couldn't move.

"You place too much value in mortals." It was said gently, almost fondly.

"And you, not enough."

"As befits a House-bound." Again, amusement and fondness in Asmodeus's voice. She hadn't thought—they'd been close, but she hadn't thought they would ever talk to each other that way.

"You came for the baby, didn't you?"

"You malign me."

"Bathed in Fallen magic. She'd be such a fine recruit for Hawthorn, wouldn't she? Perhaps even that rarest of things, a mortal who's a natural at magic?"

"She's yours," Asmodeus said, simply.

"Not by blood."

"You know what I mean." His voice was grave. "Borne by your partner, gestated with your magic, raised by you. Your child, insofar as Fallen can ever have children."

"And there's value in that?"

"If you won't leave the flat . . ."

"Asmodeus. I can't."

"You mean you won't pay the price to. That's a very different thing." A pause. "You're not safe here. You know you're not."

"I'm not playing your games anymore."

"Those games are what's keeping you alive." Again, that gentle, quiet tone.

Françoise ought to have felt something. Fear, or worry, or pity; but she couldn't seem to focus, except that they both sounded as drained as she was, wrung out, their voices flat with exhaustion.

A silence. Then, "Come to Hawthorn. You'll be protected in the House, from Astragale or whoever else gets it into their heads to attack you. And . . . I have no equal, there. Not since Samariel . . ."

"Oh, Asmodeus." Berith's voice was pitying. "You can resurrect dead Fallen."

"As can you." His voice was joyless. "You know the price of that spell. He would come back without any memory of what he was, of what he—" A pause. "—of whom he loved."

"Everything to do, all over again?" Berith's voice would have been mocking if it hadn't been so flat. "I'm sorry."

"Don't be."

The baby nestled against Françoise, an odd, electrifying warmth in the breast she was suckling, and she was drifting off into sleep, their voices receding once more into insignificance.

WHEN she woke up again, struggling to throw off the fatigue and drowsiness, she was no longer lying on the mattress, but being carried, passed from arms to arms—through the frame of the door, the safety of Berith's wards falling away like torn veils.

"Here," Asmodeus said, his voice coming from very far away. "Gently, or you'll hurt her."

What—?

Whoever was now holding her was carrying her downstairs. As if in a dream, she saw the moldy, cracked ceiling of the staircase pass overhead, felt the slow rhythm of her captor, descending step after step. She tried to twist away, but she couldn't move: nothing seemed to obey her, not her legs, not her arms.

She twisted again, a weak, uncontrolled gesture that sent her arms flailing against her captor's chest.

"Don't struggle," Asmodeus said.

He was walking by her captor's side—bodyguards, he'd come with bodyguards. One of them was carrying her; and Asmodeus in turn carried Camille in his arms, wrapped in a swaddling cloth, and further in the folds of his swallowtail jacket. The baby slept on, blissfully unaware.

"You. You can't." The words came out through parched, cracked lips. "Berith—"

"Berith is asleep. Exhausted from helping you give birth. I do apologize." His voice was grave; he walked slowly, with nothing like the easy grace he'd moved with earlier. "But with both of you gone, she will have no choice but to leave the flat."

"You. You want her weak. You want to kill her."

She'd expected sarcasm or irony, but he merely looked at her, his face creased in a mildly annoyed frown. "Of course not. She's my Fallsister. I want her in Hawthorn, where she'll be safe. And the same goes for you."

We're safe here, Françoise wanted to say, but the words seemed to have turned to smoke in her throat.

"You must realize that your situation is untenable. House Astragale grows bolder, and sooner or later, they'll find a way in." He smiled, and it was dark and unamused. "As I said, I apologize. Berith has always been too stubborn for her own good."

He. He wanted Berith in Hawthorn. For company. For comradeship. He'd said as much earlier, and of course he was never going to take no for an answer.

"You can't . . ." Françoise tried to move again, to twist out of the bodyguard's grip, but she was out of breath already, the buildings around the courtyard bending and twisting above her, as if they were going to crush her.

"Of course I can." Asmodeus's face was pale, and three streaks of blood crossed his chest, pearling up through his shirt.

She couldn't breathe, could only call on the embers of magic within her. All of Berith's protections had been stripped from her, and her partner slept, exhausted, above them, unaware of what was going on. Within Françoise, there was nothing but mild warmth, dying out.

A bodyguard carrying her, and others no doubt waiting for them in the street. And Asmodeus, worn-out and diminished, was still a Fallen, with access to magic that she couldn't hope to match.

It was no good. She tried to call on magic, on something, on anything, but there was nothing left in her but emptiness, and the weight of exhaustion, drawing all the strength from her limbs.

No no no.

PHILIPPE, coming back to the flat, pushed the door with the song of the dead in his ears, and paused when his feet slid on something unexpected. A distraction. He didn't need one, couldn't afford one at the moment. He was close. He could almost taste it. He was missing just one thing, a piece that would make it all come together, a final knot that would tie together all the disparate threads of magic and breach the boundary between the living and the dead.

So close . . .

In the flat, Morningstar sat in the chair, barely visible behind the cluster of dead, featureless faces, though the shape of his sword pierced even the wall of ghosts. *Embracing power at last. Good.*

Philippe took one step inside. The thing under his shoes shifted, and sent a spike of magic arcing through his body, a jolt that was a wake-up call. The ghosts vanished like popped soap bubbles. Morningstar wavered and disappeared, and then it was just him in a cold, dark flat.

No. No. He was so close. He needed . . .

He needed to get that thing away from him. He bent down, and picked it up from the floor: a scrap of paper filled with a pale, blue ink, and the flowing, curly handwriting from a bygone century.

Philippe. Something has gone wrong. She's giving birth early, and the midwife isn't available. Please help, I beg you.

It wasn't signed. It didn't need to be. He exhaled, willing the ghosts to come back. They did not. It was just him and the cold flat, and the message, burned across his field of vision.

She's giving birth.

The baby had been barely eight months along: premature, but not catastrophically so. The squalid flat where Françoise would be giving birth, though—the louse-ridden mattress, the infested kitchen, and the broken window that couldn't keep out the cold . . .

Philippe crossed the blood-spattered floor, his feet smudging, beyond repair, the patterns he'd drawn. No matter; he could always make more. Behind the desk was his doctor's case: he grabbed it, and ran for the door.

At this early hour of the morning, the streets were filling up with laborers and children. The lone bakery was doing brisk trade. Aunt Vy was at the counter, completely recovered from the fever that had seized her. She waved at Philippe as he passed by, to remind him she still owed him baguettes and *pains au lait*. Philippe nodded, and ran on.

The air was saturated with the sharp, biting smell of winter. The distant peal of church bells rang in the streets, calling to morning prayers. How long ago had that message been slipped under his door? There'd been no date or anything, and he couldn't remember how long he'd been away, couldn't count the days or nights since Olympe had visited him.

He was so focused on running toward the flat that he didn't pay attention to what lay ahead of him, and, late, far too late, saw the colors of Hawthorn, the bodyguard carrying a limp, exhausted Françoise away from the door, and Asmodeus, following a step behind with a newborn in his arms.

They stopped, stared at him. The cold wind bit into the myriad cuts on his arms. His hands opened, dropped the case. He felt alone, and naked, and without recourse.

"You can't take them," Philippe said.

Silence. There were *khi* currents in the street: water from the snow on the cobblestones, earth, and a hint of scorching fire from Berith's flat. Philippe drew everything he could to him, fashioning the threads into a lash.

"Philippe." Françoise raised her head, stared at him. Her face was dark, her eyes bruised-looking.

She shouldn't be up. Not so soon, not in the cold—and not the baby, either.

"Leave her alone," he said. And, before anyone could speak, drew the lash across the ground, toppling bodyguard after bodyguard.

Françoise moved then. Her elbow dug into the chest of the woman holding her. As they parted, Philippe tumbled that bodyguard, too, but Françoise was already hurtling toward Asmodeus. She'd snatched the baby from his grip before he'd even moved—how could he be so slow? And then she was running, grabbing Philippe's hand as she passed.

He followed her, still trying to process it all. This was madness. They couldn't stand against Hawthorn. Ancestors' sake, they couldn't stand against Asmodeus. Philippe had barely managed that the last time, pumped full of Fallen magic, and even then Asmodeus had been only mildly interested; not furious at being thwarted.

He had little trouble keeping up with her: she was running on sheer desperation, her breath frosting in the air. Street after street after street, people staring at them, and then at what was behind them, though Philippe daren't look back.

"They won't stay down forever," Philippe said. He was about to suggest

Françoise hand him the baby, took one look at the harsh set of her face, and decided not to. "I don't know where you planned to go."

Françoise shook her head. "Away." Her breath came fogged, heavy. "Has—to—be—some—help—"

From whom? Olympe? But she wasn't headed toward Olympe's flat, or anywhere in la Goutte d'Or where other Annamites congregated. Rather, she was making her slow, painful way out of the neighborhood. "You need to stop," Philippe said. "There's nothing out there." Just the ruined Gare du Nord and Gare de l'Est, and, farther on, la Villette Basin, and the Saint-Martin Canal, leading to the dark and murky waters of the Seine.

They stopped, finally, on a bridge—rue de Jessaint, Philippe saw, with his heart sinking. Below them were the tracks, and the wrecked trains, and on the cobblestones was the charred circle he'd escaped from.

Françoise leaned against the railings, breathing heavily. "Bastard," she whispered. She clasped the baby to her chest. "Not going anywhere."

All Philippe could see was *khi* metal and earth, coming from the trains below them. They were weak, not replenished since he'd drawn on them. Rue de Jessaint was a small side street over bundles of tracks, of little interest to anyone.

Footsteps, on the bridge. Asmodeus was walking toward them. No bodyguards that Philippe could see—only the shadow of wings at the Fallen's back, limning him into sharp contrast, light glinting on his glasses, on the paleness of his face. His jacket was bloodied: three gashes across the cloth. Philippe didn't remember Françoise touching him, other than snatching the baby from him.

"This isn't your fight," Asmodeus said, as he drew near. The stones started to shake under Philippe; he sent earth into them, to steady them. Light streamed from Asmodeus, pallid and wan, the radiance of a spent winter sun. "I'd advise you to leave while you still can."

Philippe's hands had clenched into fists, his fingers curled around the scars Asmodeus had given him, once. "You were kidnapping them."

"Merely giving Berith an incentive to come to Hawthorn." Asmodeus smiled. He gestured, and the railings twisted around Françoise, holding her in an unbreakable embrace. "She will understand."

The cobblestones buckled again under Philippe, sending him sprawling to the ground. He pulled himself up, wincing at the pain in his arms. Some of the cuts from the ghosts had reopened.

There were no *khi* currents anywhere. No, not quite true. Earth and metal, and a feeble trickling of wood that had pooled on the bridge as the sun had risen. Asmodeus was still walking toward them. Philippe sent a ripple through the *khi* metal, hardening the currents into an impassable wall. Or tried to: Asmodeus frowned, and slowed down, but didn't stop. The light coming from him intensified, throwing Philippe's makeshift weave into sharp contrast.

Philippe turned to Françoise. She was struggling, futilely, against the railings that held her and the baby pinned. The magic Berith had infused in her was all but gone, like dying embers, and there was nothing but a mortal, weary woman who had just given birth.

"You shouldn't move," Asmodeus said, gravely. "Your friend—the Annamite woman—she had to give you extract of ergot when you started bleeding heavily. You're not healed yet, and you certainly shouldn't be struggling."

"Shut up," Françoise said, her breath hanging in the air, a cloud of vapor in the cold. "Stop acting concerned and friendly. You have no right. Not after this."

The railings had fused to each other, forming an embrace of black metal that trapped Françoise. It wasn't tight, but she couldn't get out.

"I hadn't even started," Asmodeus said, mildly. He *pushed*. Philippe's weave shattered, with a sound like thunder, the threads of *khi* earth snapping and writhing like beheaded snakes.

Philippe's hands were still on the twisted iron railings. Metal. Fire overcame metal. He needed to find fire. A blazing midday sun. A summer day. The heat from dry, cracked earth. None of that here.

Asmodeus was still walking, straight toward them. No fire. He'd worry about that later. He tried to gather some threads of metal, to disturb the cobblestones under Asmodeus's footsteps, but it was too late. Asmodeus's hands seized him, threw him away. "I told you not to get involved," he said.

Philippe struggled to rise, but magic held him pinned to the ground, invisible bonds that tightened around him, constricting like the coils of a snake. Footsteps, and Asmodeus, standing over him. "I have no patience left. And you, I'm afraid, have no time." The bonds tightened around Philippe, slowly crushing skin and bones.

Far, far away, a burst of magic, the sound of metal tearing—Françoise screaming, "Philippe!"

But the dead were already rising from the hungry earth, lapping at the wounds on his arms—whispering, slowly, carefully, the words of a spell to call them back.

"Come," Asmodeus said to Françoise, and his voice wavered, too, became Morningstar's, singing about power and magic and the cost of ruthlessness.

Another sound: footsteps on the raised street. The coils imprisoning Philippe abruptly released him. He pushed himself upward, dragging the ghosts with him, dripping blood on the cobblestones. His vision swam, showed him the wreck of the station, the white, smothering veil of the dead.

Françoise, standing in the middle of a ruin of bent and torn railings, breathing hard, but not moving, the sea of ghosts parting around her like water scalded by burning metal. Asmodeus, no longer facing her—he turned, his face overshadowed, for a moment, by that of a ghost—to stare not at Philippe, but at the people on the bridge.

"Nemnestra," Françoise whispered.

There were a dozen of them, in unfamiliar House colors, with dark red swallowtail jackets and gold insignia pinned at their throats. They fanned out, like a pack of wolves, across the street. The ghosts gathered around them, but didn't touch them, as if wary. Magic rippled lazily. And Asmodeus took a step back, and another, until he stood with the iron railings at his back.

Françoise looked from them to Philippe, to Asmodeus; and then, pivoting on her heel, ran. Two of the House-bound started after her, only to be stopped by an imperious gesture from the woman—Nemnestra—who led them.

"Let her go. We'll deal with her and her partner later."

"House Astragale." Asmodeus's voice was a lazy drawl, but the ghosts were congregating around him, and Philippe could see the blood dripping from his chest. "I should have known."

"That old sins always come back to haunt you?" Nemnestra gestured. The House-bound split. Two of them made for Philippe, and the rest for Asmodeus, who watched them come with his head cocked.

"No. I was warned against you. But too late, it would seem."

Nemnestra smiled. "What a shame. The Annamite can join the others working on the wall. As for you . . ."

Asmodeus's shoulders were digging into the iron railing. He made no move or spell to defend himself. His face was pale. His voice, though, was unchanged. "You're taking me to see Ciseis?" His smile was the predator's, through and through. "I shall be pleased to see her again."

"I'm sure the pleasure will be mutual. Take him," Nemnestra said, and they closed in like vultures.

IT was a large room, and the food wasn't so bad, although everything, including the sauces, had that curious blandness of Western dishes. Except for the desserts, which were invariably too sweet and harsh on Thuan's tongue. The door, though, opened only on servants bringing and taking food away; and Thuan still didn't know when he would be allowed out, or under what circumstances.

He had the sketching book. The first pages, carefully detached from the rest, were Samariel's still lifes. But he'd never been particularly good at drawing, and demons take him if he allowed himself to fall into the mold Asmodeus had prepared for him.

He took the charcoal, and used it as a calligraphy brush instead, copying down the poems he could remember from Uc Trai and his time in Second Aunt's library—and when he grew bored with that, he composed his own.

Along the path, frost-white reeds and the moon hushed in the
  winter sky
The river stilled, its fragrance smothered beneath oily mirrors
Inside, wings of smoke on clouded mirrors, reaching out to choke the
  soul.

His tutors would have had sharp words, about the quality of it, the awkwardness of classical references, the indifferent verse, the overreliance on similar syllables that created an artificial and awkward rhythm. Still . . . it passed the time.

On the second morning of his imprisonment, the door opened. Thuan was up before he could think, thrusting the sheets of paper behind him—bracing himself for Asmodeus's mocking voice, though he wouldn't have been able to say why.

It was Nadine.

"You?" he began.

She shushed him with a wave of her hand.

"No time," she said. "He's gone from the House, so I went through his office. . . ." Her face was pale, taut. She handed him a thick stack of papers. "Here. It was in the drawer closest to his chair—not locked. He'd been working on it before leaving. You have two hours. They go back after that. They have to."

And then she was gone, the key turned back in the lock, running away before any words could reach his mouth.

Thuan sat down at the desk, and stared, for a while, at the papers. They smelled of Asmodeus, and of lips on his, and a voice whispering "unwise," the same one running through his dreams, the ones that stubbornly refused to turn into nightmares.

Some of them were printed sheets from a book that had fallen apart, their long edges still coated with a residue of glue. They'd been heavily annotated, and the rest were drawings, and writings, all in the same forceful hand, with a quill or a pen that regularly blotted on the rough surface.

A House is, after all, nothing more than a collection of wards, embodied in the person of its head—first and foremost, a territory made manifest by magic. The wards lift it beyond a simple piece of ground or of city, make it something not alive but meaningful, something that lives and dies and grows. And, without a head, there is no House.

That last sentence had been circled, and a couple of words added in the margin: "the grove. Previous heads. Uphir." Thuan turned the page. If it was all like this . . .

What, then, to make of dragon kingdoms? Or, rather, dragon kingdom, as the only other extant one, the Bièvre, didn't survive. Like Houses, they are territories where other rules apply, where water reigns supreme, and dragons and other sea creatures can exist.

Great. A travelogue written by a Frenchman. Well, at least it would be somewhat entertaining, he supposed.

His gaze was drawn to the top of the next page, and stopped.

A dragon kingdom, thus, is in many ways a nascent House, one awaiting only the presence of a strong magic user to make it theirs. And there are precedents of using a dying dependent of a House to shatter its defenses and seize its grounds (see Echaroth and House Montenay).

In today's Paris, it is impossible to do so because Houses have protected themselves against such rituals, but dragon kingdoms have done no such thing, making them summarily vulnerable. The expenditure of power involved, of course, would be staggering. . . .

And, beside that, a series of short phrases written on the paper, so deeply they'd torn it.

Nascent House.
The proper ritual?
They have no dependents, but symbolism is key.
The union of two worlds, and the subsequent death of the old.

And, in small, neat capital letters, the word "dependent," struck through and replaced by "consort," which had been underlined and circled twice.

Nascent House. He couldn't mean. He couldn't— Thuan flipped through more pages, which were formulas and calculations, Asmodeus working through the phases of a spell, adding and subtracting words in an arcane fashion that made little sense to Thuan.

Words of a spell. A spell to kill him. For something that would take fuel from Thuan's death, and tear apart all of the kingdom's defenses, exhaust all of its magic, paving the way for conquest by the House of Hawthorn. It was never going to work. The book had said that the amount of power required made it all but impossible.

With a sinking heart, Thuan remembered the power that had seized him, outside Asmodeus's rooms: an artifact, hidden away somewhere, a fuel source for a large, impossible spell.

The last page, the one Asmodeus had been working on, looked to be the end of the spell—except it was covered in struck-through words. Something had obviously been deeply unsatisfying.

He read it through, slowly, carefully.

When he was done, he piled the sheets of paper by the side of the door for Nadine to take back, and he lay on the bed, staring at nothing.

It was kindness, he supposed, to attempt to modify the spell so that Thuan survived it, somehow. It never worked, because the spell needed Thuan to be weak, to be *dying*, in order to work. Rape, mutilation, lifelong imprisonment, his tongue torn out, his limbs restrained and atrophied, a cornucopia of horrors all weighed up, and regretfully discarded. What kind of mind would work through these, one after another, and never flinch?

His hands were shaking. Death, after all, might be the greater kindness. Except that the choice wasn't his. Had never been his.

A morsel.

To be chewed on, like fish or crab flesh, and, ultimately, dissolved. As the dragon kingdom would dissolve, becoming a mere adjunct to Hawthorn.

He felt betrayed, in a spectacularly foolish way. It wasn't as if he'd been owed anything. It wasn't even as if he hadn't been warned. Asmodeus had told him. But he'd thought—he'd hoped . . .

I like you, dragon prince. More than I should.

But not enough to put his plans aside. No, that was unfair. Did Thuan really want any of the alternatives Asmodeus had explored?

There had to be something he could do, to stop this. His grasp of magical theory was good, but not the equal of a House head's.

The spell, strictly speaking, had already started, from the moment Asmodeus and he had stood together by the ancestors' altar, from the moment the contracts had been signed, when he had become consort. As Asmodeus had said, Thuan was the living link to the dragon kingdom. He was its weakness. He couldn't be sure, but his death, in some way, in any way—even if he stabbed himself with charcoal or pencils, or made a weapon from the metal in the room—would fuel the spell. It would be less elegant or thorough than Asmodeus would want, but still have disastrous effects.

There had to be something. . . . .

He slid, at some point, into a dark, confused sleep, dreaming of vast underwater spaces, and the silhouettes of dragons wrapping themselves around a hawthorn tree—pierced by the thorns and taking on the color and the shape of branches, until there was nothing of them left but a faint and unrecognizable memory.

TWENTY-ONE
INTO BATTLE

THUAN woke with a gasp. Morning filtered through the dark green curtains. Something was wrong. He reached out for the elaborate dressing gown by the side of the bed, wrapped himself in it, feeling very much as though he was putting on a costume designed by someone else: the role of the French gentleman of leisure in some unfamiliar play.

The clock on his bedside table said it was past ten o'clock, but there was no tray by the door, or any sign that anyone had tried to enter. And the papers Nadine had brought him were still there, which meant she hadn't come back, either. Why not?

He sat down on the bed again, and listened. The House should have been full of bustle: servants through the corridors, dependents going on various tasks, the laughter or frustrated tears of children in the gardens. Instead there was . . . nothing. A profound, frightening silence that seemed to extend into every crack of the room and of the wing, as if everything lay smothered under rock.

Thuan looked, for a while, at the *khi* currents in the room. They were stronger, somehow, like caged beasts that had feasted on their neighbors' flesh. The water in particular, the one he could easily read, was at an all-time high. If he didn't know better, he'd have thought the House was flooding.

Things will change, in the House. Soon.

He went into the huge tiled bathroom, immersing himself in a bath, breathing in the smell and coldness of water, a reminder of the distant, beleaguered kingdom. He didn't bother to use the towels, letting the droplets of water dry on his skin. For a moment, as they evaporated, his dragon shape broke through, revealing scales and the shadow of antlers on his head.

He considered, then, what to wear. The robes he'd worn when arriving in the House were familiar, but cumbersome: they were ceremonial clothes, designed to make him look like a rooster. He hadn't packed clothes, because he'd known, even then, that being made a consort was an irreversible break with his role as prince of the dragon kingdom.

Which left the overlarge suit, cut for someone else. Well, at least it wasn't two sizes too small. He had a halfhearted forage for sewing supplies, but of course they wouldn't have left needles or scissors where he could find them. Too dangerous. He could have made a needle by melting and reshaping one of the buttons on the suit with *khi* fire, but it would have been a crude one—ironically, probably good only for stabbing someone, if not very deeply.

Never mind. There were still small things he could do, with careful application of *khi* fire and *khi* water. Sleeves could be cut, albeit not very elegantly. The cloth at the back, over the shoulder blades, could be tightened, and the same at the waist.

When the key turned in the lock, Thuan was sitting in the armchair by the desk, looking over Samariel's sketches. He rose, slowly, carefully, with all the presence his tutors had despaired to ever instill in him.

As he had thought, it wasn't Asmodeus, but Iaris and Sare, and Nadine behind them, her face unreadable. "I've been waiting for you," he said.

Iaris watched him, for a while. "How much of this did you plan?" she asked.

"Plan? I didn't plan anything." Other people—Asmodeus, Nadine's mysterious faction—had planned *around* him. But no longer. "I don't have any idea what's going on. Other than it not being normal."

Iaris stared at him, hard. Thuan, who had, on this front, nothing to hide, stared back. At length she said, grudgingly, "Lord Asmodeus went out late, in something of a hurry. He hasn't come back."

"Surely that's not unusual?" Thuan asked. He didn't move, didn't do anything that would lessen the impression of control and strength that he projected.

"In and of itself, no," Sare said. "But there's something wrong with the link to the House. And . . ." She hesitated and looked at Iaris, who nodded. "There is no path going out of the House."

"I don't understand," Thuan said, mildly.

"There is nothing beyond the gates," Sare said. "The stairways to the quays don't lead to the river, either. Just to a wall. A dark, impenetrable wall."

"A wall?"

"It's hard to describe. You're quite free to take a look at it if you want."

They *were* desperate: adrift, with their only source of certainty removed, and under an attack they couldn't explain. Thuan looked at Nadine, who hadn't said anything. She looked relaxed, for the first time in a long while.

"You mean you want me to take a look at it," Thuan said. "In case I can do something?"

"You're his consort," Iaris said, a touch of impatience in her voice. "You must have some power."

The power of dying. But that wasn't the matter at hand. "Perhaps," Thuan said. "I'm also a prisoner of the House, so you can understand why I'm less than motivated to help." Among other things.

"You resent being stuck in here with us?" Nadine's smile was fierce. "You did spy for the dragon kingdom. That was not exactly loyal."

Was he the only one who could hear the bite in her voice? Iaris didn't appear to take anything amiss, and Sare was too busy looking at every corner of the room, as if she suspected Thuan had booby-trapped it. Which would have been rather pointless.

"Fine," Thuan said. "Let me out, and I'll take a look."

"Of course," Iaris said.

He raised a hand. "I don't mean just so I can see the problem for myself. I mean not being locked in this room anymore."

Iaris grimaced. "I had understood. I could force you, you know. The Court of Persuasion . . ."

". . . would take some time to get results from me," Thuan said. In a way, sparring with Asmodeus had liberated him. He could no longer find any room for fear within him. "And perhaps I can't do magic at all if you start harming me."

"Or perhaps you can." Iaris's voice was mildly amused: it was easy to see where she got her mannerisms from. "But never mind. In the scheme of things, I would rather have you running loose in the House than not know what we're facing."

Intrigue. Treachery. And him, at the center of it all, still struggling to make it come into focus, to understand enough of what was going on to survive. "Show me," he said.

THE gardens were deserted, too: the children sheltering on the steps before the main building of the House, running a subdued game of tag under the watchful eyes of members of the Court of Birth.

Thuan looked up, as they headed toward the Seine. The sky was blue with no trace of clouds or ashes, more disquieting than he'd expected. The air was crisp, cold, his breath hanging in the air. That feeling of something not quite right followed him as Sare pushed through thin, cracked branches, her feet crunching on the debris-strewn gravel.

And then they reached the stairs going down to the quays, and he saw what they'd meant.

There was nothing, where the river should have been. The stairs trailed off halfway through, and the quay had vanished. It was like a mist or a curtain of snow, if snow had been mixed with smoke and cinders. The *khi* currents swirled in front of it, turning back when they reached the wall. That was interesting: he'd expected them to be cut off if this was some kind of obstacle, but it was as if nothing existed beyond that wall.

Thuan didn't go down the stairs. He just stood behind the low stone railing, staring left and right—yes, it stretched on and on, and curved inward, at what he imagined were the boundaries of the House. They were quite neatly cut off from the city. As Nadine had said: not very comforting that he was included in the "them."

On the left side, all the way at the boundary of the House with the streets, something that drew his eye: he couldn't have said what exactly, but for a moment, the mist seemed to part, and he saw the skeletal silhouette of a tree with bloodred fruit, and something hanging from it, far too large to be a fruit.

No. Nonsense. That was just Nadine's stories getting to his head.

Sare, Nadine, and Iaris were waiting for him just a little way off. "What happens if I touch it?" Thuan asked.

Iaris grimaced. "Try."

Great. Moral support. Thuan reached out, cautiously. It was like touching cold stone, if cold stone had been ghostly and allowed his fingers part of the way through, all the warmth of his body absorbed into the endless mist. And a gaping emptiness that threatened to swallow him whole—no, that wasn't it—it was the hungriness, the stillness of *khi* earth; and the slow choking of *khi* metal, laced with something that wasn't either of these elements, wild and uncontrollable, and desperate, the magic of the lost and hungry.

Fallen magic.

Stone, and *khi* elements, and Fallen magic, all woven together. He closed his eyes. Thought, again, of that table where his fate had been decided; the conversation between Second Aunt and Asmodeus.

The khi *elements that choke, that bind, that bury.*

Few things are as absolute as the boundary between life and death.

"The wall," he breathed, aloud. It wasn't the kingdom they'd been trying to cut off. It was Hawthorn.

Near unbreakable, Second Aunt had said.

"Well?" Iaris asked.

"I . . ." Thuan looked at Nadine, who gazed back levelly. She wasn't worried by anything he would do. Which meant that she either trusted him or thought he couldn't break the wall, or both. Both, probably. Nadine was nothing if not methodical. "I don't know. I can look it up, if you give me access to the library. And Asmodeus's office."

Neither Iaris nor Sare looked surprised. He still wasn't going to get used to seeing them on the verge of panic. During all his time in the House, they'd both been cool and competent, and always assured. But, then again, he'd never lived with a link to a House in his head. What would he do if it abruptly went wrong?

What would he do, full stop?

As they left, he inclined his head toward Nadine, making a small gesture with his hands. *We need to talk.*

She smiled back at him, tight and controlled. *Of course.*

PEOPLE stared as Elphon and Madeleine walked deeper into la Goutte d'Or. Thin, starving faces; grimy children running across ill-paved streets; people wrapped in torn, mismatched layers of clothing, carrying heavy loads. The smell of alcohol—absinthe?—wafting from drunks huddled against buildings. Doors falling into ruin, repaired with flimsy wood; windows taped shut with patchworks or oiled papers; buildings where entire walls had collapsed, and where families still thronged, the wail of babies piercing the air like sword strokes: the misery of the Houseless, laid bare for all to see.

No angel essence, no magic: it was all too expensive for anyone here.

And, at the back of her mind, the link to the House, fiery and roiling once more, as if she were in mortal danger again. What was going on? By Elphon's barely concealed grimace, he felt it as well.

The House. The House was in danger.

Elphon asked directions from a young Annamite child, who couldn't have been more than five or six years old, thin and mud-pale, though her belly wasn't puffed up. She looked like a walking skeleton, her wide, almond-shaped eyes taking up all of her face above the sharp cheekbones. "Here," Madeleine said, and gave the child the little money she had in her purse.

She grinned, which should have made her seem younger, but merely made Madeleine want to scoop her up and take her with them, never mind that it was impossible, that the House had no time for her or her ilk. "Thank you, Elder Aunt."

The building they sought was at the intersection of two streets, one going up and one going down. It had this peculiar, eye-watering effect of being crooked. Madeleine couldn't be sure whether that was the case, or if it was simply the difference in elevation. The entrance door was missing, filled with a large piece of wood that wouldn't lie flat against the opening.

Inside, the courtyard was filled with debris, and an odd, sharp smell suffused the place. It took Madeleine a while to realize it was the smell of Annamite cooking, the same as in the dragon kingdom, only poorer and watered down.

Atop the small, claustrophobic stairs, they hammered on the door, and got no answer. "It's tightly warded," Elphon said. "I don't even think we could break through—"

The door opened, on the frowning face of a woman who looked deathly ill. "Yes?"

Elphon sucked in a sharp, noisy breath. "Apologies," he said, bowing lower than Madeleine ever remembered him do. "I didn't know—"

"—that I was Fallen?" The woman looked amused.

She didn't look like a Fallen. Her eyes were sunk into her face, her movements slow and deliberate, as if she could break at any moment, and there was none of the unearthly light that came out at random moments when magic surged through them. "I'm Elphon. This is Madeleine. We're from—"

"House Hawthorn. Yes. I can read coats of arms." She sounded amused again. "I suppose you had better come in."

As she crossed the threshold, Madeleine felt a strong resistance, as if she were pushing back against a wall, and then the Fallen woman gestured, and it lessened.

Inside, it was cramped and small, and the smell of cooking didn't quite disguise the sharper one of blood. The mattress that exuded *that* was still on the ground, and the color of rust, and it was immediately obvious why: in the blue plush armchair that was one of the only furniture pieces in the room, an Annamite woman was breast-feeding a newborn baby.

"I'm Berith, and this is Françoise," the woman said. "The baby is Camille."

Madeleine bowed. Françoise looked deathly tired, too, though no wonder, if the birth had gone badly.

"We're not here for the baby," Elphon said.

Françoise's laugh was low and bitter. She didn't let go of her hold on the baby.

Madeleine said, slowly, "A woman who died here. A while ago. Ghislaine. She was from Hawthorn, though you might have been told she was from House Astragale."

Berith and Françoise looked at each other. They said nothing. At length Françoise got up, handing the baby—who had finished feeding—to Berith, who took her cautiously. Françoise rummaged in a broken-down cupboard until she found a chipped bowl. "Here," she said. "We had two of these. House Astragale took one. They were more interested in this than they were in the body."

Inside were green shards, all too familiar, with that same odd feel to them as the one she'd handled in the dragon kingdom. "Ghislaine came to us gravely wounded," Françoise said. She settled in the armchair again; or collapsed into it, her legs incapable of supporting her for long. "And she died in the night, without saying much that made sense. I'm sorry." She frowned. "She spoke of a rot within the House, something that had been festering for twenty years. I thought she meant Astragale, but it was Hawthorn, wasn't it?"

"You have a graver problem," Berith said, shifting the baby so that Camille's chin rested on her shoulder, and then gingerly patting the child's back. "House Astragale has taken Asmodeus."

It was as if someone had punched Madeleine in the gut. "How—what—"

"Françoise saw it," Berith said. She didn't venture any more information.

The link to the House, as taut as a bowstring. "Elphon—"

Elphon glanced at Madeleine. "I don't know," he said, gravely. "Something is wrong with the House, but . . ."

Berith shrugged. "I don't have any stakes in this. Asmodeus and I parted ways some time ago." She sounded casual. Too casual.

"But Françoise happened to be there when he was kidnapped?" Elphon's laughter was high-pitched, nervous. The same panic Madeleine felt now, rising within her. It was one thing to fear Asmodeus, to know that the House was a dark and unfriendly place, but it was still a House.

"To be fair"—Françoise's voice was sarcastic—"he was trying to kidnap me and Camille."

"I think you'd better explain—," Elphon started.

He never got to finish that sentence. The link to the House flared in Madeleine's thoughts, like a warning that a dependent was in mortal danger, except ten times stronger: a knot of pain in her head that became a red-hot spike. Elphon's face was locked in a grim smile: he felt it, too. It came from outside. The southwest, where the House stood.

Madeleine made for the table, gripped it. The wood, splinters and all, still felt more reassuring than anything within her. It was ebbing away, leaving only a sour aftertaste in her mouth, but what replaced it was wrong.

There was no other word for it. It was as if the tree of thorns in her thoughts, the omnipresence of Asmodeus's amused cruelty, had been replaced by something else. Something that looked right, that even felt right, but that, on closer look, wasn't. Something that . . .

She'd felt it, once before. That gaping emptiness at the heart of her thoughts, a sense that the world had collapsed. "It's not *here*," she whispered. "The House." *Please God, no, not the House. Not again.*

"Houses don't just vanish." Elphon's face was oddly still. Fighting the same panic as she was. "There's something. . . ."

There was. But it wasn't Hawthorn. It wasn't—God help her—it didn't even feel like a House. "We have to go back," she said.

House Astragale. The dragon kingdom. The rot within the House. Clothilde. Someone, or something, had been working against them from within. She thought of the hawthorn flowers, scattered along the basin, of the mold flecked on their petals.

Berith's voice was grave. She said, to Françoise, "I need you to tell me everything that the woman said before dying. What do you remember?"

"Something about a grove and a harvest of bodies. It didn't make a lot of sense. I thought she was delirious," Françoise said.

"She was." Berith shook her head. "But it doesn't mean there was no truth in it."

Françoise said, finally, "Something about an heir, and poison distilled for decades? And a body that would make everything right. I remember that much. Why?"

"The heir." Madeleine clung to the only thing that made sense. It was hard to breathe. It was—if she paused, if she stopped thinking for a moment, it was going to overwhelm her with the sheer *wrongness* of it all. And yes, it was Asmodeus; it was a House that had given her nothing but fear and pain. But she was on the verge of the abyss, and reason didn't help. "Uphir's heir. Ciseis." The woman who would have succeeded Uphir, if Asmodeus hadn't seized the House first. Who had sought sanctuary in House Astragale.

Berith said, slowly, "You reap what you sow. Do you know what the grove is?"

"No." Elphon was taking deep, shaking breaths. "Does it matter?"

"It depends how much the future of Hawthorn matters to you." Berith's voice was amused.

"*I* don't care," Françoise said, abruptly.

Berith shook her head. "Françoise."

"I know." Françoise made a face. "She said they were coming."

Berith rocked the baby gently, one hand supporting the back of the neck. "You can't stay here. We've already had this discussion." Judging by Françoise's closed face, not happily. And, to Madeleine and Elphon: "Neither can you. House Astragale is coming for me. Soon . . ."

Elphon said, "Tell us about the grove. Please."

Berith looked at Françoise. "He's my Fall-brother. I—"

"It's all right." Françoise's tone suggested it wasn't, not quite.

"I don't know everything," Berith said. "But the grove . . . the grove is where Hawthorn lives, and dies. Where heads of Houses die, and where their killers—their successors—take control of the House, if they so choose."

"You mean Ciseis is trying to take Hawthorn?" Elphon said.

"Or ensure Asmodeus no longer has Hawthorn. Or both." Berith leaned against the wall, looking winded and tired. She looked almost human, and not in a good way. "That's where Ciseis will have to take Asmodeus. But you won't find the grove easily."

Elphon's face was a study in horror. "It's stories," he said, slowly. "They're . . ." He shook his head, as if to dislodge a persistent thought. "They're not meant to be true!"

"Of course they are," Berith said. "They always are. You need to get to the grove and stop Ciseis. It's hard to find. But not impossible, if you know what you're looking for."

Madeleine's hands still gripped the table. She tried to think, to process something, anything, through the fog of her thoughts. Ciseis was going to kill Asmodeus. She wasn't going to weep over this, over any of it.

But.

But he had come back for her. Mocking, sarcastic; out of his own self-interest, he had said, looking to set into motion whatever complex plans he'd had for the dragon kingdom and his consort. But still.

As principled as ever, Asmodeus's voice whispered in her mind, but it had none of the usual bite to it. *Do I still have your loyalty?*

She didn't know. She didn't know, not anymore.

THERE was no fast way to get back to Hawthorn. They took an omnibus, and that got bogged down in traffic, and all the while Madeleine could feel the altered link at the back of her mind, could feel it rubbing at her thoughts, sharp as jagged shards of glass. Elphon leaned against the window, staring at nothing. They were jammed in with artisans, and the occasional House dependent, but no one from Hawthorn that she could see. There had to be someone, anyone, from the House, who could help them. . . .

The omnibus dropped them at Pont de Passy, and they walked the rest of the way. But, even as they neared the straight line of the quays, it became obvious what was wrong. Where the House should have been, at the inter-section of Pont de Grenelle and avenue de Versailles, there was nothing. A mist had risen from the river—dark, tinged with greenish reflections—and swallowed everything behind an impenetrable wall.

Madeleine stared at the shards of the halberd, now cutting a line into her hand, and back at the wall.

The boundary between life and death.

"The rebels aren't seceding," she said. "The wall—they built it around Hawthorn."

Footsteps, behind them. The disk against Madeleine's flesh pulsed and twisted, as if it'd been jolted alive.

"Well, well, well." It was Clothilde, coming up the stairway leading down to the quay. She wore a cloak over a flowing dark gray dress with stripes of silver highlighting the narrowness of her chest. Her face still looked smooth and ageless, but her eyes were deep-set, angry. "I thought you two would come back from your little jaunt, at some point."

"You—" Elphon leaped for her. Clothilde didn't even move. She twisted—and, for a moment, something large and dark seemed to accompany the movements of her arms—and Elphon stumbled, and went down on one knee.

"Elphon!" Madeleine was up and running, kneeling by his side. Blood ran from his nose and mouth. His eyes stared at her, slowly focusing on the gray skies above.

Clothilde glared at Madeleine, as if daring her to do something. "No?" she asked, shaking her head. "You're pathetic. Both of you. The dead Fallen, and the essence addict who doesn't know which way to turn. All I have to work with." She cocked her head, looking at the wall. "Well, this is obviously not coming down on this side. We're going to need to tackle its foundations. In the kingdom. Great. I could have done without facing Yen Oanh's little band of rebels."

"You—" Madeleine started, stopped. "Elphon told me—"

"That I was a loyalist? The operative word is 'was,' Madeleine. I'm not a fool. No one wants another three years of purges." Her face was harsh, but her voice dipped, a little, on those last words, as if she was remembering unpleasant memories.

"There'll be purges anyway," Elphon said. He pulled himself out of Madeleine's embrace; stood up, woozily. "Because someone in the House is working with Ciseis and Yen Oanh. And if it's not you . . ."

Clothilde rolled her eyes, as if the comment were too stupid to dignify with an answer. "I'm loyal. Whether that's enough for him . . ." She let the words hang in the air for a while.

"You were Samariel's," Elphon said. He tore up a strip of his shirt, used it to stanch the flow of blood from his nose. It turned a bright, painful red. "Lord Asmodeus will never forgive you for that. But he'll not hold it against you."

"Because he's fair?" Madeleine couldn't help the words. "You forget that he's the one who killed you."

"I haven't." Elphon's voice was weary. "I told you, we can't keep fighting a twenty-year-old war."

Unless, obviously, you were Ciseis. *You reap what you sow,* Berith had said.

"If you two are finished . . ." Clothilde made an imperious gesture toward the steps. "We have a wall to bring down."

TWENTY-TWO
THE RUIN OF LIVES

GOING into the dragon kingdom should have felt familiar, like a taste of the home Philippe had left behind a long time ago: words spoken in Viet, the smells of fish sauce and rice and sea-things; the embrace of *khi* elements, and a magic that was weak and exhausted in the rest of Paris.

How it felt, ultimately, was draining.

His captors locked him in the barnacle-encrusted cabin of an old barge, and left. The wood was smooth, everything saturated with *khi* water, the old, old kind, all claimed by dragons or crabs or other sea creatures.

And, everywhere, there were ghosts. The smell of death, rising around him, a dank, gagging odor that filled his lungs to nausea, and white figures coalescing out of the wood, dripping like pus through the oeil-de-boeuf window, rising from the slick, moldy parquet like miasma.

They spoke to him, once more. The wall between life and death was thick, but it was there; it could be reached; it could be breached. If he could find the missing piece . . .

"You're going mad," Asmodeus said, matter-of-factly.

He was propped up against one of the walls, where they had left him. Blood was soaking through his jacket. His face was pale and bruised, almost alien in its naked hunger—little of the effortless, frightening elegance he always displayed.

"And you're dying," Philippe said, before he could think. Three ghosts were bent over each of his bare arms, featureless faces touching his skin. He could hardly feel the blood they were drawing from him.

"Not yet." Asmodeus's smile was bright and terrible. "To every thing there is a season, and a time to every purpose under the heaven. . . . What did Berith give you?"

He could have sparred, endlessly, with the Fallen, but they were at the end of the road, and there was so little left to either of them. "A promise. That death should have no dominion . . ." The words rose from a deep place in his mind, a memory of some missionary's preaching, somewhere in the Mekong Delta, of a church by a village's communal house, cramped and miserable. . . .

Asmodeus's smile didn't leave his face. "Poisoned gifts. Oh, sister mine. I'm afraid she'll have to fend for herself, eventually, against House Astragale, and the new House Hawthorn." He sounded almost worried. Weary.

Not that it changed anything he had done, or would do if he were free. Philippe stared at the wooden surface under him, soaking up words that slowly coalesced into meaning.

The door opened. The pair that came through them was as unexpected as the one he made with Asmodeus. A dragon in dark orange robes, her head bare, with no cap or insignia of rank, and a Fallen, side by side and with hardly any animosity. The dragon was glaring at Asmodeus with ill-disguised fury, the *khi* currents around her curled into points.

Asmodeus spoke to the Fallen. "Ciseis." His face didn't move. "You have me at a disadvantage."

"As planned." Ciseis was small, slight, with long, flowing hair so fair it was almost white. Her eyes were also pale: a blue like ice or a midday summer's sky. "You'd do the same if our situations were reversed."

"You'd be dead," Asmodeus said. He moved, to curve around his blood-soaked midriff. "Much as I like . . . prolonging some pleasures, I have no desire to see my position challenged."

"Oh, but it is," Ciseis said. "Challenged. Won, even."

Asmodeus said nothing. It was the dragon who spoke. "Vulnerable," she said in a hiss. "If we didn't need you alive—"

"Yen Oanh, I trust that halberd thrust has healed?" Asmodeus grunted, as the *khi* water in the room tightened around him.

"Yours," Yen Oanh said, with a touch of malice, "has not. Because Fallen magic doesn't heal. Can't heal. It's a cancer, gnawing away at the foundations of the world."

Ciseis strode into the room, still keeping a wary distance between her and Asmodeus, and knelt close to Philippe. The ghosts scattered in her wake, briefly, before congregating around her again. He stared at her—tried to, but the weight of the ghosts was bowing him down again, and all he could hear was their whispers. "This one doesn't look like he's going to last much longer."

Yen Oanh snorted. "Mortals are so fragile. Not that it matters much. The wall is almost finished," Yen Oanh said.

"Fair point." Ciseis made a gesture he couldn't see, and he was half dragged, half carried by guards through the door.

Outside, light, layers of shimmering radiance the color of ice. *Khi* water, swirling around him but escaping his grasp; a heart-wrenching drop over the side of the laundry barge. And he felt it, long before he saw it.

It rose step after step from the silt at the bottom of the river, looming over him, the weight of its presence pressing down on Philippe's shoulders like invisible, implacable hands. He flopped in his captors' arms, his eyes streaming with tears: so many ghosts, pressing themselves against a dark, impassable wall the color of jade, the color of blood.

Philippe.

It was Isabelle's voice. There was a hole in the wall, a door that had been left open, and she stood on the threshold, watching him with burning eyes. Behind her was the shadow of Morningstar, the Fallen's fair head ringed with *khi* fire, his sword shining in the darkness—and behind them both, the dark shadow of thorn trees.

"Isabelle." He was on the ground, struggling to breathe under the weight of ghosts, watching Ciseis and Yen Oanh and Asmodeus cross the threshold, and dark, featureless silhouettes scurrying. And then his vision cleared for a moment, and he saw they were Annamites, just like him.

Someone kicked him. "Get up."

Philippe pulled himself up, legs wobbling. A swarm of ghosts came with him, clinging to his skin.

"No scroungers. You work, just like the others."

It was Viet, but drowned out by the song of the ghosts, and his eyes were still on the door, on the fading shape of Isabelle. Workers were carrying bricks of quarried jade, shimmering with *khi* earth and *khi* metal, and slotting them into the opening. He fell in with them, moving mechanically.

There was a hole in the ground, where packed earth and coral were shaped together into bricks. He carried one such brick, then another, to the end of the line, where a dragon in human shape and a Fallen in the colors of a House he didn't recognize laid their hands on the coral until it became the sleepy green of jade.

Philippe.

One brick, then another—the workers were speaking to one another in low voices, the familiar cant of Viet, all but drowned out by the whispers of the ghosts. Faces swam by: he must have seen them in his surgery, workers coming in for twisted backs, or broken arms, or the myriad things that could happen on the docks. He must have . . .

Hands steered him away from the bricks, and sat him down by the side of a small knoll. Everything reeked of death, and ghosts. Two workers watched him, looking worried. One of them, whose face was vaguely familiar—had he treated her, once?—handed him rice pressed into the shape of a roll, and algae that smelled of rot and mold. "Here, doctor. You'll feel better," she said.

Philippe looked up, struggling to breathe. The ghosts had latched on to his chest, slowing his heartbeat, and he could barely move for the weight of the wall on his shoulders. The two workers were watching him, warily. "I'm fine," he said in Viet. "Thank you." They relaxed a fraction, but still watched him.

"He's with us," a familiar voice said. "Child? Child, speak to me." And then, more firmly, "Pham Van Minh Khiet."

"Olympe?" The word tasted wrong on his tongue, dried paper instead of meat.

"You shouldn't have gone to Berith," Olympe said. She sounded . . . sad? Angry? He couldn't tell, anymore.

"What—" He tried to say something, but his tongue felt dry and bloodless in his mouth, like burned paper.

"This is where we end up." Olympe's voice was mirthless. "Where our myths, and our guardian spirits, and our fairy tales, all end. Where they take us as needed, and discard us like so much chaff."

Like the French, recruiting workers to cut into rubber trees, to bake bread, to lay down roads and railway tracks.

"What . . ." Every word hurt. "What happens now?"

"I don't know." Olympe sounded weary. "They invited me and a few others to join House Astragale."

"And you said yes?"

"I'm not a fool." The words were sharp, cutting. "I asked them what would happen to the rest of us. They said 'too many mouths to feed.' I doubt the rest get to go home. Workers have died, already. The first were buried in the foundations. Now they just dig graves by the wall, and dump them in."

Of course. Take what you need, kill the rest. How very like a House, or perhaps it was merely the language of power, spoken in different tongues but ultimately always the same.

The wall pressed down on him, unbearable, a boundary that shouldn't exist, a veil that needed to be torn away. He saw that the hole through which Ciseis and Yen Oanh had passed was almost sealed—no, not sealed; locked, like a door they didn't want anyone to open. And, beyond the door, beyond the wall, Isabelle, and the mocking shadow of Morningstar, the blade of his sword as bright as a fallen sun.

For a moment he was back in Françoise's cramped flat; and, for a moment, he stood among the bookshelves of Berith's dominion, with the soft touch of paper under his hands. And, as if the paper had suddenly burst into flames, illuminating everything, he suddenly *knew*.

"I can call her back," he whispered. He stopped, looked at Olympe again, and said, finally, "A friend of mine died, because of me. I asked Berith—"

"How to bring her back?" Olympe's voice was toneless. "Oh, child. The dead don't come back. Except as hungry ghosts, feeding on our blood."

So many of *those*, a sea of white faces, of small, stunted bodies clinging to him like twisted children. "I know," Philippe said. "But Fallen magic . . ." His voice trailed off.

Olympe said nothing.

"I can do it," Philippe said. He stared at the wall looming over him, at the boundary that shouldn't have been. "Except. Except—" Except that he would have to reopen that door. The wall . . . the wall, he knew, was an obstacle to what he wanted to do, everything that separated Isabelle from him made manifest. "It will tear a hole through the wall. It will bring it down, piece by piece." He paused then, seeing the workers by their side get up, ready to go back to picking up bricks. "This isn't what you need."

"Philippe." The ghosts parted, for a moment, letting him see Olympe's face, small and slight and wrinkled, and dark with repressed fury. "This won't help us. But. But they built this wall with our sweat, and our blood, and our dead, to bring us into a fight between Houses we care nothing about. I don't give a damn about the wall. Bring it down. Bring it all down."

THANH Phan was waiting for them at the gates to the palace, her face unreadable. She led them, in silence, to the courtyard where Ngoc Bich had first welcomed them—and to the throne room, where Ngoc Bich sat on a raised dais, in a curved chair of delicate golden traceries, its arms ending in the shape of two golden dragons, with no trace of rot or of mold, merely the crushing weight of a kingdom at its height.

Behind her, a crowd of dignitaries: a sickening press of officials in blue robes adorned with the faces of dragons, of parasol carriers, of attendants with fans, guards with spears and conical hats. The antlers of dragons mingled with the pincers of crabs, and the oily, glistening scales of fish. Not everyone was wholly human, and few seemed to care.

Ngoc Bich's face was covered in a thick layer of white, her antlers glinting with red lacquer. The entire room, from pillars to engraved canopy, seemed to vibrate with her anger. Madeleine followed Elphon's lead, bowing to her. Clothilde barely bothered with courtesy, her own bow perfunctory.

"I have little time," she said. "You're aware that the House is under attack."

"You mean the kingdom?" Ngoc Bich said. Her smile was assured and frightening, reminding Madeleine of nothing so much as Asmodeus's, of a predator's. "As I said to Asmodeus, the world doesn't revolve around Houses."

Madeleine saw Clothilde open her mouth. She was going to say something sharp and wounding, something about the city still standing.

"We're allies," she said. And stopped when once again all the attention in the room turned to her. "We're supposed to fight this together."

"Are we?" Ngoc Bich's expression was enigmatic.

"Please," Madeleine said. Within her, the link to the House twisted and turned, flailing. "We need your help."

The look Clothilde threw Madeleine could have frozen stone. "We don't. But it would be good to have it. As Madeleine says"—again, that look that suggested a hard conversation later—"we are allies."

"And you would, no doubt, be grateful for support in your hour of need."

"They're your rebels," Clothilde said, pointedly.

"For which we sought help from *you*," Thanh Phan said.

"Enough." Ngoc Bich raised a hand. "Clothilde is right in one respect. There is little time left." She paused, for a moment. "And I've had enough of Yen Oanh's little rebellion. What do you want to do?"

"Break the wall," Clothilde said, simply. "Get into Hawthorn. Prevent the House from changing hands. Ciseis won't be kind to the dragon kingdom and she has no reason to safeguard Asmodeus's consort."

"Surely alliances last more than one reign?" Thanh Phan's face was a mask of fury. "It's good to know we can trust Fallen to keep their word."

"Alliances with other Houses? Yes. With heathen primitives? Probably not worth the paper they're written on." She raised a hand. "Not my words, or Lord Asmodeus's."

"Of course not." Ngoc Bich's voice was deeply ironic. "So you know how to break the wall."

"The halberd broke when Lord Asmodeus poured enough Fallen magic into it," Clothilde said. "I think the wall would do the same."

Except one was a small blade, the other an edifice that was so huge it had cut off Hawthorn. "You'd need a lot of power."

"I don't have a lot of power," Clothilde said, sharply. "Every other Fallen is inside the House. So it's Elphon and me and you, and the artifacts I've brought with me."

"And angel essence," Ngoc Bich said.

That stopped Clothilde. "How—"

"There's no lack of it in the kingdom." Ngoc Bich shook her head. "We'll provide you with what angel essence we have, if you're ready to pay the price for its use."

The sweet, sickly smell of it, a memory of lying on the wooden floor of the cabin, breathing it in, finding no comfort—only fear, only decay. "I can't," Madeleine said, before she could think.

Clothilde's voice was cold. "You're not getting essence. I'm not dragging an addict on a high along with me, Madeleine. You can have angel breath. Elphon and I will deal with the essence."

Stung, Madeleine opened her mouth to protest, and then stopped. Did she truly want essence?

"We'll leave you to work out your differences," Ngoc Bich said. "I'll provide you with soldiers to get closer to the wall. After that . . ."

After that, of course, they were on their own. But they'd known that all along.

AFTER Madeleine and Elphon had left, Berith turned back to Françoise. "We need to talk," she said.

Françoise didn't want to talk. She wanted to lie down in the armchair; to sleep, as Camille was sleeping in her arms, wrapped in her scarf, finally getting the rest she'd been denied.

"They'll come back," Berith said. "Nemnestra said as much. With Asmodeus gone, and Hawthorn in turmoil . . ."

Had the storm they had feared or ignored, or both, finally come to their door? Françoise stroked Camille's back, slowly, carefully. "You said we'd run, if worse came to worst."

"I—" Berith's face twisted. "You should leave, Françoise. You and Camille."

"And leave you here to face them by yourself?" Françoise didn't bother to keep the anger out of her voice. "Was that the plan?"

"You . . ." Berith looked awful: bruised circles under her eyes, cheekbones protruding, a flimsy coat of flesh over bones. But then, Françoise, bone weary, still shaking with the memory of giving birth, wasn't much better. "You have to realize that they'll come after me. They'll always come after me. Because of Asmodeus. Because there is always a risk that I'll want to help him, or avenge him, or both."

"And I—" But she already knew the answer. She was mortal, and powerless, and she might be able to borrow Berith's or another Fallen's power, but ultimately she mattered so little, in the grand scheme of things. She'd been happy with that knowledge, never seeking more, except that now it made her want to smash things. "I can't let you."

Berith shrugged. "You've always known I could die."

"Not like this!" Françoise tried to gather thoughts that seemed to have fled. Every word felt like the wrong one. "Look, we can run. We can leave the city. We . . ."

There was nothing beyond the city, beyond the suburbs. Devastated countryside, other cities in equally bad state. "You can't," Françoise said, stubbornly. "There has to be another way."

Berith rested her hand, for a moment, on Camille's wrinkled face, gently rubbing the skin. The baby gazed back at her, brows furrowed as if in thought. "I'd have had a different answer a few months ago, but we have a child," she said. "Please. Françoise."

"You could uproot," Françoise said.

"And leave you with a newborn and a Fallen so weak she can barely walk? The flat is all that sustains me. Beyond it, I'm useless." Berith's voice was ironic.

"There's still time." Which they were wasting by arguing. *Please, Berith. Please.*

Berith closed her eyes. The flat wavered, became bookshelves again for the briefest of moments. "It's too late," she said. "They're in the street. You could—"

"Sneak past them?" Françoise snorted. "As if that would work."

"So you're going to fight them with Camille in your arms?" Berith's voice was harsh. "Think for a minute, Françoise." She moved from where she leaned on the table, bent toward Françoise, and kissed her, slowly, deeply. Magic welled up, twisting on shared breath, filling Françoise's throat and lungs.

The world wavered. Everything hung on a knife's edge, the flat stilled for a moment. In Françoise's arms, Camille gurgled, her face relaxing as though she were feeding.

Berith withdrew. She was oddly blurred, as if seen through tears. "They won't pay as much attention to you now. It's not invisibility, but it's close."

Françoise meant to protest, to say something, but Berith was already at the door.

And, on the other side . . .

They were waiting, as they'd waited on the bridge: rich brocade and cotton clothes, a vivid red, a gold so bright it shone in the gloom. Three of them: Nemnestra, the gaunt-faced human called Célestin, and another one, a beefy woman whom Françoise vaguely remembered.

"Only three of you?" Berith asked.

Nemnestra smiled. "For now." She put both her hands in the space of the doorframe, probed as if at a wound. "Or perhaps forever. You're weak now, aren't you?"

It wasn't a question. Françoise breathed in magic. What would happen if she stood up? Her legs no longer shook, and Berith's kiss had infused energy into her, but how far would that go?

And how far was she willing to run?

"Not so weak," Berith said.

Nemnestra *pushed*. Françoise saw Berith flinch, bit her lips not to cry out. "Oh, but you are. I warned you, old woman. Hawthorn's time has passed. Asmodeus's time has passed."

"Charming," Berith said. She withdrew from the door, moved to lean against the table. Could the others see the tremors that went through her? "I was never Hawthorn, you know." The flat wavered and buckled, and light streamed toward her, her pale skin becoming gorged, translucent. "Or cared much about it." She made a short, stabbing gesture with a long glance at Françoise.

Get down.

Nemnestra pushed again; and again, and something gave way.

Berith screamed, a sound that was almost a wail, tearing at Françoise's entrails, and she was up from the chair, common sense be damned.

She didn't even take three paces before the door exploded.

The frame collapsed. Splinters flew all around her, and a shock wave sent her sprawling to the ground—where was Camille?—she had to protect her; a newborn couldn't possibly endure all of this—dust in her lungs and in her eyes, the world a blurred, painful aggregation of tears—and Camille screaming, a small, high-pitched sound that wouldn't stop. "Ssh," Françoise whispered. "Ssssshh. Everything—" She wanted to say everything was fine, but the knot in her throat wouldn't let her. She found, by touch rather than by sight, Camille's slight shape, tried to feel her head, her neck, her limbs. . . . "Ssshhhh."

Camille quieted, gradually. She was going to be fine. Françoise couldn't feel anything wrong, couldn't see any blood. Breathe. She needed to breathe.

Berith.

She looked up. The doorframe was a sharp, jagged blossom of splintered and warped wood. Beyond the threshold, on the murk of the staircase, lay the body of the third woman, her head at an impossible angle for anything living. Célestin was leaning against a wall, breathing heavily, one hand on his ribs. Blood mingled with the vivid red of his suit.

In the flat, the explosion had broken the table, and thrown everything in the cupboard to the floor. The chessboard was facedown, the pieces of their game scattered over the broken parquet slats, and the bowls in the cupboard lay in shards—after all the trouble they'd gone to patch them. . . . No. Useless to think about. What mattered was surviving.

Berith faced Nemnestra. The other Fallen barely seemed inconvenienced: a few drops of blood on her white gloves, and some dust on the sleeves of her dress. "Impressive," Nemnestra said. "But not, I fear, sufficient. Where did your partner go?"

Berith's face didn't move. "She ran away."

"Smart," Nemnestra said. "One mortal in a sea of mortals . . ." She let the words trail away. "We might even have better uses of our time than run after her."

Françoise could feel it in her guts: the power flowing to Berith, the flat slowly bending out of shape, the ruined walls becoming bookcases, not grand or imposing, but battered, too, splintered and broken like the doorframe, with the shadow of torn pages fluttering in the air.

She moved, slowly, agonizingly slowly. She was going to be spotted; they were going to call her out—but nothing happened. No one moved.

Slowly, carefully, she unwound her scarf—wrapped it, time and time again, around Camille, securing the baby tight against her chest. Brown eyes looked up at her, gaze unfocused, before Camille settled back with a contented look on her face. She looked normal. Assuming that was what passed for normal with newborns. Françoise knew so little about them, in spite of all the toddlers she'd helped wrangle.

Hold tight, child. We're going on an adventure.

"You will do as you please. And certainly not make me lose my temper." Berith gestured, and Nemnestra stumbled, catching herself on the table, and then withdrawing as if it burned. On the wood of the table, the shape of a star shone for a brief moment, before fading into nothingness.

Françoise had managed to kneel by the shards of the bowls, cradling Camille's head with her hands. A quick glance upward: Célestin was still leaning against the wall, still trying to stand. Not the kind of wound that could be brushed off, then. Which suited her.

Berith and Nemnestra were still locked in their odd battle of wills. Françoise felt magic ebb and flow above her, currents that pushed her left and right. Nemnestra was holding on to half the table, her fingers digging holes into the wood, her face twisted in pain. Berith leaned against the wall—a wall of ruined bookshelves and torn pages. Her face, limned in light, was elongated and skeletal, frighteningly alien.

They'd had only one knife in the flat: a long, triangular blade that had gone dull with years of use. But a bowl had broken in two, leaving the raised circle at the bottom almost intact. A raised ceramic edge. Françoise picked up the knife, and passed it several times in succession against that edge at a steady angle, hearing the faint sound of the blade sharpening.

There.

Then—*Don't look at Berith don't look at Berith*—she pushed herself upward, on shaking legs, and walked toward Célestin. It was impossible that he not see her. He had to look up; he had to hear her, had to—

But he didn't. Merely those same gasping, heaving breaths from him; the blood, dripping drop after drop onto the parquet floor. When Françoise was almost close enough to touch, he frowned, as if something was wrong.

"Who . . . ?" he asked. He frowned. Magic—some artifact or charged mirror, emptied before the fight—rose within him, sharp, unexpected. Too much magic. She couldn't hope to fight that.

She stopped, heart in her throat.

Who was she fooling, anyway? Weak and trembling, barely able to hold herself steady, a newborn at her chest, and a bone-deep weariness only thinly plastered over by Berith's magic.

Except no one else was coming. It was her and Berith and not much else, against the wrath of Astragale.

She drew in a burning breath and—before she could change her mind or wonder anymore whether Célestin had seen her—drew the knife, swiftly, across his throat.

It caught. It was too heavy, too blunt. He turned, the words of a spell rising to his mouth—but Françoise, with the strength of desperation, pulled the knife again, dragging it with everything she had until it hit the carotid artery.

A spray of blood fountained up. Célestin stared at her, eyes focused on her. "You—" Lips shaping around a word, the spell dying, only a faint blast of heat on her hands. Ten, twenty, thirty agonizing seconds before he finally toppled, and she could breathe.

Hands grabbed her, twisted her around. "Well, well, well. The little Annamite has claws." A spell tore at her, undoing layer after layer of protection, until everything was sharp again, until there was nothing left to her or Camille. "Clever," Nemnestra said. Her hands rested at Françoise's throat, sharp fingernails prickling the skin.

No no no . . .

Berith stood up from the wall, in a flutter of paper and leather bindings. "The baby," Françoise said.

Nemnestra's hands tightened around her throat, hard enough to bruise. "Don't overestimate your value as a hostage."

"Is that all you see?" Berith's voice was soft. Almost too soft. It wasn't weariness but anger.

The armchair was a throne again, and the ceiling of the flat was receding: sharp, blue sky with flocks of birds, and the smell of freshly crushed grass. She was dragging them into her dominion. No, Françoise suddenly realized, her heart going cold. She was stripping the flat of everything, every ward, every protection, gathering all the power she could for one spell. Nemnestra couldn't see it, because she didn't understand what the flat was, didn't understand how it sustained Berith.

Berith. She couldn't get the words out.

"I see death," Nemnestra said. "For you. For your Fall-brother. For your partner. The baby, perhaps, we can spare, for who would teach her vengeance?"

The books were fading, one by one, from the bookshelves, the torn pages absorbed into Berith's skin. Her face glowed like a sun, and the sky overhead darkened, clouds gathering to block the sunlight.

Berith, no.

Berith smiled. It was joyless, and ghastly, the rictus of a Fallen whose heart was being removed from them. "Who will teach her vengeance? You don't understand, Nemnestra. It's not about Houses dying or rising, or time passing. It's never been."

Nemnestra didn't move. "You want to kill me? I'll snap her neck before you even have time to cast a spell." A slight pressure on Françoise's neck, with the unmovable, inhuman strength of Fallen.

"You'll kill her anyway. Won't you?" A wind rose, the few remaining torn papers gathering themselves in a spiral, weaving themselves around Berith like a small storm. They'd turned a glistening blue. Words flashed on Berith's arms, becoming featureless smudges. The bookshelves were all but invisible, faint traceries of light on the cracked walls.

"Would I?" Nemnestra asked. She shook her head. "The time to make your move is long past."

Think. Think. Berith couldn't do anything to Nemnestra without killing both of them, all three of them, baby included. She needed an opening. A distraction.

If Françoise hadn't been shaking with fatigue or carrying a baby, she would have hit Nemnestra in the crotch, and dived out of the way while she was still dealing with the surprise and the rising pain. But that was out of the question.

Hands at throat. She needed these away. And it would take something painful.

"Berith, I'm sorry." Françoise made her voice as weary as possible, which didn't require much faking. Nemnestra's hands tightened, relaxed again. She thought Françoise was giving up, that she was going to plead for her life. Her mistake. "I just can't."

She dropped down, as if she were going to faint—her upper body going limp, but her heel moving, sharply, with all the strength she could muster—onto Nemnestra's right foot, pressing down on the instep.

A crack of breaking bones. Nemnestra screaming. Françoise pushing herself out of the way, running as fast as she could, as far as she could.

"You little—"

Magic, rising at her back, the heat of a spell—and then, in front of her, Berith spreading her arms wide, her eyes streaked with silver, light streaming out of her in the rising wind, and all the smudges on her arms exploding outward like ink splattered from a broken pen.

Everything flashed a bright, painful white.

When Françoise managed to open her eyes again, she found her hands over Camille's face—what if the baby went blind? She waved them, several times, but nothing seemed out of the ordinary: still the same unfocused brown gaze, mildly irritated now. "Ssh," she said. "Mommy is here. Ssh. Ssh."

She raised her eyes.

There was no flat left. The walls had collapsed, wide-open to the cold outside, and every piece of furniture was thrown aside or broken, or both. The floor had buckled and broken in multiple places, and slats protruded like spikes. Françoise threw a glance backward, to where Nemnestra had been standing. There was nothing left, just a smudge of black on the floor.

The blue armchair was cleaved in two, and Berith leaned on one half, breathing heavily. "Berith? Berith?"

Berith looked up, and her face was a grinning skull; her skin so taut Françoise could see the bones underneath. "I'll—I'll—be—fine. I—just. Need. Rest." And then she fell silent, and there was only the noise of the winter breeze, whistling amidst the ruins of their lives.

TWENTY-THREE
REBIRTH

BEYOND the wall, in the grove of Hawthorn, Ciseis knelt, drawing a circle around a tree.

She had left Asmodeus, Yen Oanh, and two guards a little way off, by the tree that bore the thin shape of Uphir in its embrace. Asmodeus's face was pale, his glasses askew, his shirt drenched with blood from wounds that wouldn't heal. He watched Ciseis without expression.

Yen Oanh said, "They say old sins always come home to roost."

Asmodeus shrugged, and grimaced, one hand going to his chest. "Old sins, new sins. I regret nothing." He tried to push himself away from the tree; stumbled, and would have fallen if one of the bodyguards hadn't caught him.

Yen Oanh smiled. "You care about your House, but you're too weak to stop us."

"Don't count on weakness." Asmodeus smiled: a quick, tired expression, a pale shadow of his bright, terrible former self. "It may not last."

"Mocking us? You're in no position to do so."

Ciseis's voice rose and fell, drawing out the words of a spell. The tree at the center of the circle grew sharper, branches twisting, bowing down toward her, blossoms fading away and becoming the vivid, flaming red of berries—

and Asmodeus grew paler and paler, dangling from the bodyguard's grasp like a corpse with all its bones shattered.

"I'm surprised you would ally with a Fallen," he said, softly. "Or a House."

Yen Oanh's face didn't move. "Who else would I ally with? The Houseless, the hungry, the powerless? Needs must, Asmodeus."

"As long as they apply, yes." Asmodeus's voice was malicious. "You do know she and House Astragale were behind the angel essence traffic into the dragon kingdom? The very thing you so decry, used as the foundations of your rebellion . . ."

Yen Oanh's face froze into stillness: the intent gaze of a predator. "Not at the beginning, no." One hand foraged into her wide sleeve, brought out the engraved hilt of a knife—just a fraction, but Asmodeus saw it. He laughed, softly.

"And all bonds shall fall to dust, all alliances be torn asunder. . . . What fun we shall have. . . ."

"You," Yen Oanh said, viciously, "will be dead."

Asmodeus raised his head, met the unwavering, cornflower blue gaze of Uphir's corpse. "Or worse than dead. They're all still alive here, preserved for the good of the House." His voice ought to have been mocking, but instead it was in earnest, stripped bare of pretense or posturing. "And, in the end, we all come here, all give ourselves for Hawthorn. Isn't that so . . ."

"Asmodeus." Uphir's voice was the whisper of the wind. "I see you have learned your lesson, after all these years."

Asmodeus laughed. "Older and wiser, Uphir. Or perhaps just older."

In the center, Ciseis's circle now glowed red, and blood stained her hands. When she moved, the branches of the tree moved with her, crowning her with thorns and flaming berries.

"It's time," she said, her voice echoing in the grove. "Bring him."

THUAN was in Asmodeus's office. Iaris had made a face, and Sare had looked outright uncomfortable, but no one had forbidden him outright. Their body language had been quite clear: he could risk himself, and it would be on his head when Asmodeus did come back.

It was impressive, the faith that he would come back. Even as the House descended into chaos—as the unnatural blue sky and the dry, stale, recycled feeling in the air took hold—they clung to the knowledge that he would stand by them. They didn't *like* him, would never stop fearing him, but he was still their bulwark—even absent, even diminished.

Asmodeus's office was that of a gentleman of means: bookshelves with leather volumes, all carefully dusted; a few cupboards and a secretary desk on Persian rugs, a low table with two wicker chairs in a corner, and a huge desk of polished wood with a leather surface.

Most drawers and cupboards were closed, and sealed with strong magic. When he ran his fingers over the wood, he felt the slight jolt and catch of Fallen magic, and a faint smell, a memory of orange blossom and bergamot. A voice, whispering "unwise" in his head, the touch of lips on his.

And a ritual that would end with his death, and the death of the dragon kingdom.

He spread the papers he'd brought from his room carefully on the desk. He was sitting in one of the wicker chairs, not the large plush one behind the desk: he would have felt like a thief, consort or not.

He should have paid more attention in magic classes, both in the kingdom and in Hawthorn, but he'd always assumed that he'd never need to wield or shape Fallen magic, merely oppose it with *khi* currents. He'd thought of pitched battles and magical duels, and not of rituals in which he would be caught, unawares. Second Aunt would laugh at him if he confessed to such naïveté.

He stared at the papers, again. Nothing. Nothing he hadn't seen originally.

"You have some nerve." Nadine's voice was amused. She came into the office slowly, glancing left and right, as if unsure whether she'd be chastised.

"You don't sound like you have much," Thuan said. Calmly, he set the papers over a pile of other, current ones: expense accounts for the House, and memos from the different courts.

Nadine threw a worried glance at the chair behind the desk. "If you're not court and you come in here, it's generally not for commendations."

"Did he ever summon you here?" Thuan asked.

Nadine pulled one of the wicker chairs, sat in it. Her whole body had gone rigid. "When I was a child, and a bunch of us brought down an entire set of shelves with magical artifacts in them and incinerated the laboratory. He wasn't head of Hawthorn then, just the leader of the Court of Birth. I don't remember much. Mother says he's never done anything to children, except put the fear of the House in them." She didn't sound as though she believed it. "People go straight from this office to the cells, sometimes."

It sounded like a myth. Like something so often told it had gotten deformed. He didn't want to ask who, or when—they were all old, stale fears—didn't want to sound as though he was making excuses for any of it. But he was starting to understand what the House ran on. And what, ultimately, had brought it to this juncture.

"You're very interested in his papers," Nadine asked. "The same ones I brought you?"

Thuan had already given it some thought. "Yes," he said. "His plans for me. He . . ." He scowled, with a worry he didn't have to fake. "He wanted to know how dragons' bodies worked."

Nadine's face was haunted. "An operating table and a knife?"

"Several types of knives," Thuan said. "And a long time in which to test things. He had understood we can heal ourselves, like Fallen. It was an added attraction." Again, a scowl, just enough fear to mirror hers, to play on what was already there, her preconceived ideas. It wouldn't last, if she did read the papers. But she had other things on her mind.

Not, of course, that what Asmodeus outlined was any better or any more desirable than a live, slow dissection.

"Figures," Nadine said.

Thuan laid both elbows on the sides of the wicker chair, bending toward her. "Tell me what's going on."

Nadine looked at the door again. It was closed, but that didn't seem to make her more relaxed.

"I don't think your mother or anyone else is likely to come in here." Thuan felt like an interloper, but at least he couldn't be in any more trouble than he already was. And he had no history with this place. "And I'm rather unlikely to go straight to him and tattle, even if I knew where he was." He couldn't afford to wonder where Asmodeus was, or how he was doing. There could be no pity, no compassion, no ambiguous desire getting in the way.

At length, Nadine said, "I told you. Things are changing." She leaned back against the chair. It made a creaking, cracking sound. "Twenty years ago, the House was taken from Lord Uphir. He had an heir. Ciseis. She escaped to another House. House Astragale."

"I remember," Thuan said, softly. Old history. Not his, but he'd learned never to underestimate the power of the past. "And now she's come back? Why support her?"

Nadine's face didn't move. "You're the one he dragged all the way here and planned to experiment on, and you ask this?"

Because he didn't have any proof that Ciseis was any gentler. No, that wasn't true. He already knew that she and House Astragale ran the angel essence traffic into the kingdom. He closed his eyes. "So this is . . . a take-over? A change of masters? What happens to the servants of the old?"

"It has to change." Nadine's voice was feverish. "We've lived in fear for twenty years, Thuan."

She'd been a child when Asmodeus seized the House. She'd admitted as much. How much did she remember?

And what was he doing, trying to find holes and cracks in her story? It wasn't as though he needed to be convinced of Asmodeus's ruthlessness.

"There'll be"—Nadine took a deep, shaking breath—"positions for people who took the right side at the right time. New courts drawn. New blood."

She didn't say what would happen to the old blood. It was obvious. Hawthorn, ruled by fear and purges—and even Ciseis would be molded by it, in the end: a string of overthrows leading to the same climate within the House.

"I see." Thuan said nothing for a while.

Did any of this include a chance of survival for a consort? He weighed it, for a while. There would be a new head of House, but the ritual would still exist. He could burn the papers and hope no other traces subsided in the drawer, but there was a chance Nadine would remember them before he could. And consorts of deposed heads were embarrassing remnants that never survived long, in any case. There'd be the fear of retribution by Second Aunt if he was harmed or killed. But the kingdom was weak, and who knew if it could afford a war? Who even knew if, with the Houses at their throat and too much to lose, Second Aunt wouldn't judge it politic to merely ask for blood money?

"I'm not sure where I feature in this," Thuan said, slowly. "Except for not liking Asmodeus." It wasn't quite a lie, but not quite the truth, either. Was fascination truly dislike?

Nadine laughed, nervously. "It's a start. Look. You could help us."

"How?"

"You're a dragon. You have magic."

Even if he wasn't too sure how much use he could make of it. "And you want me to use it?"

Nadine said nothing, for a while. "I like you, Thuan, lies and all. I don't know how much I can trust you."

"To save my own skin? Rather a lot." Or not at all, if their scheme involved removing the dragon kingdom, or harming Second Aunt. "What do you want?" It wasn't a time for subtlety, or finesse.

"Mother and Sare and the other dependents are trying to break the wall around the House."

"And you want me to defend it?"

"The wall prevents anyone from getting into Hawthorn, and people from Hawthorn from interfering with Ciseis's ritual. Asmodeus isn't coming back, Thuan. The future lies with Ciseis. We need to hold," Nadine said, with a grimace. "Until it's over and the House has changed hands. Until . . ."

Until Asmodeus was dead, until Thuan was marginally safe from any arcane rituals. Except, of course, that he would remain vulnerable. No, he couldn't afford to wait until Ciseis came back, triumphant. Nadine was a child, in many ways, caught in a storm not of her making and trying to weather it with little knowledge. He would have felt sorry for her in other circumstances.

"What happens," he asked, because he had to, "to Iaris?"

Nadine's face hardened. "Mother made her own choices and her own bed. Let her sleep in it."

And see the end, too, of that easy familiarity with Asmodeus, which Nadine hadn't approved of, the neglect of her own child in favor of the House. Thuan didn't say it aloud. He didn't dare.

He couldn't trust Nadine. He couldn't trust Ciseis. She might well listen to Nadine, be convinced that Thuan had helped them, but eventually the situation would be the same: Thuan would remain a pawn within the House, and an expendable one at that. Gratitude, as he well knew, seldom featured in the calculations of the powerful, especially in those of a new head of House, busy purging her new territory of everything that might remind others too closely of her predecessor.

When the wall came down, when it was all over, Thuan had to be back to his only place of safety: the dragon kingdom.

But nothing would defend them against the onslaught of the House, if Ciseis decided to come after him.

Except . . .

He remembered his night wandering within the House; remembered power surging upward, even through closed doors: a hook pulling, bringing him to his knees. The power Asmodeus had been counting on, to finish his ritual and bring the dragon kingdom down.

The expenditure of power involved, of course, would be staggering. . . .

If he took that source of magic, if he could steal it, bring it back with him, then the House would hold little to use against them. And who knew? If worse came to worst and all the other Houses continued to encroach, they could ask Véronique and the others to make use of it. It was Fallen magic, but not the corruption of essence: not safe by any means, but, in the absence of better defenses . . .

How easily we give in, he thought, bitterly. No easy way to win, or to remain as they were. If they had ever been pure of all Fallen influences. Perhaps that had been the illusion, from the start: the idea that they could hold themselves within the city, yet separate from it and its powers.

"I might be able to help," he said, slowly, carefully. "But I'll need access to Asmodeus's bedroom."

Nadine's head jerked back. "If he finds out—"

"I thought he'd be dead?" Thuan said, smoothly. "And he'll blame me, in any case."

"Not if I go in there with you."

"You don't have to," Thuan said.

Nadine gave him a long, hard look. "I do." Of course she didn't trust him. But, at this stage, that didn't matter much. "Why do you want to go there?"

"I saw something," Thuan said. "When I was there. I'm not sure. . . ." He let the words trail, for a while. "But I think it could help you defend the wall."

"An artifact?" Nadine asked. "It's probably heavily defended by wards."

"Maybe," Thuan said. "But it's worth a try, isn't it?"

Silence, for a while. He might have pushed too hard. Might have not seemed casual enough. But at length Nadine said, "You were always too curious." She sighed. She didn't sound quite convinced: she would keep an eye on him in the bedroom. But she had relaxed her guard a fraction, and that was all he needed.

Thuan felt the *khi* currents around him, the slow, gathering strength of water, patiently waiting until everything lay quiescent and cold. He could wait, too; for the proper moment to strike.

THERE was only the wall.

It pressed down on Philippe, its shadow vast and unknowable and *wrong*. He wanted to claw at it, to tear it apart piece by piece, but he couldn't. Ghosts pressed themselves against him; he hardly felt, anymore, the blood they were taking from him.

They'd been gathered in a makeshift shed, a little way from the quarry, little more than a roof over four slender sticks, and beaten earth underneath. The dragon and the Fallen who were infusing the blocks with magic had left, and now it was just a handful of dragon and crab guards, looking bored, secure in the knowledge that a few mortal Annamites weren't going to be a threat. Olympe was having an urgent conversation with a burly female docker who looked distinctly sour, while two younger ones stared at the diseased coral and mother-of-pearl buildings with some of the wonder of seeing myths come to life. He knew them both: Hortense had come in with a broken foot after stepping on a magical trap, and Jérôme's back, never strong, needed frequent straightening out after he'd carried crates all day.

Olympe had brought him tea earlier, watching him carefully. "You have some time," she said. "Before Yen Oanh comes back."

He'd wanted to tell her she pinned too much hope on what he could do, on how he could help them, but the words had remained stuck in his throat.

Philippe knelt, and traced the shape of a star in the churned earth. Ghosts ringed it, slowly filling its contours like paint sinking into paper.

There were words, on his tongue, spoken in a language that he couldn't quite understand, burning like acid as they came up his throat. There was . . . Berith's voice, slow and measured, reading from the pages of a huge leather book that held all the names of the Fallen, all those who had been flung down from Heaven, a hundred falling stars in the sky above the world: Lucifer Morningstar, Echaroth, Calyce, Uphir, Asmodeus, Selene, Hyacinth . . .

Isabelle.

The wall stood between them, an unbearable divide, a pain that needed to be excised. Philippe raised his eyes, struggling against the weight that bowed down his head. The line of dark stones went on and on without interruption, saturated with *khi* earth and *khi* metal—shot through with the thin, billowing shapes of ghosts—and, where Ciseis and Yen Oanh had crossed, one thin, familiar silhouette holding herself unmoving, with that familiar pent-up energy, a sense that she would never sit still if she could run or act.

I can take it down.

Brash words, Asmodeus whispered in his mind. *The words of a madman. Poisoned gifts.*

But he'd always known the gifts were poisoned; because Berith was Fallen, because, no matter how weak, how human she seemed, she couldn't be trusted.

Around the star, his hands had traced words in a spidery, unfamiliar writing. He didn't remember writing them, didn't even remember how long he'd spent, kneeling. Olympe's conversation had finished, and there was a faint smell of jasmine rice and fish sauce wafting from the circle where everyone else sat. She'd come to bully him into eating, soon.

No time.

He raised his eyes again. Within the wall, over the lintel of what had been the door, the white shape of the star had appeared, limned in silver. It was askew, blurred—tumbling down from its proper place, holding the white shape of Isabelle in its shadow.

He'd promised her this. In the ruins of House Silverspires—in the shambles of their friendship, forever broken—he had sworn to turn back time.

He rose and picked up the cup of tea by his side. Then he knelt within the star. It was crossing into another country: a faint resistance as he stepped over the line, thin, featureless arms that looked like branches or tentacles reaching out to embrace him, a wet cold spreading through his shoes to the soles of his feet. Berith was still speaking, in the background, her voice growing fainter and fainter.

He stood, in the dark, under the shadow of the wall, watching the star he'd traced on it grow larger and larger, and the *khi* currents swirling around a curious emptiness that had to be the Fallen magic. By his side were ghosts, not thin or featureless, but people. People he had known, such a long time ago in Annam, ancestors who had died: his mother and father, his grand-parents, his great-grandparents, faded portraits on the ancestral altar, now standing, larger-than-life, with a hand on their descendants' shoulders.

A smell of green papaya and coconut, and burning incense, and the wet, swollen sound of a river at monsoon time, and abruptly he was back a thousand years ago, before he ascended, before he became Immortal—when he was just a child, sneaking into the ancestral shrine and trying to grapple with the enormity of death.

Your desire cracks open the wall between life and death.

But it wasn't a wall, not anymore. That was a Western view of it, the inviolability of the boundaries, ghosts and spirits in their proper places, science and magic neatly labeled.

It had never been a wall.

The ghosts by his side reached out, and the weight of the wall—the unbearable thing that fought to make him abase himself—receded. The wall itself, the dark, shimmering stones, faded, but where he'd expected cliffs, or the shadow of stairs leading up to the quays of Paris, there was instead a large, diffuse shadow, with a red pavilion at its feet.

A wheel. A huge wheel, not the red lacquered thing he'd imagined in the Courts of Hell, but a wooden one, the kind found on water mills, bringing up *khi* water into the city, every spoke loaded with ghosts. And a faint sound, a bell in a distant pagoda, every peal sending a thrill through him. He knew this place. He had not been there. He might never go there, for he didn't age, didn't die, but it was within him, as within all who had once been mortals.

Philippe walked up to it. Slowly, carefully, reverently, for what else could he do? In his hands, he still held the cup of tea, which now smelled different: a pungent odor tinged with just a hint of bitterness. The cup of forgetfulness, the tea of herbs that made a soul forget its previous lives, before its rebirth.

Isabelle was waiting for him at the bottom of the wheel, on the steps of the pavilion. Her face billowed in the wind like a spread cloth, not one feature remaining constant or in focus. She looked human, with nothing of the magic of Fallen about her, no unearthly light, no wings, no coiled power: just a girl from Marseilles or Montpellier, with the olive skin of the Mediterranean. At her back, not the shadow of Morningstar, with his mocking smile, his facile, glib truths about power, but a wooden statue of the bodhisattva Quan Am draped in folds of cloth, her face creased in the benevolent, reassuring smile of one who heard everything.

"Philippe."

Behind him, a string of ghosts: his ancestors, his compatriots lost in the war. Ahead of him, only the wheel, churning its load of water and souls into the city, and back again.

Isabelle held out her hands for the cup. Philippe stared at it, for a while. "No," he said. "I need you to remember. Silverspires. What happened between us." How he had failed her, time and time again, and everything they had shared, too, the kitchens and the kneading of bread, and the card games where she always lost, too earnest, too sincere.

She stared back, fey, enigmatic. "But not this." Her hands moved, encompassed the wheel and the wall, and the growing light of the star above them. "Never this." Gently, she took the cup from his hands, and drained it in one gulp. She handed it back to him. "You know what to do."

And, for a single—perfect—suspended moment, he did.

He tightened his hands around the cup, crushing it into fragments. There was a single, high-pitched scream—a scream of a newborn, brought into a universe of blinding lights and unconfined spaces, where breathing *hurt*. And the vast, larger sound of something cracking into a thousand pieces.

The wheel was gone. Isabelle was gone, and the ghosts, and the ancestors, and the feeling that everything made sense. He was on the ground in the middle of a smudged drawing, the shards of the cup wedged into his hands. His fingers and palms were a mass of glistening, fiery pain, dripping blood on the earth.

The sound of everything cracking was still rolling in the background. He forced himself to look up, utterly drained, and saw that the cracks were spreading through the wall: the shape of a huge star, and then other cracks spreading from it, a network of fault lines that swallowed bricks and mortar in its wake. Entire sections toppled toward the ground, in a cloud of sand and silt and dust that cut off everything.

And then silence.

When he opened his eyes again, the wall still stood—barely, riven with fissures, its line dipping up and down where bricks had toppled. Except in one place: the door Ciseis and Yen Oanh had gone through, which was now open again, a hole surmounted by the shape of a star.

And in that hole . . . in that hole, curled up in a fetal position, the white, pale shape of a body.

The feeling of oppression had vanished, and his mind felt clear, for the first time in days. His body, though . . . He tried to rise, fell back, drained of everything. He couldn't seem to heal, couldn't seem to stop the bleeding in his hands. . . .

Ahead, at the doorway, the body unfolded. It was *her*, the gestures heartbreakingly familiar as she pulled herself to her feet and started, stumblingly, to walk toward him.

"Isabelle," he whispered, through lips that had gone dry.

But, even before Isabelle reached them, he knew that something was wrong—knew, in fact, exactly what it was.

She looked exactly the same as she had, at the wheel. Her skin was dark, her hair cut short, and there was no aura around her, no oppressive light, no unearthly elegance. She didn't walk lightly upon the ground, barely touching it; didn't have the glazed, distant expression of newborn Fallen, or the ruthless gaze that came later, surveying all that it touched and wanting it all for itself.

Mortal. She was mortal.

TWENTY-FOUR
WEIGHT OF THE LIVING

IN the grove, Asmodeus was kneeling, bowed under the weight of thin branches from the tree, wrapped around his arms and sinking into his flesh. Ciseis laid a hand on his forehead. It left the bloody imprint of a dozen thorn prickles. Asmodeus jerked, and tried to pull away, but the branches held him fast.

"Time," she whispered. "Twenty years, Asmodeus."

He opened his mouth. Twigs and berries arched from his throat, choking him from within, the House growing within his own body. His voice was almost inaudible. "Some people had it harder than you."

"Those you purged?" Ciseis's voice was hard. "The Seine running red with blood and ashes . . ."

"While you found refuge in a House that courted you and preserved you for its own ends? Dined and wined every night while others bled and screamed in your name . . ."

"You know nothing." She laid her hands, not on him, but on the thin network of branches anchoring him to the tree. It started to pulse, gently, like veins infused with blood. He half rose, struggling; she pushed effortlessly, sent him back onto the blood-covered ground. "And your time is ending. From Uphir to you, from you to me, your mastery of the House is passing; your mastery of its wards is passing. . . . From Echaroth to you to me, the House is given in trust, and I am given to it, body and soul. . . ."

The tree shivered, stretched. Asmodeus opened his mouth to scream: it was filled with brambles and thorns, and only the thinnest of sounds came out. His arms went taut with the effort to resist, but the branches inexorably extended, dragging his arms with it, away from the cold earth, until his entire chest lay exposed like that of a crucified man, his folded knees centimeters away from the ground, his ankles dragging in the dirt.

Yen Oanh stepped forward. Her hand was wrapped around the hilt of the knife. The bodyguard from House Astragale lay unconscious on the ground, blood seeping from where she had stabbed him.

Ciseis was bathed in cold, red light, and Asmodeus was fading, shrinking, the skin of his hands tightened over the bones, the shape of his body warped and pressed, a network of thin, thorny branches sprouting from his mouth and nose. The tree's boughs shook with his efforts to free himself, but he was growing weaker and weaker—as the blood left his body, the skin of his face grew translucent, outlining sharp cheekbones and the recessed eye sockets of a skull, and the branches of the hawthorn grew fatter, ruddier, their hold on him like a vise.

"It is the season of blood, the season of thorns, the season of berries that are poison. Your mastery of the House is passing; your mastery of its wards is passing—"

Ciseis stopped. She gave a strangled gasp, struggling against the hilt of the knife Yen Oanh had sunk into her side. The dragon withdrew it, stabbed her again, higher this time; and pressed down on her, bearing her all the way to the ground. Ciseis's blue eyes were wide-open, glazing in shock, the same color as the merciless sky above. Her mouth worked, trying to speak around a flow of blood.

Yen Oanh held her down, wordlessly, as her struggles ceased. Then she moved, to stand in front of Asmodeus—knife thrust back in her right sleeve, the broken antlers around her face thick and yellowed, like ivory. Ciseis's circle had sunk to nothing, and the network of branches holding Asmodeus had gone slack, lifeless.

"Put not your trust in dragons. . . ." Asmodeus's voice was almost inaudible, still choked by the tendrils growing within him. He'd managed to pull his right hand in front of him, the skin of his wrist torn to bloodied shreds. His fingers—long, insectile—flexed, slowly, carefully.

"I'm not a fool," Yen Oanh said. She shook her head. "You're all the same, deep down. Ciseis at the head of House Hawthorn would have been no better than you."

"And you would . . . claim . . . that dominion?"

Yen Oanh reached out, and laid her fingers on the branches holding his arms, pushing until he gasped in pain. His right hand, which hadn't stopped flexing, brushed the skin of her wrist, withdrew as if scalded. His face was taut with more than the pain—a terrible effort to move something, anything, away from the tree's grasp.

"You misunderstand. I have no interest in Hawthorn. None at all."

Her hands shifted, became overlaid with gray scales the color of rot, her fingers sharpening into jointed claws. Frost climbed, from her fingers toward the hawthorn tree, swallowing everything in its wake, covering branches and berries and flowers with a thin layer of shimmering *khi* water—and from the tree to the others, locking body after body in the stillness of death. Asmodeus's face went white, ice crystals creeping up the temples of his glasses, fogging the lenses with intricate patterns like colorless embroidery. "You would destroy us," he whispered. The frost climbed into his mouth and sealed his lips.

"One fewer House," Yen Oanh said. "One fewer threat."

Asmodeus made a choked, low sound. He shifted, pulling with him the branches in one drawn-out, spasmodic movement—ice shaking on branches, thorns rubbing against his skin, drawing red, vivid blood.

"No . . ." His voice was a hiss. A faint, dying light streamed out of his skin, magic shriveling branches in its wake; but they only grew back, faster than he could burn them. Yen Oanh shook her head, vaguely amused.

"Stronger magic than yours, I'm afraid."

The light died down. Asmodeus jerked back, his breath coming in short, spasmodic gasps, and pulled. There was a tearing sound from his right wrist as flesh parted all along the line of the thorns' embrace, revealing the glistening shape of bone. His fingers, stretching, grabbed the hilt of the knife from Yen Oanh's sleeve. He drew it, his mouth a thin red line of taut pain, and dragged it in one swift gesture across the right side of her neck.

Yen Oanh grabbed the blade, twisted. Asmodeus held on, grimly, pushing with all his strength, the knife slowly cutting through flesh and muscles. His body jerked and turned, branches snapping, growing again into a thicker, denser network. Yen Oanh's face had gone white as well, as she struggled to hold him at bay. "Nothing will save the House, Asmodeus," she whispered.

He said nothing, merely continued to strain against her. The knife hit the jugular. A spray of blood fountained up, swiftly absorbed by the branches, lapped up eagerly like water on a parched and cracked earth. Asmodeus's strength finally gave out: his fingers opened, convulsively, and the knife fell to the ground in front of him, was swallowed by the onslaught of frost.

Yen Oanh leaped back, pressing one hand to the wound. "We don't die so easily, even by these blades."

Asmodeus's mouth was now completely choked, his eyes rolled back into their orbits behind glasses seized with frost. Blood had drained from his face, leaving his skin sallow, with the faint bluish tint of a corpse. His breath, faint, inaudible, barely shook his lean frame, or the branches that held him.

Yen Oanh stood, shaking, her hand covering the wound, pressing so hard it had gone pale, with only a faint tracery of scales between the knuckles.

"It's started," she said. Patterns of frost continued spreading from the tree, to cover the entire grove. "And soon it will end."

FROM the hill, the laundry barge looked smaller, and battered down, and diminished, the skeleton in the iron cage almost obliterated by distance. It felt insignificant, irrelevant.

It should have.

But it had been Charles in that cage, eaten up by fish and crabs. And the boat was where she'd been imprisoned, where she'd felt the life ebbing out of her.

Madeleine's hands were wrapped around a mirror containing angel breath, feeling the warmth of it in her fingers. A comfort, but all she could smell was the angel essence tucked away in Clothilde's and Elphon's clothes—a sharp, acrid odor that couldn't be covered by silk or cotton—and the memory of it, sweet and sickly, spread over her clothes: lying down and trying not to breathe it in, with nightmares of what would happen to her if Asmodeus found out—and then the kiss, and his magic filling her up like an empty glove, a puppet being picked up.

There were no strings left now: Asmodeus was gone, the House in disarray. But no, that wasn't true. Of course promises remained, and old habits; and everything else binding her to Hawthorn. And the gaping emptiness in her mind, the sense of urgency that she had to do something, anything, to fill it before she went mad.

"I count forty of them," Thanh Phan said. "At least." The crab official wore battle armor: a cracked, lacquered breastplate, and two swords crossing behind her back. Her face had been painted white, but in such a thin layer it did nothing to disguise the places where her skin had sloughed off, and the sharper, messier white of bone. She didn't look happy, but then, she seldom did, whenever Houses were involved. They might have an alliance, and a contract, but Thanh Phan would hate them all the way into her grave.

The price of survival, of the politics that the House played, to remain powerful, to remain havens in the wastelands of Paris. Madeleine was no fool. Not always.

Thanh Phan's force was small: ten soldiers. Among them was Anh Le, who didn't even bother with a semblance of human form, her face covered in blue-gray scales and mottled with rust, her shape sinuous and flowing.

"You can't take them all," Clothilde said. She'd changed her clothes, from a formal dress to a straight tunic that looked like a newer, sharper version of the clothes worn by the kingdom's officials: dark gray with ornate buttons, and the same side slits at the midriff. Even from where she sat, Madeleine could feel the heat emanating from her, the treacherous rush of power granted by angel essence.

Thanh Phan looked as though she was going to roll her eyes up. "Obviously not. We'll cause a distraction. . . ." She pursed her lips. "The hospital would be ideal, but I'm not keen to slaughter the dying." Her eyes narrowed. "There."

It was a small shed, crammed full of people—Annamites, though Madeleine couldn't make out their faces.

"Dragons?" Clothilde asked.

"Mortals," Thanh Phan said. "They shouldn't even be here. So much for our secrecy."

Somehow, Madeleine doubted any of the mortals were going to make it out of the kingdom.

Clothilde said, "Your secrecy is past. As soon as Asmodeus presents his new consort—"

"Which assumes he survives," Thanh Phan snapped.

Madeleine opened her mouth to ask a question, and then the entire hill shuddered, like an angry leviathan, and threw them off. The world shook white and green. For a moment the spell that kept them upright and breathing faltered, and she was inhaling brackish, polluted water, desperately trying not to choke.

When she looked up again, the line of the wall was . . . not gone, but severely damaged. Cracks had spread to the entire structure of the edifice from a central nexus somewhere to the left of the shed, and a hole vaguely shaped like a door had opened underneath, leading into glistening darkness. The rebel camp was in shambles, people picking themselves from the scattered debris, silhouettes vaguely seen through the rising cloud of silt and sand.

Clothilde pulled up her gray gloves. Magic shimmered, at the tips of her fingers, and her arms were surrounded by that same dark aura as when she'd thrown Elphon to the ground. "Now," she said.

The first rebels who moved to block their path fell to her. Then Thanh Phan's force moved in, driving a wedge behind her, aiming for the shed, now covered in stone shards. Behind them, dragon kingdom soldiers dropped to one knee, the crack of rifle shots whizzing past Madeleine, downing rebel after rebel.

Madeleine struggled to follow Thanh Phan. Even with angel magic coursing through her, she could hardly breathe, and certainly not run as fast as they did.

They passed the makeshift coral buildings—the hospital, with its lingering smell of death and corrupted essence. Every step Madeleine took seemed to be through tar. Ahead of her, Thanh Phan was engaging a guard, coolly wielding her two swords like extensions of her hands. Clothilde and Elphon had peeled away, heading for the opening. Anh Le had fallen back, keeping a wary eye on her—coiled halfway, standing on her tail as though on two legs. Madeleine didn't need to look at the dragon's face to feel her exasperation.

She was never going to make it. Never mind that she was supposed to be some dubious kind of last resort, that Clothilde considered her next to useless—she just was going to run out of breath long before . . .

She stopped then.

For, slowly walking out of the mass of rubble, a little ahead of her, was Isabelle.

"Isabelle?"

It was impossible. Isabelle was dead. Madeleine had been there when she'd been cut down: a surprised look on her face, and that slow, agonizingly slow fall backward, a spray of blood fountaining from the two fist-sized wounds in her chest. Asmodeus could resurrect Fallen, if he so wished, but of course he had no interest in doing so for someone from another House, someone who had opposed him at every turn.

Isabelle turned, to stare at her. She was unchanged, dusky skin under black hair, wide eyes open in wonder, and yet . . . "Madeleine." A guard made for her. Anh Le sprang, wrapping herself around him from the midriff and choking the life out of him. Isabelle walked on beside her, oblivious, as if dragons with broken-off antlers and raw patches of skin under green scales were an everyday occurrence.

"You . . ." Madeleine fumbled for words, gave up. "You were dead. I saw you die." A hundred words rose, were choked in her throat.

"I remember." Isabelle's gaze was unfocused, still with a distant glaze, as if she wasn't quite there. "Death isn't a barrier. Not always." She looked back, at the shed, where Thanh Phan and the others were now engaging a host of guards in draconic form. Anh Le, finally losing patience, was trailing after them, swimming rather than running. "Philippe. Philippe called me back."

Madeleine hadn't seen Philippe since the destruction of Silverspires. Hadn't seen anyone, in fact, save for that brief glimpse of Aragon and Emmanuelle. "I'm sorry."

"What for?" Isabelle looked puzzled.

For, ultimately, failing both Oris and Isabelle, her apprentices who had died, unable to find any protection or comfort in her; for watching, powerless, as Isabelle fell and breathed her last. For . . . "I should have protected you better. I should—" She closed her eyes, trying to find comfort in angel magic, finding none. "You got me out of Hawthorn, even if it didn't last. I got you killed."

"I made my own choices." Isabelle shook her head. She laid a hand, gently, on Madeleine's shoulder. Her skin was warm, soft. No coiled magic, no power seeking to take over Madeleine. Small comforts. Small gifts. "And so did you." She looked, for a moment, at the shape of the wall beside them. Clothilde and Elphon were both standing, staring at the opening. "You should go. There isn't much time left."

"Time?" Madeleine asked.

"For Hawthorn." Isabelle's smile was fey, enigmatic. Where had Madeleine seen that before?

And then she remembered. It was the smile on the Buddhist statues from Annam, the alien, disturbingly serene faces of their gods. What had Philippe done?

"Go," Isabelle said. She pulled, slightly, at Madeleine's clothes. "Go face your dead, Madeleine."

"I can't."

"You have to." Isabelle was walking away from her, toward the shed. Madeleine stared at her, at the wall and at the hole within it, felt the frightening emptiness within her, the absence of the House—and, like a puppet propelled on someone else's string, or an addict looking for her next fix, she walked toward the wall.

WHEN Madeleine reached the opening in the wall, only Elphon remained. He was staring into the darkness. "Clothilde?" she asked.

He turned to her a face as white as funeral sheets. "Went ahead. I can't, Madeleine."

The shadow of the cracked wall covered them; this close, it was alight with Fallen magic, a faint, flickering light that seeped through every stone and every mortared joint until the stone itself became translucent. The opening was a jagged rectangle like a door drawn by a child, and nothing lay beyond but impenetrable night. From within, a familiar smell, blood and things burning, and a faint echo of arms clashing. "Why?"

Elphon's hands shook. "I—I have been here before. I see nothing. Oblivion, and darkness, and no way back. I can't."

He remembered nothing, he had told her. Nothing from his time before, nothing from being in the gardens with her, nothing from his death—and not, either, wherever he had been when Asmodeus decided to raise him again. And yet.

He loved the House, far, far more than she'd ever done. To her it was a refuge by default, a place that kept her from the streets. To him . . . His loyalty to Asmodeus was absolute: respect and adulation and even a kind of affection, all things she couldn't ever imagine feeling for the head of Hawthorn. If Elphon balked now . . . "We can't leave Clothilde," she said, slowly. From the shed came the noise of battle, dying down now. It was almost over, which meant that people were going to turn their attention to them, soon.

Isabelle had been right. No time left.

Elphon said nothing. Tears ran down his face, and his hands shook, drained of all color. From the doorway, Madeleine still couldn't see anything, but then, she didn't fear death. She never had.

And she wasn't Selene, or Asmodeus, or Clothilde. She couldn't push him, not if he couldn't bear it.

"It's going to be all right," she said. She hugged him, held him until he stopped shaking. "Keep an eye on things, will you? I'll find Clothilde."

It was only after she left him, walking ahead of him into the darkness he couldn't face, that she realized she hadn't even asked him for the angel essence he carried.

*   *   *

DARKNESS rose around Madeleine, absolute—no barrier or resistance: she was through the wall, and climbing the stairs leading up to the House, her feet trailing small clouds of silt. They weren't the same stairs she'd taken. She didn't even know where they led. They were old, and worn, and crumbling in places. She had to make the occasional leap of faith over the ones that had disintegrated, trusting the water of the dragon kingdom to buoy her. In spite of everything, it was still alien and disturbing to see the laws of physics simply lose their hold.

As she walked up, she felt . . . something, at the back of her mind. Instead of the gaping absence of the House, the abyss that threatened to swallow her whole, there were flickers: dim flames guttering before going out. The presence of Asmodeus, muted and weak, a bare, wordless whisper with no bite. She shouldn't have missed him, but she did. Damn him, but of course he was Fallen, and probably already damned. She had no way to know, in spite of the priests' reassurances that they were on earth to redeem themselves. In Asmodeus's case, it didn't really seem to have worked out.

When she came up, out of breath, she found herself, not on a deserted quay, but in an enclosed room. She had been there before.

In the doorway stood Asmodeus, not the head of the House, not the dark presence in her mind, but the leader of the Court of Birth, wearing the orange scarf that he had given to his partisans, just as he had stood, watching, when his thugs killed Elphon. He looked at her with gray-green eyes: the gardener, the insignificant girl who had slumped against the secretary with shattered ribs, bleeding from knife wounds and struggling to breathe. . . .

"Madeleine."

She was back there, among the dead.

Zoé, the head of the Court of Gardens, lying in a pool of blood, her eyes staring at nothing. Frédéric and Pierrette, side by side, shirts and jackets drenched scarlet, their arms covered with knife slices. Monnis, his head blown away by a well-placed bullet, beyond any capacity for self-healing.

"Madeleine."

She looked away; forced herself to, shaking, looking for that lacquered cabinet, behind the red Louis XV armchair, the one she'd dragged herself to.

He wasn't dead, but breathing shallowly, exactly as it had happened, twenty years ago. Two sword strikes, into his chest. Madeleine had crawled to him then, struggling to breathe through her own wounds, keeping the darkness at bay through sheer stubbornness. Now she was upright, with no wounds except those within her own memory, and yet she was struggling to breathe.

"Elphon."

He was outside the wall. He was waiting for her. For the House of Hawthorn—for Asmodeus—to be saved. He wasn't there. Asmodeus wasn't there, wasn't standing in the doorway, waiting for her to cross.

There was nothing, within her mind. A weak, impalpable link to the House, a terrifying sense of being on her own, with no comfort, no essence, no magic to cushion anything. Her calf was shaking, old pains rising up to the surface, the knife wounds that hadn't healed, that would never heal.

Elphon stared at her with glazed eyes. The light was going out of him, streaming through his skin and mouth and eyes, until nothing was left. And his labored breathing, too, fell silent. If she knelt, if she could somehow bring herself to move, she would find him dead again, with no pulse that she could feel. With no hope. A faint, forgotten prayer, words that made no sense, to a God that wasn't listening, that would never listen.

Ahead of her was the door she had crawled through, in another lifetime. The one where Asmodeus was waiting for her, gray-green eyes impassive behind horn-rimmed glasses. The only way out, to the gardens, to Ciseis. To save the life of the Fallen who had turned Hawthorn into an abattoir—who owned her, as casually as he owned fine porcelain and weapons—collecting broken things and bloodied trophies, lining them up on cracked marble mantelpieces, and never, ever letting go.

She walked, slowly. Halfway through, her calf gave in. She started limping, and then the pain of her shattered ribs rose again, and every breath sent scalding agony through her chest. She . . .

She wasn't going to crawl. Never again.

She found, by touch rather than by sight, the container with the angel breath, broke the clasp, inhaled.

It should have been a slow, gentle comfort. Instead, as she struggled to breathe, it was agony, as if someone were tightening bands of red-hot iron around her chest. She wasn't whole enough or strong enough, to hold it all.

You never left, Madeleine, did you? Always crawling away from the wreck of the House, twenty years ago, never leaving the shadow of the past.

Not. Crawling.

Slowly, agonizingly slowly, she walked. Dragging her useless leg behind her. Fighting the weakness in her limbs and body, the fire in her chest. Watching Asmodeus, who wavered and danced in her field of view, blurred through tears. Leaving the dead behind, all her dead, numbered and named and forever beyond her.

Every step, she thought that she would fall. That the pain raging within her was finally going to fell her, that the fire in her chest, the bones rattling within her, what felt like a thousand cuts on her skin, would bring her down to the floor. That she would fall, and not get up; lie there with the dead, in the ruin of Hawthorn . . .

But she had walked—crawled—away from the House, once. She could do it again.

When, at last, she came to lay one shaking hand on the doorframe, Asmodeus had faded away almost to nothingness. "You don't own me," she whispered, through the excruciating pain in her chest.

Commendable, he had whispered when she'd first told him that, newly returned to Hawthorn, filled with the inescapable knowledge that he would do what he pleased with her. But now he said nothing, his image slowly fragmenting—the orange scarf going last, replaced by the shadow of dark stones, and then that, too, faded away as Madeleine stepped through the door.

And found herself at the top of broken stairs, standing in a frost-covered grove of hawthorn trees.

TWENTY-FIVE
SAFE PLACES

THUAN was standing outside the huge doors of Asmodeus's bedroom, watching Nadine fumble with a set of antique keys, when the temperature suddenly plummeted.

Nadine looked up, shock-still. "Thuan?"

He shrugged. "Don't look at me. I have absolutely no idea what's going on. I take it that's not normal?" The *khi* water around him was growing, every turn and eddy sharply limned, a wealth of familiar power that made him feel giddy.

"I don't know!" Nadine said. She'd dropped the keys, blowing on her hands to keep warm. Thuan, who was used to freezing temperatures below the Seine, merely gathered *khi* water to him, and waited. "I wasn't taking notes the last time!"

It was getting colder and colder. On the lower half of the wainscoting, frost crept like a hundred—a thousand—snakes slowly crawling across the wall, drawing spirals and circles, and complex patterns that almost felt like a hidden language. "It's in the House, too."

"I—" Nadine shook her head. "I have to know what's going on, Thuan. We'll do this later." She picked up the keys and was gone, running before he could stop her.

Thuan walked to the nearest window. The sky was still that cold, un-earthly blue; and he could guess at the presence of the wall beyond that, still blocking off the House from Paris and any help that might come. But the gardens, and the other buildings . . .

Everything was covered in a thin, glistening layer of frost. It spread across trees and grass and windows—and caught people, too, stopping them in their tracks like statues, gently coiling over their skin, leaching the color from their eyes and skin and clothes.

No, not frost. *Khi* water, honed to a killing edge.

What in heaven was going on?

Thuan looked down. The frost had spread across the dusty parquet, and was starting to root him to the floor. *No.* He drew on *khi* earth and laid it around his feet, a halo that choked the water as it tried to climb up his legs. It felt . . . familiar. Draconic. He hadn't thought there was another dragon in the House, but of course the rebels were involved with the wall. One of them had to be causing this, somehow.

Frost was going around him now, heading toward the doors, and shriveling back as if it'd met the edge of a knife. The wards on the doors, whatever they were, still held. Thuan walked to stand in front of the doors: the dark gray background, the two falling stars that wavered between silver and red. Gently, carefully, he laid his fingers, one by one, on one of the handles. Magic welled up, slowly, like blood from a wound, or heat from glowing embers. He'd expected some of the same familiar feeling he got from the drawers in Asmodeus's office, but there was nothing, merely a slow, gentle warmth that reminded him of home, and being held in loving arms.

Nadine hadn't had time to open the door. And, ordinarily, it would have been a problem—except that, with the *khi* elements so strong, and particularly *khi* water, Thuan was no longer in a position of weakness.

Water was stillness. Water was winter and the frost under his feet; but also the winter of life, and the slow creep of old age. The handle grew colder under his fingers, a cold that spread into the mechanism of the lock and into the wards surrounding it. A fine, gray dust spilled outward, and the door slowly, silently gave in, the warmth of magic fading to nothing on his skin.

The office was one thing, this room another. Thuan understood now how Nadine had felt. As he entered the bedroom, the smell of bergamot and orange blossom wafted up, so strong he turned, for a moment, to check if Asmodeus was standing right by his side. But of course there was no one.

Unwise.

The kiss?

The confidences. But thank you.

The chair where Asmodeus had sat lay half in shadow. Thuan approached it, heart in his throat, expecting, at any time, power to seize him and hold him still, the touch of fingernails raking his cheeks. But it was empty, too. He breathed out, not sure whether to be relieved or disappointed.

He turned, to check: the frost was creeping in behind him. He didn't have much time.

He stood in the center of the room, looking at the faint traceries of *khi* currents. They were weak; they had always been weak in this room that was saturated with Fallen magic. And what little there had been was being twisted out of shape by the approach of the cold. Not much time. No time, not even to save himself.

Breathe. Breathe.

Buddhist mantras, over and over, prayers to his ancestors, the sound of his breathing sinking away to nothingness, the quiet, black place where he meditated or prayed. He opened his eyes, and stared at the *khi* currents again. Faint, faded traceries on the oak wood parquet, but there was one place where they were fainter than they should have been.

Not under the bed, or the chair, but by the desk, stacked with books and scattered papers. There was a space in the wainscoting that felt soft, and pliant under his fingers, that gave way as he pushed, revealing a long, wooden chest, so charged with power and wards that it glowed in his sight.

Water. Water and stillness. Water and cold. Thuan laid both hands on the sides of the chest, and waited. *Khi* water spread from his fingers. Scales on his skin flashed in and out of existence, and he knew his antlers would be appearing and disappearing, too, and his teeth sharpened into the fangs of predators. Not that anyone, anymore, had any doubt that he was a dragon.

It wasn't like extinguishing *khi* fire: the Fallen magic refused to sink down and die. It kept pushing back, struggling to survive against the on-slaught of the water in Thuan's hands.

He was going to run out of strength, or *khi* water, or both, in spite of the House overflowing with frost. His hands were shaking, his fingers sharpening into claws; he was losing control, and the Fallen magic kept pushing and pushing, trying to find a way in. He had to stop. He had to withdraw from the room, before . . .

The chest opened, with a click that sounded like a gunshot. The Fallen magic fell away, leaving Thuan pushing against nothing. He stopped himself just in time, before he drowned whatever was inside with water.

Inside, laid on velvet lining, was a sword.

But not just any sword. Hawthorn was full of swords and knives, of old, prewar things hung above chimneys like trophies, their blades tinged with rust, their handles broken or so fragile they would never bear to be taken down. This was different.

It was huge, and lethally simple: a large, two-handed weapon with a curved guard, and a grip engraved with a thin spiral—the only concession to elegance, for everything else about the weapon was straight, and brutal, a statement of strength and power rather than beauty. Faint letters shone on the blade, in an alphabet that was utterly unfamiliar to Thuan, and the whole thing radiated so much power it was like standing next to a furnace—no, not a furnace; there was something oddly attractive about it, something of a flame to a moth. He had only to reach out, and he couldn't help himself, so he did—and the magic climbed through his hands, into his heart, a memory of tumbling down from Heaven; dreams of a distant city, bathed in golden light and the presence of God, to which he could never return, nostalgia and loss turning to sharp bitterness, the edge of a knife to cut himself and a hundred others; and then the magic withdrew, leaving behind a name that tasted like fire and brimstone on his tongue.

Lucifer Morningstar.

Thuan's hand shook, wouldn't go back to being human, his claws raking the hilt. No wonder it had been such a powerful feeling. No wonder Asmodeus had been so confident. What couldn't one do, with all of this at one's disposal?

He lifted the sword out of the chest. It was heavy, and yet it didn't feel it, more like it had always been meant for his hands.

The room was now covered in frost, the sheets and curtains shimmering with the harsh light of ice, and the oak wood floor almost vanished beneath a thin layer of whiteness. But, around him, as he walked with the blade in his hand, the frost died in a circle, utterly obliterated by the magic saturating him.

The House would be in sheer chaos. Any people who weren't frozen would be too busy trying to save themselves. It was unlikely anyone would try to stop him, and if they did, he could easily blast them unconscious.

Thuan walked on, heading toward the gardens, and the distant safety of the dragon kingdom.

IN the ruined flat, Françoise knelt by Berith's side, slowly searching for a pulse that seemed to elude her. She was alive. She had to be. It would just be so stupid of her, to come all this way and fail. . . .

"Berith. Berith."

Camille was warm against her—snug and small, completely trusting in her mother to fix whatever was wrong. If only she knew.

"Berith."

Berith's eyes opened. Silver flecks shone for a moment, and faded again. "I'm—fine. I—" She took a deep, shuddering breath, her hands convulsively gripping Françoise's. "You should have left."

"Not without you." The same old, tired argument. "Did you—did you uproot?"

"Not quite." Berith pulled herself up to a standing position, pushing the armchair's remnant out of the way. "But soon. I can't sustain . . ." Her legs shook. Françoise fought not to cry.

"Let's go."

"They'll come back."

"And find a ruined flat full of corpses and scorch marks. We can hide. You"—Françoise struggled to speak—"you don't look like a Fallen anymore." If she had ever looked like one. If she hadn't been dying. The flat was a ruin, the cupboards splinters of wood, the wall blown open to snowflakes and cold wind, her ancestral altar askew, the offerings scattered, the small pictures of her grandparents overturned.

"Of course not. I—" She shook her head. "There's no safe place, Françoise."

Françoise tasted ashes, and dust, on her tongue, and the bitter taste of defeat. "There is. Hawthorn."

"Hawthorn is falling."

"Not yet." Françoise stroked Camille's head. She thought of Asmodeus's smug, self-satisfied face as he calmly told her that she would find it no easy thing, to raise her child, Berith's child. That their situation was untenable, and that their only safety lay in Hawthorn—even as he stole them away to force Berith to come to him. "They wouldn't have come for you if they were sure of winning. It wouldn't have mattered." Every word felt dry, drained of substance, hard pebbles she couldn't face swallowing. "You said it yourself. A lone Fallen can't stand against a House. If they had Hawthorn, if they truly knew that they had wrested control of it from Asmodeus, they wouldn't have cared a jot about you."

Berith's face didn't move. "A lone Fallen can't stand against a House. I'm dying, Françoise. There's so little that I can do."

"And you would rather die here than elsewhere?"

"I would rather know you were safe!"

"Safe, and starving in the streets?" The words were coming out fast now, all the things she'd left unsaid, all the wounds she'd never torn open, the resentment and the fears she faced at night, while Berith slept fitfully—the choices she'd made and was no longer sure she could live up to. "Tearing my fingers into pieces with sewing trying to earn just enough coin to live? Going hungry so that Camille can feed? Is that better?"

It was unfair, every word hurting Berith like a hurled stone, when she was no longer in a state to parry anything, or offer any coherent response. But it was that or letting her die here. "I don't know," Berith said. Her face twisted into the heartbreaking expression of a hurt child. "What do you want?"

A long, happy, prosperous future for the two—the three of them. A childhood of games and laughter and carelessness for Camille, all the things

Françoise couldn't provide, Berith couldn't provide. "A future," she whispered, finally. "Any future that isn't death."

The wind was rising again, biting at her bare fingers, insinuating itself in the space between her clothes. It brought the smell of snow and rain.

"A future." Berith's eyes were flecked with silver again, and the armchair was a sundered throne on a dais choked with ashes. Instead of a ruined wall, there was the shadow of bookshelves, and the faint smell of parchment and books—and a sound, almost on the cusp of hearing—voiceless, toneless, like a distant swarm of bees. Light streamed toward Berith, limned her in shades of gold and orange—erasing the bruised eyes, the raised shape of bones beneath translucent skin. "Come," she whispered.

Françoise climbed the three steps, stood by Berith's side. She could almost see the flat if she squinted: an overlay of the dingy, ruined room against what remained of the dominion.

"There's so little left," Berith said, her voice echoing in the emptiness. "Despair, and anger, and emptiness."

"I know," Françoise said. The noise was growing, fragments of words and sentences in a language she couldn't understand, like being thrown into deep waters, not knowing how to swim.

A price, Berith had said. There was always a price, even for small, diminished wishes that weren't heart's desires.

But they had so few choices.

Berith kissed her, slowly, gently. No magic, nothing, just warm, supple lips on hers, arms wrapped around her, holding her safe for a single, suspended moment. "There's nothing here that will ever shake the foundations of the world. Nothing large or earth-shattering."

"Ssh," Françoise said, and kissed her back—and for a while there was nothing but the three of them, an illusion of a happy family, safe and sound and feeling nothing of cold, or hunger, or hopelessness. For a while, nothing but gentle warmth, suffusing her and Camille and Berith.

But all things ended, in time.

Berith laid her hand against Françoise's forehead, gently tracing its outline. "I can't give you your heart's desire," she whispered. "You know why."

Because there was a price. Because there would always be a price to pay, and she couldn't afford to pay. Because she'd already been granted it, in some way. Berith and Camille were still alive, still with her. So many things. "I know," Françoise said.

Warmth rose, within her: the comforting presence of Berith's magic, bathing her in its glow. "This is yours, for safekeeping," Berith said. "What little there is, with my blessing. Because nothing here is shallow, or meaningless, either."

The dominion was fading again, but this time there weren't even traceries left, and the flat itself was shaking. The floor shifted under Françoise's feet, became covered with a thick layer of dust. The broken throne became the armchair again, wavering to the pale color of the sky, its flower patterns reabsorbed. And then it was gone, faded as though it had never been.

Berith stumbled, caught herself with a grimace. She raised her hands again. Light flew to them, ten thousand flecks of silver rising from the floor, sinking beneath the skin of her arms, of her legs, briefly imprinting themselves on her face before being soaked up. Françoise reached out for her, but Berith pushed her away, shaking her head. *Not now.*

The distant noise Françoise had been hearing grew and grew, became the rush of a wave—and then a sharp, wounding sound, like a huge stone table snapping in two. And then silence, and stillness, and a spreading sense that the world had just been hollowed out.

There was something left, around them. It was as though it were the ghost of a flat: every piece of furniture was still there, all the broken walls still in place, but her gaze slid right off them, unable to focus on anything. Like a chameleon on a background, always fading away, never coming into focus. Her eyes watered, trying to keep up.

Berith stood up, shakily. Her face was sunken, her movements tentative. Françoise reached out, again. With all the magic sloshing out of her, she could strengthen her; she could—

Berith shook her head. "Don't," she said. "I can't hold it. It would burn me alive."

"There has to be something."

"Not until I find another place to anchor myself." She grimaced again, gripped Françoise's hand hard enough to bruise. "Let's go."

*   *   *

PHILIPPE was lying on a cold surface, feeling currents of *khi* water swirl around him. He'd given up trying to pull himself upward—winded and drained, his hands aching with the wounds he'd received when breaking the cup.

Noises of battle, screams, and the smell of blood. The *khi* currents around him became tinged with metal and water, the familiar pattern of approaching death.

"Philippe. Philippe." Someone raised his head on her lap. It was Isabelle, staring down at him.

"You." He swallowed, feeling only the dryness in his throat. "You're alive."

Isabelle shook her head. "Later. You need to get up."

"Why—what's happening?"

She pulled him, centimeter by agonizing centimeter; left him, finally, standing—shaking—in the darkness of the shed.

There were no guards left alive. And Annamites had fallen, too. He caught a glimpse of Jérôme, unseeing eyes staring upward. The remainder of them were gathered at the back of the shed, behind Olympe, who, quivering with anger, was facing down ten armed dragons and sea creatures.

Their leader, a crab official Philippe didn't recognize, held two swords, one in each hand. Her cheeks were the blue-gray, mottled color of a crustacean's shell, cracked and broken in patches that even a thick layer of ceruse couldn't disguise. "I may not have been clear," she said. *Khi* water swirled around her, currents bound to her will. "You may stay here. Shelter and accommodation will be found, and I suppose we always have a use for servants. Or you can die. There is no going home."

Olympe's face was set. "We're not servants. And we didn't ask to come here." She turned, briefly, to the people cowering behind her. "Anyone who wants to take that offer is free to do so. But I'm not dying in the name of absurd secrecy. You're the ones who took us from our homes!"

"*We* didn't," the crab official said, pointedly. Her expression said, very clearly, that she got to clean up other people's messes. "And it doesn't matter."

No better, in the end, than Houses, but then, why had he thought it would be the case, that the dragon kingdom was somehow immune to the tangle of small and large cruelties Paris had become, after the war?

Philippe considered, for a moment, walking away, while the crab official's attention wasn't on either of them—halfheartedly, and without conviction. Other people's messes, indeed.

"Grand Chancellor."

Her head whipped around, to stare at him, surprised that he could read her title even from the small patch on the uniform she wore. "Another mortal? This is getting tiresome. Get with the others." Two soldiers moved, around her, made for Philippe with bayonets at the ready.

He would get only one chance, one throw of the *mat chuoc* tiles, one colossal bluff. Because he certainly didn't have the energy for more than one. As the guards moved, Philippe yanked to him *khi* earth and *khi* metal, the unclaimed currents in the shed, and drew them through the guards' legs like scythes. No finesse or subtlety, just brute force, of which he had so little.

The guards toppled, bleeding. The crab official's painted eyebrows shot up.

"I'm not mortal. And they're under my protection." He used, not the Viet Annamites spoke, but the older, ornate language of the court of the Jade Emperor; when he had been an envoy, bearing decrees of execution into dragon kingdoms. He hadn't spoken this way for years. The words felt odd, on his tongue—comforting, too, the mantle of an illusory power.

She watched him, for a while. Her hands, wrapped around the hilt of the swords, were long and jointed.

"You're weak," she snorted. "In no state to dictate anything."

"Am I?" By his side, Isabelle was quiet. She might have remembered how to wield power, but she no longer had any, and this deep into the dragon kingdom there would be no Fallen magic anyway. He planted his feet, firmly, in the silt of the Seine, feeling his entire body anchor amidst sea currents. He'd sat, once, in a cave on a mountain, fasting and meditating, and opening himself to the elements. There was something left of that unyielding balance; of being a quiet, utterly unmovable center through which everything passed.

The crab official grinned. "Don't stall for time."

Philippe hadn't been stalling for time, but for strength. He cast out again for *khi* currents, but this time he aimed straight for the *khi* water by the crab official's side, the currents that she claimed for her own. Startled, she tried to hang on to them. He pulled again, in another direction. Balance. Strength. He couldn't hold for long, wasn't going to have the energy, but . . .

The threads snapped, coming to rest in his hand, where they became blue flame, dancing on his fingers. The crab official's nostrils flared, her antennae stiffening.

"They're under my protection," Philippe said, again.

At length, the crab official shook her head, and made a dismissive gesture. "Houseless mortals," she said, with a snort. "It's not as if anyone will believe you if you talk of spirits and dragons. Come. We have better things to do," she said, and she and her men left the shed, heading for the wrecked wall.

Olympe walked to Philippe. "That was exceedingly foolish."

Philippe closed his fingers. The blue flame died. It was all he could do to keep standing, knowing that if he collapsed, the crab official would see his weakness, and that nothing would stop her.

The others were watching him with something like wary awe, their faces lit up with an expression that made him uncomfortable. "Grandmother," Hortense said. "He's—"

"A fool," Olympe said, without breaking stride.

"You were the one who told me to get involved. Grandmother."

"Killing yourself in the process?" Olympe rolled her eyes upward. She held his gaze, for a while. "'Grandmother.' How old are you?"

Philippe didn't feel like debating the finer points of who used what form of address to whom. "We can discuss that later. Please. Let's get out first."

Olympe snorted. Then she looked at Isabelle. "My apologies," she said in French. "You are?"

"This is my friend," Philippe said, throat dry. "Isabelle."

"Grandmother." Isabelle bowed, slowly, never taking her eyes off her.

"Isabelle." Olympe rolled the name on her tongue. Then she shook her head. "She'll do. And you're right," she said grudgingly. "Let's go home."

*　　*　　*

MADELEINE stood, breathing hard, in the midst of the trees. Frost rimmed them—garlands of ice, white patterns on thin trunks, glistening thorns covered with water, pink petals hardened to the texture of crystals.

And hands and arms, too. Even with the covering of frost, it was obvious that the fruit of those particular trees wasn't berries. And, even with the cold, some of them were still moving, trying to reach out for her with sparkling hands, to grab her and pull her upward, into the thorns, her blood sinking into the trees to replenish the wards. . . .

Madeleine leaped away—stumbled on her bad calf, went down, biting her tongue. They were slow, because of the cold. That was the only reason she was still alive.

Echaroth. She'd grown up in the House. She'd heard the tales, and the legends, and had never thought that some of them might be true. No, that wasn't it. She'd heard tales of heads of Houses, and leadership, and had thought they would never apply to a mere gardener.

The pain in her ribs and calf was . . . not gone, just faded away to its faint, usual levels—for these wounds had not healed, would never heal. The drawing room where Elphon had died was gone, and Asmodeus's image with it. It was just . . . the hawthorn trees, and the blue sky above her, and the link to the House, a cold, empty thing in her mind, sinking further and further out of reach the more time passed.

There were noises, ahead; and, with angel magic still coursing within her, she could feel the faint heat of spells being cast. She walked toward it, because she didn't know what else to do.

Among the trees, Clothilde was fighting Yen Oanh. She was limned in dark, textured light, a fine coating over her arms like the feathers of a blackbird. They were locked in some alien, beautiful dance. Yen Oanh's neck was bleeding, but it didn't seem to make her any slower, or less dangerous. She was still in human form: hands with nails that were slightly too sharp, and patches of scales on her face, and the oily reflections of the river in her hair.

Behind them was a hawthorn tree; and bound to it by a network of ice and roots was Asmodeus. His face was white—not pale, but completely white, the speckled color of frost, lenses of his glasses sparkling like diamonds, frozen branches clenched between his lips. He didn't move, or look up, or give any sign of life.

But. But he was alive. Had to be. Otherwise the link to the House would be gone, completely, or in Ciseis's grasp.

A few more steps, and Madeleine saw the body, lying on its side in the opening between two hawthorn trees. She'd seen Ciseis only once, from afar, in the gardens, but there was no mistaking her. Or the red wounds in her side, the ones that had killed her.

She was no fighter. She couldn't take on Yen Oanh, even if Clothilde hadn't been keeping her busy. She shouldn't even have been there!

As she watched, Clothilde and Yen Oanh's fight moved away from the tree that held Asmodeus, and, for a moment, out of her sight.

Madeleine moved, fast, before she could stop to consider the folly of what she was doing. She ran for the tree. She had been ready to burn the threads with angel fire, but there was a knife, planted in the ground in front of Asmodeus, its blade the same dark brown with green streaks as the stones of the wall. She picked it up, feeling power coursing up her fingers.

The tree loomed over her, branches slowly stretching, slowed down by the frost. Yen Oanh and Clothilde were still fighting, not paying any attention to her.

Madeleine hefted the knife, with a confidence she didn't feel, and cut one of the threads that bound Asmodeus to the tree.

Or tried to.

It fought back, twisting and writhing out of her grasp, its thorns raking her skin. She cut at it again; and again and again, until it finally fell still, gorged with the light of magic. Blood spurted out, staining her fingers—his blood?

Another thread, another struggle. It wasn't ice, wasn't roots. It was red, like a frozen capillary. Slick and smooth, it kept slipping out of her grasp, the blade narrowly missing her own fingers. The blood coating her hands just made it worse.

She looked up. Clothilde and Yen Oanh were still out of sight. But she didn't have much time. They would come back. And Clothilde might be able to distract Yen Oanh, but Madeleine didn't have much that would stand against any attack.

It should have been . . . it should have been Elphon, or anyone else within the House. Not her. Never her.

She cut a third thread, a fourth, struggling to grasp them. Blood stained her shirt, her hands, her arms, a rank, animal smell, a sticky, slippery coating that threatened, again and again, to make her lose the knife. How many were left? Ten, twenty? She was never going to make it. . . .

A blast of ice froze her hands, narrowly missing her face. Yen Oanh and Clothilde were back in sight, and Yen Oanh looked furious. "Two of you?" she said. "It won't be enough, to defend Hawthorn."

Clothilde grabbed her, deflecting the next blast of ice. Yen Oanh's cheeks were hollowed out, like Ngoc Bich's, showing white bone and rotting scales.

"The House still stands," Clothilde spat.

"Not for long."

Another blast of ice: Madeleine raised her hands, drawing crude, shivering wards from the magic within her. The wards held, barely. She could feel them bending in with every blast Yen Oanh was sending her way.

Clothilde bore Yen Oanh to the ground, pinned her arms and hands away from her. Clothilde's arms were now completely black—no, it wasn't her arms, but something at her back, the same black wings Madeleine had once seen around Asmodeus, spreading behind Clothilde until she hardly seemed human anymore. When she moved, there was a sound like a rush of wind in the heavens, thunderous and terrible.

Madeleine continued, mechanically, to cut thread after thread. The world had shrunk to her and the tree; and the branches, writhing and cutting under her touch. The blood on her hands was the tree's and hers mingled, and she wasn't going to hold out long, at this rate. Everything was wobbling and tightening, with that peculiar sharp throbbing that came on the edge of unconsciousness. . . .

"Madeleine!" Clothilde screamed.

Madeleine jerked awake with a start. The knife had fallen on the ground: she had to twist it away from the tendrils that had wrapped themselves around the handle. They snapped with the wet, slurping sound of a cut windpipe. But, as she turned to Asmodeus again, she saw that the first thread she'd cut was knitting itself back together.

No. No.

She had perhaps six threads left. An eternity, with Yen Oanh's ice battering away at her inadequate defenses, and the entire tree trying to put itself together again . . .

Help me, she whispered, to the God she so seldom prayed to. *Please.*

Above her, Asmodeus stirred. His face was still that odd, speckled white, but the ice on his glasses melted, and his eyes, no longer gray-green, but colorless, focused on her. His mouth worked, trying to shape a word. Her name?

Six threads. Madeleine gave up on trying to protect her fingers, and slashed at random, as hard as she could—again and again, until her hands were slick with her own blood, and pain was shooting up her arm—and Asmodeus's body flopped in her arms, with nothing to hold him upright anymore, mouth still filled with thorns and pale, glistening berries.

Yen Oanh was up again, her hands held in front of her, sending a wave of ice toward Madeleine.

Her wards caved in. Frost seized her fingers, hardening congealed blood all over her hands. She flexed them, trying not to scream at the pain that shot up. Once, twice, and again and again until a thin network of cracks spread across the frozen blood.

Clothilde threw herself on Yen Oanh, pinning her to a tree where a blue-eyed body—Uphir's—dangled, hands futilely trying to break the spell of cold, to reach down and take either or both of them. In Madeleine's mind, the link to the House stirred, briefly, and sank again, utterly spent.

Wake up. Wake up, damn you. There was no one else, to take the House. She or Clothilde, she supposed, if either of them thought that way, grasping what was offered, grabbing at power for power's sake, but they didn't. They weren't Ciseis.

She had magic. Not much, not enough, but it was fire. It was warmth. It might be enough to burn away whatever held Asmodeus. Madeleine cleared away branches from his face and mouth, heedless of the way they dug into her skin. And then laid both hands on his frozen chest, and without stopping to think, or ask for a permission that he couldn't have given her, she bent down and, laying her lips on his, poured everything she had into him.

It wasn't a kiss. It didn't even feel like resuscitation. He wasn't moving, wasn't speaking, and frozen thorns brushed against her lips. Her mouth filled with the salty, animal taste of her own blood.

She withdrew, panting. Nothing left. If Yen Oanh targeted her again . . .

The link to the House flared to life, a slow, quiet thing within her. And, at her feet—slowly unfolding, limb after limb, spitting out fragments of thorns and branches on the frost-covered earth—Asmodeus rose.

TWENTY-SIX
A TREE OF THORNS

BERITH didn't speak as they stumbled away from the flat. She just grew paler and paler, the hollows under her eyes grayer, her skin thin, translucent, like rice paper sprayed with water.

On the omnibus, Françoise cradled Camille against her chest, letting the baby feed. Even the rush of euphoria associated with that couldn't overwhelm the gravity of their situation. The only thing she'd taken from the flat was the pictures of her grandparents and Etienne, scraps of papers retrieved from their frames, faded photographs snug against her skin, dry and bloodless and cold. Her only link, anymore, with the past. Berith had taken the chess book, grimacing; had looked, for a while, at the dictionary. "Too heavy," she said.

"I—" Françoise started to say she could carry it for her, but they both knew she couldn't. "I'm sorry."

"We'll find another one," Berith said. She clung to the book as though it were a lifeline. "I'm sure Hawthorn has Annamite dependents."

Hawthorn. With every bus stop, the House grew closer; with every street they passed. Asmodeus. Cruelty, casual arrogance, the province of the thoughtless, nonchalant powerful. Those who took and took, and gave away only when it suited them.

The walk from Pont de Passy to Pont de Grenelle was almost too much for Berith. She had to stop, several times, leaning against the railings of the low walls that separated the city from the Seine. "Berith?"

Berith shook her head. "I—I'll be fine."

She wouldn't, unless she found a way to root herself once more, to a place she wouldn't be able to leave, just like the flat.

Hawthorn.

The word tasted like blood.

When they reached Pont de Grenelle, there was no House. Merely a shimmering, black wall with the hint of cracks across its surface. People milled outside it: Hawthorn dependents in dark gray and silver, laborers, curious passersby, none of them daring to approach the wall.

Françoise pressed her hand against it, felt the slight yield, the hint of choking, of decay—the fire of angel magic, mingled with it all. It was weak, even weaker than the blade fragments she had given to Madeleine.

"Françoise, you shouldn't. . . ."

If she pushed, with Berith's magic and strength within her, if she laid her hand flat, as Nemnestra had done, trying to enter the flat . . .

Cracks appeared around her fingers, spread like spiderwebs across the surface of the wall. She pushed again, and entire fragments of green, brittle stone came loose, falling at her feet with a tinkle like broken glass.

Again, and again, until she'd cleared an opening large enough for the two of them. The crowd watched in silence. The only sound was Berith's labored breathing.

Behind it, the wrought-iron gates of the House, the ones she'd walked through, a lifetime ago, when things had been . . . different. Less desperate, or perhaps she'd only been less aware of the situation.

"Come on."

Inside, the overgrown garden she remembered was covered with frost, and full of—statues? No, not statues, people caught by the cold where they stood, the colors of Hawthorn drowned by the ice.

Berith took a sharper breath as she crossed between the open gates. "It's dying," she whispered. "He's dying."

"It'll be fine," Françoise said desperately, a cold, comforting lie. Every few steps, she had to pull harder, so that the frost wouldn't root her to the ground. She sent magic into her legs: angel fire, to keep away the cold.

Berith shook her head. "Deeper. We need to go deeper." She leaned on Françoise as they stumbled through the gardens, her weight growing larger and larger as they walked. Between Berith and Camille and the birth, Françoise wasn't going to hold for long.

Glistening hedges, white paths, the ice hiding the flecks of dirt and debris in the gravel; fountains that had become alien concoctions, their stone transmuted into crystals, their water cut off. Fewer and fewer people: it was just them, and the House.

One step, then another, one breath, struggling for the next one . . . Cold had seized her feet, her shoes feeling full of biting water. Every movement felt through tar.

Berith's weight lifted, abruptly, from Françoise. Not because she'd stood on her own: she was on her knees in frost-covered grass, the chess book fallen by her side, open on two pages replete with drawings of game boards. "Berith!"

"Can't." Her voice was a hiss.

"You." Françoise held her breath until the world seemed to burn and crinkle around her. "You need to root. I'm sorry. You have to."

Berith shook her head. Frost curled up around her, anchoring her to the ground. It was creeping up her body, turning her into a statue, like the dependents they'd seen in the gardens. "He has to let me."

No need to ask who "he" was. "I doubt he's in much of a position to object," Françoise said, through gritted teeth. "What do you need?"

"Time," Berith said. She stared at the grass under her, and back at Françoise. "And less fear would be good, too. I haven't done this in—so many years. And never in a House before."

Françoise squeezed her hand, gently. "You can do it," she said. "You've done it before. And . . . for all that's going on, we might as well not be standing in a House. Remember we still have a game to finish."

Berith forced a smile, haunted and curt and joyless. "Figuring out how to beat you? I couldn't even beat a beginner, Françoise. We both know it."

Not enough, then. But why had she thought it would be? "Here."

Françoise undid her scarf, and held Camille out to Berith. The baby gurgled, snuggling against Berith's chest. Françoise kept a wary eye on the frost, ready to snatch her if necessary. "If not the game . . ."

Berith's eyes, flecked with faint traces of silver, were dark and unreadable. "The future," she whispered, one hand tracing the contours of Camille's face. "Any future." She laid a finger into Camille's mouth, let the baby suck on it for a while, a look of raw contentment spreading across both their faces; a heartbreaking expression, for it wouldn't last. It couldn't.

"Thank you," she said to Françoise.

"I can give you back the magic," Françoise said.

Berith shook her head. "It was a gift. Here." She handed Camille back to Françoise. Camille, scandalized, looked as though she might cry for a moment, but then her mouth opened, seeking Françoise's breast.

"Hang on," Françoise said. She shook her feet to remove the frost, and undid her scarf again. Camille wailed, a short, high-pitched sound—hungry hungry—and then Françoise managed to hold her against her breast again, and the sounds of weeping gave way to profound, contented silence.

Berith's eyes were closed. She was whispering in a slow, harsh language that Françoise couldn't understand, words dragging at her ears like barbed hooks. Slowly, gradually, her skin lit up, a faint, almost invisible radiance that gripped her, sharpening the silver flecks in her eyes. Beneath her, the frost was melting in a circle; and, somehow, it seemed to go beyond that boundary, everything slowly becoming sharper, more present on the path, all the way to the Seine and the shadow of the wall.

Berith plunged both hands into the earth. They went up to the wrists, a faint blue shimmer rising around them, a smell of churned earth. "There is nothing," she whispered. "Almost nothing. No wards. Oh, Asmodeus." She looked as though she might weep.

"Berith. You have to go on."

There was no frost left around Françoise, either. Shadows rose, around her, dark and blocky, the bookshelves of Berith's dominion, with a faint odor of parchment and glue, and a faint memory of a thousand voices speaking. The sky was blue and clear, with no hint of pollution.

There was no throne. But, at Berith's back, a growing shadow that might have been wings, black, opaque ones like the ones Françoise had seen behind Asmodeus. For a single, agonizing moment she was in the flat again, lying on her back and watching both of them bend over her, limned with their power—for a moment she was in pain and dying, and denied comfort. . . .

It passed, like a released breath. Françoise forced her heart to stop shaking, and held Camille tighter against her.

Berith withdrew her hands from the ground. They came up with a handful of shining earth. And, as she did so, the shadow at her back became sharper and sharper, growing apart from her, slowly growing and blossoming.

Not wings. Never wings. But the shape of a huge hawthorn tree, bearing flowers the color of ivory, its branches spread around Berith, like arms reaching out to enfold her in thorns.

Berith's eyes were fully silver now, with no trace of brown. She pulled herself up, slowly, gracefully. The branches of the tree moved with her, the entire structure opening up like a hundred hands. Françoise watched, transfixed.

Finally, Berith exhaled. There were no bruises under her eyes, no trace of fatigue. She looked almost unearthly, shining with a faint light. Like a Fallen, a House-bound, someone who would never bother with the likes of Françoise. And then she frowned, and it was all gone, familiar annoyance and worry taking over.

"Berith." Heart in her throat, Françoise walked to her, hugged her, hard. Frost had died around them, the hawthorn tree sharply defined in the midst of bookshelves.

Berith smiled, stroking Camille's head. "It will be fine."

"How?" Françoise forced herself to speak; found words that wouldn't come. "The House."

Berith took her hand, laid it, gently, on the trunk of the hawthorn tree—and Françoise felt a bare hint of warmth, in the midst of ice and cold and stillness. A hint of the thaw, which became a distant, sarcastic, and all-too-familiar presence, struggling to pull himself together.

"Now we wait," Berith said. "It's not over."

*   *   *

TIME seemed to slow down to treacle; suspended, as Asmodeus pulled himself to his knees. Behind him—beyond him—Clothilde was still fighting Yen Oanh, with less and less energy, the little magic she'd taken with her running out.

The lenses of his glasses were fogged with frost, his eyes barely visible beyond the fog. He laid one hand onto the earth of the grove. Frost shriveled and died around it, a thin contour of mud in the overwhelming whiteness around them. Without thinking, Madeleine held out a hand, to help him stand.

He smiled, and it was a fraction of his old expression, amused and cruel.

"Madeleine. Still no bandages for the bleeding?" His touch should have been like fire, should have brimmed with thoughtless power, the same thing that had filled her back in the dragon kingdom. But there was nothing. Dying embers. The link to the House in her mind, barely palpable. It had all been for nothing; she'd walked through water and the dead just to watch him fall. . . .

Asmodeus gripped her hand, and pushed, so strongly it almost sent her back to her knees. He was upright now, and couldn't hide the tremor running through him. She could hear—labored, slow—his breathing, when she'd never heard anything from him before. He'd always been silent as a hunting cat, making no noise or warning.

"Tell me you have something," Madeleine said. "Tell me . . ." *Tell me we're not doomed. Tell me it was worth it.*

Yen Oanh had forced Clothilde to the ground, and was straddling her, one hand on her throat, ice spreading from her outstretched claws to cover Clothilde's skin above the straight collar of the tunic.

Asmodeus didn't move, for a while. "Do you trust me, Madeleine?"

She feared him. She loathed him. And yet, despite that—"You keep the House safe," she said, slowly. "I don't have to . . ." She didn't have to like him. She didn't have to be less afraid of who he was, of what he would do. She would *never* not be afraid of him, never attain the easy familiarity of Iaris, the unthinking devotion of Elphon. "What do you want?" she asked, instead.

Asmodeus laid a hand on the hawthorn tree that had almost killed him. His lips were still red with dried blood, cut by the branches he'd spat out, his voice a thin, reedy whisper of sound. "The trees are the foundations of the wards. The strength of the House. The strength of its head." His expression was still distantly amused. "And there is a new tree, in the House, new roots extending into my dominion. . . ." The fog on his glasses was melting, and something passed from the tree into him, not the light of angel magic, but something that made him look sharper. Better defined, as if more than frost had melted from his shoulders.

"You want me to distract Yen Oanh," Madeleine said, heavily. It wasn't as if that were new.

Asmodeus looked, for a moment, at Yen Oanh and Clothilde—Clothilde's arms, scrabbling, ineffectively, to push Yen Oanh off her, the shadows around them fading into featureless white. His mouth tightened. "You misunderstand." He knelt, picked up the knife; rose. The tremor was barely visible this time.

And, without another word, he walked away toward Yen Oanh, leaving Madeleine at the foot of the hawthorn tree.

"Killing the weak?" he said, to Yen Oanh, as he neared her.

"The corrupted," Yen Oanh said. She took her hands from Clothilde, and stood up. Clothilde wasn't moving, but perhaps there was still a chance. . . . Madeleine dug her fingernails into her hands, to prevent herself from running to Clothilde's side.

"The kingdom of diseased coral and decaying palaces." Asmodeus's voice was slow, hypnotic. He had the knife in his hand, but made no move. Simply stood, watching her. At his feet, frost melted, slowly, gradually, the trunks of hawthorn trees returning to shades of brown, flecked with fungus and mold. "You have odd notions about corruption."

"Ask yourself how we came to that point."

"Isolation. The delusion that you could stand apart and hidden from the city forever."

"We could have. The wall—"

"All walls come down, in time. And all edifices have flaws."

"Like Hawthorn?"

"We're no different. And I claim no moral superiority."

It was like watching him with the leader of the soldiers when they'd fled Yen Oanh after her imprisonment. Poking and needling and playing on fears—or, in this case, Yen Oanh's anger—until he could strike. And yet . . .

And yet, he'd wanted something from Madeleine.

A distraction?

You misunderstand.

Do you trust me?

He had the knife. He was going to stab Yen Oanh, for why else would he have picked it up? But he was weak, and slow, and would summon nothing of the effortless speed and elegance he'd had—and even that, in the dragon kingdom, had failed to do more than slow Yen Oanh down. She was going to move away, and let him exhaust himself, and start, again, the slow process of killing the House.

He was the distraction. The one person Yen Oanh wouldn't take her eyes from, the symbol of everything she wanted to tear down.

"Your House certainly has flaws." Yen Oanh's voice was malicious. "Do you think you've earned more than a reprieve? You're weakening as we speak."

"Not quite that fast," Asmodeus said, mildly. "Or that conveniently."

There was a hawthorn tree behind Yen Oanh, the one that held Uphir's frozen shape. No. If Asmodeus held her attention long enough, it wasn't going to be frozen anymore. The magic spreading from him would have banished the frost on that, too.

Blood. The blood of heads of Houses. Of dependents.

Of dragons.

"And what do you hope to achieve, even if we die? Your wall is broken, and other Houses will rush to fill the vacuum we leave. You'll fall, one way or another."

"You know nothing."

"On the contrary. I've had several mortal lifetimes to watch power games."

The line of brown reached the branches where Uphir hung. Madeleine took a deep, burning breath, and started to run. She'd have screamed, but she had no energy left in her wasted lungs. Not that it mattered: Yen Oanh looked up at her—a fraction of a second—and then dismissed her as no threat, and focused back on Asmodeus.

Who moved, feinting, the blade in his hands aiming for her chest. Yen Oanh danced away, once, twice, again and again, smiling coldly all the while. Asmodeus's hands were shaking, his face pale again. Yen Oanh had been right: he was going to collapse again; there was no time left. . . .

Madeleine covered the last of the distance separating her from them—and, heedless of the knife weaving its way in and out of the fray, grabbed Yen Oanh. Borne by her speed, she pushed her against the trunk of the hawthorn tree and held her, panting, for a fraction of a second.

Yen Oanh's lips moved. *Not enough,* she was going to say, mockingly. Not enough to defend much of anything.

But then Uphir's pale, thin hands reached down, the entire tree stretching, branches extending like thorny arms, wrapping themselves around both of them, and pulling.

For a moment—a single, timeless moment—Madeleine hung sideways, as if flying, and then the thorns were biting into her flesh, and pain shot everywhere—a scream scraping her throat raw—the grove, seen upside down, the frost receding from Clothilde's body. Fire on her skin, a hundred—a thousand—bites on her arms and legs, and branches wrapping themselves around her chest, cutting off her breath—it hurt to breathe, but she was still struggling to get some air—to live, in spite of it all.

Do you trust me?

Of course she couldn't. Of course, the good of the House always came first. Blood for wards, blood for spells, blood for the strength of its head.

Within her, the link to the House flared into life, a pyre that consumed every thought, made the blood in her veins liquid fire. Her hands spasmed, fingers stretched past endurance, arms and legs bending into painful, impossible shapes. The tree was taking her in, branches weaving over her lips and clogging her nostrils, a hundred prickles under her eyes as thorns climbed up her cheeks—they were going to sew her eyelids shut, or to puncture her eyeballs, or both.

And then it all vanished. The tree let her go, and she was falling, clinging to the trunk, scraping her palms against its surface. Hands grabbed her, threw her away. She scrabbled upward into a sitting position.

Asmodeus detached himself from the tree, took a few, shaking steps out of its reach. He watched her, for what seemed like an eternity, gray-green gaze transfixing her like a spear. Behind him, in the tree, Yen Oanh hung—brown eyes open, antlers covered with a thin network of cracks like broken eggshells—her flesh pale and sickly, her body twisted out of shape by the branches that held her, her mouth open in a scream that looked as though it would never cease.

Her. It would have been her, too, endlessly kept alive for the good of the House she had tried to destroy, sucked dry to replenish the wards that kept Hawthorn safe.

Nausea welled up, uncontrollable, knifing Madeleine in the stomach, and she was on her knees again, vomiting, coughing up fragments of twigs and thorns mingled with bile.

"Such a shame," Asmodeus whispered, each word cutting into her flesh like a knife blade. "A waste of strength, some might say. But I always stand by loyal dependents."

Madeleine, still with the curdled taste of vomit in her mouth, raised her head.

Slowly, inexorably, Asmodeus sank down to one knee in the midst of the half-frozen grove; and didn't rise again.

THUAN was almost at the Seine when he stopped.

Ahead of him was the abruptness of the wall. The dark surface was now shot through with cracks, like eggshell porcelain, or the walls of the palace in the dragon kingdom. There was also a larger opening, a door that seemed to lead back to the Seine, though he could see nothing but darkness within.

Except . . .

His eye was drawn, again, to the left, at what should have been the boundary of the House with the streets. It was still wreathed with mist, but he caught a glimpse of the same thing he had before: hints of skeletal trees from which dangled large, indistinct shapes, and berries the color of fire.

Something . . . something was pulsing, softly, in that direction, drawing the blade in his hand toward it, as surely as a hound scenting blood.

Power brimmed within him, slow and dark and cruel, the desire to reshape everything to his will. He could easily push through, go back to the kingdom and find Second Aunt.

It would have been the sensible, reasonable thing.

Instead, Thuan found himself walking toward the mist.

Like the frost, it shriveled around him. He was hardly aware of channeling angel magic into it. Cutoff *khi* currents flailed, and awkwardly reshaped themselves into smaller, weaker eddies, and still he walked.

Ahead of him, the trees became sharper: hawthorns, some in flower, some in fruit—and some bearing twisted, contorted bodies that held only a passing semblance to life. The outermost were covered in frost; as Thuan walked deeper into the grove, the layers of frost became thinner and thinner. Hands and branches reached down, slowly, trying to scoop him up, but withdrew as if scalded when they neared the blade.

Ahead, nothing but silence; but at last he reached two trees that were entirely free of frost, and a circle of green grass and churned mud. And, within . . .

Three women: two dead, the *khi* currents around them saturated with metal and water, and one on all fours, coughing and struggling to breathe. And a little way from them, Asmodeus.

He was on one knee, head bowed, both hands driven deep into the earth. Magic—faint, insubstantial—rippled out, currents of *khi* water shriveling and dying around him. He didn't move, not even when Thuan walked closer: too weary, too spent to do so.

Thuan looked up, at the tree behind Asmodeus—saw Yen Oanh caught there, her mouth open in a soundless scream, her entire body twisted and contorted.

"Asmodeus." Thuan's voice came through a dry, burning throat.

Still nothing. Then, at last—at long last—a slow, ponderous rising of his head, gray-green gaze focusing on him. His face was pale, skeletal, cheekbones sharp, lips chapped and reddened with blood.

"Dragon prince." The voice was low, spent—raw. It made Thuan feel as though someone were scooping his innards out with a hook. "What a surprise—always showing up at . . . inconvenient times."

"Inconvenient times. You. You were going to kill me," Thuan said. Still might, for all he knew; still might hound him all the way into the kingdom. "You . . ." He struggled for words. "You and your ritual and your conquest. Why did you even have to take an interest in us?"

Asmodeus made a sound, low and rasping. It took Thuan a moment to realize that it was laughter, not cruel or malevolent but genuinely amused. "You have the sword," he said.

He did. He looked, again, at Asmodeus, felt Morningstar's power surge through him, hungering to take, to cut, to hoard—anything to fill that gaping hurt, that unbearable loneliness. "You want me to take the House?"

Again, that amused sound that sounded like lungs tearing up. "I'm . . . not . . . in a position . . . to stop you."

Weak, and struggling, and the House itself already in the grasp of Yen Oanh's *khi* water—except that Yen Oanh was dead, or worse, and he could take it all for himself with little effort. If he killed Asmodeus, here, now, drawing on the magic of the sword, he would make Asmodeus's spell work in reverse, claim the House for the dragon kingdom; would, in one fell swoop, make sure that they were safe, and inviolable, and taking their place in the order of things in the city—ruling in his own name, like the Fallen. . . .

The sword was warm, in his hands, thirsting for blood, for power, for undisputed, unshared dominion.

Like the Fallen.

No worse, no better than them.

Asmodeus's eyes were on him, the only things that seemed to be alive in his face—the same gaze that had, dispassionately, considered whether maiming or imprisoning Thuan would be better than outright killing him— who would have strung Thuan up in these trees, to hang emptying himself of blood, feeding the power of the House.

He knew then.

"I'm not like you," he said, slowly, savagely. "Never."

And, gathering to him all the *khi* water in the grove, he bent down, one arm scooping up Asmodeus from the ground—hardly any weight to him, bones as light as a bird's—the other driving the sword, up to the hilt, into his chest.

Asmodeus gasped, coughing up blood. But Thuan's lips were already on his, catching warm, electrifying breath, the blade itself followed by a weaving of *khi* water, a surge of magic into Asmodeus's heart that was both Fallen and dragon, keeping him alive even as the sword transfixed him.

Reshaping the world. Thuan wasn't good with Fallen magic, but he didn't need to be, not with this amount coursing through him. He knew what he wanted—such a small thing, compared with what Asmodeus had had in mind, such a small, localized change—and he just needed to let his desire guide him.

Not conquering, not killing, not taking over. Merging. Sharing.

On all the trees in the grove, the frost melted, leaving only warm puddles at the feet of the trunks—swiftly absorbed, lapped up as eagerly as blood—and flowers, gray and green, the color of moldy algae, blossomed like a thousand hands opening. And, outside, on the quays, the Seine growled and shifted, while water seeped out of the earth to drown the lawns and pathways of the gardens, and the fountains filled up with oily, dark brine.

Asmodeus's lips moved, trying to shape themselves around a word, which Thuan caught, swallowing it like live fire. And, slowly, gradually, as the power within the sword drained away, sinking to impalpable embers—as the *khi* water he held sank down to bare, thin threads—something rose, within his mind. It was . . . Asmodeus's amused, distant cruelty—and, beyond, deaths in the grove and in the gardens, each of them an open wound—and a dozen—a hundred—lights lined up like lanterns at the Midautumn Festival, which he had only to touch to reach, and snuff out: the dependents of the House, so many frozen, so many hovering on the verge of death. . . .

No.

The power spread, encompassed the House, pushed, again and again, against the cracked wall, melting frost like wildfire. Lights shivered and wobbled in Thuan's mind: a dozen—a hundred—emergencies as dependents, freed from the frost, fell shivering and gasping and dying to the ground, wave after wave of imperious desperation. He had to do something for them; he had to do it *now*.

Thuan withdrew the blade, dropped it. It was dark now, all its magic spent. The network of *khi* water hung together for a moment longer, knitting together the flesh of Asmodeus's wounds, until he lay, dangling like a rag doll, in Thuan's arms, pale and light and *brittle*. He hissed, gaze lifeless and unfocused. "Consort," he whispered, and then his eyes rolled up, and he fell silent.

Consort. Thuan knelt, laying Asmodeus down on the ground—brushing, gently, the hair back from his face. He looked at the hawthorn trees all around him, feeling their roots, and the wards they kept together, the drowned gardens near the Seine, the remnants of the wall that would have to be torn down piece by piece.

Consort. Head of the House. Joint heads, to a House that was now Hawthorn, and a part of the dragon kingdom, neither and both of these, new and raw and frightening.

I'm not like you. Never.

Unwise.

"I know," he said, aloud. "I never said I was wise." And, rising, and brushing his bloodied hands against the jacket of his suit, he went to see what could be done, for the House that now half belonged to him.

TWENTY-SEVEN
Open Paths

PHILIPPE came back to find his flat largely untouched, and unclaimed—through fear of Olympe's wrath, combined with disinclination to touch the bloodied patterns brimming with magic that he'd left on the floor.

Olympe, flanked by a couple of dockworkers, walked them to the door. She said nothing, watched Philippe find a rag and start cleaning the patterns in silence. "Under your protection," she said.

Philippe shrugged. "I just said that to get her to stop."

Olympe said a word, finally: *tien*, the Viet one for "Immortal."

"Not any longer," Philippe said, softly. "As I said, don't feel beholden to me."

"I don't." Olympe's voice was sharp. "But word gets around. They might even build you a temple."

Philippe shivered. "Not if you disapprove."

"Perhaps I don't."

He looked up, found her face unreadable. He was older than her, he suddenly realized, and she feared that he would take her place, effortlessly pushing her into the background. "I just wanted to help," he started, but she cut him off.

"I'm not a queen in my own country, Philippe. I just look out for people, because that's what I've done all my life. Because someone should care. Because someone should speak up."

"I—" He swallowed. "I can't do that. That's your dominion, not mine."

"I know," Olympe said. "But you did stand up."

And he wanted to tell her he regretted it, but he wasn't even sure he could do that, and not have it feel like a lie. There was no way he could have walked away from the shed, and the massacre or enslavement of the others.

No, not of others. Of his countrymen.

"I was a messenger," he said, finally. "A minor Immortal in the court of the Jade Emperor. Not the kind who sends blessings, or rain. And that was before they cast me out."

Olympe's face didn't move.

"I can keep an eye out. I can do some magic, but nothing loud or obvious, or the Houses will come looking for us again."

At length, Olympe shook her head. "Be a doctor, Philippe. Be *here*. That's all that can be asked, really."

He'd already done that, he wanted to say, and then saw the patterns on the floor, and the blood—alien and meaningless now, things he had once known intimately but that no longer made sense. "I can try," he said.

"Good." She smiled, sweetly. "It will be New Year soon. You and your friend can come help with the rice cakes."

Because, whatever happened, Olympe was Olympe, and he would never, ever change her. He smiled, in spite of himself. "Perhaps."

"You'd better."

After she left, he stared, for a while, at the floor, trying to regain a long-lost sense of balance.

Isabelle, sitting on his desk, watched him. "Do you have a broom?" she asked. And, when he didn't answer, went foraging into the broken cupboard. "Mmm. I see you don't."

"I had one," Philippe said, wiping the last of the patterns away. His hands ached, but it was distant pain that barely touched him. "Probably stolen."

Isabelle snorted. "I'm not clearing the debris by hand."

"I'm not asking you to clear anything."

"I know." She shrugged. "Though you might get the other Annamites to do it for you."

Philippe shuddered. "I hope not. You heard Olympe." He got up, stared at her for a while. "Isabelle?"

"Mmm."

"How much—how much do you remember?"

Isabelle cocked her head, in a heartbreakingly familiar gesture. "I remember Silverspires. I remember being dead."

Not the wheel of rebirth, or her apparitions as a ghost, but then, he hadn't thought she would. "You're mortal now."

"Yes." She bit her lips. "I don't know why. The ritual, probably."

Probably not. He knew, already, why.

Your desire shakes the foundations of the earth.

It was the magic that had torn them apart in the first place: her status as a Fallen, and her growing allegiance to House Silverspires, her arrogance and lack of compassion, making her into a mirror of the tormentors who had dragged him to France and forced him to fight in their war.

"I'm sorry," he said. He wanted to say it was his fault, but he would lose her if he did.

Isabelle shrugged. "Don't be. Most people don't get reborn. Thank you."

Some did—Morningstar, other Fallen. He didn't know the rules, didn't know anything, in spite of Berith's promises. Because of what he desired, she'd been reborn powerless and weak, in a world that respected only power. As surely as if he had killed her, he had doomed her to be part of the poor, the Houseless. They were choices he had made for himself, and now would be hers.

"I'll take care of you," he said, slowly, carefully. He was going to say, "I promise," but he'd made her so many promises, and kept so few of them. "We'll work something out." With Olympe, and with the other Annamites.

Isabelle watched him, for a while. "The two of us?" She smiled, and it was like the sun, rising, filling the entire flat. "Oh, Philippe. It'll be fine. Honestly."

"It will be fine," he repeated.

And, for a long, slow, treacherous moment—watching her balancing on his desk, smiling and hopeful, and exactly as he remembered her before things had gone sour in Silverspires—he allowed himself to believe it.

FRANÇOISE sat by Berith's side, watching her sleep.

They'd walked from the gardens into the House, finding it in utter disarray, and were triaged into the hospital wing, where Berith was given drugs by a rather disgruntled doctor, and sharply told to rest. Françoise wasn't given anything, except food and water, and a look that could have seared flesh. She sat in a chair, winded, feeling Camille suckle at her breast, the baby unaware that anything had gone wrong with the world.

The hawthorn tree had gone, but Françoise knew it was still there, part of Berith's new dominion. Part of the House, the new boundaries they had imposed on themselves. Because she'd asked her to, because she'd led them to Hawthorn.

A price. There was always a price.

A knock at the door. Françoise turned, half expecting Asmodeus, but it was another Annamite instead, his hair styled in a topknot, wearing a suit in the colors of the House. They stared at each other, for a while. "I'm sorry," the Annamite said, in fluent Viet. "I had no idea. . . ." He used an odd pronoun to refer to himself, not "child," which she would have expected given his youth, but an archaic one that she didn't know.

Comprehension dawned. "Oh. You're here for Berith. I'm Françoise. This is Camille."

"My name is Thuan. I'm . . . the head of the House."

"Asmodeus?"

"Also the head of the House." He frowned. "But unlikely to get up from his bed anytime soon." He stared at her, at the baby. "I've come to tell you that you have the shelter of the House. And its protection."

"As your dependents?"

"As whatever makes you comfortable. It would make my work easier if you were dependents, insofar as protection goes." Thuan raised a hand, cutting off whatever she might have said. "You don't have to decide now."

He was so young, barely in his twenties, and yet he projected a confidence that was beyond his years, the quiet ease of someone taught to wield power. Where had he come from? She wasn't sure, couldn't be sure; and then he shifted, and the shadow of antlers grew from his head, and a faint scattering of scales came into focus on his skin.

"*Rong*," she whispered, and he smiled. "That's unusual."

Thuan was silent for a while. "For a House? Things . . . will change, here. They'll have to. And you and Berith will be part of it."

"Things will change." Françoise shook her head.

Thuan smiled. "Fear begets fear, and nothing changed in the twenty years since he took the House."

Françoise said, "House Astragale thought they could change things, too." And had been, in the end, no better than the other Houses. "Sorry."

Thuan shrugged. "House Astragale is going to be in disarray for a while. Licking their wounds, you might say. As to changes . . . we all do what we can with the power we have, and are held responsible for it. It's only fair."

The power that raised them up, that corrupted them. Françoise said nothing.

"Anyway, I'll be back. When things have cooled down. But I wanted you to know"—he gestured to her, Berith, and Camille—"that you have shelter here."

"I see," Françoise said, slowly. "Thank you."

If he'd been Asmodeus, he would have smiled and said something sarcastic; but instead, Thuan merely bowed, in an old-fashioned Annamite gesture of respect. "Blood stands by blood."

After he was gone, Françoise sat, watching Berith sleep, thinking of the hawthorn tree in the garden, now sunk back into invisibility, a dominion only waiting to be called back. Hearts' desires, and granted wishes, and bittersweet endings, and the House that she was going to tie herself to for a lifetime, for Berith's sake. For Camille's sake.

A future. Any future that doesn't involve death.

There's nothing here that will ever shake the foundations of the world. Nothing large or earth-shattering.

But nothing here shallow, or meaningless, either.

The world was blurred, and a little painful. She stroked Camille's small head, not sure whether she should weep or laugh or both.

"We can't have everything we want," she whispered, into the silence of the room. So seldom did, in fact. But there would be food, and warmth, and a childhood that wasn't teetering on the edge of poverty and starvation. And, perhaps, in time, a form of happiness; or at any rate of peace with the choices they'd made. "But it will have to do."

THUAN hardly felt the days go by. Dependents—those who had survived—were slowly, painstakingly taking apart the wall, with the help of some rather bemused dragons. He'd sent a message to Second Aunt, and received an amused answer with her personal seal, congratulating him on his new position and wishing him luck.

Which was, truth be told, a weight off his chest. He'd been half-afraid she would carve chunks out of his own hide.

They counted the dead, too, and buried them—distant acquaintances, and utter strangers; and friends and fellow students, too. Sare, caught in the gardens, freezing to death before he had ever been able to dispel the frost.

His mind was numb, filled only with thoughts of the House. From time to time, he would realize the enormity of what had happened, of what he'd gained, of what he'd lost, and then balk again, and find refuge in the work that needed to be done.

And, as part of that work, he called Nadine into Asmodeus's rooms. He'd drawn the frayed curtains on the large four-poster bed, leaving Asmodeus sleeping deeply on blood- and sweat-drenched sheets—and sat in the chair that Asmodeus had once occupied, a quiet statement of the new order of things in the House.

Nadine wore a simple gray dress, with barely any hint of the colors of Hawthorn. She stood, her whole body taut with fear, knuckles white, hands shaking. She'd taken sides against Asmodeus, broken the vow of loyalty she'd sworn to him. She knew that her offense was grave and unforgivable. "Thuan," she said.

Thuan nodded. "I think," he said, gently, slowly, "that it would be best if you left the House."

Nadine's head jerked up. "You're showing me mercy? *He* wouldn't approve."

"This isn't about him," Thuan said. "And"—he smiled, dark and unamused—"ask me again about mercy when you've lived among the Houseless for a while."

"There are worse things." Nadine shook her head. A pause, then: "You—you don't even want to know who else was involved?"

"I already know," Thuan said. It hadn't been hard. There'd been plenty of eyewitnesses, even in the confusion of the attack on the House, and even before. Not that many people, considering. Two of the nurses in the infirmary, and a handful of students who might not even have understood the consequences of what they were doing.

"I see," Nadine said. "Sparing me from bloody purges, to salve your conscience."

"Bloody, probably not. But there will be gestures made. Statements." He could ill afford to do anything else, not when it would be construed as a weakness.

Nadine's expression was thin, and joyless. "I preferred you when you were a student, all things considered. Do you truly think you're better than him?"

I'm not you. Never. "Perhaps not," Thuan said, mildly. "But I'll have tried, at least."

"Just as I did." Nadine laughed, but there was no joy in it.

Thuan shook his head. "I'm not going to argue over this." He reached out, in his mind, found the light that was hers—and, taking hold of it, gently snuffed it out, cutting the link to the House from her.

Nadine stiffened, took a slow, long breath. A hint of panic in her eyes, swiftly crushed. Of course, she had never known anything other than the House, the omnipresence in her mind. "I see." She bowed, stiffly. "Goodbye, Thuan. I don't think we'll see each other again."

The doors closed on her, and she was gone.

"She's right, you know. In most cases, I wouldn't have approved."

Thuan turned, and was only half-surprised to see the curtains drawn, and Asmodeus watching him, propped up against embroidered pillows. "In most cases?"

Asmodeus tried to shrug, grimaced, and abandoned the gesture. "I'm . . . fond of Iaris. Making an example of Nadine would have left her in an untenable position."

"Fond." Thuan's voice was flat. *I like you, dragon prince. More than I should.* "As a master is fond of his hounds."

Asmodeus smiled. "Do you want me to have a heart? You'd hardly be the first to make this mistake."

He had let Nadine go, in spite of everything—to spare Iaris, when it would have been in his best interests to set an excruciating example, something that would forever dissuade people to betray him, that would clearly state to the House that even the children of his favorites wouldn't be spared.

"I—" Thuan found his throat had gone dry again. He could feel Asmodeus in his mind—as, no doubt, Asmodeus could feel him—but it wasn't telepathy, merely a general presence, a sense of who the Fallen was rather than of his thoughts. "I need to know."

"What I'm going to do?"

"I would rather not wake up with a dagger at my throat. Or in my chest."

Asmodeus laughed.

Thuan rose, came to sit by his side on the bed. The smell of orange blossom and bergamot didn't quite hide the older, more animal one of blood and sickness. Not that he'd put it past Asmodeus to have a knife and use it, even when weakened, but . . .

"I don't know what you did to the House," Asmodeus said. His voice was blunt, without a trace of irony. "And I have no desire to experiment and see what would happen to Hawthorn, should one of us die."

"Because the House is what matters. Because—" He licked his lips. "Because you would have killed me, wouldn't you, for the good of the House?"

Silence then. He found Asmodeus's hand, resting by his side. "You misunderstand. I will take whatever is necessary from outsiders. I will give whatever is necessary, too. But I will never ask the same of my dependents. I'm not Morningstar." He sounded amused again, with a tinge of old, tired anger.

"The trees." Thuan thought, for a moment.

"The eventual fate of all heads of Hawthorn." Asmodeus shrugged. "I knew the price. I knew when I took the House." Thuan's fate, too, now, but that was a worry for another time.

"That doesn't answer my question. How much can I trust you?" He found himself bending, his lips seeking Asmodeus's, for a kiss.

Unwise.

Asmodeus turned his face up. They met, again, lips on lips, no blood or swords, just flesh on flesh, and a familiar thrill of power and desire running up his spine.

Thuan was the one who broke it; his heart in his throat. Asmodeus took his glasses off, laid them on the table by the bed. His breathing was labored, heavy, his hands clenched on the sheets.

"How much? You're the one who stabbed me."

"You're the one who wanted to kill me," Thuan pointed out.

"True. One for one." Asmodeus smiled again, almost boyish, almost carefree. "Let's give this a try, shall we? And see what happens."

Thuan's lips shaped around the word "unwise." It remained stuck in his throat, because, sometimes, unwise things were the only ones worth doing. "Might as well," he said, with a nonchalance he didn't feel. "Might as well."

MADELEINE took some flowers to Clothilde's grave.

It was on a knoll above the drowned gardens, in a row with all the other new ones, the graves of the dependents who had fallen to Yen Oanh's attack. Everything around her smelled of rain and water, an oppressive smell that reminded her, all too keenly, of her time in the dragon kingdom—of her time in a cell in a laundry barge, of angel essence on her skin, and the inescapable knot of fear in her belly.

There was a headstone, simply engraved with two wings, and a hawthorn flower, and Clothilde's name. She knelt, for a while, feeling the pain in her unhealed calf, the slow rhythm in her mind of the link to the House, some-thing slower and different, sleepy waters mingled with Asmodeus's presence. And a prayer in her mind, to the distant God who might, or might not, be watching over them all.

"Be kind to her," she said. She and Clothilde had never been close, but it felt wrong not to acknowledge her, after what had happened in the grove.

"Still as sentimental as ever, I see."

She hadn't heard Asmodeus approach. He stood on the knoll, leaning on a cane with a silver pommel, his grip on it tight. Still recovering, then. His face, though, was its old self—the one from her nightmares, lean and sharp, gray-green eyes behind horn-rimmed glasses.

"I—" She stared at him, for a while, and wasn't sure, afterward, why the words came welling out of her mouth. "I don't know what she would have wanted."

"To survive," Asmodeus said. His smile was bright and terrible. "To live, for the future of the House. Don't we all?"

The House. At the foot of the knoll, she could see Thuan, kneeling in the water, the waves curling around his hands like snakes.

Do you trust me?

You keep the House safe. I don't have to trust you.

"The future." She couldn't stomach the thought of essence anymore, but her lungs were still wasted, her life expectancy counted in years rather than decades.

"You have one that doesn't end today, or tomorrow. Be thankful." Asmodeus sounded amused again.

"Because you won't end it?" It was rote, reflex, almost without fear to it.

"Why would I?" He shrugged. "In other circumstances, it would have been you, in that grave."

Loyal dependents. Defending the House. "I had no choice," she said at last. It was a lie, and he knew it.

Asmodeus was silent for a while, facing the grave. "You did well. For all that I failed you," he said, finally—to her, or Clothilde, it wasn't clear. And walked back to the foot of the knoll and the waiting Thuan, without saying anything more.

The air smelled of rain and mud and rot, and a faint memory of orange blossom and bergamot, already fading.

"The future," Madeleine said, again, tasting the word on her tongue: odd, alien, and unknown; and—in spite of everything—heady and exhilarating, and just a little bit addictive.

Acknowledgments

I would like to thank everyone who helped this book come into shape: Alis Rasmussen, Dario Ciriello, and M. Sereno for their fast and enthusiastic beta reading, Vida Cruz for her comments on the opening, Tade Thompson for his comments on the first chapters and his very helpful suggestions on the history of medicine, hospital routines, and doctors in general.

I would also like to thank Karlo Yeager Rodriguez, Benjamin C. Kinney, T. Jane Berry, Anatoly Belilovsky, and Steve Bein, for helping me brainstorm a (hopefully) accurate death method for Ghislaine, as well as Sylvia Spruck Wrigley, Anatoly Belilovsky, Wendy Nikel, J. Kathleen Cheney, Amy Sisson, S. L. Saboviec, Katie Sparrow, Kate Heartfield, and Diana Pharaoh Francis for brainstorming childbirth complications for Françoise. And thanks to Cheryl Morgan for helping me with Berith's character.

DongWon Song very kindly provided me with an on-the-spot Word conversion so I could reread the manuscript on my iPad while traveling.

For general support, thanks to D. Franklin and Zoe Johnson, Zen Cho, Cindy Pon, Karin Tidbeck, Nene Ormes, Alessa Hinlo, Isabel Yap, Kari Sperring, Stephanie Burgis, Fran Wilde, Ken Liu, Elizabeth Bear, Mary Robinette Kowal, and Victor Fernando R. Ocampo.

ACKNOWLEDGMENTS

On Twitter, I had numerous conversations ranging from weaponry to sorting out French translations into English: I would like to thank everyone who contributed, most particularly Alan Bellingham (for tactics and firearms, propping up the scene where Madeleine and Clothilde attack the wall), John Hopkins (for sorting out the translation of *bateau-lavoir* as "laundry barge"), and Margo-Lea Hurwizc for numerous helpful comments. Thanks as well to Boudewijn and Irina Rempt for brainstorming and dinner, and to Christian Steinmetz for the best author photo ever as well as translations of all the House mottoes into Latin.

I also owe thanks to everyone who read, reviewed, and/or spread the word about *The House of Shattered Wings*, and made me feel like a minor celebrity by attending my events of 2015/16.

Like the previous one, this book wouldn't have come into existence without Rochita Loenen-Ruiz's encouragement and suggestions. Thanks as well to my agent, John Berlyne, and my editors, Gillian Redfearn at Gollancz and Jessica Wade at Ace, for firming up the structure and closing up plot holes; Alexis C. Nixon, Sophie Calder, and Jennifer McMenemy for putting up with my wild promotion ideas; and both the teams at Gollancz and Ace for all the work from cover art to marketing (and to Nekro for the gorgeous cover art that adorns the U.S. edition).

Finally, this book wouldn't have been what it is without my family: my sister, who tirelessly brainstormed titles with me and fed me dim sum and pizza while I hammered together Madeleine's journey into the dragon kingdom; my parents; my grandparents; and Ba Ngoai for all the books.

And to my husband, Matthieu, and my two sons, the snakelet and the Librarian, many thanks for helping me write this one, too!

FURTHER READING

I based the relations between the dragon kingdom and the Houses on the early history of French ingerence into Vietnamese affairs in the nineteenth century, as well as on the opium traffic run by the British into the Chinese empire that led to two Opium Wars. The court and its various factions are based on a sinicized version of the Nguyen court of that time period, in order to reflect the earlier origins of the dragons. It is of course vastly more equalitarian gender-wise!

The geography of Paris and its suburbs in the Dominion of the Fallen series is roughly that of the late nineteenth / early twentieth century, though shifted to take into account the changed history and context. Historically, there is of course no Annamite community in la Goutte d'Or, and the city had changed quite a bit by the time the large migration from Vietnam started in the late twentieth century. I took the liberty of putting the Annamites in la Goutte d'Or for plot purposes, and as a deliberate nod to Émile Zola's *L'Assommoir*, which deals with the precarious life of the working class in an era of glamorous salons coexisting with crushing misery.

The interior and the layout of House Hawthorn are based on period *hôtels particuliers* on a much larger scale, though there is of course no equivalent to the interlocking system of courts and their attendant responsibilities.

*　　*　　*

SOME (but not all!) books and articles I read in the course of researching *The House of Binding Thorns*:

Ton That Binh, *Life in the Forbidden Purple City*

Marc Breitman and Maurice Culot, *La Goutte d'Or: Faubourg de Paris*

Geoffrey Chamberlain, "British Maternal Mortality in the 19th and Early 20th Centuries," *Journal of the Royal Society of Medicine* 99 (November 2006)

Caroline de Costa, "St. Anthony's Fire and Living Ligatures: A Short History of Ergometrine," *The Lancet* 359 (May 18, 2002)

George Dutton, Jayne Werner, John K. Whitmore, eds., *Sources of Vietnamese Tradition*

Anne Martin-Fugier, *La place des bonnes*

Hien V. Ho and Chat V. Dang, *Vietnam History: Stories Retold for a New Generation*

Huynh Sanh Thong, *An Anthology of Vietnamese Poems*

Huynh Sanh Thong, *The Tale of Kieu*

Alexandre Lalande, *Histoire des ports de Paris et de l'Ile-de-France*

Fabrice Laroulandie, *Les ouvriers de Paris au XIXè siècle*

Le Huu Tho, *Les Vietnamiens en France: Insertion et identité*

Nguyen The Anh, *Monarchie et fait colonial au Vietnam*

Erica J. Peters, *Appetites and Aspiration in Vietnam: Food and Drink in the Long Nineteenth Century*

Roy Porter, *The Greatest Benefit to Mankind: A Medical History of Humanity*

Nghia M. Vo, *Legends of Vietnam*

Choi Byung Wook, *Southern Vietnam under the Reign of Minh Mang*

ALIETTE DE BODARD is one of the Writers of the Future, has won two Nebula Awards, a Locus Award and a BSFA Award. She has also been a finalist for the Hugo, Sturgeon, and Tiptree Awards, making her one of our most-lauded contemporary fiction writers. A writer by night, by day she is a qualified engineer, specialising in Applied Mathematics.

• • •

She lives in Paris, in a flat with more computers than she really needs.

• • •

You can learn more at www.aliettedebodard.com or by following @aliettedb on Twitter.

ELIZABETH MAY

The Falconer

Heiress. Debutant. Murderer.

A new generation of heroine has arrived.

Lady Aileana Kameron, the only daughter of the
Marquess of Douglas, was destined for a life carefully
planned around Edinburgh's social events – right up
until a faery killed her mother.

Now it's the 1844 winter season and Aileana slaughters
faeries in secret, in between the endless round of
parties, tea and balls.

But the balance between high society and her private
war is a delicate one, and as the fae infiltrate the
ballroom and Aileana's father returns home, she has
decisions to make. How much is she willing to lose –
and just how far will Aileana go for revenge?

• • •

**'A riveting world, a fierce heroine, and electrifying
action – I burned through this sparkling debut!'
Sarah J. Maas, *New York Times* bestselling author**

'A stunning debut and very firmly recommended'
Starburst Magazine

SONGS OF THE EARTH

The Wild Hunt: Book One

Elspeth Cooper

Gair is under a death sentence.

He can hear music – music with power – and in the Holy
City that means only one thing: he's a witch, and he's going
to be burnt at the stake. Even if he could escape, the Church
Knights and their witchfinder would be hot on his heels while
his burgeoning power threatens to tear him apart
from within.

There is no hope . . . none, but a secretive order, themselves
persecuted almost to destruction. If Gair can escape, if he can
master his own growing, dangerous abilities, if he can find the
Guardians of the Veil, then maybe he will be safe.
Or maybe he'll discover that his fight has only just begun.

• • •

'*Songs of the Earth* is a stunning opening to a new series, from
a debut writer who already possesses a unique and talented
voice. A fast-paced book that wears its heart firmly on its
sleeve, and is all the more refreshing for it' *Fantasy Faction*

'A true storyteller' Alexander Kent

'*Songs of the Earth* is a rather stunning debut fantasy novel'
Starburst

'*Songs of the Earth* is a fascinating and thoughtful
fantasy debut quite unlike many others in the genre
and the author has a unique voice that separates
her from the competition' *Walker of Worlds*

'Fans of Karen Miller, Emily Gee and Patrick
Rothfuss will all welcome Ms. Cooper to
their shelves' *Pornokitsch*

JOHN HORNOR JACOBS

The Incorruptibles

In the contested and unexplored territories at the edge of the Empire, a boat is making its laborious way up stream. Riding along the banks are the mercenaries hired to protect it – from raiders, bandits and, most of all, the stretchers, elf-like natives who kill any intruders into their territory. The mercenaries know this is dangerous, deadly work. But it is what they do.

In the boat the drunk governor of the territories and his sons and daughters make merry. They believe that their status makes them untouchable. They are wrong. And with them is a mysterious, beautiful young woman.

For Fisk and Shoe – two tough, honourable mercenaries surrounded by corruption, who know they can always and only rely on each other – their young companion appears to be playing with fire. The nobles have the power, and crossing them is always risky.

• • •

'5 * *The Incorruptibles* is a rare thing: a clever story *and* an action-packed one' *SFX*

'This is strange alchemy, a recipe I've never seen before. I wish more books were as fresh and brave as this' Patrick Rothfuss

'Fantasy needs writers who push the envelope, and Jacobs finds the edge and tears right through it. If you want original, you've picked up the right book' Myke Cole

SIMON MORDEN

Down Station

MARY. One slip away from prison, fighting to build herself a future from nothing.

DALIP. The gentle son of a warrior tradition. A young man who must fight for independence from his family.

STANISLAV. A fierce and capable man carrying the wounds of a brutal war.

Simon Morden's extraordinary new novel is a quest for meaning and identity. It is a thrilling journey into the secrets that could change us all.

• • •

'Morden has written a book full of mysteries that are just waiting to be discovered' Fantasy Book Review

'Once again Simon Morden takes the fantasy genre and moulds it wonderfully . . . What makes Down Station so great is the immaculate pacing and the way character shapes fate for each of the well-drawn main characters' *The Sun*

ABOUT GOLLANCZ

Gollancz is the oldest SF publishing imprint in the world. Since being founded in 1927 Gollancz has continued to publish a focused selection of bestselling and award-winning authors. The front-list includes **Ben Aaronovitch**, **Joe Abercrombie**, **Charlaine Harris**, **Joanne Harris**, **Joe Hill**, **Alastair Reynolds**, **Patrick Rothfuss**, **Nalini Singh** and **Brandon Sanderson**.

As one of the largest Science Fiction and Fantasy imprints in the UK it is no surprise we have one of the most extensive backlists in the world. Find high-quality SF on Gateway written by such authors as **Philip K. Dick**, **Ursula Le Guin**, **Connie Willis**, **Sir Arthur C. Clarke**, **Pat Cadigan**, **Michael Moorcock** and **George R.R. Martin**.

We also have a strand of publishing in translation, which includes French, Polish and Russian authors. Gollancz is home to more award-winning authors than any other imprint, with names including **Aliette de Bodard**, **M. John Harrison**, **Paul McAuley**, **Sarah Pinborough**, **Pierre Pevel**, **Justina Robson** and many more.

The SF Gateway
More than 3,000 classic, rare and previously
out-of-print SF novels at your fingertips.
www.sfgateway.com

The Gollancz Blog
Bringing you news from our worlds to yours. Stories,
interviews, articles and exclusive extracts just for you!
www.gollancz.co.uk

GOLLANCZ
LONDON